SORRY, IT'S A GIRL

SORRY, IT'S A GIRL

A. A. Khan

Matador
9 Priory Business Park,
Wistow Road, Kibworth Beauchamp,
Leicestershire LE8 0RX
Tel: 0116 279 2299
Email: books@troubador.co.uk
Web: www.troubador.co.uk/matador
Twitter: @matadorbooks

ISBN 978 183859 113 7

British Library Cataloguing in Publication Data.
A catalogue record for this book is available from the British Library.

Printed and bound in Great Britain by 4edge Limited
Typeset in 11pt Baskerville by Troubador Publishing Ltd, Leicester, UK

Matador is an imprint of Troubador Publishing Ltd

PROLOGUE

IN MY COUNTRY whenever a girl is born, the doctor heaves a sigh, the nurses all look at each other despairingly, relatives plaster on fake smiles, and the new parents are given the news as an apology.

It is as if the lack of a male organ has cursed their tiny little baby for the rest of her life. Indeed, where I am from, being born without a penis is tantamount to being born with a disability. Except there is no therapy for this handicap – the child can never be fixed because at the moment of that discovery she ceases to be a full human. From the moment her gender is revealed, she becomes a commodity.

But that is only half the story.

You see, marriage in my country is a not-so-subtle means of exchanging, fortifying and attaining power. Women, or more specifically potential brides, are the commodities used in these exchanges. Owing to this tradition, women have themselves become players in our convoluted power game by suggesting this pairing or that, establishing who is or isn't worthy of a certain dowry price, and even wholly excommunicating families from the incestuous circle of marriage based on the most mundane of social faux pas. All this occurs in a bid to claw their family's way to the top of a ziggurat that is quite obviously falling apart. In the running of this societal rat race, it is often, surprisingly, the women who are most wicked to one another.

And so this story isn't so much about how men treat women, but about how women treat one another.

You see, dear reader, when a person has no option but to succumb to a lower status of existence, this lesser state of being, perpetrated upon them by society (not by the rules of Nature or God), tends to form the rules to which

1

the afflicted person becomes accustomed. The individuals plagued by this system pass its iniquities on to their children and their children's children, and the never-ending cycle continues until we are left with a mere shrill husk of a society.

Indeed, this is where Pakistan is today.

When you think of where I'm from and where a good part of this story takes place, there is no doubt that the first thing that will come to mind is Osama Bin Laden. And reader, I do not blame you. Indeed, by now, two movies and numerous books on the hunt for the terrorist mastermind have been released. Those tomes no doubt tell you the story of Pakistan as an impenetrable hinterland of the Hindu Kush, filled with scimitar-bearing Islamic radicals hell-bent on destroying the West. Those books will tell you of glorious battles and spine-tingling espionage by heroic individuals who contributed to the demise of the world's most wanted terrorist.

What those stories won't reveal is the complicated way a society makes its bed upon a mountain of hypocrisy, sheets thrown up and cracking in corruption. Ordinarily, when societies descend to this level, history tells us a person comes along who heroically strives to rectify it through the stinging judgment of the written word. This is part of our promise as human beings, our God-given tabula rasa, I suppose. After all, the French Revolution had its Hugo; Russia its Tolstoy and Solzhenitsyn.

But let's get one thing straight.

I am not that person.

Nor does my tale have Navy SEALs or scimitar-wielding Islamic radicals. What it does have is a bevy of bitches who in many ways are just as lethal. Exchange the Oakley sunglasses and M-4 battle rifles for Versace tints accessorised with Fendi handbags, swap the Qurans and scimitars for copies of *Fifty Shades of Grey* and shopping trips to Dubai, dear reader, because the world we are about to enter promises to turn your traditional definition of Pakistan on its head.

I am here to tell you about a whole different kind of war.

First and foremost, let us establish that, despite my duties as teller of this tale, I am most certainly not a hero. As you shall see, our journey shall require us to pick at the carcasses of failed romances and broken spirits rather consistently.

So if what I am about to tell you becomes the chronicle of a time, a class of people, even a nation, then let me be the first to surrender myself to history's judgment: I'm just a twenty-year-old and I'd never be caught dead without my Prada, Jimmy Choos, or iPhone. I consider myself a part of the problem and I have no clue to the solution. Therefore, what I am to you is a spy in the most literal sense, as in many cases you will be hearing quite intimate details of characters who would die before revealing them. As the poet Anne Sexton said, 'A writer is essentially a spy. Dear love, I am that girl.'

I will also use this occasion to apologise about the fact that I will seldom mention names in this book. It is an attempt aimed at protecting the identities of the guilty. I truly hope that my censure of their actions, and that too public a one such as this, will prove enough of a punishment, and will perhaps lead to a mending of their ways.

This tome is a great deal of reflection on the real-life events that I, or those near me, have experienced. Where my discourse departs from events as they have actually occurred, or where I appear to have intended to exaggerate or create a situation, trust me when I say that it is not fantastical but an actual portrayal of the lives of many that inhabit – or rather, lord over – my homeland of Pakistan.

With all that said, rest assured that I could spend an eternity telling you of the hypocrisy and the injustice that has insidiously charmed its way into the hearts of a beautiful people, but my characters and, even more so, my inner narrator are getting impatient.

They wish to be free to tell their stories and I will no longer hinder their rising passion to make you intimate with their musings.

DON'T BET ON BOYS

HER HANDS CLENCH and unclench in spasmodic rhythms matching the senseless beating of her heart and the subsequent impatient collapse and rise of her diaphragm. Beads of sweat profusely trickle down her forehead as her panting reaches an escalation. Her cries and moans get sharper now and she finally grabs onto the nearest object and clutches it with a frenzy, which makes the blood rush to her eyes and blot out everything from her vision, everything from her widely parted legs to the wall opposite her.

A woman's screams as she pushes forth a newborn represent both her pain and the realisation that she will get little, if any, sleep for many nights to come; that in effect, her soul is now halved, shared between herself and this new being – that little bundle of problems-to-be. Yet, when she holds her baby in her arms, a woman realises she has received her life's greatest calling: she is a mother and is no longer just responsible for herself and her own life. The mother looks down at the blotchy-pink diminutive, helpless creature she holds and immediately feels a rush of warmth as she realises that she has the ability to start from scratch, to help aid this delicate expatriate and to shelter it from all those ills that have befallen her. Her fondness stems less from the fact that the child has been growing inside of her for nine months and more from the realisation that it is an extension of herself and thereby a second chance for her to make amends with whatever tabula rasa she might have ignored or been forced away from in her own pre-childbirth life.

Humans come into existence through a mother's act of giving birth, but characters are born very differently – they come from situations. Like books, the pages of a baby's life are blank slates, but unlike books, their fate exists in a reality outside of written history or forethought. This novel is successful in

4

merely happening to portray a scant portion of their existence and yet I feel one must start from the beginning.

I begin my tale with a memory. One that begins in 1995 when two women of equally distinct worldviews and personalities, yet also the best of friends, gave birth to their daughters side by side while they held each other's hands.

This sort of thing was unheard of in Pakistan, and indeed it would have been greatly shunned as somehow being *haram*.*

But these were not ordinary women, or more specifically they did not possess ordinary lineages. Mrs K and Mrs N were members of two of Pakistan's 'inner-circle' families. The concept of 'inner-circle' families was much the same as it was in any country: a few families controlled and circulated power amongst themselves – that power being a share of politics, industry, and foreign trade.

However, in Pakistan the idea had its own cultural twist. Whenever a daughter was married off, if she was an only child or the eldest among only other girls then the control of whatever industry, trade monopoly, or even political office that belonged to her family, could pass entirely to her husband's family. This meant two things: one, that women prayed for sons first, lest they have to repeatedly bear children until graced with a boy; and two, whenever some unfortunate family approached this tenuous position of having only girls, those with eligible sons would line up like scavengers at a rotting carcass, eager for their chance to gobble up the beleaguered estate.

N had already had her boy but K had so far only had a girl by the name of Laila. The particular disposition of the women's families seemed to correlate with a typically Islamic sense of viewing the world. You see, K wore her faith on her shoulder, forcing others to follow suit, while N, on the other hand, was an inwardly pious yet politically liberal woman who had pulled many a friend out of situations that their rather shameless greed had gotten them into.

Not surprisingly, the same servants who feared K considered N to be an angel of a woman who was ever too kind to them and always thought of their families back in the villages. Every *Eid* holiday, Mrs N ensured their villages overflowed with treats for the feast and their wallets were filled with rupees to buy their relatives gifts. Indeed, Mrs N was such a pious and kind woman, it was no wonder Allah had blessed her with a boy on her first try.

---

* Unreligious or un-Islamic.

And it was for that very reason K had requested they follow through on a pact they had made as naive young girls. K hoped that N's 'boy – having blessings' would pass on to her if they held hands while birthing their second children. It was serendipitous, after all, that they were birthing at the same time – never mind the fact that K had ordered her doctor to induce labour a week early once she heard N's waters had broken. This time, however, it seemed sin trumped the path of piety, because instead of N's blessings transfusing into K's womb to magically change the gender of the tender child that lay within, things backfired and both women ended up with beautiful baby girls.

The funniest part about the whole thing was that unbeknownst to K, Mrs N actually wanted a baby girl this time, after having her boy. Perhaps the superstitious magic hadn't failed after all.

And so on June 5, 1995, two sisters in spirit came into the world, born from different mothers but as much the same as if they emerged from one womb. Indeed, as the doctor cursed silently to himself while he cut their umbilical cords – he had proudly put down half a month's salary on the women having two boys in the very illegal and extremely un-Islamic hospital betting pool – the first sight they gazed on in this world was each other.

From the beginning, the girls acted as one and were in many ways inseparable. Gradually they grew into their individual selves, different yet connected at the spirit. In the time before their differences could be crowned by names, they were interchangeably *she* and *her*.

Eventually we would know them as…

Ah, love. If it but had a heart of its own that beat and broke, perhaps out of pity it wouldn't inflict others with its blessed curse. Where does fortune goad on either of love's directives? What does it finally let 'love' culminate in? Is it the joining of two harmonious souls or the tears of a forlorn farewell? That is up to fortune and fortune alone. All we know is that the journey of love is full of every twist and turn the imagination can conjure up and the mind can experience.

A WOMAN AMONGST MEN

MAYA TOOK IN the crowd, the energy, the hope; and the diverse multitude of people gave her a heady feeling. It reminded her of being a girl a decade earlier in Lahore.

Her mother was nicer then, more beautiful as well. Not the woman she was today. Botox must sap the sweetness and love from women's hearts. She mostly remembered the colours of the rallies they attended, and the warmth – physical as well as ephemeral. In Lahore she felt the heat like she were wrapped tightly in its bosom.

It was the return of Benazir Bhutto, and her possible return to democratic governance for Pakistan. On that day, her mother had dressed her personally – producing a light pink *shalwar* from a magnificent box and the most beautiful slippers. She remembered how soft her mother's touch had been on her skin when she held her arms up to slide on the *shalwar* – as the dress came down and Maya felt its intricate embroidery slightly tickle her skin, she giggled and her eyes met her mother's.

It took her a decade to begin to understand what her mother's gaze meant. As she looked around at her present audience she began to feel it.

Mrs N, her mother's best friend, had come over and brought with her Arzoo, whom Maya thought of as inordinately loud, if not a physical manifestation of Jasmine from Aladdin. Arzoo wore a bright orange *shalwar*, with a small shawl usually reserved for older girls. She sat proudly across from Maya. Maya's mother easily brushed her straight, obedient hair, leaving a large part down the right to partially cover her forehead in the Benazir style. Arzoo's hair had slight wavy curls at the end, breaking the symmetry of her forward part. Her mother placed a flower and headband

7

to even it out. Like her orange *shalwar*, Arzoo's hair seemed determined to stand out, to be seen.

"Maya, New York and New Jersey are in! Come take selfies! We've got to document every state. By the end of the night I want to have one for every state she wins!" Arzoo's hair had only got louder in the decade since they had attended their first political rallies together with their mothers. Her skin had a radiant and inviting bronze tinge; people naturally liked being around her and so as soon as she whipped out her phone, three other girls and a guy piled in the shot with their 'With Her' signs.

Maya remembered her mother then, and then winced at the thought of their present impasse. She understood now that her mother saw in Benazir liberation – not for herself but for Maya. It wasn't that her mother held a poor existence, or was abused, or was unhappy. Maya knew well enough that her mother understood that the norms of the Lahori elite were stifling, that they were a self-built prison of insularity that kept individuals and even Pakistan itself from something *greater*.

Arzoo and Maya had sat in the foyer of the house. Their mothers had tied pretty little red, green and black bows in their hair – the colours of the PPP flag.* The house was abuzz with life as, of course, they were late. Arzoo rummaged through her mother's handbag and produced a bright purple fliptop device. She waved Maya over.

"My older cousin gave it to me. It's a Polly Pocket diary. I'm going to use it to find a prince," said Arzoo, as she entered her secret password. Arzoo pressed the slightly worn buttons several times and scrolled to the secrets section of the diary.

"Would it be bad if I Tindered right now, Maya?" Arzoo had to yell, as things in the conference hall were getting louder. People seemed to be conversing as to why Pennsylvania and a few other states in the 'Blue Wall' hadn't been called for Hillary yet. "I mean given present company. I think most of the guys here are gay though. Sigh, I wish Republicans didn't have such a monopoly on straight rich guys."

The feelings were years apart but Maya felt happy she could connect with her mother's feeling of hope around Benazir. Sure, Hillary would only be Chief Minister of the United States, and not Pakistan, but she would be the most powerful person on Earth. A woman. That meant a hell of a

---

* Pakistan People's Party, formed by Zulfiqar Ali Bhutto in 1968.

lot in itself, but what excited Maya was that it meant an end to the prison of women constructing a sub-realm of their own making with which to constrain themselves. It wasn't saying girls were stronger than boys, it was saying that girls would never dictate terms to each other that subconsciously satisfied the desires of *only* men.

Something was wrong in Lahore. They still hadn't left for the day's rally, the security guards in the house were yelling at each other and her father had a worried look on his face. Something had happened at the rally. Maya's father approached her mother and whispered in her ear. She snapped her head up and looked at her husband, her eyes registering disbelief then stunned acceptance. She sat on one of the long couches and looked around as if gasping for an anchor in the room until she saw her daughter – she looked at Maya and then just as quickly averted her gaze. She was falling apart. Out by the front door, Arzoo's mother fainted and men ran to attend to her.

The face that looked back at Maya seemed to be one resigned to a life of defeat – it was the face Maya knew all too well in the present day. Her mother seemed panicked, on the verge of breaking down; Maya could not look away. She watched as her mother fidgeted and fought back tears at the same time, she watched as her toes twitched. She watched as her face slowly began to return to normal. Finally, Maya's mother ran her hands over her gold bracelet and something resembling a smile began to appear.

"Maya, chains of gold work vastly better than iron. Do well not to forget that." Maya didn't really understand.

"Of course, Mother, because of the weight. It's so much harder to lift gold than iron," replied Maya smartly, already top of her class in the first form of Lahore Girls' Grammar.

"True, but gold also weighs more heavily on the heart than the body. You see, not everyone will know that being shackled in gold is actually worse than iron. Many will just think of how beautiful their prison is – and forget what they have lost. I don't know why I'm telling you this, daughter, perhaps I read it in a book somewhere, but this bracelet on my arm is just so pretty right now, I wish to fly to Dubai next week and buy another."

It was a panicked rant, an urge to say something in the uncertain moment of defeat and the heart of a loss. Benazir Bhutto was dead. Blown to bits by a suicide bomber. Maya's mother never remembered the conversation. A few days later, Maya's mother took her books on the Mughal Empire, her poems of Rumi, and her archaeological tomes on Mohenjo-Daro and Harappa, and had the servants burn them in the backyard. She even took that trip to Dubai and bought a matching bracelet. She never attended Benazir's funeral or spoke her name again.

Back in DC, things had gone from bad to worse. People were starting to openly weep. Arzoo sat holding a blonde friend's head in her lap. For once, her phone was nowhere to be seen. It was obvious by this point Hillary wasn't going to win. A mix of disbelief and uncertainty began to infect the convention hall. For Maya this meant the weight of her present predicament and her on-going struggle with her mother – who had become the greatest champion of the Lahori way and demanded an arranged consanguineous marriage for Maya. Watching Hillary win would have perhaps been a temporary reprieve from the wall that had emerged between them since that day in 2007. Maya's mother had never acknowledged how deeply the loss had affected her; she put on the appearance of being fine. Arzoo's mother might have fainted on hearing the news of the attack but she had never once attempted to pressure her own daughter in the way Maya's mother did. In fact, Arzoo attended college on the west coast at Stanford and while Maya had desperately wanted to join her, her mother decreed that Harvard would increase her marriage prospects, so to Boston she went.

So with no victory party to attend, the girls would go back to their lives the next day as if nothing had happened – no existential change incoming. Arzoo would hop on a flight first to LA to visit her cousin Fadhi, then head off for a quarter of study at Oxford. With her best friend predisposed in Britain, Maya would be alone in facing her mother's wrath. They left the convention hall together, perplexed and bewildered that the next leader of the free world was a self-admitted pussy-grabber.

MAYA, ARZOO, NILE (AND A VERY UPSET FADHI IN BURJ'S EYE VIEW)

"I HONESTLY THINK it's because you're gay, Fadhi, I just don't see it," said Maya to her best friend's cousin as she sat up awkwardly, looking at the impacted urban skyline around her.

"The logic's lost on you, Maya," sighed the cousin, "and how many times do I have to tell you I'm pre-transition non-binary. I mean, you've got hairier legs than me. What does the one who I won't speak to think?"

The four were lounging on day chairs at one of the open pools at the Burj towers. They had just returned from the annual *umrah* or pilgrimage to Mecca. An annual affair that involved the entire Lahori and Karachi colonies of both the K and N families themselves packing into the First, or if not available on the plane, Business classes of an Emirates A380, whether out of Pakistan, London or, in Arzoo's case, San Francisco.

Despite the piety of the trip, it routinely involved a stay at the Burj and an orgy of shopping for everyone's parents; and for Arzoo, Maya, Nile and Arzoo's cousin Fadhi, it meant basking in the Middle Eastern sun and humidity to get the most 'Snapchat-able/Insta-filter ready tans ever.'

Arzoo's father always told her that being Pakistani – and pre-partition Pakistani at that – meant she had traditions to uphold. When he said this in front of Maya she almost always would agree. Arzoo would always say to herself it just meant having awesome skin. And the three of them were absolutely radiating right now.

Of course, Laila never accompanied them on these trips; her husband 'loved' her company a little too much to let her out of his sight. They were all preoccupied with thoughts of exactly what they had prayed for during *umrah*. Of course, for Maya that would be Ali; and of course, Nile had his eyes set on Arzoo; while Arzoo, well, she only had space in her heart for one person and that was herself. Nile had got Arzoo into current disfavour with Fadhi.

"You mean Arzoo? Arzoo's her name, Fadhi, and being your cousin she loves you very much, you half-Saudi butthead. You cannot possibly still be mad about having to move to SF. I mean you are, wait, what again?" said Maya playfully.

"Okay, first of all, the parents of the one I won't speak to anymore are scared she's going to run off with some American Gora up at Staaaannford. She doesn't have any brothers to watch over her. Me, I'm having the most beautiful time in Los Angeles planning my transition with the best Persian plastic surgeon in Beverly Hills and seeking ways to get in Kylie's crew – and suddenly someone's dad uses eldest male sibling privileges to force my mom to transfer me to… ugh… Santa Clara. I mean do you have any idea what my dad paid to get me into USC? San Francisco is absolutely provincial. Bitch, I'm turning over."

A year and a half previously, Fadhi had convinced his father that the best place for him (to not be stoned to death) was in LA. It wasn't that Fadhi had a problem with Saudi Arabia – he didn't – but being half-Pakistani meant he was only meant to be a side-piece, once he transitioned, for some rich old bugger – never getting the proper social media kudos and fanfare he knew belonged to him. In the Kingdom there was a certain hierarchy that he couldn't stand.

Arzoo, on the other hand, had aced her A and O level exams and had promptly been accepted to the Leland Stanford Jr University – a little place called Stanford for short.

Elated (because yes, even rich people get elated at having a child attend Stanford), the entire cadet branch (Google it, people) of the family was ordered by her dad to find ways to be closer to Atherton. The problem was they were the cadet branch for a reason – there were no men in the family except for her uncle, who was far too afraid to say anything to her. Her four older cousins, all women in their early twenties, sat around their house all day doing a combination of online shopping, watching Turkish and Hindi soap operas, daily prayers, and generally passing their time until their number in the Lahore arranged marriage draft came up. In short, Arzoo had no one who could really supervise and, to be fair, how her father thought that moving Fadhi closer would be of any consequence was lost on her.

"Okay, I get it," said Arzoo, gesturing with her golden cinnamon-coloured arms to the pointed buildings around her, "he's right, Maya. It's total bullshit. Even for me."

Nile gave Arzoo a wistful look. "I think the skyline is wonderful here, Arzoo. You two are being pessimists."

The earnestness in Nile's gaze was of course lost on Arzoo. "Fadhi's right. The Emiratis have more money than Allah himself and they spend it all building huge fucking dicks. Like enormous ones!" Arzoo emphasised the word and playfully mimicked an enormous phallus, which horrified Maya, who immediately averted her eyes and squealed.

"Oh my, Allah, Arzoo, no!" said Maya, as she adorably shook her head and tried to conceal her laughter at Arzoo's suggestive political tirade.

Arzoo stood in contrast to Maya; somehow, blondish, light brown streaks and more than the normal curl had wound their way into her Pakistani hair. She had picked up an extra piercing or two and had glossed her lips more fully than Maya's. In short, she adopted a bit of California flair over her slightly more conservative almost-sister.

Arzoo used her hands to make a gesture of a large phallus and pointed at a tower in the distance. "Just look at that one, it even has a pair of balls at the base. It's a huge erect member just giving it to the sky! Just humping it like a lusty Arabian stallion. 'C'mere sky, I want your booty,' it says!"

Maya finally recovered as Arzoo's tirade wound down. "Well, I think you're right. But the same applies to us too. As Muslims we're blessed by Allah with so much money, but we spend it all on what? One day this stuff will be gone and we'll have never changed. And then the Western world is just gonna laugh at us."

"Allah, it's total bullshit, there's a million other things you can do with your money. I mean, like Emirates, the airline is awesome, right? I don't know why they couldn't build more of those."

Nile, always willing to be Arzoo's supporter, said, "Maya, I don't know why you assume everyone and everything has to revolve around your inflated sense of piety…"

Maya rolled her eyes, not understanding why her brother was such a predictable little puppy. She would be heading back to college, Arzoo for her quarter abroad, Fadhi to California and Nile back to Lahore to finish the last year of high school. The four continued to banter, not realising that, like the setting sun, their time of fun and games was about to take a deep plunge. For you see, good or bad, nothing ever lasts.

HOP ON, HOP OFF

ARZOO LOOKED AT the carpet, the mahogany table, the chandelier that dimly illuminated the hotel's Victorian-era promenade. She looked toward the other end of the hall, past pictures of stuffy long-dead English colonialists who would probably be pissed that an Egyptian Muslim owned the building their portraits rested in. Arzoo looked at the columns and noted how they plainly looked like an old England reaching out desperately for the opulence of Rome. She looked at the bar and scanned the display until she found in the top right, next to the Cointreau, oddly enough, Old Tom gin – her favourite brand for her favourite cocktail, a Tom Collins. *Ah, mission accomplished, girl*, thought Arzoo as her mind started to drift away from the moment towards frat parties at campus and clubbing with Fadhi at Ruby Skye and her favourite escapist fantasy swimsuit photo shoot of the Stanford Men's Water Polo Team (with a few guys from the Crew Team thrown in to boot). Arzoo was completely becoming disconnected from the moment when, to her total and overwhelming dismay, she felt slight pressure on her hands and looked down into the puppy-dog, sad-faced, desperate eyes of a buffoon who wouldn't take no for an answer.

"But, dear, how many times am I to tell you! I am extremely flattered that you find me beautiful" (she wasn't – he was but the thousandth person to tell her so) "and I am equally delighted by the lovely time we spent at The Promenade for high tea" (she hadn't been – in fact, she had looked at her phone a hundred times and snapped about it exactly none); "but I just can't."

The *can't* barely made it out before he started increasing the pressure on her hands and whined, "Oh no, Arzoo! But please don't say no. I wish to marry you. Why don't you want to marry me? What is it about me that you

15

find so distasteful as to resist my charms? Tell me and I will change it within a moment's notice. I've been told on numerous occasions I am the Shahrukh Khan of Lahore high society. My dear, we would be such a power couple."

The live jazz filling the room wasn't enough to drown out his incessant whining.

She tried disentangling her hand from his firm grasp, but he would not relent. She sighed and thought to herself, *Okay Shahrukh, let's get started. Well, it's the way you're sitting – your knees are pointed in, looking like the quintessential picture of a weak man (she meant one who had never trodden water for an hour straight in his life), the way your eyes, warm and soft as they are, are just too damn eager (she meant he'd never spent considerable time in a chlorine-filled pool, emerging with an epic tan, tousled sun-dyed blond hair and yes, red-ruddy eyes). It's nauseating, the way you are holding my hand (this guy's definitely not a five-metre man). Most of all, I abhor how you are trying to force yourself on every fibre of my being (gosh, real men have, like, at least three other options going at any point in time, five on weekends). Every second that I am with you leaves me yawning! I need a drink. Even if you were the most attractive and well-off man in this room I still wouldn't marry you. I need excitement, sex and – yes – even love, but now? No, no, no, not now. I have yet to learn and know my goals and myself; even if you are the perfect man for me, you come too soon.*

Aloud ,she said, "Look! I don't mean to be rude because there is nothing wrong with you. You are a perfectly eligible bachelor, but I just really can't do this. I don't know who has been giving you these false hopes. My mom? Your mom? I am in college for God's sake! Not to mention I just met you for the third time in my life as a courtesy to our parents. I'm too young to get married anyway."

"Oh, but then I will wait for you. I have never met anyone so mesmerising as you. I will wait."

"No, no, please!" said Arzoo. This time she firmly snatched her hand away. She could feel the blood rushing back into the places where he had applied pressure. "Even if you wait, I still can't marry you." And then, mumbling, she added the old, obvious classic line, "It isn't you. It is me."

On that pronouncement, she rushed out of the lobby, nodded to the doorman and – breathing a sigh of relief – ruffled through her bag for her packet of Virginia Slims and lit a cigarette.

Clicking in her knee-length Jimmy Choo shoes, she walked up and down and was momentarily conflicted about the best way to approach her mother and the fact that she was so stressed she had started killing herself by smoking cigarettes again, but then she thought of the joint nestled in her Gucci fur coat and her perfect brows smoothed themselves as she ditched the Slim and walked into a deserted side street for a quick Jamaican treat. Quickly smoking it, she had the immediate whim to sit atop a double-decker and feel the breeze brush through her hair and, because Arzoo does as Arzoo feels, on this beautiful yet slightly cold London day, she did just that.

It was while she felt the wind harshly slapping her face and screeching against her ears that the bus stopped at Piccadilly; there was some kind of a hold-up. And while she felt nervous with both the sudden slowness in momentum and the silence, she remembered she had to call her mother.

"Mom, what in Allah's name were you thinking? Thankfully Allah gave me enough of a mind and the tact to end things before you enabled them to begin."

"Arzoo *beta,*ᐟ what on earth do you mean you want to end things? Look at Maya! She is such a dutiful daughter, so obedient! Honestly, I told your father that you are not the kind of daughter who would willingly go through with an arranged marriage and you're clearly proving me right."

"Well, Mother, it's 2017, I want to live my life in ways you never dreamt. For me, life isn't just about sitting around in Pakistan spending my husband's money and not truly engaging with the world. I have more to offer. You had more to offer. Mom, please, just say no to their proposal."

"Arzoo, this is the hundredth proposal that you are saying no to! The other day Mrs S was telling me that with your track record, you are going to become so independent that it will be virtually impossible to find you a husband! She has been warning me of your impending doom ever since I can remember."

"Jesus, Mother! Why do you even listen to her? I don't believe a word that comes out of that conceited, pompous little preacher's mouth! She's like a permanently duped pro-Trump Twitter troll! Are you sure she's not working with the Russians? On their payroll?"

Arzoo, having uttered the ultimate insult by comparing Mrs S to the United States' 54th Chief Minister, caused her mother to lose her shit and yell into the phone, "Arzoo, Mrs S is not a Donald Trump! He is a son of a bitch,

---

ᐟ Child.

that wicked immoral man. Not like that sweet Obama – such a nice Muslim he is. Mrs S is an angel and the backbone of Lahore's humble business and political classes. May Allah ever bless her and may he change your mind to say yes to this lovely proposal!"

"My answer is a resounding no! I don't like him! Forget him! And for the record, when I marry I will marry for love – none of this other materialistic Lahori society shark mentality."

"Okay. Well, dear, you know I cannot and will not force you. It is your life. I told your father you will never listen, but then again I wonder how much of this is our fault. Okay, Arzoo, you win. I will say no to them. I just can't help feeling a little disappointed," she added with a hint of regret.

"Okay, Mother. Yes, do tell them no!" And she rolled her eyes in annoyance again now, as she always did; she couldn't wait to call both Maya and Fadhi and tell them about this recent intervention by Mrs S. To be fair though, to a certain degree, no matter how much Arzoo wished to bury and conceal her regrettable guilt, she did feel an inkling of a conscience, which reminded her that perhaps she was not worthy of the freedom that her parents had bestowed on her. Perhaps it came as a gift in return of a brother she never remembered meeting. She had many friends who weren't afforded this luxury of freedom. But she had limited capability to deal with both grief and woe. No sooner had she hung up than her friend called and invited her out for the evening.

In an instant, Arzoo's thought process changed from dealing with existential questions of marriage, and how she fit into a world that demanded she walk an indeterminate line between East and West, to how she was going to set up the instas/snaps with the girls when she went out that night.

Followers, after all, need to be entertained.

PEOPLE DON'T SCARE ME...
TRAINS DO

"Arzoo, man, where are you? We are already late. This is our final history of London expedition before we go back to the States, and you're seriously late?"

"I forgot, I forgot! Chill out, Charlotte. I am in Piccadilly. Meet me at the Tube in ten, okay?"

Of course, Arzoo's ten meant twenty, because having the munchies, her stomach grumbled and she stopped in at the Nando's by King's College – the contents of the high tea were already one of her stomach's forgotten memories.

"Arzoo, honestly," said the blonde, tapping her foot.

"Check your privilege, bitch – I had Eastern girl probs that delayed me. I'm here now. Now give me a kiss, sexy." She gave her a kiss on the cheek and no sooner had she sat than she started devouring the bagel with cream cheese.

The girls took their seat on the train and Arzoo, unable to check her Insta/Snapchat for updates in the underground, looked up and found the seats across from her overtaken by two first-year investment banker types. The boys were still young and eager-looking – in that space between just leaving all the idealism of university and coming to terms with adulthood. The juxtaposition of how well they wore their suits, no doubt tailored at Savile Row, and their youthful yet serious faces as they alternated glances at the *London Evening Standard* and Arzoo's bronze legs made them seem attractive to her. It wasn't so much the guys themselves but the life she was afraid she wouldn't have, the mistakes she'd never have a chance to make and recover from. She remembered reading a science fiction book about a race of mole people who finally made it to the surface of their planet and, after glancing at the sun and all the stars in the sky, promptly turned around and ran back into the darkness in fear. There was a certain horror in seeing before oneself all the endless potential in life – some would dive into the empyrean depths of potentialities while others would seal themselves away in the darkness of superstition forever.

Arzoo's mind wandered to her dearest friend Charlotte as the Tube hurtled through the darkened tunnels. *Her dirty blonde hair was smooth and silky and how I secretly wished mine was as straight as hers, while I know she felt the same about my dark chocolate to almost black mane, which is neither straight nor curly and thus can be moulded into either. Ah well! We must do with what we are given, though, in this world of cosmetic advancement, I still prefer maintaining the assets that nature has blessed me with; I only like embellishing them with Mac or Bobbi Brown. I smiled at her and she smiled back. She too was an American, a Californian, but at heart she had the most Eastern soul that anyone could think of. She loved eating spicy foods, loved Pakistani jewellery, clothes, music, wished to have a Pakistani wedding and, if food and clothes seem superficial too – which they are not, reader, for to be a Lahori means to appreciate food and culture – she imbibed the true traditional and familial values of a Pakistani. She was just blonde and I was just brown/olive skinned, but we were more meant for the place that the other was born in, as I unfortunately disagreed with being trapped and bound within my traditions.*

I believed in an evolving society that respected its values, but learned to evolve and adapt with them as time went on; my dear American friend, on the other hand, firmly believed in a fixed notion of morality, which surprisingly coincided more with my grandmother than even my mother! It was for this reason that she so abjectly decried our current predicament (considering that it was brought upon us by my insistence that we party into the wee hours of the morning with a bunch of supremely abdominally-gifted Cambridge rowers the night before).

"Arzoo, I can't believe we missed the 9am train into London. Dr G will be so upset."

"No worries. How many times are you going to say it? It already happened and can't be undone," Arzoo replied. "We're his favourite duo. And knowing his attention to mundane details, I'm pretty sure he hasn't covered much terrain on the walking tour. We're really only an hour late. Besides, I already took a class on Gothic architecture, so I'll fill you in with whatever remains amiss in that oh-so-blonde head of yours."

Arzoo's countenance was one of mock seriousness, lips stretched in a feigned glum line with one eyebrow raised.

"Shut up!" Charlotte laughed playfully. "And what remains amiss in yours?"

Arzoo was laughing but as she truly thought about the question, the confusion resurfaced, the intrepid fears regained control, the feelings of loss and the realisation that her identity was no longer hers to shape made her momentarily shiver. She smiled but the smile was forced.

Arzoo turned her face the other way – toward a mother trying to shush her little baby. The Tube line ended at Monument, but Arzoo's thoughts were far, far away. They vacillated between her father and mother and the abrupt turn that her life had taken.

Her name, Arzoo, meant 'wish or desire' and at that moment she desired nothing more than to have everyone else stop placing their own desires on her life. She wished so desperately for someone, anyone, else's life (perhaps an American's), not because of some misplaced covetousness but because of her own inability to be the daughter her parents wanted her to be. You see, the biggest problem wasn't Arzoo's parents; the problem was Arzoo.

Yes, it's funny that we are born where we are. It is but by an act of fate that we are begotten in the race, family and, yes, even time that we end up with and yet how silly of us to use these arbitrary measures as a means of identity, and even more a reason of distinction, pride, and arrogance. These arbitrary measures are the reasons for ethnic cleansing from colonial enterprises to the Holocaust, from Native Americans to Africans, from Cambodians and Sudanese to the Israel and Kashmir conflicts. I wish to laugh at mankind throughout the ages, for man never changes and history repeats itself.

You pride yourself on your race, your country, and your religion. You pride yourself on something that was never yours or anyone else's achievement. Is man nothing but an arrogant, arrogant fool?

Arzoo looked around the Tube – at its well-used interior, at the amalgamation of varying ethnic faces and socioeconomic backgrounds, and was reminded of the first time she ever sat on a train. It was in Lahore and the train was bound for Rawalpindi. She was fourteen and, tired of dress-up and her mother's insistence that she lose weight, she had cut her hair, packed her bags, and decided to run away. The dirt and grime and homogenous ethnicity of that train she rode all those years ago was in many ways similar to the one she sat on now, but her realisation of the poverty on the train from Lahore to Rawalpindi was an atrocious understatement.

She vividly remembered sitting huddled in a corner trying to hide her Prada bag under the big Louis Vuitton shawl she had wrapped around her. Even so, frustrated men – further to that, being immensely embittered at the vagaries of life for the poor in the Hindu Kush – can smell a young girl miles away – especially one who is reeking of fear. Two or three such blokes spitting *pan** and twirling their moustaches came and sat next to her, upbraiding her with greedy lustful eyes as if she were a calf before *Eid ul Azha*. Even though she tried to signal to the police officer, who was sitting down the compartment, he merely grinned and turned around to the person sitting next to him. He waved his baton, his gun nestled carefully next to his crotch, using his policeman status to extricate funds for his greedy hands.

Three heavyset women hopped on the train in a huff, carrying massive bags and chatting loudly among each other in Urdu. The women bundled on board, unescorted, with a throng of children. They carried bags immensely too big for themselves, their hands and fingers were fat and worn. Their children, an innumerable number of boys and girls alike, attempted as best they could to help put their massive bags on the luggage rack.

The women laughed and argued and debated how best to seat their luggage before finally hoisting one piece in place and then another. As the little tribe worked toward their solitary goal Arzoo, watched as the youngest of the girls went over to the final bag by herself and, without the aid or prompting of her brothers and sisters, attempted to pick it up. The little girl tried and lifted, tried and lifted, but the big bag would not move, but she would not give up in her singular purpose.

When her large and domineering mother finished racking the other bags, she shooed away her other children and looked behind her for the last bag. She saw her daughter trying to lift the bag and Arzoo could have sworn the woman paused for a second – that perhaps she saw something poetic or prophetic in what the little girl was trying and failing to do. The woman

---

* Beetle leaf delicacy eaten in Pakistan.

called her daughter forth and then gestured to her friends to help with the final bag. Then they began looking for seats.

The women moved through the train with authority. The leader had replaced her smile with the judgmental half-scowl of a proud and pious woman from the rural Punjab. Her sisters, be they blood or in-laws, herded the bevy of children before and around them. The woman zeroed in on Arzoo and with a grunt she moved her hefty frame briskly towards the young pre-teen surrounded by a pack of would-be predators.

In what was surely a concerted attack, the men were quickly inundated by children before the women peppered them with slaps and admonishments for their *haram* designs on an unescorted young girl. As the men fled, they pleaded with the women and protested that they were only keeping the sister *safe* from other such nefarious men as ride the trains with hearts full of wickedness.

Having trampled upon the salacious designs of the brigands, the women and their children all sat next to Arzoo. The leader sat directly across from her and to Arzoo's surprise the little girl from before crawled into her mother's arms, denoting her spot as her mother's favoured child (a spot usually reserved for boys).

"Salaam, sister. I am Ayesha, you have here my sisters Salma and Bilkees," she patted the pride and joy sitting in her lap, "this is my Noor," and then she waved her hands like a proud chieftain, "and Mohamed, Ahmed, Abdul, Bint, Naeem, Husain, Marwan I and Marwan II."

Arzoo nodded and smiled at each child, mesmerised by how each of them was their own individual, moving and writhing and laughing or sleeping and everything in between.

"Hello, I am Arzoo." The children broke out in a cacophony of 'Archoo', 'Artoo', and 'Arzoo' as they all tried to say hello. Ayesha watched each sternly to ensure they at least made an attempt to say their greetings as good manners afforded.

Arzoo wasn't sure if all the children belonged to Ayesha, but she seemed to be the type to run a village. In the bags they carried were tightly sealed saffron satchels destined for Islamabad markets. Ayesha explained to Arzoo that their village was in Sindh province, in the southern part of Pakistan. They lived halfway up a mountainside over a valley with an onerous river that had a proclivity to flood its banks. Thrice a year, they would dry and package the saffron in vacuum-sealed bags, stuff them inside nondescript luggage and just the women would take them to Islamabad. "With this many children, they assume the bags are filled with their changes of clothes, toys, knickknacks, not millions of rupees' worth of saffron," said Ayesha.

"If our husbands carried our shipment, bandits would surely waylay them on the road. Several men carrying such large satchels invite easy attention. The other option would be to pay for security – which goes either way. You pay them once and you must pay them forever, for they know what you carry and will relieve you of it themselves if you think yourself too spendthrift to continue to afford their services.

"So, my dear Arzoo, it is by the same law that these wolves surrounded you with their ill intent on this train that allows for my sisters and I to trade in peace. Women are a commodity in Pakistan. We who are obviously older, married and with children have our value spoken for. You, however, are a fat open bag of saffron for all to see! So I find it strange that you would be on this train so far from home all by yourself."

Ayesha said what she felt to be her duty and plainly reinforced to Arzoo what she had quickly come to learn – young unaccompanied girls have no place on such trains.

Arzoo got off at the next stop and as she said her brief goodbyes to the women and their small tribe of children, Ayesha's youngest child offered her a waxy wrapped parcel of knickknacks. The delicately sweet scent reminded Arzoo how hungry she was and despite her manners, she eagerly took the gift.

"*Jalebi** fried in syrup, flavoured of course with saffron. It's my specialty. You go to the station chief and have him call your driver. Then you sit in his office and do NOT move until someone you know comes to collect you, girl. Trains don't scare me, people do."

Arzoo did as Ayesha said and bounded right up to the station chief. She looked up into his bronze face and perfectly groomed moustache, took one deep breath, then another, and then burst into tears.

The next two hours she spent waiting in the station chief's office. Finally, her driver came and exchanged words with the station chief; a few nods and '*theek hai's*' later and Arzoo was inside her father's Land Rover being driven straight back to Lahore. As they rode she licked the bits of saffron-flavoured syrup off her fingers. The taste mixed with her dried tears was actually pretty good. She thought of Ayesha and her children and lives no different in a century or millennium.

---

* Local sweet delicacy.

As her eyes wandered and flickered over the Paddington Tube, Arzoo visualised that train of her childhood. She imagined Ayesha's youngest child watching sternly over a flock of her own as they dried and processed saffron. Arzoo glanced at her reflection in the mirror, slightly entranced by her exotic beauty as it simultaneously held her in Ayesha's world and beckoned toward another. Yet, as is always the case with Arzoo, her more eudemonic musings were replaced by worldly, lesser nonsense. In looking around, she accidentally made eye contact with one of the suits. He smiled and moments later, he and his friend had produced business cards, replete with their cell numbers written on the back, and invited the girls for drinks that weekend.

The Tube finally came to their stop and, as her arm interlinked with her American other half's, Arzoo stepped out onto the platform to look for their eccentric (in an atypical Oxford way, of course) professor and other comrades. Her friend tore up the phone numbers, tossing them in a nearby trash can – obviously underestimating Arzoo's capability of future planning and memorising the numbers.

As she walked out of the Tube, Arzoo was plagued by yet again another thought – the memory of the performance of *The Taming of the Shrew* by the Royal Shakespeare Company that she had seen the night before (where she met said abdominally-gifted rowers – one of them was an aspiring actor). The play had been a magnificent interpretative, interactive, contemporary reading of the text and yet had successfully maintained the Shakespearean quality and brilliance. The stage literally played up the metaphor of the bed and as the actors tumbled up and down, the stage bed they enacted physically reverberated with the sexual innuendo prevalent in the plot.

I thought, in all seriousness, what would be the stage of my life? What would be the focal platform from which to metaphorically view it all? As I thought of the Tube station and my ill-thought childhood adventure, my life was very much scattered with false stops and starts, but I suppose there would always be one final destination. The only thing that one truly had to look forward to was all the hundreds and thousands of people who hopped on and hopped off the same train as you, crossing paths and imprinting a bit of themselves on you and taking a bit of you with them. Sometimes their paths intersected with yours and sometimes they didn't, sometimes they meet briefly only to completely diverge, and sometimes they seem disparate and are actually the same, but one thing is for sure – big or small, saffron farmer or investment banker, they always leave an impact.

FLIBBERTIGIBBET

The Flibbertigibbet is perhaps the most fascinating creature of all Lahore society. This demon lurks within the highly raised eyebrows that passively mock and feign outrage, within the rouge-plastered to perfectly-lined lips that readily issue their scorn with flailing tongues that dart back and forth, spreading malicious rumours with utter disregard for the lives torn asunder by their vitriol.

Yes, the Flibbertigibbet is quite a crucial element of Lahori society, though for an outsider to that society, I must warn you it is the one kind of creature – or rather, woman – that must be dealt with using the most extreme cautionary care. The lips of idle women are one of history's bitterest weapons, dear reader, and as you shall see, those unfortunate souls that underestimate the tricks and traps set by the Flibbertigibbet invariably pay a heavy price.

At a quarter past four, the parade of Dolce and Gabbana, Jimmy Choo, Fendi and Dior commenced. Cosa Nostra, a posh Lahori restaurant, named after a major Italian crime syndicate, was teeming as always with all variations of people – the young, the old and the ancient. Unlike most places in the world, in Lahore it is of the *utmost* fashion to be *unreasonably* late.

Nearly a week before the event, the hostess of the party had informed the throng of designer carriers that the late lunch/early tea of the committee* would commence at 3pm. It was presently more than an hour after the posted start time and, aside from one or two slightly elderly women in their late forties or early fifties who were oblivious to this fashion of lateness, the

---

* Kitty Parties are very common amongst the women of Pakistani's social scene.

sectioned-off area of the restaurant was empty. Even the host of the event herself was yet to arrive! She was at that moment sitting in her car, parked a little way off from the restaurant, awaiting the perfect amount of 'lateness' before she graced her own party with her presence. And let me be clear, under no circumstances would she be anything but late.

At 4.35pm the clicking of heels, made evidently louder by the adjusted steps required to walk in their over-hemmed *shalwar kameez* could be heard climbing up the stairs. The glass doors opened and, in groupings of twos, fours, and eights, beautiful Prada and Chanel handbags, accompanied by their crass owners, emerged from the doors accompanied by the ear-splitting crack of high heels noisily slapping into the wood floors as they tapped their way toward the tables.

Suddenly, the quiet air of the restaurant was cacophonous with the shrill cackles of their laughter, hisses of their disfavour, screeching of clenched teeth – even the force of their fake smiles could be heard in the posh restaurant (that's how fake they were). The Flibbertigibbet happily resides within these women. It has lived for centuries and eons and never met so many in number, so many who were such gracious hosts of gossip.

These women represent the quintessential 'Lahori aunty'. How the name 'aunty' succeeded in being applied to this bunch is beyond my knowledge; perhaps it is out of reverence for these women who, in spite of their evolution into adulthood, remain transfixed permanently on cultivating gossip and innuendo as they did at the age of sixteen? It's a mystery.

Clad in either the most stylish *shalwar kameez* – and believe me, even the traditional Pakistani dress can be made to look highly provocative if it misses a back or barely has a front – or, in the case of the usually younger members of the committee, newly married and in their mid-twenties, in Western wear ranging from Karen Millen or Zara jackets to, yes, even those cherished garments adorned with the sacred Louis Vuitton emblem, the women fill the tables. Their diamond ring-plastered and bracelet-laden hands push designer sunglasses further and further up powdered foreheads – despite being indoors and quite away from the sun, these women will not put their glasses away and will persist on keeping them perched on top of their heads where their brand can easily be spotted.

As waiters pour mostly Diet Coke, audible thumps resonate as the women place (or more like, conspicuously slam) their designer handbags on the table in a show of force that would makee the greatest of chest-thumping warriors proud. To this bunch, the handbag is one of the greatest testaments to both their husband's spending capacity and their own supreme tastes.

I must equivocally point out that, to these women, being wealthy and, even more importantly, to live a designer-addicted life was the basis upon which respect was doled out in their community. Unlike most educated wealthy elsewhere in the world, who purchase a bag or shoe because of the beauty in the craft of its design or the elegance of the shape or the handiness of its material, here an accessory is purchased when its brand logo is easily visible or when, in spite of its ugliness to the majority, the item is limited and expensive. Thus, designer items such as the Fendi bag with the company logo needlessly printed everywhere or the Chanel glasses that screamed their Chanel-ness were displayed as standard issue at the table.

After the Diet Cokes were poured and the pointless side conversations reached a new peak, all the excited and extremely envious glances and their accompanied 'oohs!' and 'ahs!' became transfixed upon Mrs U's newly acquired Hermes Birkin bag. It was her sixth Birkin! Whatever she did with the first five was a mystery, because with Mrs U, merely having brought them forth in public view once meant that their worth was considerably lowered, and there was no way she was ever going to repeat a bag more than twice and, quite often when she willed it, not even more than once.

"OH MY ALLAH! You are the luckiest woman ever. Your husband bought you another Hermes!" exclaimed one of the women.

"Isn't it your sixth Hermes?" chimed in another socialite.

"WOW! The Auvergne colour is so attractive," exclaimed Mrs K. What Mrs K did perceive was how horrid a colour it was for a Birkin, but it was a Birkin so there really wasn't much room for being critical. She had already examined it for any sign that it was a fake, but had come to the unfortunate conclusion that it wasn't.

Mrs U sat there smugly and, for the first time in a very long time, felt an ever so slight tinge of warmth for her husband. As I mentioned earlier, marriages in Lahore are often brought about for every reason under the sun other than love. Sometimes, there are the lucky few who marry those whom they desire, but in most cases, the marriage is a socially formed contract, an alliance between families. The unsuspecting girl is married off into a family of greater wealth and prestige, which is a symbol of respect to her own family and their 'honour'.

Honour – horrid word. I despise the very essence of that word, not because I am a dishonourable person, but because so many have been sacrificed on the altar of their perceptions of the word. The matchmakers who sit at other people's marriages to ally more marriages are, in my opinion, dishonourable for, until and unless they are approached out of genuine need, who has given them the right to carry out their designs on other people's fates?

Just the same, those parents who agree to a union without their daughter's knowledge or who force a consent unwillingly are dishonourable, for what right do they have to toy with their daughter's emotions or her life? Islam permits a woman's own choice of marriage or, as is one of my favourite and extremely horribly delightful stories, even allows a woman to divorce her husband if she doesn't like the way he looks.

Ignoring the taboo that divorce has become, marriage in many areas of Pakistan is seen among the lower classes as a means of blood money or repaying a loan where the child bride may be wed off to a man twice her father's age. But we are for the time being not talking about the poor and the desolate, but the crème de la crème of Lahori society. Many of these women too are dishonourable, for they willingly submit to this injustice; after all, they reside in a much more preferable circumstance where, rather than being married off in the hopes of ending a blood feud, they are merely greedy vultures taught since birth that money and the pursuit of it is the be-all-end-all of society. They are taught the art of entrapping a man, to make him oblivious to their charms. Their entire life is structured around being the perfect wife, the perfect daughter-in-law, the perfect daughter, in that very order of hierarchal importance.

There is one clan, for instance, that is one such example of this explicit kind of training in the warfare for a perfect husband. Much like the Marine Corps takes pride in producing outstanding infantrymen, this clan is the most admirable in their training of skilled enchantresses. Now I don't attempt to single them out in an attempt to ridicule them, for there are very many fine young women who are a part of the clan. I mention it so that you, dear reader, can be made aware of the current renown that exists within Pakistani society regarding these women.

I also provide them as an example to illustrate the extremes to which some go to perpetuate this system for their own material advancement. I consider these girls dishonourable when they marry in attempts to gain more riches, forgetting and blatantly neglecting the noblest cause of marrying for love.

The forty were beautiful women who looked, as I said, much younger than their considerably advanced years. Interestingly enough, the secret behind their youth comes from a natural process rather than the expert work of a UCLA-trained Parsee plastic surgeon, as you'd expect. Their beautification starts the moment they wake up, commencing with a morning workout (which is really progressive uphill walking on the treadmill), a strict dietary regimen (whatever *Cosmo* is telling them *not* to eat this week) and of course, countless visits to the salon.

Ironically, as these women gracefully age, their husbands become more and more unkempt as time passes, growing babies that will remain unborn in the form of their potbellies, but as long as they provide and provide in millions, the marriage exists. It publicly works on the principle that the wife remains beautiful and the husband provides for the riches, and that's all that is socially required or expected.

What happens behind closed doors usually remains unknown.

The culmination of these socially and politically arranged marriages is often long hours of silence, months of sexless nights, and hardly a moment of true connectivity. Those rare and heart-warming moments shared with their children are perhaps the only times when they remember they are a couple. Misunderstandings and miscommunications serve as permanent barriers, enforcing an unfortunate relationship where each partner looks to his or her own needs, never knowing the essence of the 'us'.

So when Mrs U sat smugly thinking of her bag, she did for a moment acknowledge the lack of communication she and her husband had had for such a long time, but then she heard the praise over the bag and all else was forgotten.

"So why did you get it, U?" asked the slightly more stern and direct Mrs S. S was the host of the event and the tone of her voice sought to establish her position as the leader of the bunch.

"Oh! No reason – just like that," she said, shrugging her shoulders to make it appear as if an Hermes Birkin was an everyday occurrence in her household. To be quite fair, she had received the bag as a gracious thanks from her husband for their son's academic success: the six-year-old had got straight As and was invited to the prestigious tea ceremony with the school principal of the renowned Aitchison College.

The conversation in fact now turned from bags to children and, like the bags, the children were transformed into the means of indicating one's supremacy over the others.

"My son got nine As in his O levels," announced Mrs B.

"Well, that is excellent, dear B *jaan*,* and my daughter got eight herself," interjected Mrs H. (Even if she didn't quite think that education was that important for daughters; nor did she plan on letting her extremely hardworking daughter go for higher education abroad, especially if the girl managed to warrant a handsome match; eight As in O levels merely showed her daughter's brilliance and was ironically a means and method of increasing her market value.)

As a symbol of acknowledging the market value both women had ascribed to their children via their O levels, all the women nodded their heads in approval. Mrs W was the extremely rich and proud mother of an unfortunate-looking twenty-two-year-old good-for-nothing who constantly flaunted his father's money, spending it from Dubai to Lahore without any sort of conscience. W started praising her son's extravagance to Mrs H, whose flicker of interest was mounting to unknown limits.

"Our daughters are quite happy at Stanford and Harvard," Mrs K interjected.

She was referring to her and her best friend Mrs N's daughters. Clearly, O levels can offer no comparison to such world-renowned institutions. Mrs K, whether she believed in the value of education or not, had played her ace card. The entire party nodded in approving reverence (except of course those who were aware of Mrs K's other daughter's current situation).

Now the host, Mrs S, of course couldn't allow such an announcement to upstage her. O level exams were one thing but how would a daughter that went to such a prominent world institution simply come home and consent to their way of doing things?

S was a smart woman in her own way and she knew she had best nip such dangerous rebellion in the bud. So, adopting an austere tone, she began, "Oh my! I don't know why the two of you don't worry; such young daughters getting ideas into their heads. Next thing you know they'll be telling us in patronising tones that in a marriage men and women are equal! As a mother,

---

* Word of endearment, local substitute for darling.

yes, a woman has more rights, but as a husband, a man is the breadwinner and a wife must be submissive to her man, who has been gracious enough to provide a roof over her head, bread to eat, and, of course, diamonds to wear."

Mrs S let the word *diamonds* sink in, while she expertly caressed her face, displaying her ostentatious wedding ring that more than a dozen poor Africans probably died to mine. Once she noticed that the other women were sufficiently enchanted, she continued.

"No really, K and N, you two are my best friends, which is why I warn you to keep your daughters in your control before it is too late. It is good you took them to pilgrimage in the middle of the semester, but you never know, they might even come and tell you one day that they don't wish to be married, especially in their twenties, and want to work, in which case do you think they will get proposals after they are twenty-five?"

Mrs S shuddered at that. No, it wasn't just an exaggerated expression of disapproval, but quite actually a natural outlet of horror at the thought of women getting married in their late twenties. Oh the horror!

"So Harvard or no Harvard, Cornell or no Cornell, I think a woman's most important role is to be a good wife."

And just like that, Mrs S brought the entire party back from the brink of their temporary dalliance with the possibilities inherent in sending their daughters to elite overseas universities. Mrs K and Mrs N were left quite speechless but, in true Flibbertigibbet fashion, were extremely relieved when the conversation turned to the latest breaking news – an exhibition by some upstart designer.

"I mean, I am not saying her fashion isn't up to the mark – it is the quality of the material she uses," said Mrs S. Of course her words on anyone were divinely inspired and not open to much interpretation.

"Yes," interjected Mrs K, eager to regain her lost social ground.

"We need fresh new faces in the group. I think she is a very inspired young girl and in fact," and here she inserted the argument clincher, "the Chief Minister's wife would undoubtedly agree with me. She bought at least ten *kameez* from her!"

"Ahhhhhhhhhh!" cooed the buzzards. Case closed. The Chief Minister's wife was the most important woman in Pakistan's upper crust. She was a queen above all others and this was why she didn't grace events such as this little gathering. The Queen never came to the group: the group came to her.

"Speaking of which," interrupted Mrs U, for you see she was eager to show her own social value due to her supposed close relationship with the Chief Minister's family, "who has been invited to the dinner that they are doing this Friday?"

She was slightly both envious and shocked that every member of the committee raised her hand.

"Well," she said, still adamant about enforcing her social value, "I knew about this dinner two weeks ago. As you all know, I am so close to the wife…" They all didn't know, but of course Mrs S used the pause of everyone trying to come up with something wittier to say as the perfect lapse in time in which to bring forth her own agenda to the committee.

"Listen, listen ladies. I called you here for a reason. I strongly feel that the members of this committee must pledge to support my project for the Kalam-Swat river valley. After all, you all know that region is my father's legacy and I wish to enhance the agricultural productivity with my irrigation project."

The other women were stunned. They had never thought S would stake her character on such an altruistic ideal. Well, that certainly was the case as she continued, "Ladies, you all know how profitable government construction is. I urge you to think of your families and the benefits such a noble project will provide in terms of guaranteed government rupees."

The swarm of toadies nodded their heads, each spellbound by Mrs S's ingenious idea. Of course, as is the case with Mrs S, her project wasn't just a two-layered venture but indeed it was layered with multiple agendas. After all, it was just the other day that one of the maids (from her village) informed her that one of the girls' schools was torn down by Pakistani Talibs – those bloody infidel terrorists needed to be countered with progress and development.

She smiled at the group and many pledged to support the project, but Mrs U brought up the topic of the Queen as the political clout needed to send the army in to secure the area and issue permits for construction, even in the hinterlands. No doubt it meant support from her husband's office was a necessary prerequisite to the project beginning. S quickly realised that the Friday dinner at the Queen's residence would present the perfect opportunity for her to secure the support of the project's most powerful benefactor.

Another absolutely necessary component to the irrigation project was Mrs K, as her husband's company enjoyed a construction monopoly in the urban areas of NWFP. However, before S could secure Mrs K's pledge of assistance, she and Mrs N were getting up to leave, as they were invited to some other tea and thus had to leave.

Of course they had barely left when the world of the downtrodden was completely forgotten and the more prevalent news of the divorce of Mrs K's elder daughter spread.

"Did you hear she got a separation?" the newly married Mrs A remarked. "I mean, art or no art, how could she leave her husband? My, he is so handsome and so rich!"

Mrs A was only twenty-one years of age and even if her husband was richer than the gentleman she was referring to, he was eighteen years her senior and not of an extremely appealing exterior or interior.

Mrs S interjected, "That's why I say women shouldn't be made to have all these liberal thoughts. Education – ha! What is the point of this education when it can't teach these women the concept of being good wives? Tsk, tsk. Pointless."

Mrs U, more as a means of a rebuttal against Mrs S than in support for the poor subject matter at hand, said, "But we don't know the story and if she wishes for a divorce, Islam is the most liberal of all religions in that regard."

"Yes, but it is also the thing that is allowed but most displeasing in the eyes of Allah," replied S, smug in her knowledge of Quranic discourse.

Yet Mrs U remained unconvinced, now fully displaying the stubborn liberal streak that had led many to avoid picking a fight with her. "What Allah 'feels' is not for us to decide. We don't even know what each of us truly thinks or feels, so how can we think of ourselves to be so incredibly wise as to try to fathom the Great Creator's feelings on the laws he has given us."

"That is not what I meant. I was just trying to imply how improper divorce is for a woman. What is she to do?"

Mrs S simply could not contemplate a woman's life without a husband. *Suttee** may very well be on its way to extinction in India, but the stigma attached to a divorce in Pakistan is so excruciatingly difficult that one might as well burn a woman after she gets divorced.

"Well, what can she do? I am sure she was an immoral woman. I have seen her many a time staring at other men," Mrs R replied, quite the reputed

* Suttee is an archaic Hindu tradition whereby the wife of the deceased is burned alive.

liar. She just loved spreading malicious gossip and for the only reason that it made her feel powerful and in control of her fellow Flibbertigibbets.

"Tsk, tsk, she must have no shame," said pea-brained Mrs B, gulping her Diet Coke. Mrs R thought Mrs B went at the Coke a little too quickly – 'like a damn peasant' was the exact thought that came to mind. Mrs R smiled at Mrs B and said, "It is hot today, no?"

They both knew it wasn't and Mrs B blushed and got flustered, putting her drink down as if it had suddenly grown venomous fangs and bit her on her pouty lips.

"Not at all," joined in Mrs A, with a disdainful glare in the direction of Mrs B. Mrs A wished very much to gain more of Mrs R's friendship, whom she idolised.

The waiter was coming around for the orders and after bringing out numerous 'salads with Caesar dressing on the side', he found himself bringing out pizzas and burgers with French fries next – a cultural nuance here, as the most mundane and simplistic of American dishes is solely the purview of the glitterati here in the exotic East.

"Mrs S, I heard your maid is extremely good. Does she have any brothers or sisters?" asked Mrs J, deftly avoiding the impetuous slender young girls; her lack of acknowledgement actually moved them into an embarrassed silence.

"Ha! That girl is good for nothing. Trust me, her worthless family is even more *kaam-chor** than she is."

"Speaking of worthless, I can't believe Mr Y married that good-for-nothing half-foreigner," chimed in R, eager to make up for her imbecilic attempts to embarrass the pleasantly plump J.

"I mean, imagine – he is the sole heir of the B and B Board of Companies, ranging from oil and properties to textiles. And so, so, so handsome; the most eligible bachelor," sighed Mrs R's little sycophant Mrs A, who was again thinking about her own husband's unattractive countenance. All the young committee members had a thing for Y, even Mrs R.

And as the women fawned over this now unattainable man, his better half walked into the room. Her stunning beauty elicited muted hisses, while her bewilderment at the intricacies of their social circle goaded them into conspiratorial plots.

---

* Lazy.

"Oh, well, look who the devil brought in," said Mrs R, changing her acid countenance to one of feigned joy. Y's wife's Pakistani father and American mother called her Ariyana and in Arabic the name meant vivacious.

With her white skin and lithe body, she was the quintessential outsider, but as Mrs S saw her she could see the millions of dollars in USAID money that accompanied her American ethnicity. Like every wise entrepreneur, Mrs S always knew a good opportunity when she saw one. She waved, smiled, and pointed the woman toward the seat right next to her that Mrs K had just vacated.

THE INSIDER VIEW ON THE OUTSIDER

MRS R WAVED at the figure entering the glass doors, doing a sweeping check from head to toe as she did so.

To the women's (especially R's) delight, this is what Ariyana wore: loose, baggy jeans accompanied by a pair of flat sneakers, a jean jacket – vintage Jordache, praise Allah (and I say this with much relief) – with a thankfully bouncy ponytail, and no makeup.

Perhaps her simple dress was a function of her bohemian mother, or the fact that she was not, and never would be, a full-fledged member of Pakistani high society. Her father had sinned twice over, first by marrying outside the circle, thus rejecting the unofficial rules of incestuous wealth sharing, and second by actually loving her mother.

Her attire was so exceedingly frumpy that it seemed as if her choice of clothes was an attempt to mask the appeal of her body in order to not seem so 'proud' – no doubt a tactic Ariyana wanted to use to reduce the number of enemies she would have and increase her potential friends. After all, she wasn't stupid. She knew she was envied, she knew her husband was coveted, and she knew those two things made her a target.

Yet her attempt to appear less stunning was a fruitless endeavour with these women. They were, after all, trained in the art of X-ray bitch-o-vision, which enabled them to enviously make out her shapely model-like body under the Pakistani Zara-bought clothes she wore. Nevertheless, Ariyana temporarily let her guard down. Her eyes were the same colour as her hair and twinkled with excitement at being included in this honourable gathering, and her skin, the other women thought with even greater covetous acerbity, was flawless and white. Her half-American blood had given her one of the most coveted traits on the subcontinent: white skin!

Ugh, whatever, thought Mrs R. Mrs R's shameful and un-Islamic carnal desires upon Ariyana's husband led her to despise the fairer woman something fierce. R's hatred was fuelled by the internal shame she felt over the fact that if she ever had the opportunity to corner Ariyana's husband alone... let's just consider R's internal musings regarding the man to be the definition of *haram,*˙ or something out of *Penthouse Diaries* to those of you reading in the West.

Mrs R issued one of her thinly veiled dual-purpose insult-compliments. "A bit tall, isn't she?"

"More like a horse," chipped in Mrs A, laughing.

"Hush now, girls," Mrs S sternly added. "You can't be rude to guests. If for nothing else but for the sake of her husband, hush!"

"Oh! What a little temptress – I am sure she trapped her husband!"

"I am sure she slept with him and convinced him with her bed trickery," said Mrs R under her breath. As Ariyana stepped within earshot, the duplicitous R exclaimed, "Oh my God! I love your shoes. Are they Gucci?" She knew they weren't Gucci, but wanted to embarrass the other woman.

"No," Ariyana replied, smiling and shrugging at the same time, "they're Skechers, much more comfortable. I am sorry I am late, Mrs S."

Her sincerity sickened the other women, and of course Mrs R couldn't resist saying something. "My dear, why ever would you apologise for being late?"

The whole table broke out in loud, obnoxious, unbecoming laughter. They each forgot their turn at being butchered under a gossip's knife. It's interesting how man's and, especially, woman's nature is made up of such inconstant, fickle matter that it forgets the plight it once felt and is thankful when another is made to feel that pain. They all at some level felt horrible for what they would end up doing to that girl, but for now, they rejoiced in another's misery; their darker selves fed off the despondency wrought by their ill will. So when they laughed, they laughed as much at her pain as at their joy that they weren't the subjects of it.

---

* Unholy, forbidden, un-Islamic.

UNSTABLE RELATIONS

MRS K ALMOST tripped on the wooden stairs as she carefully made her way out of Cosa Nostra in her four-inch Dior heels. Holding the rail, she regained her composure slightly even as she glanced at a couple of barefoot street urchins staring at her, no doubt humorously confused as to why the rich woman would choose to hobble in her 'foreign' shoes when Allah blessed her with bare feet that worked just fine.

K shooed them away and considered swinging her handbag at one, but couldn't countenance the thought of the leather being besmirched by coming into contact with their damned dusty selves. Mrs N, who was already on ground level thanks to her far more practical heels, extended her hand and helped her friend down the last two steps.

They passed the security guards and the valets ogling their wealth with jealous eyes.

The women paid no attention because that sort of thing was an everyday occurrence anywhere people with money stepped out in Lahore; it was the price of being princely. Already grumbling regarding the fact that her vehicle was not waiting for her on the street, Mrs K took out her iPhone and called Zafar, her driver.

As she waited for the driver to pick her up, K looked up and down the main road to see if the buffoon had somehow got himself stuck in traffic. It was the early evening, which meant the insufferable Lahori rush hour was upon them: rickshaw drivers yelled the latest news, sang to their passengers, or sometimes hurled insults at competitors as they pulled their carts to and fro. Cheap diesel-powered Honda motorbikes zigzagged their way through traffic, and donkey carts vied for road space with the occasional Porsche Turbo.

Zafar had not picked up Mrs K's call. She was about to start yelling at the valets – someone had to bear the brunt of her displeasure – when her S-Class Mercedes Benz, driven by the poor six-foot-eight-inch *Pathan** squished behind the steering wheel, rounded the corner. Zafar was a gentle giant whose height was about the only daunting thing about him – he was an adorable simpleton with perhaps the slightest tendency for indolence, which of course always led him into trouble with his unrelenting *bibi ji*.**

Despite his height, Mrs K demanded that the utmost legroom be reserved for her and her guests in the back of the car. This meant that poor Zafar had to operate the vehicle with his car seat pulled all the way to its forward position. To make up for the nearly impossible contortions required of him to operate the vehicle, whenever he got the chance, Zafar would roll down his window and drive with his head sticking out of the car. Mrs K hated when he did this, as she despised the fact that the car would be filled with 'the stink of Lahore's streets and the diseases of the poor'. Nevertheless, poor Zafar drove in this way whenever she wasn't in the car. He spotted Mrs N and reflexively waved hello at her while smiling profusely; dust had already mottled the colour of his moustache, and his 'driving glasses', as he liked to call his cherished pair of knockoff Ray Bans sent to him from a cousin in Philadelphia, were also obscured by the city's seemingly endless dust.

"There that idiot goes again, driving my Mercedes like a damned donkey cart!" groused K to her friend.

Zafar waved and smiled as he expertly swung the car around a truck dangerously overloaded with live chickens to pull up to the curb. "*Salam aleikum, bibi ji.*"***

"Zafar, where were YOU?"

"*Maafi, bibi ji,***** it was kind of hot—"

"YES, I KNOW. I have been standing with poor Mrs N out in this heat for the past EIGHT MINUTES!"

"Sorry, *bibi ji*, I dozed off—"

"You slept while on duty! IS THIS WHAT I PAY YOU FOR, TO CATCH A LITTLE SHUT-EYE? I am going to cut your salary for this week."

---

* Man hailing from the Western Frontier of Pakistan.
** Madam.
*** *Salam aleikum* is hello in Arabic; it translates to 'May Allah's blessings be upon you'.
**** Sorry, Madam.

Zafar leapt out to open the door for Mrs N; he was slightly late in opening it for Mrs K, and with a rolling of her eyes, Mrs K shut the door on Zafar's face.

As they sat on the leather seats and Mrs K heaved a sigh of relief, sticking her neck out in front of the air conditioner, Mrs N leaned nearer to Mrs K and whispered, "I think you shouldn't cut the poor man's pay. I know they do get on our nerves but he is such a good man—"

"Yes, yes," she said, "I know. I was merely threatening him. His wife has cancer and I have actually been helping him with the treatment, poor thing. But all the same, a little threat now and then keeps them on the straight and narrow, as you know."

"Well, anyway, why did your *samdhan** to-be invite you over today? Didn't she just get back from an overseas trip today?"

Mrs K was quiet for a minute. She still hadn't told N of her daughter Maya's recent antics and how the girl's aloof disregard for her cousin-fiancé had come to the attention of her mother-in-law to be. I suppose the future mother-in-law had wanted to meet Mrs K in order to receive assurance that both families still equally valued the match. Of course, to Mrs K, the woman's son was the best thing that she could have hoped for her daughter; he was (in terms of his wealth and social status) exactly the match she had always had in mind for her daughter and she would not let this opportunity for her daughter's own betterment slip by.

But Maya's reluctance to give up on this damned boy she claimed to love was risking everything. Mrs K needed the counsel of her best friend prior to the meeting, so she said aloud to Mrs N, "Let's talk in the other language." By that they meant English, as they didn't want Zafar to overhear and perhaps pass information on to some other drivers who would gossip to their own *bibi jis* – a natural social phenomenon in Lahore.

She switched over to English and continued, "You know Maya's future mother-in-law is just such a dear. She really wanted to have us over for tea, as she said she really missed us in Paris."

"Oh K, you are so lucky. Maya is such a dutiful and obedient daughter, isn't she? Not wild like my Arzoo at all."

"Yes, yes," replied Mrs K, smiling, fanatically conscious of both her social image and prestige, and too embarrassed to relay to her friend that perhaps

---

* Child's mother-in-law.

another one of her daughters would either fail to marry or, in the case of her eldest, Laila, stay married to whom they were meant to.

"You know, I really wonder about Arzoo. She just does whatever she fancies. Maybe it's my upbringing. I probably shouldn't have sent her to school in California – all those flower children, dear," said Mrs N in apparent exasperation. She did think that the reason Arzoo was so indulged was because after what happened to her son, what more could parents do with a single child?

The genuine concern for Arzoo in Mrs K's voice temporarily caused N to drop her guard; after all, the women had been friends since childhood, and without thinking, K spoke to cheer her up. "Come, come, dear, stop the worrying – no two children are the same. Look at my Laila."

Bringing up Laila was a mistake. K wouldn't have done it if not for her reflexive desire to let her friend know she wasn't the only one with a daughter to worry about. All the same, Laila's impending divorce was a big deal and even Mrs N felt awkward about the girl being brought up by her.

"Well, yes."

And with that, Mrs N determined to veer the topic away from Laila and bring it back to her own daughter. "But this is about the eighth guy I am showing Arzoo. I just want her to say yes already so we can all rest easy knowing that she will be taken care of."

"Wait, you already introduced her to the Karachi industrialist's son? The one we agreed would be a pushover in marriage and have us divvying up his father's company inside of a decade?"

Mrs K's unabashed greediness made N laugh.

"Oh my Allah, K, you and the money, dear! But, yes. She is at Oxford for the term and I introduced them; he took her out on three dates. His mother told me he was going to pop the question today; let's see what happens. But," she shook her head, "I think Arzoo will reject him," and then she laughed as Mrs K looked at her with a slightly horrified expression. "She says he is a bit of a bore for her. I suppose I can't wrong her on that score."

Shocked and appalled at her friend's willingness to let such a honeypot float down the Indus, K folded her arms in protest.

"Well," she said, "no wonder Arzoo keeps rejecting them if you keep supporting these decisions."

"No, no, I don't support it. I just believe that it's her life and not a question of a day or two. Let them enjoy their lives – before they know it they'll be our ages and the only thing they'll have to look forward to are committee lunches full of gossiping stooges desperately holding onto their teenage years."

Before Mrs K could reply, the car arriving at the huge gate of the cousin-fiancé's mansion saved her. She hopped out of the car and signalled frantically to Zafar, ordering him to hand the presents in the trunk to the guards who rushed out to greet them. Then she plastered a huge and subservient smile on her face for the benefit of her daughter's future in-laws and wondered how in Allah's name she was going to both keep Maya's potential union from falling apart and also send Laila back.

HELL HATH NO FURY LIKE A HAND SCORNED

THE PAIN IN her stomach was much too unbearable and yet she knew if Mrs S were to return to the house from her committee party and find her invariably without a *takki** sweeping the floors – as her mistress had time and time again caught her modulating her work schedule, once for a hair-braiding session, once for her little *bibi's* doll admiring one, and, yes, once even for an apple-eating one – her fury might goad her to beating the little servant girl.

She did not want another encounter with Mrs S's hand, and what a hand it was. It was large, with fingers that extended like a vulture's talons and yet the long horrid nails were neat and well-kept, though their manicured edges had sporadically clawed their way into her skin.

Those same fingernails were used for other ventures too, including the occasional journey into the derriere or in the burrowing of her nose to root out all the miscreants embedded inside. Both pastimes seemed to give Mrs S no limits of joy. Of course Mrs S would carry out these pursuits when she felt she wasn't in the presence of other human company, but the little servant would always catch her *bibi*. But then again, people of Mrs S's class and noble birth forget that servants too are human and that they see and know everything.

It was true – one smack from that hand was enough to send your head spinning, and the little girl wasn't the only one who would suffer the plight of facing that masculine hand of the ironically small-framed lady; the other

* Wet rag used to manually sweep the floors.

servants, her children and, yes, even Mr S would upon occasion feel a roaring in the ears and blood creeping up to form a bruise upon the unfortunate piece of flesh that had felt the wrath of the hand. So I hope you now know why this little twelve-year-old, Fehranaz, whose name meant 'joy', would feel intimidated about attending to the pain in her stomach; even while Mrs S wasn't present, her hand's presence had forever imprinted on the little girl's mind. One would expect a twelve-year-old servant girl's thoughts to not be this articulate, and indeed Fehranaz hadn't been to school much, but she had a secret benefactor who occasionally indulged Fehranaz's thirst for knowledge in everything, especially in the English language and in stories of magic and swords. They had not quite prepared for this moment.

I kept thinking about her hand, I kept thinking about the last time I was so brutally slapped and only because I picked just one apple from the tree in 'her' garden. Why was bibi sahiba* such a mean mistress? I hadn't had anything to eat all day that day and had been feeling faint from want of food.

Was stealing an apple so wrong? The apple was as much my right as the air I was breathing and yet in this house I would often fear doing even that. Sometimes even, when Mrs S would raise her eyebrow at a bit of dust on an ornament I had been polishing, I would gasp and hold my breath for fear that even the movement of my chest would make her hit me; the entire time my eyes would be locked on the hand and my gaze would be steady. Maybe if I stared at it and wished hard enough I could will it to not strike.

The pain was there again. My stomach had hurt spasmodically all day and now the pain gripped not just my stomach but my back too. I could feel a sticky wetness between my legs and felt a great urge to relieve myself. Forget the hand – this pain was more sharp, more obstinate, more aggravating than the momentary slap of her hand and, unlike the hand, which was a prospective courtier of pain, this ache had already seized my body; but, where to go... where to go? The servants' quarter was too far away and I feared I wouldn't be able to walk there, much less run, before bibi got back. Could I use her toilet? It was too late to think of what I could or could not do.

My own hand, shuddering from both pain and anxiety, dropped the takki and went to the nearest toilet, which in this case was, unfortunately, none other than bibi shahab's. Flustered both with the prospect of the jarring pain in my groin and the inalienable expectation of Madame Kaiser's return, I scampered

---

* Respectful term for Madam.

as fast as I could into the toilet and shut the door. I walked over to the pot and pulled down my shalwar and, much to my horror, saw blood there.

At first, the girl was quite shocked by the appearance of the blood, then she started sobbing and her body trembled with the wails that took control over her little torso. She rocked with each tear, her hands clenched into fists. She raised them to the skies, begging Allah for an answer why. She was completely resigned to the fact that she was going to die, that there was nothing in the world that could save her now.

They say life flashes before your eyes before you're about to die; well, this little girl's twelve years flashed before hers. Fehranaz recounted the very first memory she had of her home, of the smell of cow manure lining her abode, of the aroma of her sister's cooking, of the smiles of her desolately poor father, of the warmth of her mother's bosom, of running around in the fields feeling the long blades of grass under her feet as she played *look-chupai** with her other four sisters. Her elder sister was eleven then and old enough to aid her mother in the humdrum chores and her youngest sibling and only brother was barely four months old, so those two siblings would be naturally excluded from the frolicking endeavours of village squatter children.

Her five sisters, excluding herself, were all a year or two apart in age; her father had, as is quite common among these illiterate semen holders, wanted a son, in the typical belief on the subcontinent that a boy would aid him in his old age. Thankfully the seventh child was a boy, and her mother was now at ease from her husband's obsession and frenzied lovemaking (or rather body bashing) – frenzied in the hope that the more energetic the copulation, the more likely his wife would produce a noble heir to his squatter shack. Another mistaken and common belief among the more elevated and logical species of the illiterate Pakistani populace was that women, or more specifically, their state of mind at conception, ultimately determined the sex of the child.

Fehranaz was the second youngest child and the only one who, with fierce green eyes and light brown hair, resembled her Pathan mother; all the others were dark replicas of her Punjabi father. Being a beauty even at the paltry age of five, her parents had big hopes and dreams for her. Yet money was short and when her father got fired from the ministry work at the road construction site over a minor brawl with the *thekaydar,*** her parents had

---

* Hide & seek.
** Contractor.

no other choice but, to put it politely, to relinquish their daughter, their five-year-old daughter, to one of the wealthiest houses as a servant girl.

She remembered her last memories from home – her father's smiles turned into straight lines of grim melancholy, her sisters weeping alongside her, and her tiny five-year-old hands clutching her mother, hanging onto the breasts that had given her sustenance, as if pleading with them to not let her go. But her mother calmly disentangled herself from the frail distraught girl and gave her a tight slap. She remembered having stopped crying at that point, allowing herself to be nudged by her father out of the house and onto the road where the driver awaited.

She remembered looking back just once and seeing the expression on her mother's face – it was stone cold; it would have melted the Himalayan icecaps. That was the last time Fehranaz ever saw her mother's face. What she did not or could not have known was the anguish her mother let fly once she left, or the fact that her mother still clutches her clothes every night, murmuring her name in between desperate, forlorn sobs.

She recalled her departure from home and the end of her childhood with greater acuity than her stay there. She recounted the pain she felt at the way her mother plucked her off her body and how, in spite of the seven years that had passed, she would refuse to meet her family even on the rare occasions that they would come to collect their share of the salary (80% of it, that is, for the other 20% was retained by Mrs S for room and board). You see, Fehranaz was only twelve years old, so was not entitled to even the 20% that, as unfair as even that paltry dividend was, was her right.

Fehranaz was in effect a dependant of Mrs S and the charity that accorded her was even more sporadic than her family's calls to the mansion.

Completely consumed by the agonising lamentations that had taken a hold of her, Fehranaz failed to hear the car pull up in the driveway, even though the bathroom window faced it. She failed to hear the sound of heels as a pair of Gucci-clad feet climbed up the stairs; she failed to hear the pause outside the room, failed to hear the gasp at the sight of a wet *takki* ruining the newly-bought Persian carpet, failed to hear the calm assessment of the frightened wails. She too did not hear the clenching of teeth at the realisation that the crying was coming from the bathroom, nor did she hear the turning of the handle or the fact that there was someone else inside the bathroom now gaping at the terrified little girl sitting on her toilet, contaminating the seat with whatever venereal diseases the poor carry (as the rich truly believed). She did not know that Mrs S had returned until the hand slapped her face. And as her ears rang with the sound of it, and the skin of her face tightened with the numbness of the blow, she briefly stopped crying, only to start up again with the ferocity of a Chennai monsoon.

THE RETURN OF THE TIME OF NO CALM

AND CALM ONLY lasts for a while and it too must pass like all else does.

Maya's relationship with her mother had begun to slowly deteriorate as she had failed to connect with her chosen cousin-fiancé.

The January following the election, he visited her in Cambridge. Maya herself was still a little stunned over everything and her reception was less than ideal. However, cousin-fiancé, being the asshole he was, persisted in trying to force himself on her in innumerable ways.

The thirst was *real* with this one. All the time. Maya could not so much as wear an ankle-length dress without him trying to grope her with some aggressive hug or hold her hand for an excessive period of time.

And his texts! They were as incessant and unnecessary as his abuse of the 'puckered kiss' emoji. Maya swore cousin-fiancé should have known better than to send that emoji in every other conversation because every time he attempted to manoeuvre in for a kiss she instinctively turned her cheek so that he impacted the back of her cheekbone just around her ear.

The trip had ended abruptly when cousin-fiancé, frustrated at his attempts to cop a feel and get Maya's body to have anything but a rigid and inflexible posture around him, decided to leave a few days early. On the surface Maya was amused because she had it on good order that cousin-fiancé was off to spend the extra days in Dubai quenching his 'thirst' with some Ukrainian call girl. However, at the back of her mind she knew there would be hell to pay with her mother, who of course had immediately flown in with Nile to act as 'chaperone' during the days that the fiancé would be there.

She could not tell when, or how, the levee would break but Maya knew simply from the additional smothering and slobbering from cousin-fiancé that the marriage negotiations had reached their terminal stage. As such, her faux pas would incur a disappointed parent's wrath...

Their feigned normalcy was agitated by an innocent, and in fact complimentary text asking her mother what the secret was to her childrearing from cousin-fiancé's aunt (who was oblivious to the inner drama playing out within the engagement circle and merely thought herself doing her part to sweeten Mrs K up by graciously praising her truly amazing children).

The text was well-intentioned (and in fact, well-deserved) because Maya's mother, Mrs K, had sent her youngest daughter to Harvard, married off her eldest, Laila, to a wealthy scion of the Allama Waterworks Company, and was raising her youngest son, Nile, to be an above-average catch, despite his addiction to FIFA.

The issue was compounded by the fact that Maya, in a moment of daughterly weakness, had revealed her true feelings to Mrs K with regard to cousin-fiancé and her desire to be with Ali. At the time Mrs K had taken it in with the moment, not chastising Maya or showing an ounce of judgement on her face. She respected the moment. Yet Maya knew her mother and knew that her honesty would be deposited in her bank account of pain – just like her feelings when Benazir was killed, just like her own suppressed and forgotten loves, hopes and dreams. It was from this vast store of internalised pain that a tempest of fury would emerge whenever Mrs K was triggered.

Despite the benign nature of the text, reality slowly crept up on Mrs K, reminding her that Maya wasn't just her little princess anymore; she was another person. Yes, she was her daughter, but the girl didn't belong to her anymore – her mind was independent and not afraid to think on its own. Mrs K's body had self-aborted as Maya broke off into her own space and individuality. Mrs K's pain was further compounded by Maya's refusal to conform to her mother's wishes on who she would love and marry. To Mrs K, this sort of betrayal was the body gnawing at itself – and such was her fury fuelled.

Maya watched her mother's face as she looked at the WhatsApp. She watched what could have been an appreciative smile stop abruptly and morph into a face tinged with hurt. She watched the face she had seen fight back tears with a twitch of the left eye countless times do just that. Maya watched the woman who had loved her more than anything, who would have poured her entire soul and being into her out of love and who considered her, Maya, as an extension of herself more than any of her children. She watched as her mother inhaled to swell her tiny diaphragm in preparation for the coming onslaught. She watched the woman who now hated her because of who she chose to love.

"You are a whore, do you get that? You are a whore to even think you love someone else. Love – what is love? You are a disgrace to me! What face do I show everyone? I feel like telling this woman" (who had just texted her) "what you really are – A SHAME! A shame to ME, a shame to YOUR FATHER, a shame to your WHOLE FAMILY!"

For a moment, Maya retreated within herself, drawing upon memories of her past. Trying to plead her way through this impasse. Feeling the pain of tearing herself from her own mother's bosom and dealing with the simultaneous joy of freedom and pain of hunger. Her mind wandered...

I am so tired of my life, so tired of being miserable, so fatigued with putting up an armed fortress, which is composed of nothing but an elusive web to keep all pain out. But pain is the trickiest of all the elements in nature – it weaves itself and camouflages itself into everything we know; into our friends, into our lovers, into our brothers and into our sisters, into our fathers and, yes, most of all into our mothers. Pain hoodwinks the kind lids that guard our eyes, placing suspicion where infinite trust once lay. How else would they doubt or learn how to suspect that which they have always known and had full faith in?

Mother, you break my internal resilience. I come from you and while I wish for you to understand my dreams and aspirations, my hopes and my desires, you merely concentrate on the other half of me you know so well – my weaknesses. I hear the words coming out of your mouth, I hear the venom coating every syllable, the pinch in every consonant, the acrid flavour in every vowel, and yet I stay quiet, clenching my fists ever so tightly, wondering if you ever gave birth to me.

"And why is that? Why? Merely because I don't wish to wed that ASSHOLE! I am in love with someone and have been in love with him for FOUR years, *Mother*!" Maya's sneering use of the word 'mother' pounded the war drums of open rebellion.

"You are so selfish, do you get that? So FUCKING selfish. I hope you remain unhappy for the rest of your life. I do hope you get married to the ASSHOLE you want and he teaches you the meaning of hardship."

"Yes, and I hope I never get to see your face again, *Mother*."

Slap!

That first physical blow in the latest skirmish in the battle between the titans of the K household resulted in Maya whirling back at her mother with a proud, defiant stare.

"Yes, I do hope I *never* get to see you again."

Slap! Backhand! Slap! Backhand!

Seeing so much of her own face looking back at her, denouncing her with such resolute confidence, rattled Mrs K to her very core. Considering this, her response to Maya this time was off the cuff and littered with the telltale signs of a mother losing control of her commanding disposition over the family as well as her place in the world.

"I don't want any relationship with you. I don't have a daughter. Why have I cared for you all these years? Why have I got you so many things? Why did I get your facial appointment when you just want to go and live in that impoverished state upon a pile of dung? And let me tell you this: the day that you go into that house, your bad *sama** will start! Not only will you be completely disrespected and abused, but you will have no family to back you."

Maya picked up on this immediately and perhaps out of pity or some subconscious connection that mothers have with their daughters, she steered the conversation back into a realm of rationality.

"How can you wish ill on your own daughter? How do you know what will happen to me? How can you be my family if me not marrying this stupid cousin of mine has led to such a huge catastrophe? It is my life; my decision and choice with whom I want to spend it. Why am I viewed as a bad person just because I wish to be noble in love and marry my love?"

"There you go with this 'love' again. What about what you *owe* to your parents?"

"I don't owe my entire life to you. I love you and would always be there for you but that doesn't mean I will shackle myself into an unhappy marriage for you."

"You will never be happy without your parents' blessings, with killing them, mark my word! You will never be happy! I spit on this love of yours."

"I hate what you stand for. I don't even want to speak to you. Why won't you leave me?"

---

* Time/experience.

In this matter of egos, mother and daughter forgot their relationship, their very intimate bond that ought to have withstood this crucial, yet in many ways trivial, issue. Maya truly believed that whomever she married was her right, and yet she knew she would never choose that right over the prospect of losing her mother's love.

She had given her cousin-fiancé countless chances and knew that his wealth and the promise of a better future wasn't enough to convince her to live a life with someone she wasn't emotionally, mentally, or, unfortunately, even physically attracted to; even now she was appalled by the fact that he had told her mother every word of Maya's honest assessment of him, an assessment that included an earnest description of what she wanted from life. He had callously broken her trust. Despite that, Maya wished no ill to him either and felt extremely unhappy that he had been caught in the midst of this. He just wasn't right for her on an existential level.

On the other hand, the malleability of Ali, her lover, made him the perfect sieve for her own empowerment and thus the empowerment of her family. Maya's lover stood to become a liberator in the long run, beneficial even in the strategic political sense as well. To be sure, he was less wealthy than her cousin but he was a free man, flexible, open, and uncorrupted by Pakistani society life; he represented a literal and metaphorical freedom. Why couldn't her mother see that in Maya's choice of a life partner lay her own self, lay the part of her that wanted to take control of her life and lead it the way she wanted to but couldn't because of the gilded prison in which she resided?

It was disheartening to think then that all this was because her mother simply wasn't ready to accept a 'no' from her 'child'. Mrs K had seized upon the concept that she had lost Maya to a world of intellect and ideas.

Perhaps you think that Maya's mother believed that she had no influence in the world of ideas, that she believed Maya was walking on a razor's edge, and that on either side was the abyss of misbegotten modernity and its empty promises of fulfilment bought at the expense of liberation from family, from culture, and most importantly from her mother. Other things must surely be happening with these two women to succour such enmity. The thing was that they were both fighters; both possessed opposing auras with identical wills. That was their curse.

Maya stormed out of the living room and into her room, but not before she stopped momentarily to glance at the den. Her brother Nile was lying on the couch playing FIFA on the Xbox – high out of his mind, with not a care in the world. As the youngest child and a boy he was doted upon by both parents, which meant he could do pretty much whatever he wanted. Thus, whatever he said was taken to be true, whatever he would do would never be questioned, and whatever he would ask of them would never be denied. They were two years apart in age and yet sometimes it felt that they had completely disparate lives with parents who wavered in their discipline and remained inconsistent in their treatment of son and daughter.

Now, compared to the other louts his age in high-society Pakistan, Nile was a good kid. Maya did admit it for he had a good soul. But that didn't mean he even came close to measuring up to the stringent standards to which Maya was held. She thought of his erratic academic performance in school and the fact that he was held back a grade so his workload would be easier, making him three years behind her instead of one. She thought of his pothead friends and his countless girlfriends (from much lower classes, yet he was a boy and even if he would want to get hitched with any one of them, he wouldn't have to leave his home, so the girl's status would never be a problem). And yet she had not once heard her mother scream at him or her father be disappointed in him, and Nile (who could do so much better) was allowed to stew in his mediocrity solely because he was a boy. Already in an emotional state, she was angered even more by this Xbox-playing reminder of the unfair circumstances surrounding boys and girls in Pakistani society. It wasn't her fault that she was born without a penis, was it?

She tried going to sleep in between sobs; Maya realised that her god, Love, had cursed her. She had to sacrifice one love for the other and yet despite being a regular adherent to the altar of Love's worship, she knew not how to sacrifice it in any of its forms, so instead her mind revolved around in confusion about all the hurt she had felt and caused and how she wished she could be far from it. After anger dissipates and only the hurt remains, you start having kinder sentiments towards the person that aroused the fury in the first place. She never wanted to make her mother anything but proud. She wanted to see her mother weep with joy, hold her in her arms, and say, "I love you and always will."

After a couple of hours of restless thought, transfixed by an uncontrollable need, Maya leapt out of the bed and tiptoed softly, quietly, into her mother's bedroom and stood watching her as she slept, wanting so badly to tell her how much she loved her. And after a few minutes, she just as quietly opened the door and left. Her mother woke up the second she shut the door; the elder K had no idea of her daughter's uneasy heart. She had woken up to a dream of her daughter when she was a little girl running around in pigtails. "Mommy," the little Maya said, "I will always, always, always love you."

The next morning she decided that they would head back to Pakistan as all this education was doing Maya no good. She secretly knew that there was a semester break and that her already-straight-A-student daughter would not suffer in any way. According to Mrs K, a trip to Pakistan would just exact the right amount of pressure to tip the balance in her favour. Anything for her little girl!

THE CEREMONIAL REGALIA
OF CONTENTIOUS EMBLEMS

I LOOK INTO the mirror and at the cascade of long brown curls that flow down and lightly touch the back of my knees. This is the most alluring thing about me; this thicket of hair – hair that is dead and yet still so captivating. Every time I bend down to wear shoes or pull up my pants I can feel it lightly brushing, whispering, telling my face that it owns it, my body, myself.

Hair. I can never rid myself of this exquisite ceremonial regalia, this pestilence that binds me to it and defines my existence, defines my gender. Why am I different than a man – is it the swelling of my breasts, the lack of male genitalia, the lack of a beard? No, to me I am different because of my hair. In my religion, or rather in Arab culture, covering one's hair is considered pious. I've always wondered why that is. Perhaps it's because hair is the first discernible feature between a man and a woman, the first thing that sparks a man's interest because, after all, a woman's hair is a flamboyant display of her gender. Is it our blessing or is it our curse? I look at my reflection again, at the locks of hair surrounding my face and calmly yet ominously tumbling down my shoulders. Those locks are my prison. They restrict my unbound perception of myself and for that they have to go.

Yin and yang, black and white, right and wrong. Society cleaves itself along such stark divisions, ever refusing to acknowledge the greys. I am both male and female and yet neither. I know that now. I look at the deep pits of black, at the fathoms of both pain and joy, and look deeper, deeper into my eyes until I see myself. I don't think the essence, or soul, of womankind is either male or female. If all babies begin their point of inception as the same essence of female, then why should later mutation, whether it be better or not, enable such different views, reactions, and treatments from others? Why should the exterior define the internal self?

I believe our souls are too precious to be dichotomised into either male or female. The soul might exist on a scale of maleness and femaleness where the person is either more of one or less of the other, but always contains both in whatever combination or percentage that can never be arbitrarily and prematurely defined based on what their outsides are socially polished to be.

If a man wishes to wear lipstick let him do so; if a woman wishes to grow a beard let her do so. Why allow a society to dictate the internal expressions that a soul wishes to seek and display? We are all, men and women, young and old, the same in our own respective uniqueness though, I thinkt with a smile, women will always succumb to the ideals of beauty propagated by not just their culture but the desires of this more global culture, while men, even more homogenous and generally more quizzical about experimenting, will always take – or socially show to take –pride in the generally accepted norm of masculinity.

We perpetuate the gender stereotypes that we remain critical of and while the world propagates a universal adherence to respecting differences, it supports and perpetuates an extremely uniform ideal of beauty; the buff man with his six-pack abs and the 36-24-36 figure of countless Instagram and Snapchat profiles is fast approaching a universal acceptance rate. Beauty no longer lies in the eyes of the beholder but in the viewing frame of an iPhone or the pages of a magazine.

I look at my hair again – painful as it is; even I take pride in its beauty, and yet I would rather be true to myself than be beautiful. I take a pair of scissors and swiftly, without any remorse, start chopping away. A few minutes later and the floor is full of long tresses more dead on the ground than when they were hanging on my head – I have removed them from feeding off my life source. I brush my fingers through the short stubs that remain and laugh. I make quite a pretty boy, I think. I always wanted to be a boy and now I am a pretty one. I laugh some more. I pick up the brush and start painting away.

Not thinking, I let the brush take command of my hand; till today I never understood how my aura was connected to the brush and how the brush served the inner recesses of my heart, forcing my hand to succumb to what it knows I desire. I am but a medium, a middle person, and an instrument of the muse that guides me. I always wonder why I am chosen to be this proxy,

*this interlocutor. Maybe it's because I am unafraid of myself, or who I can be.
I shudder when I think about him and for a moment I feel my hands clench;
for a moment I feel fear, as the memories of what was to be the most beautiful
moment of a young girl's life rush back to me. I remember his heaving damp
breath, the pain, and the smell of the poison running in his veins. I remember
the horror of my innocence being violated, corrupted, defiled, and murdered,
I remember the submissive whore who was obscenely birthed that night – the
night of my wedding.*

It was five years ago, her wedding night. Laila was sitting on the bed in
the most beautiful maroon and gold *lehnga.** Her hands were ornamented
with henna, and from head to toe she appeared to be the perfect model for
a gold exhibition. (An artist requires such descriptions.) The *matta patti***
annoyed her and the earrings were too heavy, and yet she knew and realises
that soon they'll be all off. She smiled shyly and yet there was a certain
coyness to her abashed thoughts.

Where is he? Laila thought, as nervousness combined with impatience. He
was rich, handsome and extremely affable, what her society referred to as the
'perfect package'. Capitalism today, even in Lahore, exists not in terms of the
exchange of physical commodities but rather in the exchange of marriageable
people, and by those standards of valuation her newly-acquired husband was
quite effectively a *killer-app*. She was terrified of succumbing to any individual
other than her own will, and yet this man, with his soft words and polite
actions, had won over first her family and gradually herself. Even so, she had
not fully submitted control of herself over to him.

He had first seen her at her friend's wedding and, like he always told
her, had fallen instantly head over heels in love. She didn't know whether
she was in love or what that even was, but she did acknowledge that she
was happy – almost blissfully happy. *Where is he?* she thought again, a little
more frantically than before. Just then the door opened, and she lowered her
glance, staring at the floor, smiling the entire time.

It took her a few seconds to realise that something was wrong. As he
staggered inside, she could feel the stench that accompanied him. Horrified,
she looked up into his eyes – gold rims adrift in a red abyss. His handsome
face was no longer full of life but contorted into a lifeless, inhuman
expression. Startled at this sudden change she started backing away from

---

* Traditional wedding wear skirt.
** Traditional wedding head gear.

him, but he caught a hold of her wrist and twisted her arm. "AHHH," she screamed, gasping and clutching at her hand. "You're hurting me. Let me go. Please. Let me go."

He smiled, his face coursing with a litany of wicked and perverse thoughts and desires. "Ah, ah, ah, dear Laila. Vows have been exchanged, the wait is over, you're mine now, and I'll have you *now*."

As she frantically tried to extricate herself from his grasp, he grabbed her hair, pulling her locks toward his face, then inhaled lustily. "No," she said, "please, please stop." He smiled and drove his face so forcefully into her hair that his mouth impacted with her head, leaving her with a sharp pain. Tiny rivulets of blood appeared on his lips, and as he spoke he licked them clean, savouring the rancid mixture of the blood and alcohol on his breath coupled with the exhilarating scent of her mane. "Your hair is fascinating. Hmm. It was the first thing that I noticed about you." This caught her off guard, but only for a second. That momentary relaxation of the muscles was all he needed. In a flash he grabbed her arms and twisted them behind her back. Truly frightened now, Laila screamed, yet that was futile as her cries couldn't be heard above the din of the revellers outside.

The more she screamed, the more he laughed. He pulled at the earrings, cutting her ear lobes, he grabbed at her neck and bosom, breaking the necklace he had bought for her, and he groped and probed at her body and tore everything that he could grasp hold of. Like a rabid animal he bit, clawed, and even punched her as he proceeded to mark his territory in every possible way he could think of. Beaten and battered, she lay silently and winced when he finished on top of her, gently kissing her forehead, smug in the security of his new possession. He spoke softly in her ear, "I love you, Laila."

While he slept soundly and, thanks to his advanced state of inebriation, snored next to her, she lay paralysed and awake all night, a victim of 'shock and awe' in the truest sense. She had been bombarded and mercilessly ravaged with the intent of simultaneously instilling in her a sense of fear and obedience – it was, after all, how he was trained. Despite it being his perverse pleasure to do it, he could always claim a clear conscience thanks to the unspoken Pakistani code of creating a submissive wife. He knew that she was one of those who hesitated in succumbing, who had always been born free, unhinged by society, by family, by expectations, and yet that night, he slept soundly – confident that he had dealt a mortal blow to the most important part of her – her spirit.

I finish the painting – it's the portrait of an androgynous person. The atmosphere is dark and cloudy, almost as if it's night; yet the person in the painting seems to embrace this night. The eyes of this man/woman are sad, they've seen a great deal of anguish and yet they are powerful in their newfound discovery. They have finally found strength within themselves, as have I. My quest for finding my other half is finally over.

I am now my second half.

A DREARY VENTURE

THE BEST JOURNEY is often the one that you make in the name of love, for not only do you get to explore an entirely new person, but you finally discover someone infinitely more significant: you.

They say that all souls were created long before the creation of bodies and that these souls interacted with one another to form relations or measures of dislike. That is how they explain an instant like or repulsion felt toward someone without ever knowing the exact purpose of such emotions toward a believed-to-be stranger. Perhaps that is one of the most simplistic reasons for the intense love shared by soulmates, the intense fear that separation from that person will cause a tear in the person, rendering them only half of a one. Yes. Love teaches you a lot. Empathy, sacrifice, passion, sometimes even patience, but most of all it teaches the person the extremes that they are capable of.

Maya was, of course, sitting in her room contemplating the vagaries of love. She looked around the room – the round princess bed with a canopy and silk bed curtains, the floor wooden with Persian carpets adorning most of it, two flat screens clinging to the walls and lavish fabric wallpaper scraping them. The whole room was a combination of off-white and gold and nothing that one wouldn't expect of a princess of today. (After all, her name, Maya, meant princess and, like a princess, she had every single luxury that money could afford except the one of freedom.)

Why couldn't they understand the fact that all she wanted to do was be with the person who made her feel complete. No, not complete in the way that without him she would never be capable of being her own person, but that he gave her an inner joy, peace and confidence, which was a rare combination that any other person had the capability of attracting in one.

Why is it so easy for the adult world of rules and tradition to be so terrified of love? After all, what was it about love that was so rebellious to them?

They said that she was wrong, that she must marry for the family, but why couldn't they love her enough to respect her wishes and her decision for her life?

Maya was, of course, weeping, and right then the eight-foot wooden door to the chamber opened and in walked the maid with tea. Her hair, full of silver, was tied in a long braid behind her back, and a thin veil covered part of it. Wrinkles had started blessing her smooth white skin, but her smile was still as mischievously pure as always. She supported a tray carrying tea, sandwiches and biscuits on her hip and walked over to the centre of the room and up the steps to the side of Maya's bed.

"Maya, *shehzadi*, you haven't eaten all day. Please have some of these knickknacks I got for you." It was then that Dai gee (as Maya called this beloved woman who had raised her since she was a kid) looked at her face and noticed the tears that streaked her face. "Oh no, no, *meri beti*," she whispered, lifting Maya's chin, wiping away the conveyors of pain and grief. "You must not cry. You must be strong and show them what you want. Yes, you must."

"Oh, Dai gee." Maya threw her arms around the elderly woman. "I don't know what to do. I don't know what to do."

"Oh, but you do, dear. You always do. You just have to be brave enough to find your own faith and not be afraid of yourself. You are in love – fight for it. No one in this house has ever had either the courage to fall in love or the determination to seek it. No, you must not give up. You must prove to them what you truly are. All your life, *meri beti*, you have put up a false front to please all those around you. I fear now it is time to be yourself." She kissed the top of Maya's head. "Well, now I will be on my way before your mother hears us talking and feels like I am trying to influence you."

Of course Dai gee knew her mistress too well, but she, of course, had no idea that her conversation with Maya was keenly heard by Mrs K, who not only felt jealousy that Maya had found a mother in the woman who had quite honestly been one to Maya while she, Mrs K, was busy in her social philandering, but was more affronted by the fact that this woman actually had the audacity to put ideas in her daughter's mind. The woman, of course, had a greater understanding of Maya – one her biological mother would not have the patience or desire to grasp.

Dai gee was one of those poor innocent souls whose sole purpose in life would always be as an 'aider', to assist the rich and spoilt and in particular her

62

very own *shehzadi*. Dai gee herself was the proud mother of eight – a brood that had been constant in its inception since she was fourteen years of age. So even though she was in her mid-forties (an age at which most mothers in the West plan their prospective families), she was a grandmother, and yet none of her flesh and blood came quite as close to instigating the maternal instincts and love that Maya did. Having spent every waking minute with Maya except for, of course – as Dai gee regretted immensely – her time at Harvard, the care and protective inclinations were to be naturally expected. Equally as plausible was Maya's desire to reveal herself to her Dai gee and to find a parent in the arms of this surrogate mother. Ironically, Mrs K was like many other women who end up being bitter about their child decreeing someone else, and a servant nonetheless, a mother.

So it shouldn't come as a surprise that a week later, poor old Dai gee was checked by the security guard at the gate of the house, who found to her astonished surprise several diamond solitaires and a ruby ring in her little pouch. She was of course instantly fired, much to Maya's chagrin and painful cries. But her accentuating grief, of course, always fell on deaf ears.

She, of course, still wouldn't leave Maya's life, but that's for later, much later, and as I digress, let us return to Maya and the present. As Dai gee left the room, Maya once again thought about the man who made her feel like a woman, who loved the part of her that she loved. If nothing else, she would always have their memories together that had made her feel so alive and full of joy. After all, she was glad that she had been loved. She would never have had it any other way. Yet peace was a fleeting prospect as at the same time she was constantly bombarded by a litany of negative comments scolding her and predicting that their love was star-crossed and sure to end woefully.

"You cannot marry him."

"He is the same age as you. You know older guys are better husbands."

"He is not as rich as you. That's the problem, isn't it?"

"Maya, how dare you? Maya, what is everyone going to think?"

"We don't know their family – for all we know they could be rapists and serial killers."

And the one she disliked the most: "His supposed love for you, it is a ploy to get your money."

Funny thing, that last objection, considering that they'd first professed their love to one another five years ago. *I suppose on my parents' planet sixteen-year-old boys are well-trained fortune hunters.* She laughed. It was a scornful little laugh. He was well off enough and yet was the only person she knew in their society who scorned this obsession with money and made her realise the importance of being modest, sincere, and charitable – concepts that were as foreign to her family as the New World was to Columbus or accountability and integrity to our politicians.

"Maya this! Maya that! Maya! Maya! Maya!" Angry faces, scowls, and clenched teeth flooded her vision. She screamed, clutching her head, slowly calming herself down with thoughts of him.

And lastly his words, "Maya, please understand that you must tell the truth. Stop hiding. I love you so much."

"I love you too," she whispered.

She had taken his advice and shed the skin that she had worn so comfortably that it had allowed her to forget her real self. All she had faced in response was anger, contempt, and a complete disregard of all her emotions and freedoms. As days turned into weeks and weeks into months, her precarious situation kept degenerating. Yet she would not and could not give up on the self she had found with him and him alone. Her lavish dream room day after day had now become the very disabling factor for her peace. She longed for Harvard, for her friends, for the new emancipated woman she had met inside herself, and most of all for him.

They also say that when you dream, your spirit leaves your body and is only connected to your body with a single ray, a ray that makes all the difference between living and dying. *Perhaps*, Maya thought, all alone in her thoughts, with a woeful smile that gave her beautiful face the most haunting allure, *perhaps I can meet you in my dreams.*

She wept into the pillow and fell asleep with fresh tears still wetting lines on her face. Whether it was because she had just been thinking about him or because her spirit and his searched and found each other, she did dream about him.

But how many prisons of a prison can one create? The answer to that easily rests with my parents. They gave me life only to steal the very essence of it away from me because – and only because – I defy their will.

It is a conundrum of a family when love is overshadowed by a testing of wills, when it becomes no longer a matter of the bonds that tie us but a fragile issue of the 'self' and the self's perception of right and what's best. I fear all parents suffer from a superiority complex: they forget that they too were once children, tiny frolicking nobodies who had hopes and dreams that went tainted by the reality of the system.

Must I spend every tantalising minute alone in a solitude that affords no comfort? Must I be incessantly blamed, taunted, and jeered at with no solace? Must I be an expatriate, an outsider to the people whom I hold most near and dear to my heart?

Is it but destiny that some people must learn the hard way, or is it but a consequence of their own lacklustre, short-sighted, frugal and futile attempts?

How trapped I feel and yet with no cathartic impudence on fate's part that my home is the very prison that traps both my body and soul?

I am a person. I repeat it to myself again and again and again so that I don't start confusing myself with the nameless identity of a thing.

The battle is as always between the 'I' and the 'me'. The me has the series of social identities thrust upon it and the I – the more elusive I – remains the culmination of all one grapples with when one attempts to think about and define oneself.

If I shut my eyes I can almost hear them – the sound of family, laughter, happiness, love, and then, just like that, it's gone and all that remains is pain. Pain. Oh, if only it didn't exist to remind us invariably that we are but human. I cry and hug myself ever so tightly because there is no one else to. I think of poor old Dai gee and wonder how she must be getting on. I cry more and then I remember the words she spoke to me the first time I ran, arms flailing, to my room in tears over some long-forgotten and assuredly inconsequential offence:

"Life is but a shadow within the storm of hope, little *shehzadi* – it blows and huffs and puffs but can never blow down an entire house of dreams."

Seems like Dai gee's words of wisdom were not without their essence of fortuitous blessings. After the summer of insults, abuse, torture and permanent house arrest reached its culmination, Maya's mother announced to her that even though they had initially told her that returning to Harvard was now a lost cause, Maya would in fact be enrolled in Harvard for the fall semester. As she rejoiced in her naiveté, Maya remained oblivious to all the reasons that enabled this miracle. Of course the fact that people would talk played such a significant role, but even so, Harvard was a means of ensuring that Maya felt 'grateful' for what her parents had offered her. Her right to an education would be used as the ultimate blackmail weapon in convincing her of the inescapable match made in hell.

TOUCH ME NOT

I HAVE NO idea why he wished to follow me to Boston AGAIN; clearly my more than apathetic response, my extreme horror and uneasiness, at his coming was lost on him, everything seemed lost on him and that too EVERY SINGLE TIME.

I always wonder if human beings are to a certain extent telepathic because often I have experienced thinking things and had the other person not just understand what I have been visualising in my mind's eye, but also convert my musings into – surprise, surprise – reality. This often happens with my parents; I often think of telling my mom that I want to eat a particular food and the next thing I know, she is making it.

My dad somehow is even more tuned in to my inner cognition than anyone I know. He observes and understands every cough of discomfort, every smile of nonchalant inclusion, every blank look of pain – perhaps I am most like him. Perhaps it isn't just telepathic connection but our connection with the universe that makes us aware of each other's covert desires. It isn't just when I wish for the cute boy behind the counter to smile or my professor to call on my raised hand or the waiter to come around to me first without any apparent effort save for the mere mental strength I am emulating.

We picked him up from the airport. I only wish I could tell you the extreme horror that was taking hold of me. Why was he coming? Why? I didn't want to see him! I wanted absolutely nothing to do with him. And yet, in spite of the ferocity with which these thoughts clamoured their way around my head, echoing and hitting the sides of my skull only to reverberate with greater force, my dear cousin appeared oblivious to them. After all, I had even already told him that I loved another and was being forced to marry him. In spite of hearing the truth, he wished to be oblivious to both my heart's pain and our own collective future unhappiness.

He gave me an awkward hug; his audacity at trying to put his arm around me didn't go unnoticed, and as my insides recoiled, my outsides (under my mother's stern gaze) managed a frosty smile and a weak hello. If he had the ability to read minds, he would have undoubtedly understood my palpable discomfort and sat on the same plane to take him back home, but as it had for the past year and a half, his stupefied frontal lobe merely stored the memory for a later reactive outburst.

As I walked alongside him to the car to take us to the hotel near Harvard, I was no longer Maya the unfortunate princess but Maya the queen warrior. I could feel my hair standing and I could almost visualise myself snarling at anyone who attempted to come near; I should have been highly commended for my capability of controlling the mounting disgust within me and maintaining the calm and composed social veneer that my mother required. Interceding via constant iMessage and WhatsApp message, my mother was of course all smiley emojis and excited jubilant responses. I suppose it was making up for my petulant morbidity.

The ride back home was even more frustrating than the meeting; my mother joined us and rode up front and I was left at the back to make forced small talk with him. The next day went by with the same amount of outward apathy and internal resistance. I know I did not give off vibes of particular ecstatic happiness, for I hate someone imposing themselves, yet I tried to be civil, if not for any other reason than that I simply just can't be cruel to anyone – no, not even this despotic destroyer of my life's hopes and dreams. He must have picked up on my internal dilemma because instead of making our exchanges more civil, he tried every possible way of appearing like a spoilt needy child, making it even more difficult for me to take him and his superficial conversation seriously.

So I tried a different approach, perhaps playing toward his sensibilities and secretly my own desire to stare at Zac Efron for two hours. I asked, "Do you want to go see a movie? I think Baywatch is playing?"

"No, Maya. I want to 'chill' at home, ya know?" Clearly he always had a Cali spirit, being born and raised in Pakistan and going to school in London; his pretentious American accent made no sense. If it was meant to impress me, it more than failed miserably. Desis, unlike everyone else in the world,*

---

* Urdu term for South Asian people and culture, the term is used to describe not only people but also their habits.

prefer English over their own language and suffer from an extreme complex regarding their natural accent, using every means possible to camouflage it.

A bit anguished at the thought of being stuck in one room all evening with him, I crossed my legs and sat on the edge of the sofa and tried to look as engrossed as I possibly could in the magazine I was thoughtlessly skimming through. He sat quietly on the other end and before I know it he scooted over and enveloped me into his puny arms. My body jolted with uneasiness and yet I made no apparent grimace of horror, knowing though that this churlish, callow twenty-eight-year-old would throw tantrums, complain – or more aptly putting it, 'bitch' – to my parents and put my life into an even bigger predicament than it already was. So I just sat making neither any effort to shrug him off nor to return his embrace; my fear of upsetting my parents was more paramount than having this alien touch me. So I withdrew myself, numbing my body and locking my soul. I just couldn't stop my thoughts from ricocheting with their fury. In spite of knowing and understanding my visible distress, he proceeded to allow his lust to take hold and guide his further actions, clouding not just his judgment, but his humanity.

He took a hold of my hand and, stroking it, put his foul mouth to it. I felt his beak of a nose more than his lips and as he pecked the skin on my hand, I was pretty sure some snot rubbed itself on my skin. Feeling restless with disgust, I attempted to withdraw my hand, but he held even more firmly. He then got even closer and all the while he kissed my cheek and neck, I could hear his laboured wheezy breath covering me and marking his territory like a dog peeing to mark his. Having felt my will slipping away from my hands, my shoulders, my body, satisfied, he closed in on me with even greater force. I actually felt he was going to break my ribs, at which point I told him he was hurting me, which elicited an even stronger hug. Torn between the desire to cuss him out while joyfully forcing my knee into his groin, I remained oblivious of his growing member. The next I knew, he tried to look intently into my face and I failed to even look into his eyes, disgusted both with his lust and my inability to run away from him and this pickle I had put myself into. He tried to kiss my mouth and as I turned away, he laughed and aimed a few misguided missives at me as a sort of personal mea culpa for his failure to 'score'.

None of it bothered Maya, of course, because she reigned triumphant. After all, she'd survived another day walking the razor's edge of keeping her parents happy and not letting cousin-fiancé have his way with her.

The next day went by as passively as it could for someone who doesn't wish to be with the other and the other perceiving the truth yet failing to act on it. In fact, if the respective other wishes to levy himself commandingly on someone, the friction of dislike and apparent nonchalance mixed with the frustration of not being wanted is bound to create a series of unfortunate rows. What happened in the cinema was one such example that ought to be recorded for the sole purpose of the extreme ludicrousness of the situation.

While stroking my hand, his other floppy arm wound its way around my back in a most awkward situation, with his arm forming a constrictive block between the seat and my upright back. As a matter of reflex my back shot ramrod straight as it recoiled from his slimy little hand. He looked at me with the most innocent and hurt face that the little devil could muster.

"Does it hurt?"

"No, no. It is fine." (Yes, you buffoon, my spine feels like it is resting on bricks. REMOVE your arm.)

After what seemed like an interminable amount of time, but was in fact just a few minutes, he removed his arm, only to pull me toward him.

Oh, hell no! I thought (as I obviously didn't have the authority to voice my opinion – thanks, parents). So I kept my body as rigid as possible, and upon his incessant pulling to have me rest my head on him and basically shift my body so that I would be almost lying on him, I refused to budge. Having realised he could not employ greater force on me publicly, he acquiesced to my internal thoughts and unwittingly rested his elbow on the other side of the seat, which was in the direction opposite from me. As he was still holding my hand, the ten minutes or so that he spent on the other side of the seat remained unnoticed and as I failed to register his every hand movement or every blinking of the eye, my lack of 'care' was bound to warrant his dissipated anger. After all, we only care for someone when we are aware of his or her every eye blink! I noticed his cold replies after the cinema and when he exclaimed, "I don't think you like me," as I stepped on the escalator behind, looking down at my feet, all I could say was, "I do." It was perhaps the most disheartened and affectionless tone I could muster, which would have been enough to convince anyone of my lack of 'like'. However, I again dared not convey my true feelings for fear that he would, without a moment's hesitation, ring up my parents and inform them of whatever honesty I would have attempted to share with him.

We walked back from the cinema to the hotel, conversing a little about this and that until we met a homeless man. My darling to-be-fiancé's lack of humility and demureness reached paramount levels as he refused to answer any of the man's questions and in fact mocked his poverty and mental instability. Disgusted with my cousin's own mental imbalance, I reached into the bag and withdrew a fifty-dollar bill, placing it firmly into the tattered drunk old man's hands, hoping that the slight bump in the usual charity he receives would be enough to momentarily suffice his personal injury.

We continued walking, this time again in complete silence, when I, both in an attempt to make light of the situation and to pacify my perturbed agitation at his rude behaviour, asked, "Were you mad at the homeless man?"

"No. Were you?"

"Oh okay!"

Pause.

"I was just wondering because you seemed to get mad after you met him."

Pause.

"I only asked because I was concerned." I strategically left out whom I was truly concerned about.

"If I said no, why are you asking again?"

"Because it seemed as if he did something to offend you."

"I TOLD YOU ONCE. WHY DO YOU KEEP ASKING AGAIN AND AGAIN? OH GOD! WHY ARE YOU TRYING TO BE SUCH A DRAMA QUEEN LIKE OTHER WOMEN?! I am upset about other things."

"Like?" I questioned, disconcerted with his ability to lose his temper while I had been doing a marvellous job at keeping mine in check.

"DIDN'T YOU NOTICE... umm, in the cinema, when I moved to the other side?"

"What do you mean?" I replied, controlling my desire to imagine opening the car door and seeing him roll out onto the pavement.

"I mean you couldn't see that I was upset!"

"I mean, no, I was busy watching the movie, which was the purpose of sitting in the cinema. (And frankly speaking, I would much rather stare at even a crappy movie than his face.) And honestly, if you were upset about something why didn't you just voice your concerns then, as opposed to holding them off till you see someone else so I suppose that the anger is at that person rather than at something I apparently did? And in any case whatever did I do that should have sparked such a huge outburst?"

"You know what? Fuck this shit! You should have known!"

"Well, clearly I am not the one doing drama like every other woman on this planet."

After a great deal of the same kind of nonsensical repartee, we reached the hotel; he stormed into his room and called up my mother while I waited, scared, angry, and made to feel guilty, in the hotel lobby. Of course, my mother took his side; I clearly questioned her allegiance to her own blood. He ended the conversation by quite impetuously storming out, just because he said. When I told you what the problem was you should have concentrated on that instead of bringing up the homeless man – and I replied with a simple fact – that I can't understand people's theatrics, especially those aimed at gaining attention, and if he desired for me to have concentrated on the problem, then he should have mentioned the problem then and there instead of waiting for a later time to unburden his nonsense. Clearly there isn't enough room for two bitches in a relationship – no, not even a forced one.

It was about the hundredth time that Maya had thought about their relationship since the moment that her parents announced that they were to be married; they never really asked her, just asked her how he was and she said what she, or for that matter any one of us, reader, would have politely said about anyone based on a first impression: "He is fine." They took that as a clear indication that she wished to wed her second cousin, whom she knew nothing about other than that he lived in Karachi and had recently moved to Lahore.

She thought about all the issues they had ever had. You said you wouldn't babysit me in front of my friends. Why did that Harvard guy hug you? You were fifteen minutes late for our Valentine's Day forced 'date'. Why don't you have a curfew in college? Why did you go to the concert where there were drunken people? Why didn't you pick up on my first ring?

He used this extremely pointless little tiff as the perfect opportunity to go out with his friends and get inebriated – or, as he liked to put it, "Roll with the homies and get wasted." Thank you, 1990s-era bro slang.

For all the pointlessness of our arguments, I had to walk a razor's edge when it came to him. The desire of my parents to see us married – and I mean my mother in particular – was getting stronger and stronger every day. She now construed every issue I had with him as some sort of conspiratorial act on my part to derail what she viewed as a match made in heaven. To make matters worse, every single time that I had tried to trust him with my self, a task which is excruciating enough as it is, he always let me down by dealing with that information about me in the exact manner that I would request him not to, by either going to my mother and crying about it, thereby making sure

71

to create irreparable damage to an already shattered relationship, or by using that information as blackmail and a key to gaining what he wished.

I suppose in Maya's eyes there couldn't be a bigger coward than he who is nonchalant to the plight of those around him and who would fail to rise above the present moment, using his confusion and utter lack of comprehension of events to control the situation. Both their perceptions of him were confirmed the next morning when not only did he switch his mind from 'I am not doing it' to 'I am' but he insisted on staying with them in their apartment.

What a gentleman, thought Mrs K, *he not only forgave my daughter's callous attitude, but is willing to give her another chance.*

WHAT AN ASSHOLE, thought Maya, *not only is he continuing on with this sham of a relationship after knowing everything – ignorance can no longer even be an excuse – but he wishes to increase my discomfort by invading my space now too! Why won't he just leave me in peace?*

They were strangely enough both right in their own way. Her mother saw his love, a love that Maya failed to see because of its inherent selfish volatility. Things were only about to get worse for her.

THE RESOLUTION

THE MORNING AFTER her cousin's epically diabolical performance brought with it the promise of change. For all its worth, his big finale was still a precursor to his departure, and Maya revelled in the fact that she'd soon be rid of him (at least until the next visit was foisted upon her). Her cousin's flight was the same evening and she was so happy that he was leaving that she was finding it hard to contain her excitement. In fact, she was so ecstatic about his imminent departure that she was actually making an effort to be civil to him (which he of course misconstrued as an indicator of her sudden interest in him).

Mrs K was also pleased with her daughter's sudden change in spirits and actually even smiled when they all met for brunch that morning. It was tragic that it took Maya being complacent to her dastardly cousin for her mother to exhibit any sort of love for her. That was a testament to how far their relationship had deteriorated over the whole issue. Maya smiled back while wondering to herself why parents such as her mother require goals and fulfilment of expectations to exhibit the care and love that most give unconditionally.

The goodbyes at the airport went smoothly enough; they were as always strained and superficial. Maya was particularly perturbed by her cousin's parting performance. As soon as they hit security, he suddenly started behaving as if Maya was the single most important person in his life and any amount of distance from her would drive a deep wedge in his heart. Upon announcing this, he managed to elicit a solitary tear, then proceeded to heave his face directly into Maya's bosom, 'sobbing' uncontrollably. Any rational mother would easily have seen through the façade but Maya's turned away out of respect for the cousin, either oblivious or uncaring about the fact that the urchin was using the situation as an excuse to apprise himself of her daughter's cleavage from a 'danger-close' perspective.

Following his performance, he presented a card to Maya and even though the contents of the card were soppy song lyrics, she acknowledged the sentiment (and she at least appreciated it because it took her attention off her horror at the fact that he had become quite aroused from his intrusion onto her person). At the least, the card meant he was perhaps making an honest effort to attain Maya, irrespective of how lacking his intentions were in nobility and empathy. All the same, considering that Maya was now near-delirious with joy at his impending departure, she succumbed to his gesture and passed on the card that her mother had made her write, with a truly genuine smile.

Maya's card read: "Dear cousin, I hope your stay was comfortable! I assure you your visit was a learning experience and I believe through the ups and downs I have begun to know you resolutely better. Have a safe flight. Yours sincerely, Maya."

Her sentiments were genuine and contained a great deal of deeper intentional meanings that he would remain oblivious of. The 'Yours sincerely' in particular, to most of us merely a formal way of ending a card or a letter, he took to literally mean that Maya was agreeing to be his in all earnestness.

As a result, while they waited in the check-in line, he became even more melodramatic by stealing serious glances and trying to brush her or touch her any chance he got. He was also adamant about leaving at the last possible moment, as if a few extra seconds could earn him the favour he had quite erringly lost over the past few days. Knowing that it would all soon be over, Maya kept concentrating on the fact that he'd soon be moving away from her at a cruising speed of 388 miles an hour. To be fair to him, he could be with just anyone else so why did he persist in forcing himself on her?

His absurd behaviour, coupled with the fact that she'd soon be free from his smothering, made Maya want to physically push him through the line. She looked at an elderly woman in a wheelchair and imagined the woman – wise in affairs of the heart due to her advanced years – hopping out of the chair in order to let Maya strap her cousin to it so she could shove him right through the line, past the gates and onto the plane. Somehow, she managed to control herself, and soon enough he passed through the TSA checkpoint and was finally gone.

Maya managed to not snap at her mother when she shed a tear as he waved goodbye and as she, perhaps even more infuriatingly, silently stood there for almost fifteen more minutes, sipping her coffee as she waited for him to message them that his plane was about to board. Yes, Maya managed to maintain her cool because her freedom papers were about to be signed and sealed.

On the way back to the car she even kept up appearances and she and her mother had a rather amicable conversation as they waited outside for the driver to pull round. Yet youth has its disadvantages and Maya's carefully sculpted façade came down when she saw the Emirates logo on the plane that boomed overhead as it took off. She watched in almost pure ecstasy as the white, green and red liveried aircraft climbed away into the clouds; the grin on her face said it all. Seeing the joy in her daughter's face and understanding what it meant, Maya's mother looked on in silence, plotting her next move against her own child.

The first thing Maya did on the car ride back was text Arzoo.

"The epidemic has passed and taken all calamities with it."

Arzoo, anxious to hear what had been happening since Maya had told her the cousin had arrived, replied immediately.

"RLY??!?!??!?! OMG! Been waiting for five days to hear from u. I was 2 afraid to know whether to try and get in touch with u in case ur mum thought I was trying to teach u new ways 2 be rude to him."

"No, no, I'm actually glad you didn't! I would've blown up at u 2 – he was SUCH a trial on my patience."

"Oh! You poor, poor thing. Can I call you?"

"Nope. In the car with mommie dearest."

"When is she leaving?"

"Well now that her darling son-in-law has left she won't stay more than two days I am guessing!"

"God I miss you – I wanna see you!"

"Ur right we need 2 hang."

"Oh shit. Have you spoken to Ali yet?"

"No, of course not, how could I being stuffed between the hawk and the fiancé with the emotional intelligence of a five-year-old."

"You should! Maya he's hella upset rgt now. He literally called me a hundred times in the past five days asking me how it is that you can so passively agree to have your cousin-fiancé come and stay when your whole family knows that you don't want anything to do with him."

"OMG, Arzoo, he's being an idiot. I LOVE HIM."

"Just saying, Maya. He feels that you gave up and he is fighting a lost battle; after all you did just get engaged to someone while you loved him. Dude… maybe he IS justified in his insecurities."

"WHAT???!??? Are you kidding me? Why doesn't he ever understand… I have no choice. I'm a girl, a PAKISTANI girl. There is a limit to the amount of mutiny that I can get away with. I haven't given up, I just know that in order to win in the long run you sometimes have to give in in these minor battles. And I will NEVER, NEVER stop loving him; they can chain me, beat me, coerce me in every way possible, but they can't and never will change how I feel for him."

"Yes, I know, but you know he loves you and he can't stand the idea of you not being his."

"Fuck. I wish I could see him; then none of this would even matter."

This text was followed by an unusually long silence. Arzoo's WhatsApp status switched between online, typing, and offline. Perhaps Arzoo spent the time thinking up a scheme or maybe she already had one and was savouring the dramatic nature of the moment.

"Well, maybe you can."

"What?"

"Why don't you get your mother to ask you to visit me?"

"She'll never agree."

"She will! I'll get my mother to convince her. Okay, but you're going to have to talk Ali into coming out to Palo Alto."

"I don't think he will even pick up my phone. I think I will have to send him a letter."

"Like a written one? Wow old skl dude."

"I am sure he'd appreciate that. I am so excited, it's going to be just like old times."

"Contain yourself, my dear, my mom still hasn't given her consent."

"She will, trust me! She never says no to my mom. God! I'll get Fadhi to come over this weekend also."

"*Insha Allah,*[*] I hope so." But in her heart of hearts, Maya had an inkling that she would. Her bad *sama* was dissipating with the cold winter and as spring was coming, she knew there was nothing but happiness for her during break. And she was right. Mrs N called Maya's mother up that night

---

[*] Arabic phrase that means 'God willing'.

and since Mrs K could rarely turn down any of her bestie N's requests, she assented to the visit despite the fact that she was a bit apprehensive about Maya going to Stanford by herself.

This was a hesitation that Mrs N, too, feared, yet she was so anxious about giving Maya space to breathe outside her captivity that she cajoled Mrs K and assured her that all would be fine. Of course, how she ever intended to make sure of that when she herself was thousands of miles away in Pakistan was a mystery. Still, what was important was that Mrs K agreed. With the permissions set, Maya called Ali repeatedly but he refused to pick up his phone; unperturbed, she sat down to write him the letter.

THE LETTER THAT MARKED THE BEGINNING OF THE END

My one and *only love, Ali,*

This is the day he leaves. I try and try hard to understand what it is, but I can't quite put my finger to it. I have been thinking about you. What's your agenda? We all have one. And usually I'm really good at pinpointing who wants what from me, but in your case the essence of your existence baffles me. I don't know what it is that draws me to you, nor do I have the capability to explain it profusely with my words. Being apt here would imply even being able and yet I fail to understand that which I so willingly and desperately crave to call mine: you.

I repeat, what do you want from me? With your progression in years, your incessant needs and wants waver and conflict; you require me, you need me, you hunger for me, you cry for me, you yearn for me in all the possible interpretations of the word 'love' from the most meagre and sexual to the most esteemed degrees of our souls' camaraderie. As always, me, myself and I, heart, body and soul are awaiting eagerly to be yours.

And now, yet again we find ourselves on that familiar path. Somehow I have failed you again. I project so much of myself onto you that I forget we aren't the same person, though so inseparable in ideology. My failure in preventing my cousin from coming has resulted in you once again withdrawing to the very recesses of your self, not our self, and I know it'll take much more for us to be whole again this time. I wish I could take back time and I wish I could have understood you back then. I wish I could have said no to my parents before so I wouldn't find myself in the situation where I am right now.

How empty everything feels without you, and you think I lie to you? I can and will never ever conceal what I feel for you or wrap it to suit my needs, because I have no other agenda from you than to have you be my second half. But when you keep things from me and retreat in this fortitude of doubt and anger, I feel so afraid. I feel afraid of trusting you because I don't know and understand what you're capable of. The more I give you, the more I fear for myself, and that's where we err because I shouldn't fear for me, just us. I wish I didn't think in terms of power ideology, but my love gives me courage my being never knew existed while at the same time enslaving me like a beggar whose dependence on you seems anything but laudable. Please let me in again. I promise you and you know that I will never ever intentionally hurt you.

Why can't you see that I let him come to Harvard for you? Had I opted to fight back, I could have never got the permission to come to Stanford and see you. I don't argue with you when you say that I was pacified with him coming, because I know you're hurting and no matter how much pain I'm in, I just always feel better when you vent out and at least tell me what's wrong. But my love, I've dealt with more than even I could handle. To realise that a person's gods and idols aren't to be worshipped anymore, to know that your life is simultaneously yours and yet never truly is, to know that the people you love are the ones betraying and deceiving you, but most of all to know that no matter what they do or how they shatter their image of themselves in your regard, you will still love them.

Everything I knew and took for granted: my parents, my family, my gender, my freedom, my dreams, all are expendable and easily corroded. Am I alone in this new understanding of the world and my place in it? I don't know. All I know is that I love my parents and I love you and somehow my spirit is being tested by the shape its form takes – that of a lover. Must everything I know and must my understanding of it be sacrificed to show how firmly I root myself in my belief in love? I don't know. I have even forgotten what morals are or, more rightfully, to analyse the situation through my standard of values. Who is right? Who is wrong? I don't know anymore. That's the only conclusion I have come to. We are all victims of our situations.

But tell me where you play a part in this. I will try to rid myself of my cousin and hopefully he shall go, but have you thought about the conclusion either way? What if he doesn't leave my life, but better yet what if he does? Will you be my other half in this mysterious irony of our existence? Will you always love me or will you pull away as our hopes and dreams drift asunder? I need to know that even if I find my lost self in you, will you find you in me?

I have an epiphany: I want to spend the rest of my life with you, but do you know what that means, do you know what I, Maya, mean? My name means princess and that implies a life of luxury contained in this diamond cage. How do I know that I can trust you to think about me when right now you won't even pick up the phone? I want so much to just see you.

I miss you so much and I'm going to be patient for you to come back to me. You can't be scared to trust me. I promise you. But I'm still afraid: if I choose you forever and fight for you then aap meray kuwaab pooray honay do gay,* whether it's to have grey-eyed babies with you or run for Chief Minister? Yeah sirf jo ap chacho gay?** Ap kaabhe meray liyay dard aur ehsaas kero gay jaisay kay mein kerti hoon?***

I don't know when I'm going to see you again. Hopefully you'll come to Palo Alto.

Yours through every point of creation and life we undergo,
Maya

The letter had the impact that Maya had expected. Ali didn't call Maya because, like a typical Pakistani boy, he obviously had to still behave like he was affronted at her behaviour. Instead he sent Arzoo a terse Facebook chat message to let her know that he would be 'visiting some friends at Menlo College' during break.

Two weeks from the day that she wrote the letter, Maya and her lover were both boarding separate planes bound for the Bay Area. Hello Stanford!

---

*   You will make all my dreams come true.
**   Everything will be the way you want it to be.
*** Will you care for me as deeply as I do for you?

THE APPLE FOUND IN PALO ALTO'S EDEN

"IT'LL BE THIRTY dollars and sixty cents, please."

He lifted his head. We had passed the entire taxi ride from the airport to a hotel off University Avenue in unmitigated definitive silence. Words and language are sometimes superfluous modes of communication. They are just constructs limiting us, constricting the scope of human emotions, leashing the scale of expressions and affections. I had been looking out of the window throughout the thirty-five-minute ride, admiring the mountainous terrain between San Francisco and Palo Alto, with his head nestled firmly on my lap – quite an interesting simultaneous reference to a woman's sexuality and motherhood, and I am sure all men always need a bit of both. The flight from New Jersey had probably tired him, as had mine. I arrived at SFO more than two hours before him and the cramped-up seats on local flights are always gruelling. I don't know whether his eyes were closed or open, nor do I know what he was thinking, but I know that I hadn't felt this peaceful in the longest time. His presence calmed me, reassured me, and above all thrilled me.

The second they saw each other, it was a silent pact that they made to forget about the cousin, the engagement and his anger while they were at Stanford. After all, she had waited in a feigned attempt at an apology for over two hours at the airport for his flight to land – an attempt that nevertheless won his equally concealed forgiveness.

I sensed all this love, that had lain dormant inside me, rising to the surface, leaving my body, forming this ball of powerful energy and entering

81

his, but it was all done betwixt the most exuberant of all hushes. I feared that I must stop myself from feeding too much love into this effervescent ball. The harder I tried, the more I couldn't contain this vigorous ardour leaving my body, so I just smiled and sat silently with an oddly natural stillness and let him unconsciously pick up on the secretive puissant messages that my self was sending to his self. The taxi driver jolted us both awake from this esoteric exchange. He lifted his head and looked at me. We both smiled.

He then reached into his wallet and was about to pay when I interjected, "That's not fair. You always pay."

"Shhhh!" he replied softly. "It is my job to."

"Why is it your job to?"

"Because you are my love," he whispered. "Now, no more silly talk. Hurry up and come inside, Maya. I am getting the room keys." Without another word, he opened the door and stepped out into the lobby.

I shut my mouth, which had hazarded an attempt at dissuading him, but realising that it was fruitless, made no further undertaking and proceeded to pick up my bags when I realised that my wallet was missing.

FUCK, FUCK, FUCK, FUCK, I thought, wondering where it could be. After a jumbled and hectic search, the contents of my purse lay scattered on the seat. The kind driver wasn't too perturbed by my sudden mania; perhaps it was also because he was a desi like myself. Outside their respective home countries, Pakistanis and Indians get along fairly well and tend to associate themselves as one entity rather than as two disparate nations arbitrarily divided by Radcliffe and his ignorance.

He called, "I got the key, where are you?"

"I can't find my wallet."

"All right, well, I am sure it's somewhere in your bag. I am heading to the room. It's 103; just come there whenever you are done." The phone clicked shut and I protested a bit to no one on the other end.

I stared with quite a degree of bewildered petulance at the phone. The bond of love was temporarily broken.

Ah well! The plane here must have been considerably more taxing on his Royal Majesty's nerves than mine. As I angrily stuffed everything back in my purse and picked up my clothes bag ,and the bag with the new lingerie I had happened to purchase for someone who was no longer going to get access to the privilege of seeing them, I fumed out of the cab, only to drop the bag containing the lingerie – clearly not one of my finest moments – and the wallet, which *obviously was in the last place I would have looked. As the awfully amicable taxi driver retrieved my extremely intimate articles of clothing, he was perhaps even more bashful than I was. Luckily our brown skins were too neutral to show off the red in our faces.*

"*Shukriya,*"* she mumbled.

"Any time, *bhen,*"** he said, more to the ground he was looking at than her.

She thought of the Mughal Skeikh who had abandoned her and had probably delved into the covers for a nap. Unbeknownst to her, he had actually gone inside the lobby and, in an attempt to establish himself as the 'guy', had checked in while ordering the special bouquet and champagne service. Typical man! Always neglecting what truly mattered for the bigger lofty ideals to please the woman who would never be understood.

Elegantly storming, as elegantly as one can storm, in her Christian Louboutin heels, she made her way into the lobby, handed the bags to the porter, and was led to 103. Ali was sitting on the sofa, a remote in his hand, flipping through the channels to, of course, find the football one. His flip-flops were thrown to the side; one of them was upside down. As neat as he was, she supposed he was too tired to realise that the shoes weren't properly placed, and as anal as she was, she loathed things not being symmetrically placed.

"Here you go," he said, reaching into his pocket and giving the porter a tip for executing the job that ought to be his responsibility.

Without another word, she thumped on the bed and lay there in a posture of feigned nonchalance. Her back was resting against the pillows and she began fiddling with her thumbs.

Why are you so rude? Why won't you look at me? Why won't you apologise for what you did? I swear to God I am not going to let you kiss me! He sat there, more absorbed in the football match than he should be with me, staring quietly at the images on the TV screen.

The TV was on mute. Perhaps he heard her thoughts, which were inaudible in the room but screaming inside her head. He got up, sat on the bed, and without another word kissed her.

My mouth opened and my treacherous body responded; I could feel myself getting dizzy in the head as his and my, our, passion took over. I bit his lip and

---

* Thank you.
** Sister.

pushed him back and said, "Don't you dare kiss me!" He squiggled on top of me and kept his arms on either side of my head, and as his hands reached to stroke my face, he challenged me and, looking at me straight in the eyes, whispered in a dreamy way, "Really? My little princess…"

Before he could continue saying anything, I reached up and pulled his head down and his mouth into my own. His tongue moved through every inch and corner of my mouth: searching, probing, familiarising. His lower lip curled perfectly around mine so that I could feel the fullness of it. It's a funny thing, love – it has its initiation in the body but culminates in the core of your being. "Don't call me that!" Drunk with each other's smell and taste, we stopped kissing for a brief moment. As we looked into each other's eyes, I could read something that I had not witnessed before: a conviction. It reassured me. He kissed my cheek, then my neck, and tried to fumble through my blazer and was unsuccessful. I laughed and said, "Let me."

He took his shirt and his jeans off while I took my clothes off, except for my undergarments. They were from my new purchase – blue lace Victoria's Secret. He traced the provocative lace and I knew he wanted to rip them off. He kissed my neck and traced his tongue all the way down to my stomach – sucking, licking, nibbling, doing everything and anything his desire to please me directed him to. He looked up and, with a slight smile, started to unhook my bra when I, anticipating his desire, laughed and teasingly shrugged him off.

"Come on," he whispered, kissing my hands.

"In another life," I said, reaching up and biting his nose.

"Really?" he whispered in my ear. Oh no! Not the ear. He definitely knew he had me now. I hate it when he says 'really?'; it is just a mere formality meaning 'who are you kidding?'

"Yes, really," I said, flipping him under me and kissing his neck. Oh! Now I had him.

"Really," he said again, turning me under him now.

After many more bouts of playful wrestling, I lay stark naked under him, not at all uncomfortable or conscious of my body in any way. He just made me so content with my own self that I stopped worrying about trivial things like what to do or how I looked. I just know that I was with the person who made me the happiest I have ever been by far and I just wanted him to feel what he made me feel. He put his fingers between my legs and after massaging my clit, separated the pages and put his fingers up me. The moans that escaped my body were indicative of the physical pleasure that I was feeling, but both of us knew we wanted more. His hard member lay against me. He stopped and looked at me again with that calm surety, but this time his eyes were slightly quizzical; they were asking me for an extended vow of fidelity. I suppose they must have brazenly answered in the affirmative because the next thing I knew he held me really, really tight and, never breaking his search into my eyes, began entering me. The second he blinked, I felt him moving inside me and suddenly I was overtaken by a complete harrowing fear. This was the one aspect of my 'morality' that I had promised I would never part with.

Her religion, her family, her culture condemned it ,and what is more, she had made a pact to wait till she was married, but, as she looked into his eyes, she remembered who she would end up marrying. Why keep the most sacred aspect of her existence, the most prized possession, for someone she wished to never set her eyes on? From whom her whole body cringed and shut itself off? No. She would give it to the one person she trusted and loved more than she did herself. Yet these profound thoughts did not run through her head then; it was only later that she attempted to understand the logic behind her unconscious acceptance and agreement at that moment. Her momentary hesitation forgotten, the only thing she remembered was wishing nothing more than to once and for all be one with him. As she felt the pain of him entering her, she clawed his arm and he stopped.

"Shhhh," he said, "shhhh. I am sorry. I am sorry. I hurt you." And he did. He stopped. He held her in his arms and the next thing she knew, she was crying. Her tears streaked his chest more than they did her face, but throughout the entire time he just held her and made her feel like he would never let go. When she stopped crying, he kissed her again.

Before they could say anything else to each other, the doorbell rang and, smiling at her, he put on his shirt, already wearing his boxers, and went to the door. It was the waiter with the pre-ordered service, right on time! She ducked under the covers and, when she heard the door shut again, peeked from under the sheets to make sure the coast was clear. He offered her a glass (more out of courtesy than because his Pakistani protective instincts willed it) but she declined, thankfully! She did smell the flowers and decided to keep them on her bedside. They kissed once more.

We slept in each other's arms almost right after that, still technically virgins. I remember waking up at 3am to find his face inches away from mine; our legs and arms intertwined. I just know I wanted that night to never end. I looked at the flowers next to me, at the soft petals slowly falling and floating down, and went back to sleep feeling a mixture of ecstasy, calm, and this surreal kind of sadness associated with the realisation that all good things always end too. It was the most complete I had ever felt.

OFF TO THE CITY

BUZZZZ BUZZZZZ.

"Mayaaaa," he was groaning. "Could you pleeease get that?"

Groggy and still dreaming of an exotic intergalactic star ship, Maya was in no mood to pick up her phone. She rolled over and covered her head with a pillow to drown out the incessant vibration. Ali was equally tired and in his sleepy state he reached for the phone to answer it. Which of course could be a BIG MISTAKE.

Maya was, after all, in Palo Alto to visit *Arzoo* at Stanford. If her mom found out she was with Ali, then all hell would break loose. "Fine. If you won't get it then I will, sleepy," said Ali. "I bet it's that bum Nile anyway."

She murmured in her half-sleep, "Nile really is a bum." Then she thought about Nile, perpetually sitting, loafing about playing FIFA in the family room... family... room... hous – things started coming together more rapidly as she passed back and forth between dream world and reality. House... home... mother... mother! "Mother! MOTHER!"

Maya shot straight up in bed, her eyes wide open. She glanced at the clock; it was noon, which meant it was midnight back home and way past her check-in time. "Shit!" In an instant Maya snatched the phone out of Ali's hand and spoke into the receiver, "Salaam?" And yes, as was usually the case with Maya's glorious luck, the call indeed turned out to be her mother. As she waited for her mother to respond, she glanced at her call log. There were fifteen missed calls from Arzoo and ten from her mother!

"Maya, where have you been? I just called you so-o many times."

"Yes, Mother, sorry. I was so tired I was sleeping."

"That's strange, you are such a light sleeper. You always wake up!"

"Mother, my phone was on silent."

"Anyways, where's Arzoo?"

"Uh, bathroom session." She slapped herself on the forehead for the screw-up. The plan they had settled on was to always say Arzoo was at a review session when her mother called in the mornings and to say Arzoo was in the bathroom when she called in the evenings (obviously more believable due to the extreme length of time Pakistani women take to present themselves to the world on any particular evening). Because Maya had been startled from sleep, she happened to screw up and now Arzoo was caught somewhere between the bathroom and a review session.

"She is what? In the bathroom?"

Maya, panicking by now, chose to go along with it.

"Uh, yes, she's in the shower."

"Well, fine. I will wait for her to be done then speak with her. So tell me, from what you've seen, how much better is Harvard than Stanford?" Perhaps it was instinct, perhaps it was just her own distrust of everyone in general, but Mrs K seemed determined to verify that Maya was indeed with Arzoo, which of course she wasn't.

Maya held her mother off with small talk while she figured out what to do. She made sure to mention that she thought Palo Alto was garish and obviously full of new money, which made it contrast poorly with Harvard Square. Of course, her mother gleefully took note of this, adding it to her repertoire of off-handed one-upisms she would use at the next women's gathering at Cosa Nostra.

Just then, a text from Arzoo arrived. "Maya, you stupid bitch, call your mom ASAP. I told her you're still sleeping."

"Oh shit," thought Maya. Her mother had made sure she had her bases covered.

"I'm on with her now!"

"Told her u were in the bathroom."

Arzoo texted back, "Srsly?"

"What are we gonna do now?"

"Wait – I know."

"What?"

"Gonna call you and u merge the calls! Mute your mom when I switch over!"

"What! Won't she be able to tell?"

Arzoo had already headed into her bathroom and flipped on the shower. The noise would presumably muffle the electronic feedback that would give away the fact she was actually on the phone as opposed to being there in person.

Maya glanced down and saw that Arzoo was indeed calling in. With a deft movement of her fingers as she spoke to her mother, she muted herself, answered Arzoo's call, merged the call with her mother and removed the mute.

"Arzoo, Arzoo," said Maya as she knocked on the door of her hotel bathroom. Ali looked at her with the most quizzical look on his face, confused as to what Maya was doing.

"Oh hey, Mrs K," said Arzoo, with the shower noise in the background. Maya's mom was surprised/disappointed that she hadn't caught her daughter. She was sufficiently convinced by their little ruse to finally believe that Maya was indeed with Arzoo.

Arzoo and Mrs K bantered for a few more minutes, then Maya managed to end the call. Crisis averted! And all thanks to Arzoo's quick thinking. Maya turned to Ali and said, "Arzoo, oh my Allah, that girl. Ali, you have no idea – she just saved my life. Our lives!"

"You know, Maya, I've been thinking. Let's do something nice for Arzoo today. Honestly, this is just so wonderful that we're together and she's like superwoman in terms of keeping our parents oblivious to this. Even talking to us both when we're mad at each other."

It was moments like these that justified Maya's love for Ali. He was so appreciative, sensitive and understanding, and overall prone to bouts of spontaneous kindness. She gave him a look that told him as much.

"Hmm, sure! How about somewhere in Downtown Pal—"

"Nah! Nah! Let's go into the city. Let me take care of the arrangements, dear. Can you check on trains?" Ali plopped down in front of his laptop to quickly search for a restaurant worthy of Arzoo's selfless efforts.

After about ten minutes of perusing Zagat reviews, Ali settled on the perfect place; he called Maya over and she agreed. She whipped out her phone and called up her best friend.

"Hey, girl! You just saved my life!"

"Ha-ha, nothing to it!"

"Are you hungry?"

"Hell yeah! Been waiting on you sleepyheads. Stacks?"

"Umm, what about Luce?"

"You mean in the city?"

"Yup."

"Maya. That place has a Michelin star!"

Ali looked at her sitting there – a picture of such poised dignity. Both her beauty and her softness enraptured him. Even in her undergarments, she really was a lady, a dutiful daughter responding with the appropriate 'gees' and 'of courses'. And yet he felt this immense sadness for the way she was the one who trapped herself. Even through this little phone call, the tension in her body lingered – a defensive strategy she put up to survive her family's constant haranguing. He desired nothing more than to just snatch her away forever. So when he reached in to kiss her neck, trust me, he really couldn't help it. Pleasantly surprised at his antics, she, of course, smiled and, slapping him playfully, put a finger to her lips. As he had been shooed away, he got up from the bed and began setting aside his clothes for the day's outing.

"You've done so much for us, Arzoo. We owe you a fantastic meal. Meet us at the Cal-Train station in forty minutes and no buts! And bring a few of your friends from school too."

There was a pause, and then she replied, "YESSSS! Bteedubs (BTW) I'm totes bringing dessert treats!"

As Maya hung up she observed Ali putting his credit card and a wad of cash in his coat pocket. She recognised this as a sign he would be paying for the meal, and being Maya, she, of course, was not going to be pushed out of putting her share toward Arzoo's treat.

"Come on, dear, let's split the bill."

"No way, Maya. It's my treat."

"Noooooo, dear! Noooo! It's mine!"

He stepped forward and put his arms around Maya, at once an act of love and manly assertion of what he perceived to be his duty to the friend who enabled him to be with the love of his life. "Maya, we're together now because of her; it's the least I could do. I don't want to hear any more of it. It is my responsibility." And there je went again with the Pakistani love for 'responsibility', which rivalled their equal obsession with 'honour'.

They were interrupted by Maya's phone ringing. Worried that it might be her mother again, she hurriedly disengaged herself from his embrace, only to heave a sigh of relief as she picked up Arzoo's call.

"Yes?"

"Give Ali the phone."

"It's for you."

Ali stared at the phone with a feigned sense of mockery and a raised eyebrow. "How may I be of service, dear Arzoo?"

"Just wanted to say, please make sure madam princess dresses fast."

"I—"

Yet, excited as Arzoo was, she wasn't about to let him put a word in. "Please tell her to hurry. She takes eons just putting on her makeup. I have been able to spend absolutely no time with her. I am so jealous of you right now for keeping her all to yourself. Please do hurry."

"Ha-ha-ha. Don't worry! I will dress her up myself if it comes down to it."

Indeed. He got her dressed in forty minutes. It would have been thirty-five had he not pecked her on the side of her head and made her hand unsteady and, naturally, the wing of her eyeliner crooked. Nevertheless, they were on time (contrary to her former accusations, Arzoo reached the station after them). As she caught sight of her, Maya let go of his hand and as the two squealing friends embraced, he looked behind the bundle of girly euphoria to Arzoo's three friends and Fadhi, whom he had always liked. He shook hands with the girl and tensely acknowledged the third person, a guy Ali had heard of but never seen, and who seemed to live up to the things Arzoo had said about him.

"This is Brent. He's my dealer, y'all."

"Ha ha. Guilty as charged. What's up, guys?" The boy smiled and stuck out an almost effeminate hand to shake Ali's.

Brent was skinny, wearing a well-fitting Ben Sherman shirt, skinny jeans, a pair of what looked like hand-me-down Clarks Desert Boots, and possessed a huge unruly mop of hair that slightly contrasted with his kempt beard. He was, in a word, the very definition of a hipster.

Right off the bat, Ali didn't like him; Brent struck him as a bit condescending and Ali didn't like the way that his eyes would wander then remain transfixed on Maya, a girl he barely knew. Ali thought making conversation with Fadhi at this point was a good ice breaker.

However, Maya, being free of Arzoo's clasp, stepped back and firmly clutched onto his hand and as he smiled, what may have been a whiff of his insecurity zoomed in the opposite direction of the train approaching, horn blaring and engines stalling.

EPICURES

"So MAYA, HOW has your quarter – sorry, semester – been?" asked Brent.

Maya and Ali were sitting in the seats facing the opposing direction of the train's motion and as always she felt nauseous with the incongruous momentum. They had no choice. Those were the only adjacent two seats that were empty. She looked up at Brent and into his blue eyes. They were a really dark blue – the kind of blue that comes to mind when you envision the colour blue in your mind. For the hundredth time she wondered why he had taken up Arzoo's place opposite the couple; it made her both nervous and shy.

"Ahem, good, good! A bit hectic because I got to campus a bit late and then had to take off in the middle."

"Really, why were you late?" Brent seemed genuinely interested, which made his asking the question seem even more awkward.

She gulped and looked over at Ali before answering. He was drumming his fingers against the window and humming a tune. He was purposefully being loud so as to obnoxiously block any effort between Maya and Brent to effectively communicate. Still keeping her eyes on Ali and pretending that she was looking out at the green trees and physically experiencing motion parallax, she replied, "Well, I had a bit of an emergency."

"What kind of an emergency?" It was obvious Brent just wouldn't stop, which caused Ali to tense up some more. He clenched his fists and stuffed them in his North Face, where they were out of sight.

Maya was becoming a little unnerved by Brent's slightly overbearing curiosity. *Arzoo*, she thought, *I will physically rip you into pieces. Who asked you to be such a pea-brain as to invite this smart-ass while Ali was here?* She

92

didn't even try holding his hand, for fear that it would aggravate him to jump up and throw Brent out the window.

As if on cue, or perhaps because she had heard part of the conversation, Arzoo stood up from her seat, from where she had been making goo-goo eyes at the extremely attractive suit sitting at the table opposite her.

"Brent, get up, get up, get up. I have to talk to Maya RIGHT NOW!" and bouncing her round little ass, she shoved Brent off the seat and into hers. Yet another looming crisis averted by Arzoo.

"Well, then, my darling comrades, isn't it a beautiful day to be romancing in the city, eh? Eh? Eh?" she said, nudging both of them. Maya smiled and even grumpy Ali managed an eighth of a smile. Arzoo looked at her best friend and was struck by how much they were connected. It wasn't just how they had been born and brought up together but how Maya understood and loved her in ways that even her parents didn't.

She remembered the time when, five years ago, she had been fifty pounds heavier and the butt of every joke. Girls would actually make snide remarks about how she had the most expensive and beautiful clothes but how they were unfortunately wasted on her, and each of those times, when Maya would find her crying alone under the covers, she would not only know but fight her verbal battles, even disregarding her princess-like status to use foul words she wouldn't be caught dead using elsewhere. Arzoo was much lighter now and undoubtedly incredibly tough. She would shield Maya and preserve her kind heart now that she needed protection.

She reached out and held Maya's hand and mouthed, "He will be okay!" Just then Ali reached out to answer his phone.

"Hello? Hey, what's up, man! No, no, I haven't talked to Mom and Dad. Yes, yes, of course they know I am here."

"Is it Kabir?" said Fadhi.

"Yes, it is his brother."

"Yayyyyy! Kabir is always so much fun." The glitter in Fadhi's eyes twinkled with the remembrance of all the intoxication and the joyous camaraderie that they had experienced along with the anticipation of many more fun times that they were going to experience.

"Ali, is Kabir going to meet us at SF?" Arzoo was just as excited.

"Yes, hold on. Yes, he is, Arzoo." Ali smiled.

"Great. Ask him to join us for lunch. Maya, this is going to be one hell of a trip." They high-fived.

They reached the city about an hour later and, meeting up with Ali's brother and his two friends, the group set off for Luce. As they walked they laughed and talked – recounting old times, taking pictures, and making new memories. While joking, mimicking and reminiscing, they finally arrived and were seated at their table. Arzoo looked up at the décor. Round silver light balls hung down from the sky and the marble floor exuded an aura of modern pristine cleanliness that was both refreshing and calming. It kindled in Arzoo the impatient desire to do something wonderful with her day and she turned towards Brent with a sly smile, planning the wonderful.

Arzoo held her glass of iced tea as if it were the finest Napa wine. If no one in the group was yet twenty-one, they were surely not going to act it. To underscore the fact, she proceeded to ask one of her deep and philosophical questions: "You know, I was wondering if orders of intentionality occur as much in real life as they do in a good piece of fiction. What do you think, Maya?"

"Umm… hmm… I guess, I mean we never know what another person is thinking or if they're thinking about what we're thinking or if we're thinking about what they're thinking about regarding what we're thinking about…"

"Yeah, yeah, I get it, Maya! But do you know what I am thinking about?" As Brent smiled at her, Ali could almost visualise picking up the wine bottle and cracking it open on his head. The sly hipster had obviously caused their temporary truce to be called off.

"Hmmm, no, Brent, I don't think anyone can ever know what you're thinking about." She gulped, hoping he'd take the hint.

"Well, why don't you try?"

"Arzoo, how about you tell us what Brent is thinking about." Fadhi (ever intuitive of social cues) nudged Arzoo, removing her attention from Kabir and fixating it on reducing the unbearable embarrassment associated with the awkward moment that Brent was so adamant about creating.

"Ha ha – ah, he is just super confused about his friend's marriage," said Arzoo, yet again miraculously getting Maya out of an awkward situation, though this time seemed as if it would be even more awkward.

"Well, that, my dear Arzoo, would be undeniably correct. I mean I don't get – well, he is a Mormon, so one really couldn't expect anything other than the bizarre, but to go from Stanford and the mesmerising world of our very own YAO to humdrum constraining marriage is ludicrous – even for a Mormon."

"Who smokes a ton of weed," said Brent.

"Which is totally against their religion," replied Ali.

"He must be reformed or something."

"Interesting – didn't know they had that," added Maya.

"Yup, it's a thing," said Arzoo.

"It's a thing," confirmed Brent.

"Well, look, the fact is there is nothing absurd about marriage – it is the union of two people who wish to be one," Maya snapped.

"Ha! Well, I can think of more than one way of seeking a union with someone, eh, Maya?" However, after perceiving her pouty mouth open in a grimace of shock, Arzoo rolling her eyes and Ali glancing at him with eyes that screamed murder, Brent had to choke back his laughter.

Realising that the Pakistanis wouldn't understand the comedy of the situation and would only fixate on the gravity of it, he gallantly replied, "I apologise, my darling Maya; my intention was not to offend you. On the contrary, I merely wish to please you and win your approval with my every word."

Maya blushed, Fadhi glared at Arzoo as if it was her fault and Ali's thunderous look worsened; this was a direct challenge and he had to speak up.

"Listen, Brent, Bro, Bruv," Ali replied, trying to keep his voice level though it quivered with rage. "Maya is a firm believer in the institution of marriage, as long as it is for love, and she feels that age is merely a number."

Maya nodded – she didn't want to argue with Ali, for she both disagreed with the institution of marriage back home and she didn't take too kindly to him adopting the role of being her ventriloquist. Yet he was angry and she only wished to pacify.

"Oh, yeah!" said Brent. "You guys back East also believe in early marriages."

Ali didn't answer; he pretended to engage himself with his steak, as if cutting it and chewing it was enough of an absorption to make him oblivious to what Brent had been saying to him. Maya waited for him to respond and after a couple of seconds, she realised that it would be too rude to ignore so she replied.

"Really, Brent? Wow, that's a morbidly constricted way of looking at the world! I'd expect better from a hipster. 'Back East', humph – it's the same case as if I consider all of Europe, half of Africa, and both the Americas as the West! Ah! You smile, you believe I jest. But, no, just think of the variance that exists between parts of cities, forget the discrepancy between people in between cities, states, countries, and yet you group one half of the world into one word? An Arab is no more similar to a Pakistani or a Chinese or even an Iranian than you would be to a Swiss or a Peruvian! But to answer your question, yes, early marriages are the norm in 'our society', though with increased education and opportunities people are realising the significance of delaying their marital age. Still, the society is one in transition and filial piety remains important; changes won't immediately happen, perhaps not even in my lifetime."

She felt proud at her little insight.

"Well, darling, if I were born where you were, I would never let you go. I mean, here, marriage is definitely after one has found oneself. I suppose you all believe that you need to find yourself with your respective other, but we, we don't. Hell, why people even get married here beats me. If you can get the milk for free, why buy the cow?" He laughed and even though Maya was disgusted with his callous disregard for women, she was simultaneously attracted to both his countenance and his ability to inspire this Xena warrior in her. Of course, she didn't consciously realise at that time that Brent was purposefully trying to be polemic to get her to pay attention to him, but Ali did.

By the time the dessert of mango parfait and rum cheesecake rolled up, he wished to just throw in his napkin and walk out. But Maya's fingers, perhaps sensing his conflicted despair, found their way around his and as she leaned in to give him a small peck, he smiled and Brent finally stopped talking.

After the two-and-a-half to three-hour lunch had culminated with the girls covering their slightly perturbed stomachs with their bags, Ali paid and they all Ubered to Golden Gate.

They got out of the cab and walked toward the shore of the Presidio. The four of them looked out onto the Bay as the chill late afternoon wind began to descend. To fight off the cold, Maya stood with her arms crossed across her chest. She watched as the sun sent a plethora of colours wheeling across the sky and the placid waters of the Bay lulled slowly back and forth. Ali put his arm around her and she instinctively relaxed her stance. Maya lived within the moment for a second, forgetting the pressures of family, country, and culture. For a moment it was just Maya and Ali standing on a beach in what to her was the most romantic city in the world.

Yet I digress as per usual, because the time had come for Arzoo to dispense the treats she had accrued, courtesy of Brent's day job at YAO in Stanford. He nudged Arzoo and handed her a tiny plastic baggie.

Arzoo smiled, "Ah, the goods."

Fadhi produced a set of ear buds and attached them to his iPhone as Arzoo followed suit.

"You guys get the playlist?"

Suddenly remembering their afternoon plans, Maya and Ali each plugged headphones into their iPhones and opened Spotify on their phones. Fadhi had shared a special playlist with the group that would be the soundtrack of their afternoon adventure.

As they hit play on the list, The Mamas and the Papas' *California Dreaming* started playing.

Brent smiled and talked over the music. "You guys ready to take a magical tour with a morbidly constricted Western infidel drug dealer?"

"You're totally going to love this," Arzoo chimed in. "It's the YAO scavenger hunt. If you survive, consider yourself an initiated member."

Together, they dipped into the tiny baggie Arzoo held and stared out at the shrivelled mushrooms nestled inside.

"First stop, the Hookah-Smoking Caterpillar in the Haight."

As Brent turned and led the group off toward their first stop, *California Dreaming* gave way to Grace Slick's *White Rabbit*, and as they walked, reality began its transition to relativity and the colours of the day began to melt and slowly make love.

A MIRAGE OF COLOURS

SOMETIMES IT COULD *be a bit nauseating, how much in love they were. I suppose I must admit with some reluctance that no matter how much I loved my best friend, I was slightly envious – though extremely proud – that she had not only found true love, but also actually managed to sustain and hold onto it in spite of the numerous disasters that distance and circumstance had thrown at them.*

Even though Arzoo had been the one who had coaxed Maya to partake in the edible festivity, she suddenly wanted to be alone, away from everyone. Not being one to admit the feelings that were slowly creeping into her senses and taking her by surprise, she put on her shades and walked ahead of the others into Golden Gate Park, cutting across Conservatory Road. I suppose for a bit, the sensory overflow stood at a standstill, curling, waiting before gearing up for its onslaught again, and in the interim, when reality could momentarily be grasped again, Arzoo knew human contact would only derail her personal journey.

Chasing after Maya, who had suddenly woken, was no small feat. She was just so complex, layers and layers of high, nigh on impossible expectations met and surpassed; all the tension of that now suddenly fuelling her trip as she ran about with all the energy she carried as a child whose only recourse was to excel and conform.

Terrified that in her mushroom-induced state Maya would run out into the busy street, I ran behind her, Ali and the boys close at my heels. I suppose Maya, being more suppressed, was generally more sensitive to her inner self and heard her body's transformation with greater acuity than the rest of us, and was already in the place we all desired to attain, and fearing for her safety, I rushed to protect her.

Maya had that incorrigible ability to make others feel her vulnerability, to cause others to rise up and protect her at any cost. How convenient to have this strength of a vulnerability – a protection from all hostilities. Ever since we were children, every single parent, every single boy just wished to lay themselves down to her service. I know I might seem a bit jealous – with me obviously being the beautiful princess and all – but to be quite honest I've never been a firm believer in the damsel in distress routine. I liked to remind Maya that she was Old Disney and I was New Disney. To be fair, even Nile had texted me asking me to make sure Maya had a good time. Yes, even her own little brother, who she assumed was nothing but a stoner, a degenerate who just cared about his games and friends, but there was more to him, always had been.

Maya was my best friend; we had an unquestionable bond that never saw any petty female competition or internecine squabbling come between us. From the moment I met Maya, I felt this urge to protect, this motherly instinct to nourish and provide my best friend with true companionship; it was in essence a link that can never be severed or run awry. And so I ran behind her as she ran into the park. And now, upon walking alone, my own anxiety dissipated and within seconds I could feel the colours getting more vivid as another psychedelic pulse readied its assault upon my senses.

As I sat there, I looked up and saw a purple hue mixed in with the yellow, or perhaps the white, of the sun. I looked up at the trees, at their majestic stance, at the long barks winding themselves to take the form of a rigid yet regal outlook. They looked to me like some symbols of wisdom and knowledge and I wished very much to step into the world that they were beckoning me to.

My mind was never more awake, never more susceptible to every slight movement and change in the environment. Oh! How I would have missed the beauty and simplicity of nature had I not made this special and unhinged spectacle possible. The purple hue grew stronger and stronger and I was completely entranced by a desire to lift the veil between the physical and the tree world and metaphorically enter. I could feel every ounce of my mental energy waiting for the gates to open and then suddenly there was a burst and a pop and I was in!

As I passed on through to the other side, I felt this unexplainable energy, at once nameless because people all over the world call it so many different names. The feeling of freedom I enjoyed was mental and physical – it made me light and weightless; I could have jumped from the warm soft ground to the moon and then to the liquid plasma surface of the sun with the slightest effort.

I loved that freedom, a freedom that didn't know the existence of rules, codes and, most of all, society, nor did it know the freedom of the pleasures of the body, so it wasn't freedom that was in opposition to such restrictions or even the temporary freedom that is associated with anything material or worldly. It was freedom that didn't associate itself with any of this domain of the flesh but was just pure uninhibited life and consciousness, true wisdom, streaming through me and out of me.

Having undergone the keyed-up desire to be alone to experience the 'much', Arzoo made her way back to her friends. The others were hanging around on the edge of Golden Gate Park by Kezar and Stanyan. How Arzoo managed to find them she didn't know, but she somehow *felt* them and followed the contrails of their bright essences until she saw them milling about.

Arzoo went and sat on the bench and stared at the leaves on the ground. Their brown and yellow hue made her somehow think of their crunchiness, as if the colour was belying their texture as sight became associated with touch. Before she knew it, the ground heaved and breathed, letting out sighs of pain or relief, she could never know, but still sighing at the prospect of existing. We tread on the ground, we run on it, we sit on it and walk over it, we cry, laugh, play, we murder, steal, cheat, and all along the ground silently watches and knows all that we do and have done, and at the end of it, we return to it and with open arms, the ground takes us back in… Arzoo sighed.

Maya was delirious and as she ran into the park she climbed up a tree, something Arzoo hadn't been able to even convince her to do even when she was a child. She perched on the branch and rubbed her hands along it, breathing deeply as she did, as if equating her energy with the tree's, as if experiencing the passivity of life after all the action her legs had spurred her onto was the most natural conclusion to the day's events. She watched Arzoo walking up ahead, doing an impression of a Viennese waltz toward Peacock Meadow. She watched as she sat on the bench and took a deep breath, lost in the depths of her self, and Maya reached out and her fingers stretched and stretched until she held hands with her best friend.

I could feel Arzoo's heartbeat, feel her thoughts, feel her, and yet I didn't understand if I was feeling her or feeling myself. Was this the unity with the self that makes people seek others, seek society, and in spite of rejection still yearn for acceptance? I had only felt this way with Ali, when his body and mine, when his heart and mine, when his soul and mine, became one. With Arzoo, it was different. There was no sexual underlying, no connotations of the lover, no charged passion, just the familiarity one has with one's own self.

It was serendipitous that just then my phone went off, sending huge lunging shockwaves throughout my body as I continued my trip. It was my mother and for some reason, seeing her message as I was awash in these feelings for Arzoo made me feel like I'd betrayed her in some way. In reality it was probably angst over deceiving her over the true purpose of my Stanford visit. As I struggled to comprehend all this, Brent walked up. I took one look at him and back to my phone then started tearing up. Without prompting I decided to open up to Brent about my issues.

"I love her so much, I want her to know that no matter what happens she will always be my mother. My dad, he understands, he understands me so much, but my mom, I don't know. I want to make her understand and the only way I can is by being in touch with her as much as I can and you know, it's not even college, it's so many other things. I don't like lying. I hate how my entire life has become a huge—"

"Why don't you tell the truth, then?"

Maya looked at some flowers nearby; she was tripping again. The wall was moving...

She didn't know why she had been thinking of her cousin, of their degenerating relationship, and in a flash pictured the unfortunate, bleak 'luxurious' life she could have with him, but then she thought of Ali, thought of his kindness, his love, his ability to make her feel alive. She hadn't been thinking of these things. Emerson, Kant and the Greeks had kept her preoccupied enough at Harvard but now, could she always escape it? She finally managed to answer. "Telling the truth will involve me hurting so many people, including my parents."

"Well, would you rather hurt people temporarily or live a lie and leave this world knowing that your already plastic existence was basically just a shrine dedicated to everything you *didn't* want?"

"Well, when you put it that way, I guess the former will have less damning implications on my eternal soul."

Duty, honour, integrity, and unity – they are all immaterial. Knowledge and only knowledge has the capability of surviving, of living not just as long as a man lives, but even in the next life, for an illuminated soul is a happy one. I could just lie there in the sun and feel divine light being poured down on me and yet I knew that I had to form a reasonable enough conclusion about the world that I 'currently' inhabited. Money, fame, power didn't mean much to me, but love, commitment, companionship, and of course, being liked, meant everything.

"Then you aren't confused, you're just afraid of the journey that you have to go through to achieve your goal, which is you doing you and being you. No journey is easy, especially the one that involves establishing who you're really meant to be."

"But I hate having to hurt anyone."

"That's life. You can't always win Miss Congeniality."

The tree had afforded me comfort and the desire to be up away from the rest of the world. No matter how many planes or time machines, bats or boys with scars on brooms, man can only visualise flying in his mind's eye. Do we truly live in a world when we visualise it? After all, if I think of something, do I spur it into creation, does its existence in the ghostly realm of the imagination assure its being or must it actually be materialised to be considered as being? Even more pertinent, is any impossible thought I think saved into the universe to be realised into the physical world at some probable point in the future? I don't know. All I know was that Brent was leading me somewhere that I was scared to be.

"What do I do then?"

"You tell the truth."

And just like that, he planted the seed that had within a span of moments moved her towards a resolution; she would have to take a stand with her parents about who she actually wanted to marry and not be dissuaded by them this time. It would be hard; there would be moments when she knew she would regret having removed their blissful ignorance about how much hold they had on her, but she knew over time, no matter how far the journey took her from them, her heart would be closer to them. Yes, she would have to tell them about Ali, and as afraid as she was of the prospect of truly standing her ground this time, of their faces as she finally told them that she wished to not marry their 'nephew', she finally knew that she had to do it.

I wish you could just capture time and hold it permanently as it is without any infringement from locomotion or agency, for time is often seen as a linear quality, yet it is not. All time exists all the time at the same time. I am eight, eighteen, and eighty all at the same time, and irrespective of the way time actually is, we only perceive it as a continuum increasing in magnitude and never turning the other way or standing still.

Ali walked over to her and as their eyes met, Maya knew that the moment would exist with her forever; it was a part of time that for her would always stand still.

And her parents would have to know this truth.

BITTERSWEET GOODBYES

ON OUR LAST *day together Ali and I went for a walk on campus and ended up just outside the Cantor Arts Museum, among Rodin's garden of sculptures. Hands, feet, the human body, the expression of emotionality that Rodin had wished to capture in the bronze spoke openly through layers of material conventionality.*

Bewildered, I sat on the steps of what Arzoo later told me were the Gates of Hell, but to me proved to have a rather different effect. As I sat there, I looked up and saw the pink flow itself into the yellow and orange of the sun. I looked up at the gates, at their majestic stance, at the bronze that beset them with an honourable yet harsh gleam. They looked to me like gates of a new beginning – of the door that I had opened and could no longer close.

Ali sat on the steps holding my hands; I could feel him and him me and yet we remained silent, watching together, for the second time in our visit, the sun starting to dip for a good night's rest. We didn't talk. It was almost an unspoken resolve. We both knew what we wanted. There was no longer any need to talk about it. Even so, Ali caved in to reality first.

"Ready to head back to the hotel? Arzoo, Fadhi and Kabir are waiting for us."

Maya nodded in forlorn reservation; the dreaded separation was upon them. She had no idea how she'd cope with that final goodbye and the plane ride home. Fortunately for her, the second that they got back to the hotel, Arzoo had a joint packed with finely trimmed Humboldt gold waiting for them and within seconds they were all high.

As I lay on one of the twin beds with Arzoo, talking, my eyes were always on him – moving around the room, smoking another joint, chatting with his brother. He walked to the other bed and lay down. Barely a minute passed before he said my name and it thrilled me beyond words, but still I refused to immediately follow his very basic unspoken icha.* After all, all he said was my name. After a minute of silence berating the lack of my acknowledgment, he pleaded again, "Maya, please come here." I left the bed and had barely sat on the other one when, in front of everyone, he pulled me into his arms and I willingly complied.

The next thing I knew, we were both staring into each other's eyes like we always did and became oblivious to everything that was happening around us – the fact that Arzoo sat on the bed next to us, that she, Kabir, Fadhi and Brent (who was insistent on being part of the brown crew) were talking, that they were then watching the Pakistani cricket match. Ali didn't even care about the match, and the next thing I knew was that they were sheepishly sleeping next to each other with a pillow in the middle. We just stared and talked and laughed and to date, I don't remember a moment where my soul was ever more at peace.

I was gripped by the incredible sadness that our flights were in a few hours and I began to cry, as did he. He quickly brushed his tear away and, picking me up, took me to the bathroom. He locked the door and, placing a crying me on the tub, removed both our clothes.

He kissed me and slowly bathed my body as I sat crying in the tub. I looked into his eyes, searching, and found it – the source of him and his love. He stared into mine, finding mine, and in that second my nakedness came to symbolise my soul, bare yet innocent, yearning for fulfilment but committed to love. I lay before the man who held my heart as naked as the day I entered the earthly plain, my mind teetering on the uncertain path between carnal curiosities. He moved his hands slowly across my skin, his skin gently washing away the soap. Tiny goose bumps followed in the wake of his touch as I gave in to the moment. I fully accepted that I had failed this test of my morality. I wanted to be his and I wanted to be with him forever; I wanted so desperately to consummate our union that I slowly began trembling.

But we choose how we love and times like these show that we have chosen well. For a second time he spared our honour – his commitment to that was paramount. The irony of it all came to me as I dried my naked body between tender kisses on my neck: I could always afford to lose myself within Ali; he would never lead us astray.

---

* Desire.

He picked me up and carried me back to bed. Snuggling behind me, he put his arms around me. An hour passed and we both lay in externally muted, internally loud silence. He whispered my name in my ear, asking me to turn around. I slept clutching his hand, not letting it go for all the wonders and treasures of the world.

The alarm rang a few hours later and an extremely irritated Maya woke up. Brent had already left for class and Kabir and Fadhi gone back to their respective schools, while Arzoo was still there, quietly observing Maya's despair and, even though also sad about both her friends' departure and unforgiving about her short stay, she was nonetheless trying to pacify the edgy environment as much as she could.

"Guys, honestly, can't you stay another day? Seriously, it's Sunday Funday up at KA tonight."

I was helping him pack and he was 'attempting' to aid me with mine, yet I fought over the way he folded my clothes. It could have been a mutually beneficial last evening together, but I was more consumed with our separation than our last moments together.

"Sunday Funday, huh?" asked Maya. "I would love to stay, but of course what would I do all alone at a frat without Ali, because you know he doesn't take too kindly to the brothers. But at the same time, Lord forbid that he could stay an extra day."

"Maya, darling, why are you getting mad? I told you, I HAVE to go back."

"PLEASE," she said, thwarting his attempts at giving her a hug. "PLEEEASE! You don't HAVE to do anything. You are CHOOSING to go back!"

"Maya, I have a paper I need to hand in."

"La-la-la-la-la. I DON'T WANT TO HEAR IT OR ANY OF YOUR HUNDRED EXCUSES."

"Maya. For God's sake, I didn't ask you a question so that you'd take it out on Ali," interrupted Arzoo.

"Oh, please! You think I am the one who is fighting with him? Really, Arzoo, if after twenty years of allegiance your loyalty lies with him, then perhaps you should marry him."

"Oh my Allah, Maya, I am not going to say another word." And she plopped back onto the bed in an affront of condescending pride. She fiddled with her hair. Arzoo made a point of saying 'Jesus' every time she was feigning surprise or being upset. The fact that she called upon Allah this time was a stark testament to how shocked she was at Maya's choice words.

Ali looked at her and at Maya. "Maya, that was really wrong, what you just said."

She held out her hand. "Please. You stay out of it. My friend, my choice whatever I want to say to her, got it?"

It took a few moments for Maya's controlled anger to burst out and she ran into the toilet crying and crying her pent-up anger, pain and love away.

After Arzoo and Ali's ceaseless knocking, the oh-so-sensitive Maya opened the door.

"Sorry," she whispered to Arzoo and after hugging her, without another word she leapt up into Ali's lap. He tried consoling her, but nothing he seemed to say stopped her torrent of tears. In fact, she didn't even know that Arzoo was on the phone and the cab was there until she softly nudged her. Still sniffling with wide red eyes and tears smudging her mascara and trailing streaks down to her chin, Maya, along with Ali, said their goodbyes to an Arzoo who was mostly sad at their leaving, yet buoyed about the night's coming festivities. The porter was trying hard not to stare at Maya, as were the people in the lobby, but she walked with her head held high and the moment she got inside the car, a fresh new bout of tears emerged.

I lay in his lap crying and crying and crying. I cried for all the happiness he had given me, I cried for the emptiness I would feel at this separation, I cried for fighting with him the entire morning, I cried for the injustice that my parents had done by getting me engaged to my cousin. I couldn't stand being apart from him for more than an hour. How was I going to survive till the next time I would see him in Lahore? And that, too, was a maybe. As the tears came forth in dissipated abandonment, he sat silently looking out the window, holding my hand the entire time. As the taxi came to what seemed to me an abrupt halt outside the airport, he leapt out, grabbed both our bags and paid the taxi driver. I dragged a very unwilling body out of the taxi and don't know where I mustered the strength from to follow him inside. We were walking when he suddenly pulled me behind a pillar and kissed me.

"I will miss you so much more. Please. Please. Please. Listen to what I requested you to do. I want to marry you. Why are you doing this to us?" said Ali, the pain in his voice apparent.

"I know. We can't live without each other. I know at least I can't."

"Neither can I."

"But…" and the 'but' was left on both of their lips, so she changed the topic. "When will I see you again?"

"Just three months, in Lahore."

"Okay, in Lahore," replied Maya. Seeing each other in Lahore was a thought easier said than done, for in Lahore the power of her parents and her cousin's family was virtually unlimited. Their spies and agents would be behind every pushcart, within every restaurant, and at the pinnacle of every muezzin. A rendezvous in Lahore was dangerous, but their desperation had steeled their resolve.

Love teaches one more about oneself than any other trial or joy – it brings forth the extremes not just of human emotion but also of the person's own capacities. It is within itself a paradox, especially as a polarity of both pain and pleasure. To love, to truly love, is the bravest and most trying of all endeavours and yet it is often a bittersweet pain – a pain that I would feel sorry to have spent my life without ever experiencing. When he boarded the plane, I could feel the most significant, vibrant part of my life being sucked from me. They were not three months, but more like 91 days, 2,232 hours, 133,920 minutes.

"Until Lahore, eternal love…"

A LIFELONG ACQUAINTANCE

"PASS IT ALONG, pass it along! Let's not get greedy here, now."

"Hold on, Arzoo."

"Seriously dude, now, we pass the love, we don't start being a glutton, that was actually your fifth hit. Dang… hope you didn't ninja lip this shit, Tre, you fucking pledge." She started laughing as the bong was finally passed over to her. It was one of those very expensive, very unusual glass bongs, with multiple compartments that made sure the hit was as concentrated as ever. They called it the Dawn Treader and after she took a hit, the ship of her thoughts set sail on a new path full of mysterious queries and new avenues to explore.

Her six best friends were sitting around in a circle in one of the frat rooms. The friends were all boys save Dominica and Charlotte, her best girlfriend after Maya (the one whom, reader, you were introduced to in Oxford).

"Arzoo, how's Maya doing? She didn't seem quite herself when she left here last."

Arzoo blew the smoke out and coughed, as it burnt her throat a little. "Man, it's just so tragic. About a month ago she was under house arrest and not allowed to go back to Harvard. But she had a visit from the asshole – the cousin-fiancé – it went well and my mother finally convinced her folks to let her visit for the weekend."

"So sad she couldn't come for Funday!" said another one of Maya's little crushers. Obviously the magnanimity of the situation was lost on him, though not on everyone else in the circle.

"What do you mean? Can her family actually do that? Can they actually stop her from going to school?" said Tre.

"Her parents? Yup. They sure can. It's how we Pakistanis roll. Wait. Why the fuck do Charlotte and I not have fresh margaritas right now, Tre?"

Tre sprang up to attend his duties. Keeping the house sisters stocked on premium cocktails was a Stanford sigma tradition that fell to the pledges aptly given the moniker of 'Booze Bitch'.

"But she is twenty-one, isn't she? Can't she just do what she wants? Um, we're out of Cointreau."

"She could. But she never will. She will sacrifice her happiness before appearing any less dutiful than she already has to her parents," said Arzoo, before taking another man-sized rip off the Dawn Treader. "Oh and make it a Casamigos on the rocks for my party monster beside me and I'll take a Tom Collins. You know, it's pretty fucked – Maya's parents ought to see where her happiness lies, not where society demands her place to be."

"Yeah, fuck society! Every person is an individual unique in his or her own way. Why must we conform to the multitude when we each can contribute so much more to the whole by being ourselves?" Everyone stared at Tre after this little outburst. He double-timed on Arzoo's Tom Collins.

"I wholeheartedly agree," said Arzoo. She was upset about what Maya had to go through but knowing that there wasn't anything that she could do during the moment to help her, she let it slip for another day.

"That orange is such a beautiful colour," she said, staring at the poster.

"What, that? Oh yeah! It is."

"Do you think we actually all see orange? I mean, what I am calling orange might actually be brown and what you are calling orange might actually be white." She smiled. "We will never know what is the sensory experience that the other is experiencing. We never know if our sensory experiences will ever be the same."

She turned to her friend (the one she had been hooking up with along with many, many others) and asked him if he could escort her to the toilet. Of course, her purpose in doing so was more than just a walk down the hall.

But her sweet delightful American replacement of Maya interjected, "I could take you, Arzoo. I mean, I want to go too."

"Oh! Wel, in that case, let the bong come to me one more time and as soon as I take another hit, we will join the progressive downstairs."

All five of the boys burst out laughing. Realising that they were mocking her, Arzoo raised one of her perfectly-shaped thick brows and enquired, "Well, what is so funny? You! Tre! You little shit. Tell me what's so funny!"

"I can't believe you're in a sorority, Arzoo. I mean, how did they ever recruit you? You hired a doppelganger, didn't you? I can't even imagine you for hours just standing there with a false smile plastered over your face and making small talk with hundreds of girls." They laughed some more.

"Yeah," Arzoo sighed. "Made me think of home all over again and honestly, I would rather go to boot camp. The only reason I joined a sorority was because of the events and, as exotic and beautiful as I am," she said, sticking her neck up in the air, "they were by default going to take me." Shedding her mock pride, she sat up properly again and said, "Now, on a serious note. I wish I could have joined a frat. You guys are so much more chill! At least when one person leaves the room the rest of you don't start discussing that person, tearing them apart piece by piece, limb by limb, till they cease to be less a person and more an object! I hate that. It is what I can stand least about Pakistani society. Also, I like bagging on Tre."

"No, I get what you mean. I feel the same way about our sorority," said Dominica.

"I mean, don't get me wrong, there are some great girls."

"Yes, but they talk about people and boys talk about ideas and situations. I had much rather do the latter."

"Agreed."

"Arzoo, do you really want another hit? I mean, you are going to be pretty cross-faded; you had a shit ton to drink."

"Chill out, girl! I'll be fine. I am fine." She kept on insisting that she was fine even though her speech was slower and her words slurring. Charged by some unknown quantities of alcohol, she leapt up, grabbed her friend's arm, and, telling the boys that she would be back, made her way to the dance floor.

The account of the next two hours is a bit vague – it was all a bit of a blur. She didn't know whether she danced with the track team black guy (*not* Tre, that fucking eager pledge) and made out with the football player or lap danced the crew guy and grinded with the two Asian girls. Honestly, she probably did all of it. All she knew was that there was a lot of house music playing and, letting her body take over her mind, she lost herself in the music, her own impulses synchronising with the electronic sounds booming out of the speakers. When she exhausted all of her energy and when a semblance of reality (or the mind regaining control of the body) started emerging, she stopped grinding midway with some guy who was in her history class and realised that she was on the table.

A little flustered, she searched for her friend, only to realise that she was nowhere to be found. She looked around and saw some of the girls looking at her. Feeling hot, claustrophobic, and annoyed at their duplicity (because she was sure that they were discussing how many guys she was trying with, or rather envious about how many were trying with her), she went back up the stairs and into the room of her five best guy friends, glad to see them. Most reliable fact about stoners: you will always find them exactly where you left them.

She went and gave them a hug, telling them that she was really glad that they were her friends. She had barely lain down on the bed (her black miniskirt riding a bit too high so she consequently pulled it down) when the door opened and in walked Adonis.

Arzoo had never seen an American guy be that beautiful; no, 'handsome' was too lifeless a word to describe this Greek god. She stood gaping at him and sat up straight, one leg on top of the other, and ran her fingers through her hair, appearing as nonchalant as ever. She was talking to her guys but kept staring at him from the corner of her eye. His long blond hair was messy and unkempt; his blue eyes sparkled and twinkled as he surveyed the room and his body – till today, Arzoo hadn't met anyone who could compete with hers, but he sure could. She took out a piece of gum and started calmly chewing, trying to enhance her 'don't care who you are' demeanour. She noticed that he smiled as he saw her and walked over to her dealer friend and asked for an eighth. She kept looking the other way until he stuck out his beautiful long-fingered hand, and as she looked up into his face and saw him smile, she knew that for the first time she was done in.

Of course, at the moment you meet the person of your dreams, they always have to go right after. For you see, at this point, his eighth was prepared and he proceeded to pay the amount and leave. He did and Arzoo could do nothing about it. She couldn't really be like, "Hey mister! Could I get your number, please?" No, that's something that he'd have to do. Her phone rang and she rolled her eyes when she saw it was her 'little' calling. The respective pledge she was in charge of maybe, her little, but she sure came with a lot of problems.

"Arzoo," she said, crying. She could picture her blue eyes blurry with tears, her blonde hair matted with sweat, her red lipstick smudged with her attempts at cleaning her tears and runny nose. "Arzoo, please take me home. I want to go home, home." Yes. She was blacked out. Again.

"Oh, Georgina, where are you?"

"I don't know, I don't know. Hey! Hey! Where am I?"

A moment later a guy took the phone. "Hey. We're in room 312. Your friend seems pretty wasted. You should probably take her home. Hopefully she won't need to be hospitalised because *that* puts us on probation." She could feel him roll his eyes and her own anger mounting.

"Do you know who you're speaking to?"

"Uhhh, no. Am I supposed to?"

"Well, in that case I do hope my little gets hospitalised and you learn to fear the prospect of always getting girls wasted. Let's roll, Dominica. Tre! Ande-fucking-Lay, you're on lush duty."

Arzoo hung up and she, Dominica and Tre stormed into room 312 like the *Hawaii Five-O* team. Her little was sitting on the sofa and two KA pledges were standing next to her. (They were pledges because she knew of the existence of every single initiated member.) She presumed the taller, lankier one to be the one she spoke to.

"Yes, well, where is my little?"

"Oh, Arzoo. I didn't know it was you."

"Yes. I know." The trio picked up Georgina by her arms and before walking out the door, she spied a bottle of UV vodka completely finished on the ground. Disgusted, Arzoo turned around and said, "Fucking UV? Seriously? We're gonna have to pump my little's stomach for $20 vodka? Tre, you need to teach these assholes how to properly treat ladies like a gentleman – now go bring my Beamer around, dude, toots-suite."

"Arzoo, I loooove you," said her little, tottering and slurring, falling both against Arzoo and the wall in the corridor.

"Well, Georgina, let's get you home and in bed."

They had barely made it to the parking lot when a little bile spurted out the contents of Georgina's over-abused stomach on both Arzoo's Fendis and Tre's Beamer. Rolling her eyes and sighing, she opened her trunk to find some Kleenex.

A hand reached out from behind and lightly touched her shoulder. She was about to take the wrench out and smack whoever it was on the head when, curbing her instincts, she realised it very well could be one of her friends. She turned around and found herself face to face with and only inches away from the Adonis of earlier. Both the putrid vomit and the half-sobbing, half-blank Georgina were forgotten. Priorities, people. Besides, Tre was pre-med.

"Hi. I am Ian. What's your name?"

"Ummmm, Arzoo."

"Well, Arzoo, that's a really beautiful name for such a beautiful girl. All the guys in the house have such wonderful things to say about you, but I have never had the pleasure of formally introducing myself. Do you have anything in the trunk to clean up… ya? Let me help you find it…" (and continuing where he left off) "…where are you from?" He started rummaging around the trunk for Kleenex too.

"Pakistan," she whispered, acutely aware of his blue eyes turning away from the trunk and looking up at her.

"Really? Wow! That's so far away! Well, you definitely have a huge problem. I don't know much about the shoes, but the Beamer," he looked approvingly at the car, "it doesn't deserve such harsh treatment."

"Yeah. Tell me about it. Where are you from? I am definitely assuming somewhere in the States."

"Yes. From Sacramento, actually. Good ol' Cali boy!"

"Uh-huh, you play a sport?" (*You are so beautiful – where have you been my entire life?*)

"Yeah, water polo." (*I KNOW! Ditto. Didn't know exotic could make you so delirious.*)

They couldn't really find any Kleenex but she found the cloth that she occasionally used to dust the car with.

"Yeah, I could tell." She looked at his arms. (*What a great body.*)

"Here, let me."

"No. No."

"Come on, girl! It is the least I could do for such a beautiful lady." Had she been white, she would definitely be a tomato by now.

"Thank you!"

He bent around the side of the car, cleaning Georgina's stomach remains.

"And do you model?" he asked. Cheesy, but I suppose he was trying to find conversation.

"I only wish," she said, laughing.

"Could have fooled me." Having cleaned the car, he turned around and his eyes twinkled with the smile on his face.

He got up and shook her hand (with his clean one, of course). "Well, it was a pleasure meeting you, Arzoo from Pakistan. I hope I see you around." (*I will definitely stalk you on Facebook!*)

"Pleasure is all mine." (Indeed it was.)

She dropped her forgotten little at her freshman dorm and came back to KA. To her disappointment, Adonis was nowhere to be found and all Tre could say was that he was one of only two guys on the water polo team not to live in the house. She told her friends about her recent romantic interest (she of course only mentioned his name and how he helped her in cleaning), only to be annoyed at herself for doing so. The stoners bombarded her with news (at least the guys at kappa would never) of how he's definitely bad news, a tool, and how he had broken a number of girls' hearts. She kept denying her obvious attraction to him and arguing about the fact that even if she was attracted to him, she didn't care about what he did or had done. Her friend with benefits was perhaps most vocally adamant about Adonis's evil flaws, and personally, Arzoo was getting annoyed by his protective instincts, regretting the fact that she had ever hooked up with him. She shrugged her shoulders for the moment, but Adonis had become one of her primary wants and, as is the case with Arzoo, she became obsessed with the attainment of that want. Perhaps she should have listened to her friends, or perhaps not, for after three years of bitter arguments, cheating around, and hundreds of breakups, she did get engaged to him.

PUPPY LOVE

FEHRANAZ WAS INVARIABLY becoming more and more attuned with herself and her body; after all, being one of those divinely blessed, why wouldn't she? As days went by she stopped slouching at the sudden growth of her breasts, she stopped playing with the children, she stopped fearing the eighteenth of every month as Mrs S's slap and subsequent lecture had informed her of what the blood stood for the first time she flowed away her girlhood; as did, for that matter, her secret educational benefactor.

"You foolish, foolish ignorant piece of shit! How dare you use my toilet? Allah only knows what germs you've picked up living in that mud hut of yours." She railed on and on about the uncleanliness of servants and how they deserve separate toilets because of their status. It took this cold preacher about ten minutes to notice the blood stain on the *shalwar* and that even though Fehranaz had stopped crying, her face was streaked with tears, her nose and mouth red, and her eyes frenzied with a harrowing fear. "Why, whatever is the matter with you, girl?"

Fehranaz's mumblings were barely audible to her own self, let alone to Mrs S. "Speak up, girl, speak up! I can't hear you!"

Replying in English, because Fehranaz was probably the only servant well versed in the language, Fehranaz replied a little more audibly this time. "*Bibi* (madam), *bibi*, I am going to die." With that the little servant girl, pitying her early demise started wailing again.

"WILL YOU SHUT UP AND LISTEN TO ME?" As Fehranaz had no intention of desisting from her misery, Mrs S helped her out of it by slapping her out of her sobs.

"Thank God! Now." And she started laughing for a good three minutes, during which Fehranaz truly thought she was the most horrible 'she' alive.

Mrs S was perhaps unusually affected by the comedy of the situation; after all, she knew and had been educated by her classmates beforehand of the time a girl becomes a woman, so she could never know the fear a child has when they experience this life-altering event mistaking it for death, even more so when that child has no parents to calm down their fears, and take the child's pain as their own. No, her laughter was rightfully cruel to Fehranaz.

Of course, it is ironic to note how all humour has dark elements to it; it tickles one's fancy either because it transgresses a taboo or because it is at the expense of others. Very little humour is laughing with someone, and it is that tiny, hardly existent level of humour that is true humour. So perhaps we can forgive Mrs S, for, given the occasion, she was laughing at someone, but don't we all? Don't we laugh when someone falls off the stairs or slips on a peel? Don't we feel powerful when we prank-call someone, telling them that their father is dead, or when we throw eggs at someone's house? Beware! Karma's a bitch. You never know when you may face the mirror and see the reflection you try so hard to avert or, like Mrs S, when the tables may turn and you are laughed at by life in even more woeful and agonising situations.

When she stopped laughing, the cackling dissipated as suddenly as it had appeared and within seconds she dropped her Miu Miu suede bag to the floor and said in a stern tone, "Congratulations! You are now a woman. This is dirty blood that comes out of your body. You must not pray while you are on your period – that's what they are called. Even God thinks you are just as filthy as everyone during this time, so don't touch the Quran; in fact, even I think you are inexcusably disgusting and don't want you anywhere near my clothes or anywhere near the kitchen. God only knows you will be feeding us the very blood that is exiting your private part... NO kitchen. Oh! And one more thing: most women in your dirty illiterate class just tie cloths, but I don't believe in the effectiveness of these ways, so you must use a sanitary napkin, a pad. I don't want blood dripping all over my new carpets. And your pubes will start growing, so try to find ways to get rid of the hair in your underarms and around your private parts. I despise such filth and, what's more, you will stink even more. Do I make myself clear?"

All Fehranaz could do was nod her head and then not know when to stop with the persistent movement of it. There was so much she had to take in within the span of barely a minute!

"Oh, madam! Control your nodding. You are growing up now, not to become more retarded, hopefully."

"Y-y-yes, *bibi*!"

"Okay, good! Well, get to it, then! Chop chop! The pads are in the cupboard. Do you even own underwear?"

Fehranaz shook her head.

"Why am I not surprised? Well, hold on. The laundrywoman bleached my black one. It is ruined. Take it."

"Clean yourself up and go see where the children are. No, not here, go to the servants' quarters right now, abominable girl. Oh my Allah! Why have you created these servants without any brains to think for them?"

Shaking her head, Mrs S left the room and Fehranaz quickly pulled up her *shalwar* and continued about her way.

It was almost a year since that day and Fehranaz fast understood her beauty and her youth and the effect both had on the men around her. The male head cook started giving her more food; often the fruit peddler in Liberty Market would give her a mango or two for free; people on the streets would whistle whenever she walked by, much to both her annoyance and her pride. In fact, even little girls and boys wanted to come play with her more. All the women who came to Mrs S's house, or all the women who saw Fehranaz when she would accompany Mrs S and Mrs S's homely-yet-wonderfully-tempered baby, would recoil with hatred when they saw her perfect body, which hours of expensive cardio training would not attain, burn with envy when they saw her perfect skin, which no amount of treatments could ever assist them in accomplishing, or the natural ruddiness of her lips or thickness in her lashes, which no amount of makeup granted them. Yes, beauty is quite invariably a sense of both contention and awe, especially when it is in a place where most think it is undeserved.

When one comes of age, one of the most likely evolutions is in the way of one's heart. She had developed an infatuation with the new cook's assistant Mr and Mrs S had employed. He had barely started forming a moustache, but over yells from Mrs S and the making of chicken *nihari,*[*] the

---

* Slow cooked chicken stew delicacy.

two would giggle and stare into each other's eyes. Just yesterday he had got her a *gajra**. They sat under the tree as he shyly placed it on her hand; they were afraid of being caught both by Mrs S and the head cook, who like all obnoxious sycophants wasted no opportunity in exaggerating and telling Mrs S everything that had conspired when Mrs S was away on one of her social obligations. Yes, they sat very quietly.

He looked at her, thinking how beautiful she was and how lucky he was and how he would always keep her happy. Of course, he was only fifteen – the perfect age for a man to believe the promises he keeps. And she thought of nothing more than how much bliss he had given her. She kept gazing at the *gajra* and shyly looked downwards, thinking of how he would take her away from here, how he would give her a nice quiet life in the village that she always yearned for. She thought of the children they would have, how the sons would have his moustache-to-be, and out of further embarrassment she tried to keep her gaze even more transfixed on the ground (which, given her already focused attention to the grass, couldn't be humanly possible). They did not hold hands or embrace or touch in any way – they didn't need to.

Meanwhile, things in the house were taking a different turn; Mrs S was out on a rampage and Mr S was the target of her inexhaustible fury.

She picked up the newspaper and flung it on the table. "What is this? Where is the money for the factory that I gave you? Where is it?"

"I mean, um," he said, glancing at the floor. "It is in the paper... why don't you just read it in there?"

"Because I already read it, you smart-ass, I want to hear it from you. Go on! Where is the money? This was supposed to be another multimillion-dollar project that you flunked."

"No, *jaan*—"

"DON'T CALL ME THAT. I will not succumb to your non-existent charms."

He gulped and mumbled, "Bloody reporters."

"What did you say?"

"Ah! Dear wife, nothing!"

"Well," she said, ignoring the pretentious 'dear'. "Please enlighten me." She kept one hand on her hip and tapped her feet in a frenzy that matched her rising need to strangle her husband.

---

* Floral bracelet.

"Well," he said, massaging his temples, "you know I was going to go sign the contract and invest the money in the machines, but that same day my college friends invited me for a game of poker at one of the ministers' houses, all the men were going," he said with a pause.

"Oh, yes!" she said, tapping her finger on the photo in the newspaper. "Not only were you at a place where there was a *mujra** and an abundance of alcohol, but you lost all the money in an illegal gambling house and the reporters caught you. You dancing with the whore, you throwing money around her. NOT ONLY ARE YOU A COMPLETE WASTE OF MY FATHER'S MONEY, but you also don't have the decency to respect the fact that all this" (she pointed all around the office) "is based on his grace, Allah bless his soul."

"Bloody fucker left me alone to deal with this crazy," said Mr S in an inaudible whisper that eluded Mrs S.

"And you not only squander his wealth, you also disrespect this family's name and honour, my father's name. I will not tolerate such an abuse to his soul. And for God's sake, you have young children. Your daughters will be ready for marriage soon, and who will want to take the daughter of – or give their daughter to – such a wasteful good-for-nothing corrupt father-in-law. No, Mr S, I will not tolerate the misconduct of any member of this house, and as the supposed head of this house I urge you to straighten out your act."

She left. He loosened his buttons, letting out a sigh of relief, when she came back in.

"Were you sighing because I left, Mr S? You should be! Well, I am sorry to disappoint you but I know what goes on in that head of yours and I came back to tell you that I will give you more money to invest because I really want the factory project to get underway – it's for my son – BUT, Mr S, if you mess up this time, there will be no mercy, I hope you remember that. It is for my son and when it comes to him I have no room for granting redemption."

She stormed back out and Mr S was left feeling slightly shocked by his wife's erratic behaviour. Even after twenty-two years of marriage, the woman never ceased to make his adrenaline run into overdrive and force his heart to charge with fear; she was and would always be the red to his bull. He shrugged, determined to be on her 'good' side, whatever that was, and the next morning bought her a brand new leather Jimmy Choo bag. It had

---

* A sort of sexual dance done for the entertainment of men.

beautiful scales on it and the handles were studded; perhaps Mr S was truly thinking of his wife's dominating personality when he bought it.

Nevertheless, Mrs S was incredibly pleased by the notion, of course more enlivened by the bag than the fact that her husband bought it, and leaving him with a bare 'thank you' twirled up the stairs and into her room, carefully placing the bag on her bed. She would pose with it later, but for now nature was calling and so, leaving the bag, she walked into the toilet. Unfortunately, poor Fehranaz walked in the room and saw the bag at the same time that Mrs S was gladly relieving herself.

The calamitous bag was to prove to have disastrous consequences for the unfortunate girl. It just lay there gleaming, all shiny and new, inviting Fehranaz to touch it, to feel the smooth leather and glance at the studs from a nearer distance. It was a more unusual bag than the ones Fehranaz had ever seen and the nearer she got to the bag, the more it called out to her, until, not realising that Mrs S was in the toilet, Fehranaz touched it. She loved the way the scaled leather felt and, being an inquisitive little girl, couldn't help but place the bag on her shoulder. She stood in front of the mirror whirling around, liking the way the bag felt.

When Mrs S had wiped her hands on the newly laundered towels with the gold rims, she opened the toilet door and was extremely surprised at Fehranaz's audacity and was so affronted with the servant for touching her new bag. She walked up to Fehranaz and before the girl could take the bag off, Mrs S wrenched it from her arm and hit her with it.

"HOW DARE YOU? This is my new bag! I haven't even worn it yet and you are fantasising about wearing it, about possessing it. Possessing my thing? HOW DARE YOU GET SUCH IDEAS IN YOUR HEAD! I don't even give my things to my own daughters. If you want a bag, you ask for one. I don't want your grimy dirty fingers soiling my new goodies. Now off you go."

Fehranaz stood there whimpering, wondering about the perfect way to apologise.

"Well, do you want another wallop or are you going to get out of my sight sometime soon?"

Crying, she ran all the way out into the garden. She plopped down amid the jasmines and in spite of their soothing incense, she sat under the oak tree crying until she felt soft hands stroking her hair. She stopped sobbing and looked up to find the cook's boy sitting there, deeply concerned for her.

"Why are you crying?" he said, looking down at the ground, too afraid to make eye contact again.

She sat up, wiping her tears. "Mrs S beat me for touching her bag. I mean, I always have to break in the bag anyway." She was laughing now. "She has always hit me with her bags before using them." And yet she was still sobbing between her maniacal laughter.

"No, no, no," said the cook's boy, realising that no matter how much she was trying to brush it aside, she was deeply afraid of Mrs S. He grabbed her and hugged her and Fehranaz immediately stopped crying. Initially, she was shocked, but as his arms wound around her tighter and she breathed in his smell, she relaxed her head on his chest, smiling and breathing against the rising of his lungs and beating of his heart. For the first time, she was glad that Mrs S had actually whacked her with the Jimmy Choo; it had given her a moment of pure joy.

They embraced each other for quite some time; afflicted with love, they were momentarily unafraid of any and all who would be observing them either to punish or to complain. All that mattered to them was just them – the intertwined smell of their bodies and the comfort within each other's arms, which had left both of them drowsy with this new love elixir. They should have cared, for unknown to the child lovers, a pair of keen eyes was watching them from the study. Mr S pushed back the glasses perched on his nose; his eyes never left Fehranaz or her perfect body.

THE INVITATION

ARIYANA MAY HAVE graduated from Princeton with honours in psychology, but she still lacked the ability to gauge the human soul and understand its weaknesses and vices – backbiting, lying, flattering, envying, bribing. She was one of those pure souls who never had (or at least never consciously imbibed) any such thought in her own head and so it was hard for her to conceive of a situation where others would possess such deep-seated hostilities, especially any directed toward her. So she came back from the committee 'lunch' feeling giddy with excitement about finally being involved with other women. Her husband was so pleased to see her happy that it made him just as excited as her.

"Oh my God, darling! You have no idea. All those women are so beautiful. I have actually not seen so much beauty all at once!"

Her husband chuckled and winked at her. "I guess you don't look at the mirror too often then."

She playfully shoved him. "Oh, don't be silly! I mean it. And they were all so incredibly well dressed in all the latest fashions; I felt like I had walked into Lahore's own personal *Vogue*. The embroidery that Mrs B was wearing, the animal print, was truly mesmerising. And Mrs A's leather jacket just suited her so well." She just kept on going on and on about how visually pleasing the women were. Note she never once mentioned if any one of them was truly nice. Her eyes were too stunned with the visual glamour to take much notice of the fact that she was only relaying superficial elements of the lunch at that point.

"Oh! And they all seemed like pretty great mothers. They were all extremely proud of their children. Though, I must admit," and for the first time her smooth white forehead crinkled with a momentary worry, "I didn't appreciate the children being turned into trophies, but I suppose it's their own hard work that they were trying to showcase."

"Ha ha ha! Now we get to something that's really interesting, speaking of children."

She blushed. "I don't know, not now."

"Why not?"

"I don't know, I just want to be a great mother, I want to give my child all the happiness in the world that I... I just want to be sure that when I have a child I am ready for it."

"Darling," he said, taking her into his arms, "no one is ever ready to be a mother, but I know one thing: that if you are half as great a mother as you are a wife, you will be the best mother in the whole world."

She smiled at his confidence in her when she herself was quite uncertain about her parenting abilities. Every time she would think of being a mother, as hard as she would try not to, her thoughts would defiantly wander on her own.

She thought of her seventh birthday and the day the woman who gave birth to her left; it was the day that changed her life. The woman hadn't been there to wipe her tears, or be happy for her in her moments of joy. She hadn't been there when she was on honour roll or when she won the swimming championship. She wasn't present for the moment she opened her college applications and leapt with joy at being accepted into an Ivy League university, or the day she got married. Her 'mother' wasn't even there to tell her what being on one's period was or what being in love was or how to talk to other girls in a way that would facilitate successful social interactions, leading to friends.

To Ariyana, there was nothing worse for a child than to grow up without a mother who has passed away, except when that child grooms him or herself into adulthood knowing that that mother is alive and well and has rejected her own child. She thought again of her seventh birthday, the strange man who showed up, the way her mother just walked out and no matter how much Ariyana cried and tried to run after her, her mother didn't turn back once. It's hard to be a woman in the absence of the most significant presence in one's life and even though Ariyana had managed fairly well, she was forever haunted by that moment. No matter how much she tried to run away from it, every decision in her life was consciously and unconsciously influenced by the fact that her mother had left her, even if that decision was to reject the presence of that moment in her life. After all, in order to deny her mother's influence, she had to, on some level, accept its existence.

Ariyana was glad for her husband; he made her feel more sure and secure with herself than anything or anyone else ever had. Perhaps it was with his support that she could actually be the mother that she had always wanted. She reached up to kiss him.

They were sitting in the living room. Their living room was on the second floor, which wasn't in the public sphere of the house, so really her mother-in-law had no reason to be affronted. But there she was, shocked by this public display of affection, as always angered by Ariyana's 'lewdness'. I suppose it is everyone's prerogative to hold true to his or her value systems and form opinions based on those systems. Yet it is of an extremely facile and duplicitous intention to hold others by standards that you don't implement on yourself, and even if you do evaluate yourself on your own codes, it is a fallacious infringement to choke down your perceptions on others presuming that others ought to have the same values as you. Of course, Y's mother was one such woman, who, having been widowed at an extremely young age, was unfortunate enough to not have a passionate romance with her husband and so was envious of anyone else who did, especially if that someone was Ariyana, who had one with her husband.

Ariyana did suffer from not knowing her true place in society, and also whether it is the traditions of her Pakistani father or the liberalism of her American mother that she ought to associate with; clearly, with her mother gone, the choice should have been simple. Yet, no matter how hard she tried, she couldn't change her genetic makeup. Perhaps it was both this confusion and her far more than pleasing countenance that was both fascinating and beautiful to those around, especially to her husband. To him she was the eternal goddess of his desires, with white skin stretched out on Pakistani bones. Her lack of acceptance in the society is what drew her to him; what an alluring creature and so misunderstood by half of society – the female half, of course. But every love story must have a trial, and being an outsider, most of society, and especially her mother-in-law, wrinkled their noses at the match. To the 'new' and equally disappointed mother, Ariyana was no more than a fortune-seeking libertine who would never be worthy of her son and his money.

When Ariyana stopped kissing her husband, she was the first to notice her mother-in-law standing there with one hand on her hip. Without a second's thought, she pushed her husband and flung back as if his mouth had suddenly started spitting out acid darts.

"BABY, why did you do that?"

She looked down at the floor and then glanced at the doorway, hoping that her husband would turn around and look at his mother. He didn't get the hint and was about to grab her again, when his mother coughed. Extremely embarrassed, he grabbed a cushion to hide his arousal and, stammering, looked at the floor.

"Well, when you two are free, I just wanted to tell you that there are some guests downstairs to see you. If you are busy," she added sarcastically, "I could inform them that they should come another time."

"N-n-n-o *Ami*,* we will be right down."

"Humph! Also, there is a reason you have a room, Y. If your wife isn't used to privacy, then I haven't raised you like this…" she trailed off. Y's mother was, frankly, quite possessive in sharing him with anyone else, having no other form of a familial connection other than him, since her husband died when she was only eighteen and a half years old; perhaps a reappraisal of her life would make her seem not as evil and domineering as she initially would seem. Though, again, she had no right to enforce her tragedy and her insecurities on an already imbalanced girl.

Luckily the phone rang and a furiously flushed Ariyana grabbed it and ran into the room. She emerged moments later to find her mother-in-law gone and her husband massaging his temples.

He saw the huge smile on her face before asking her, "Who called?"

"That was the Chief Minister's secretary. We are invited to a dinner at his house tomorrow," she said, flinging her arms around him, before remembering that her mother-in-law might come back any moment and quickly disentangling herself. As the dinner fused itself further into her thoughts and into the female realm of needs and desires, her excitement took a sharp turn and turned to one of exasperation.

"Oh my God! I don't know what to wear. Y, I have nothing to wear. What am I going to do?"

"Hey, hey, hey!" he said, grabbing her hands. "Since when do you care about what you wear?"

"Since we got invited to the CM's house. I can't just show up in jeans."

---

* Mother.

"No, so relax. Just call up my sister. You know she is always willing to help you out."

"Yes, you are right."

"By the way, have you called your dad yet?"

She frowned. "Ummm, don't remember." *NO*, her mind shouted. "You know I don't want to."

"Sweetheart, don't lie, I know you have problems with him, but please, please just call him. He is your dad after all."

"Hmm…"

"Look at me! Please, for me, for our little baby," he said, grabbing her stomach.

She laughed, pushing him off. "We don't have one yet, Mr Too-Excited. Okay, go now, before your mother comes back up. I will call him and be right down."

After he left, she stared at the phone for a while before cursing her husband for always knowing what to say to convince her. She let it ring twice and was about to hang up and tell Y that her father didn't pick up, when he did just what she didn't want him to do.

"Hello!"

"*Aslam aleikum*, Daddy!"

"*Waleikum Asalam*… is that Ariyana?"

"*Jee, jee,** Daddy, it's me."

"How are you?"

"I am fine, and you?"

"Fine."

"How's that husband of yours?"

"He's good!"

"Still no kids?"

"No, Daddy, we were just—"

"No, no, that's good. So that when you are planning on leaving him you won't leave him with any child."

She had been waiting for him to make a comment that would allude to her mother and therefore was already prepared to snap at him, "Daddy, I am not going to run away and leave my husband. I love him."

"So did your mother, and look at what she did."

---

* Yes, yes.

"I AM NOT HER! Not every woman is bound to run away with another man, leaving her husband and child."

"Yes, but you are her daughter."

"So? It doesn't mean I am her. You know what, let's forget about it, Father! I am going to the Chief Minister's house tomorrow for dinner."

"That's nice," he grunted.

"Yeah, well, we will come see you soon. *Khuda hafiz.*"

"*Khuda hafiz.*"

As she hung up, she couldn't help but feel flustered. Ever since her mother left, she had raised herself and pretty much taken care of the entire house, including her father. When he would home come drunk at night screaming his lungs out, she would pull the comforter on him as he lay on the floor and turn off the lights. She would make sure he had three meals a day, that his clothes were ironed. She was barely eight and yet she was both his mother and wife (not sexually, of course). She had never experienced much of a childhood, always switching schools, never making friends with any girl. She never understood why, and in return all her father told her was that she was like her mother, the mother she didn't want to remember and whom she despised for controlling and overshadowing her in every aspect of life in spite of always being physically absent.

She didn't understand why she couldn't just be her own person. She had an identity that was separate from being just her mother's daughter, but both her father and society judged her based on her white half. Her entire life was spent rejecting that part of her identity and trying as hard as she could to get rid of it. All she had wanted was for one parent to have loved her enough, but her mother had never even called and her father – well, he was too busy wallowing in his own pain to think of the pain his daughter must have gone through. All he did was take his erroneous frustrations and misconceptions of the white race out on her. As a result, in spite of the fact that they loved each other, they had drifted completely apart. Her mother's one act of impulsiveness had changed their lives forever.

Ariyana wanted to understand her mother, yet knew one can't be apathetic to the person who made your life as hard as they could without ever giving another thought to you – the very life that they had consciously created. As for her father, she didn't resent him for his reaction. She was

---

* This term is used to say goodbye. It literally translates to 'May God protect you'.

only spiteful of the fact that he let all this distance and silence define their relationship. He could have moved past the hurt and created a worthwhile, loving, nurturing relationship with her, but he chose not to. She was never the one who asked to be born now, was she?

She wiped away the tears and thought about the dinner. She was going to call her sister-in-law but realised that her mother-in-law would be contemptuous at her for being late in coming downstairs when her dutiful son had already gone down, and no matter how harsh the woman was, she was the only inkling she had of a parent and she was adamant about building cordial relations at the very least. So Ariyana waited until after the guests had gone to call her SIL.* Her mind was focused on outfits and the Chief Minister's house as a means of deflecting the pain from her father.

---

* Abbreviation for sister-in-law.

BODY BLITZ

I LOWERED MY fingers between my legs and slowly began massaging the forefinger and the index in a circular motion. My thoughts were anything but pure; perhaps it was the fact that I knew that what I was doing was something mothers stop their four- and five-year-olds from indulging in that I found thrilling, or the fact that I even felt the need to please myself disturbing. Even so, there was a certain ecstatic joy about indulging in the body's hedonism; at least that form was better than the money lust and society licentiousness that everyone around me had come to require to survive, or so they had come to make themselves believe. At least I was seeking pleasure outside the framework of society.

My fingers were doing more than just satisfying my body; my mind was exhilarated with the prospect of having to live in a taboo, one of the stupid useless rules that society imposes for no other reason than perhaps because it is so much fun breaking them. Excited by the apparent 'wrong' that my body was transgressing into, my imagination picked up and as my fingers probed and moved around, back and forth, in and out, up and down, round and round, my thoughts were transfixed at breaking even more boundaries than my pages. I thought of a world of unmitigated sexual license, where the opportunity of having sex with anyone and everyone had zero social cost. I pictured my husband looking down at me while I made love to a whole host of men and women who were trained in the art of giving pleasure. It wasn't something that I was ever going to do, but the mere thought that my mind could violate norms in ways my body could not brought me closer and closer to my peak. As I imagined being in the arms of two women who would make love to me for hours, I could feel the pulse, and like a welcomed rainy season, the wave of pleasure ebbed to and fro, curling, dissipating, only to come again.

However, the onslaught of pleasure was too temporary, too short, too easily come and gone. Unlike the brazen intrepid lover in her thoughts whose moans of pleasure excited her, she only received momentary bodily satisfaction. Her heart, her soul, remained untouched and so there were no groans, no pleasure that swept away the senses and was blinding to all five. You see, she knew that no matter how skilled her hand was, she needed much more; she needed love. Love by no means requires bodily satisfaction as an endpoint or even a medium, but the best of orgasms most often require the intricacies of love.

But, really, what is love? She pondered over the question. *Can it ever exist between a man and a woman? Is it the intense feeling of belonging or letting go? Of nurture or imminent destruction? Can it only exist in the truest form, as they say, between a mother and child, though her mother had forsaken her to a lifetime of torture and pain? Can it then not exist between humans but only between a woman and the divine. But even Allah had recently forgotten her and her plight.* Perhaps it was because so had she. As she sat on the toilet seat and thought hard over questions she wouldn't receive answers for anytime soon, she heard the desperate knocking on the door.

Torn between fear and a desire to exasperate that fear by not opening the door, she kept sitting on the toilet seat and waited in an expectant dread so interminable that the only way to end it would be by opening the door. And she sat, defiant both because of her fear and because the sound of the knocks were goading her into a reluctance of any movement towards the door. The thud, thud, thud only made her more persistent.

"OPEN THE DOOR! OPEN THE DOOR, LAILA! OPEN THE DOOR RIGHT NOW OR ELSE," he hollered, while incessantly banging on the door. She could feel her heart beating faster till it matched the thump on the door; her hands started getting sweaty. They always got sweaty when she felt herself slipping away and losing control. She knew the longer she avoided the unavoidable, the angrier he would be and the more she would be torturing herself with all the waiting. Fear is but pre-emptive of the moment that follows. So, she did the only thing one ought to do when one's afraid; she faced her fear and opened the door.

He was midway in pounding on the door. His fist was raised and his mouth was partially open, his tracts ready to spout out more abuse and screaming. Her sudden opening of the door caught him off his guard and she stood there watching him as one does a cartoon frozen in time and place. He actually looked quite comical and then she looked at his beautiful honey eyes, at the red that surrounded them, and her heart started beating again at the same time that his lips contorted into a smile. Smiles are funny things; they often are used to convey the impression of a good nature, a welcoming indication of sorts. Yet they, much like everything else, are contextualised, an expression wrapped in layers of human behaviour to be unwrapped based on the person analysing the situation. As he smiled, she unwrapped it based on their interaction, both past and present, and how at this moment her husband wanted nothing more than to use her as his object of both pain and pleasure. For moments they stood looking at each other. She stood thinking of ways to escape and he stood inflamed by his ardent desire to use her as he pleased.

He grabbed her arm and as he twisted it, she no longer cried. As he tore her clothes, she no longer wept. As he added bruises upon bruises, bite marks upon bite marks, she stopped feeling and lamented her grief only in her head. As he penetrated her, she just shut her eyes. He could feel her drifting far, far away, and as much as her complete subservience, or so he thought, thrilled him, he still yearned to know that there was yet something in her that was still there for him to break. Beauty carries with it the privilege of being destroying; there was nothing more he coveted than to destroy beauty, for it made him feel just as powerful as the creator of it. Destruction may be the ultimate act of creation, but it is only fun destroying something that puts up a fight. Only the challenge on the path offers the path the capability of being worthwhile. So while he made destruction to his wife and her body, he remained quizzical of where her soul lay. She had tucked it inside deep within herself, safe and away from him.

He stopped violating her from behind and as he turned her over and looked into her eyes, she looked at him with an expression that belied both a smirk and a grimace of withdrawal. When she looked at him like that, he was reminded of a little boy. That made him want her more. He was determined to bring her out of her layers of skin and blood that sheltered her so he decided to experiment with something new today, and to verify his hypothesis, he drew a cigarette and after lighting it, burnt her back. As she screamed with the realisation of this newfound pain, a pain that her body had never been accustomed to before, he came with the most glorious orgasm inside her.

I am but a cow to be beaten, a rat to be skinned, a pig to be stuffed, a chicken to be beheaded, a lamb to be roasted. Laila closed her eyes and

132

perforated her being to the very many animals that were daily sacrificed on the altar of human greed as if they had no purpose, no life but to serve man as she had to serve her husband.

She showered, cleansing herself from the beast's smell, and was so flustered that she just couldn't help calling her mother.

"*Aslam aleikum*, Mom!"

"*Walawikum Asalam.* And how is my favourite daughter doing?"

"I– I– I'm fine!"

"Oh well! That's so good to hear after all that I have been through."

"Actually, Mom…"

"What is it, *jaani*?"

"My husband, he, he hasn't…"

"He hasn't what, dear?" Mrs K's purpose in repeating everything Laila was saying was to discourage an already hesitant Laila from saying it.

"Nothing. Nothing. Forget about it!"

"Is he, is he doing better?"

"Yes, yes, much!"

"Laila, I am so happy. You always make me so proud. Mama's heart and *jaan* you are. I only wish you had taught a thing or two to your sister. She is getting completely out of hand, Laila."

Laila frowned, worried for her baby sister. "Why? What's she saying?"

"Well, I know you know about the boy. She has made up her mind to marry him. Your father and I have employed every tactic in the book, but that selfish little whore will not be dissuaded."

"Yes, but…"

"Laila, we know nothing about his family. For all we know they are pimps and will use her as a call girl, and what's wrong with her cousin? He is the most upstanding gentleman I have ever met."

"No, you're right. It's better if it were in the family, less mess."

"I know I can count on you always, dear. Well, we are holding a family meeting soon to talk some sense into Maya."

"Yes, I will be there."

"And tell your dear husband to be there."

"But…"

"No but, Laila. What will people think? He's family."

Her mother hung up, leaving Laila in a state of morbid gloom. When you see no way out, just shut your eyes, take a deep breath and leave it to the divine. She shut her eyes and prayed, hoping somewhere, anywhere, someone was listening; she had told her family about her husband's violent fetishes and yet her family had refused to agree to her divorce even though they were the ones who instigated her to marry him in the first place. Her mother said she feared the ill repute of the divorce would tarnish their family's name, and what's more, of course her mother was looking out for her 'betterment', doing what she thought was in the best interests of her daughter. Since the day Laila told her, she had behaved as if she had no knowledge of the fact that her daughter's husband was a lunatic and Laila continued to suffer in silence, afraid of hurting her family. In the name of her family's honour she suffered the 'blitz' on her body, on her honour and her soul, only to slowly become less of a person. She wouldn't let the same thing happen to Maya. Maya had to be safe – even if it meant marrying who she didn't want to. Yes. No matter which way it went, the most important thing was that Maya had to be safe.

KITES AND SPRITES

IF YOU HAVE ever been to Lahore in the spring, you will understand the rejuvenation and the joy with which the season is embraced. Yellow becomes the official colour of the month and the entire city becomes decked out the way a bride does before her marriage – youthful, happy, and spectacular. It isn't just nature that takes on a new ensemble with all the flowers blooming, the trees and grass coloured with a brighter green, the sky adopting a bluer hue, butterflies and bees flittering and zooming in and about between roses, pansies, petunias, and lilies but man, usually the hinderer of such marvellous creations, wants to celebrate and add his own decorum to nature's unaffected allure. People roam the streets in bliss, parties are held on rooftops, but kites – yes kites – no longer bedeck the sky, embellishing it during the day the way stars do at night, as the young, the old, the poor, and the rich are no longer allowed by the government to jointly celebrate in this glorification of basant (spring). The kite string (or dor) is considered too dangerous as it could cut the necks of passers-by, but instead of finding an alternative solution, the government banned the one event that made Lahore, Lahore. There are, of course, people who will illegally still sometimes partake in such 'heinous' atrocities as kite flying, but then they are those who are far and few and usually have money to pay the police off from raiding the premises.

I was wearing a yellow dress – the quintessential colour and marker of spring. I always liked yellow – it made me feel sprightly and alive. It's funny how it is, but the colours you end up wearing actually make you imbibe those very emotions that the colours are associated with; perhaps the correlation works the other way around and you pick the colours based on your emotions. Today, though, my mind was thinking of things other than the gossip the *women were clucking about around me or the alcohol the men were consuming and thoughts of them falling off the unprotected roofs; I wasn't even thinking of the birds that chirped and whizzed or the orange peels that people carelessly dropped on the floor. (I find such disrespect of space filthy and my very vigilant mind despises visual scenes that aren't as neat as they ought to be, though what constitutes neat is, of course, up to the viewer's own desires.) I was trying my level best to not think of last night and how it had been the fifth time that it had happened.*

If something supernatural happens, and once you discredit it to your imagination, the second time you employ the same drill you assume that your mind's playing tricks on you, and as it is against your reason and prototype of what things are, you vehemently deny it. By the third time, you question the occurrence, but still shrug it off, though by this time you feel that something is off. Fifth time around and you know that you have been making yourself a fool and that there is something masquerading in the shadows of your mind, something toying with your senses, something that is fully aware of your vulnerability to rationality and therefore capable of distorting your reality.

I don't know if you believe in black magic or jinns, reader, but till the fifth episode neither did Maya. It is highly possible that as you read this, reader, you are unaware of the existence of either and disbelieve the existence of either as fairy tales and children's stories. Perhaps you don't even know what they are. Well, just in case you don't know, in Islam, and pretty much in the culture of the subcontinent – there is a belief in another of God's creations. Man is made from earth and angels from light, but there is another creation mentioned, called jinn, which is made from fire. Jinn aren't your regular vampires or witches on brooms, but an entire entity that, like man, embraces both good and evil and can be a product of either. They are seen and heard by man only when they wish it. If you take in the fact that man can only see visible light, which is a fraction of the light spectrum, and hear within the range of a few thousand hertz, what else is out there that we cannot see or whose frequencies we cannot hear? The idea of jinn doesn't seem as far-fetched as you might have thought when I first told you.

The thing with black magic is, it is even trickier to believe because it relies on the belief in the evil within man and the capabilities of the destruction that one is willing to inflict on someone else. *Nazar* is what they call the evil eye and it exists when someone feels envious of you and unknowingly creates a negative vibe in the universe for you. Of course, I am not a superstitious narrator or a Freudian in believing that every time one falls off the stairs or burns one's hand, it is due to an underlying purpose, in this case due to *nazar*, but I do believe in our connection to the universe and how one wishing ill or good on someone does materialise, not just in harming or benefiting that person, but in creating a rebound effect affecting you as well. Black magic, however, is inherently more malicious and harmful because it requires actually intending to do spiritual harm to another person. Voodoo dolls and hair plucking are frequent myths, but others include writing inscriptions, praying to the devil, and leaving the inscription outside the person's house. So beware if the next time around you see a black *taweez* (necklace) that contains such inscriptions in your flowerpot!

I assure you, whether I believe in black magic or not, I have been acquainted with plenty of such mythical trinkets myself and have been quite upset with the knowledge that someone somewhere wishes to do me harm when I try to be as conscientious as possible. There are numerous learned people who know or claim to know that they are well versed in the art of black magic and of course they receive an abundance of clients, primarily from the female populace in the country, to whom envy seems to be a severer infliction than it is to the men. I suppose women ought to be given work to do, especially those in the upper and upper-middle classes, for such calculating conniving minds rotting at home are not just a shame to the country's productivity output, but also to the woman in question who has nothing better to do than nurse her vexation at her son's new love for his wife, or her sister's rich fiancé, or her best friend's new job, or her cousin's new rich daughter-in-law or, even worse, son-in-law. The list of close relationships that spur on this wave of unconstructed envy is blasphemous. However, it is the most prevalent form of resentment that exists in all social circles.

Of course, had they an actual hobby to pursue or dreams to accomplish, other than getting married and having children, which by no means is not a hard task, but more of a duty than a life goal, they, like most of the men, wouldn't have time to ponder and think of all this useless jealousy. Antagonising someone for his or her achievements or possessions upsets no one more than the person who is feeling that envy, for it is a ridiculously consuming emotion. So these women, spurred on by their hateful obsession, seek out means to transfer it and the black magic–wielding learned people seem like the most attractive means of doing so. The means of getting at the person of their envy involves everything from that person's failure in all walks of life to unleashing jinn on them to harass and upset them, and even the wishing of death on them; I assure you many such women have had their wishes fulfilled. I don't assume to say that I believe in the dark arts – perhaps I do, usually I like saying I don't – but what I will relate to you isn't what happened to me, but what actually harassed Maya after she got back from Harvard.

The first time it happened was two days before her engagement with her cousin. She had just got back for winter break and was jet-lagged; she was depleted of all energy and by 8pm was unable to keep her eyes open. (Her cousin had informed her mother that he would be coming over to welcome her back and of course her mother would never have allowed her to tell him not to come, thinking it to be disrespectful of a soon-to-be fiancé, so all she had was an hour to nap.) Soundly sleeping, dreaming of acing an exam on Hobbes and other political theorists, Maya was woken by something that was weighing down on her body. Her hands and feet felt bound by unseen chains, her tongue silenced. The only screams she screamed were those in her head. Even though her eyes were open and were the only things that could scan the room, the rest of her body was undoubtedly paralysed. She felt a slight touch going up and down her body. When the touch stopped, she could move again, but then the toying force began weighing down on her body again. In her head, Maya wasn't scared. It's not like imagining seeing a ghost or an evil spirit; once you feel the presence, it is no longer in the imagination but out in reality and must be dealt with accordingly. So, as Maya claimed, she screamed and prayed, both swearing and begging the 'thing' to leave her. After a few minutes, it did and Maya was free to move again.

Covered in sweat, she thought about what had happened, but as soon as she turned the light on, it had already happened, and as it was too unreal to believe, she discounted it as a figment of her imagination.

But it had happened again last night for the fifth time, and yet another time was too much to be a mere coincidences of hyperactive imagination. Last night, she felt the weight reaching for her throat before playing with her body, and burdening her throat and chest again before whispering her name. It was a strange voice, since she was pretty sure it was her own, but a more eerie, chilly echo in her head. I don't quite know what the actualities of this strange little affair that Maya was going through were, except that she had been feeling this need to escape and this weight that constantly bound her and forbade her from enacting whatever her conscience told her she needed to. She felt like she couldn't be with her cousin, but at the same time she didn't know how to leave. In short, she felt as if she were silenced.

"Maya, Maya, my dear, my *jaan*, don't you look absolutely exquisite in your dress! My, doesn't she look absolutely radiant?" said a very enthusiastic Mrs W to Maya's mother.

Mrs K, pleased with the fact that her daughter was passing social approval, glanced at Mrs W and over at her son and said, "Oh! Thank you so much. Yes, she does look nice, but not half as nice as your son looks handsome." (The son, poor thing, looked anything but, being quite the awkward lanky Hans Christian Andersen in Pakistan. However, the purpose of the compliment was to give one back for the honest one received; in society even a compliment must be repaid, lest it turns to a means of the other gaining supremacy over one or of being offended.)

Mrs W wished to tell Mrs K of how much their children would have been a good match – her brains and beauty and their joint wealth. It saddened her to see such an alliance now not able to be formed, since Maya was already taken. Out loud she said, "No, no, Mrs K, you are too kind. By the way, did you go see the new lawns" (*shalwar kameez* out of lawn material) "that are out?"

Being forgotten, Maya of course took the cue to start zoning out and wondering what it was she should tell her parents. Should she tell them about her frequent supernatural encounters, which were getting more and more frequent, or about her grave wish to publicly break off her engagement? She knew the moment would be momentous in social history as aunties would gossip and speak ill of her and uncles would frown and think her family did a bad job of upbringing. Of course, they were all perfect and had never done any wrong, and of course if one commits a mistake it is but the parents' fault, for most people fail to realise parenting is five percent skill and ninety-five percent luck and that, even if society wished to tarnish her parents with disgrace, a fact that was unavoidable, it was by no means their fault as to the path she wished to take any more than it was her fault to not want to enter into an unhappy loveless marriage.

Granted, Maya knew she should not have involved another family, especially when they were her own relatives. She knew of the strain that it would put on her family, as all the relatives would have to take sides, but wouldn't it be better to face the concoction she and fate had created now, before it boiled all over and there would be no way to clean up every little stain? No, she didn't want to wait till five years after they were married and then worry about getting a divorce and how her parents and family would react then. This concept of social honour and respect an extremely trivial burdensome waste of a person's emotions because people will talk no matter what you do. They will judge because it is the most natural of human instincts. You may stop someone from throwing a punch, but it is unerringly impossible to stop a wagging tongue. The bitches will bark and all you can do is walk by and realise that no matter how much they bark, they are too broken themselves to bite. Maya both knew and realised that she didn't care about what society thought; she had rather live in truth than live based on the way others judged her. (Internal judgements are a given for every human being, but to voice those judgements and victimise a person based on those judgements ought to make people fearful, for they too could be likewise judged and socially constricted.)

She did know that her father, and especially her mother, sensitive to what people thought, could potentially let their parental instincts be overridden by society's expectations. Maybe she could try to like her husband-to-be, but then again why should she have to be in the position where she had to try to like someone when she already liked someone, when she had just recently spent an amazing time with the other? It just wasn't fair. Life usually isn't; that's what goads some to seek greater equality, like Maya, and others to just accept the unfairness as an integral part of their fate. I suppose no twenty-year-old must be faced with the dilemma that tears apart people of much older ages and wiser philosophies than her, but society fails to discriminate between age or rank, only too willing to tear apart and devour. The mob has no mentality but that of a hungry angry blob that is blind to everything save its own burning need to destroy all in its path. Society in Lahore ceases to have a moral conscience or indeed any sort of empathy for the victim (those that do unfortunately remove themselves from such mainstream company) and society functions exactly as does the mob.

Why must an individual's self be sacrificed for such blind, unforgiving, unrelenting, impenetrable social scrutiny? Are people only just products of what others expect of them? Can they not have their own goals? Is it such a sin to actually wish to marry the man you feel so secure and happy with when he isn't the socially desirable package that all the others want? Could she like her cousin, though? She knew nothing about him except that her silence and lack of effort made him feel insecure. Of course, not being loved by the person you were meant to spend the rest of your life with would be enough to infuriate anyone, yet why couldn't her parents just see it for themselves? Why did they take her love for granted and her loyalty to them as a given? After all, contrary to popular belief, especially her mother's, she was far from perfect. Why? She wanted to just scream her frustration out. She edged closer to the end of the roof. She wanted to just stand here and scream out both above and below and to all that existed between with this infernal problem that had given her sleepless nights, many moments of hysteria, excessive weight loss, and now even apparently a spirit who desired the predilections of her soul. Perhaps falling off the rooftop might be less painful than falling from grace; would it? She thought of the plunge, of the adrenaline as her body kept falling until it splattered on the ground, perhaps maiming her for life, perhaps taking her into a pitch-black hole of no return.

"Maya, Maya, Maya."

"Hmmmm," she said to her angry mother and a slightly surprised Mrs W. "I have been calling your name for a good fifteen minutes and am hoping that it would be possible for you to reply." To Mrs W, "I don't know the thoughts that the children today have in their heads. We were never like this. Our mothers used to call us once and we would be on high alert, ready to obey them at their every command."

"No, no, Mrs K, you have a very beautiful, very obedient girl. I have heard of such girls that it will make your head spin with the very knowledge of what they are up to. Just the other day I saw this girl be rude to her mother. She said – and in front of the guests, mind you – she said that she is 'no glorified maid' to be constantly serving the guests."

"Mashallah! No way!" said Mrs K.

"I am telling you I saw it with my own eyes. If it had been my own daughter I would have slapped her right then and there, but you hear of all these modern theories and laws that one mustn't hit one's children! Just think about it! *Not* hit one's children? I have never heard of such nonsense. I got plenty a thrashing in my own day and am so glad for it today! It taught me morals and principles and to display good conduct in life. *Bhae!* (Man!) That's how I have raised my children." (Unbeknownst to Mrs W, her children were far from exemplary, and that isn't my judgement but common knowledge.)

"And everyone knows how wonderfully behaved and mannered my children are. To think that you can't slap your own child! I mean that was definitely Mrs Z's method and look at her daughter – *she married a white man* – a white man! *Taubah taubah*. (God forbid!) Mrs Z could have saved herself all that trouble had she given the girl a good spanking when she was younger. To ceaselessly spoil one's child is in no one's interest, particularly a parent's."

I suppose Mrs W should have practised what she was so vehemently proposing, having given her children Prada and Louis Vuitton and phones when they were just eight, not to mention that the children do not know how to boil an egg or reach out to pick up a remote, being firmly reliant on a brood of servants who they are, to top off everything, extremely abusive to. The eldest son is perhaps the most prodigal of them all – I believe his purchase of three sports cars has been mentioned previously by me.

Mrs K merely nodded, losing interest in the elder woman's ranting on other people's children when her own were unruly to inconsiderable lengths. Nodding her head and smiling at Mrs W, she BBMed Maya, telling her to immediately go and seek out her cousin. Obviously in such a public gathering, if Maya did not interact with her betrothed, people would be extremely suspicious and prone to creating rumours. What Maya thought was immaterial was from her mother's perspective a desire that such a fate of being rumoured about not befall her protected little princess, and so she ordered this public display of an open and frank relationship with her cousin immediately. Of course Maya was extremely reluctant to seek out that which she was avoiding, but she was familiar with her mother's look – the one where she looked directly at you for a few seconds, raised one eyebrow up, and twisted her tongue to the side of her mouth to make the ferocity in the eyes even more compelling. Maya knew her not meeting her cousin was not up for discussion (even though she had been clear about her feelings toward this alliance) and for now she did as she was told.

She was standing searching the crowded roof for any sign of him; she tried looking for the man most drenched in designer ware and her eyes failed to find the most exuberant display of designer ware in the crowd – Dolce and Armani were so abundant that it was hard to distinguish one person from the next. But then she heard her name being called and turned to see her eager cousin staring at her with even more anxious eyes.

"What is the most beautiful person in the room doing standing all alone in the middle of the roof?"

"Ummmm, nothing," Maya said, staring at the floor and at her shoes; she felt uncomfortable when he stared at her that way. She only wanted one man to look at her that way and it sure wasn't him. Unfortunately, she didn't have much choice in the matter and for the time being she was just not going to say anything. (No, she wasn't even going to make him realise his lack of proper word choice having mentioned both roof and room in the same sentence.) That involved not leading him on, but at the same time not being rude so as to not hurt him, because spurning someone when they like you just isn't very commendable.

"All right," he said, "so, dude, do you wanna get some ice cream?" For the hundredth time she wondered where in his undergraduate experience in Spain he picked up the American accent.

"Ummmm, no, I don't really feel like eating ice cream."

"Well then, what do you want to do?" She could feel his voice getting more edgy and a touch of anger seeping in his false sense of collected calm and as she always wanted to avoid a fight, even though her ambivalence would always be the inherent cause of it, she replied, saying, "Ummmm, why don't we just go get ice cream, then."

His jubilant tone came back and Maya breathed a sigh of relief. "All right, buddy, let's go!"

He got a chocolate-dipped Magnum and insisted that she, too, take one and, in spite of being offered one ten times and refusing each of those ten times, to her complete annoyance she found herself with a Magnum in her hand. After the initial first bite, she swore to herself she wouldn't take another because there is no purpose of ice cream and an engagement if it must be a product of formality and not a natural flow of interaction, especially the spontaneity and impulsiveness you should be allowed to show with someone you want/have to spend the rest of your life with.

Feeling frustrated, as one would, but expected to be natural in Maya's state, she let out her internal turmoil on the ice cream stick and, breaking it in half, threw the ice cream in the bin. Inconsequential as the act was, she knew it was a waste of his money, money that she didn't like him spending on her – after all, this entire situation was due to money and she felt deep in her heart of hearts that be it the man she was in love with or the man she was engaged to or even her parents, why must she be reliant on all these other people for her livelihood?

After all, she was a fully functioning, fully capable individual and, not to sound proud, but in all honesty, she went to *Harvard,* people. She didn't need to rely on anyone to take care of her as long as she had herself. If she wanted to be with someone it would be because she wanted them and not because, like the rest of the girls around her, specifically those in her social circle, she needed them and their wealth. She was as firm on her ideals as her passionate warrior ancestors had been in their feuds with the Medes, Alexander's armies, the Brits, and some even with the Soviets; and above that, she damn sure had inherited from them her own fair share of their egotistical pride.

Perhaps it was her ego that was at stake, but loving for money was the only thing she had promised herself there would be no compromise on. She could take care of herself; just because she was a girl didn't mean that she was born with a handicap. Freud was perhaps right when he questioned women and how they spend their entire lives wishing they were men. At least women in her part of the world feel like that and forget that being a woman is their biggest asset because they are thought of as being weaker, as being incapable, too fragile, too simple, they have the capability of disproving those around them and taking them by surprise.

Men and women can never be equal, not because one is better than the other, but because in spite of the fact that they both begin this world as the same helpless state of a baby, they have been given different treatments and these treatments have offered both different roads. Perhaps those roads might switch and change, but each individual's path serves its complete purpose. Men and women don't necessarily have to compete or even argue over who is better; they are complements the way shampoo and conditioner are, the way an iron or a curling rod is, the way tights and dresses or coke and rum are, the way liner and mascara are or biceps and triceps curl.

One isn't better than the other, as both are equally necessary in bringing about a shared goal once they fall in love. If people only begin to understand this universal truth of how both are equally necessary to the other's survival and propagation, they would begin to look at the other with respect and accurately have a division of labour where house and work aren't just divided between the man and the woman, but subcategories are created within these two broader fields and they are divided so that each partakes in both realms of home and office. I guess that is the secret to a good marriage and the secret to a dynamic and prolonged happiness with the person you love – not differentiating based on gender, but treating the other as *you would like* to be treated. I suppose that can truly come to pass only when there is a certain degree of love, or at least like and respect, not a forced sort of formality, as is the case with Maya.

"Didn't you like the ice cream?" he said, with a feigned cocky expression.

"No, not really!"

"Then why did you get it?"

She wanted to tell him that she was sorry about making him spend his money, even if it was a few measly rupees, as nothing in the world upset her more, but decided against letting the truth out for fear of its inability to be contained and inevitably forcing him to flare up and sizzle in the already hot day, and so she calmly said her favourite line when she wished to avoid a situation of a highly volatile nature: "I don't know!"

"Why don't you know?" he counter-questioned, making her want to actually snap at him and tell him the truth, but, knowing that that was exactly what he wanted, she did not burst out like every other woman and decided to not give him the satisfaction of what was truly on her mind.

She just shrugged and smiled, completely diffusing the situation. "Hmmmm. It looked good but then got too sticky and I just wanted to throw it."

Just then her little family friend walked by. The boy was at least three years her junior and had always respected and idolised her. After an extremely respectful conversation about the Mughal emperors and which of the extremely ostentatious emperors had the most fascinating pedigree and rule, he spoke to her cousin and left. As soon as he left, her cousin turned around and said, "I don't like him. He was getting too 'over' with you." (Translation: 'over' in Pakistani English implies someone who is not adhering to social etiquette and stepping outside of their bounds.)

"Who? My family friend?"

"Yes. Your family friend."

"No, not at all," Maya said, finding it increasingly hard to control her irritation at this insecure person, realising that instead of creating sympathy in her heart, his insecurities only infuriated her and made her distant from him. She smiled again, as robotically as she had the first time (because a smile, no matter how genuine or fake, has the capacity to transform even the most hostile situations into containable events). "Why would you think that? Poor thing, he is so sweet and so decent. Please don't create things in your head."

"So now you're going to call me a liar?"

"Did I say that? No!" Now she couldn't help rolling her eyes.

"No, but you implied it."

"No I did not. What I alluded to was your hypersensitivity!"

"So now I can't discuss my feelings with you?"

"No, no, of course you can, when they are valid and not just a means for you to gain attention."

"So now I am a liar and an attention seeker. God! At least I am not a drama queen like you!"

"A drama queen?" She feigned obnoxious laughter. "I am the drama queen here – uh-huh."

The verbal brawl would have continued for much longer than she would have desired and, in spite of the fact that he was fuming, her delivery was calm though her words were conveying every bit the acerbity she felt toward the situation. Realising that pretty soon people would start staring and her mother, finding out that her daughter had fought with her fiancé in the middle of the gathering, might actually have a heart attack, Maya stopped presenting the truth about her feelings and said, "You know what? You are right. I am wrong," (they always seem to be the magic words in most people's case) and after that they stopped arguing.

One of his friends came over and pestered him into flying a kite (being a famous judge's son, he was obviously from the mindset of those that thought they made the rules). Maya had no desire to hold a wire between her hands that could potentially cut not just her own fingers but the neck of a hapless child on the streets, and, dull with disdain for drunk youths who should not be given the responsibility of such wires, followed her fiancé and his friend.

In conclusion, she ended up holding the stool of the wire as his friend attached the kite to the wire and ran with it before letting it go, enabling the wind to pick the kite up and her fiancé to tug the strings, encouraging it to ride God's wind and fly it as high as he could. Her thoughts meanwhile drifted over to her love and as she dreamed of being his wife, a smile came up on her face.

"Bo Kataaaaa!" someone shouted in the distance. She was woken up from her semi-trance. Apparently someone from an opposing political party had cut the kite of someone else. Not only had he cut the kite, which was a form of healthy competition, but he had shouted a whole host of insults, including those related to the person's mother (which if you but knew has roused many a hot-blooded Pakistani man to murder). Of course, insults were thrown back until hordes of men had to hold both the parties back to prevent them from falling off the roof in an attempt to get at the other.

I calmly stood amused at this flagrant display of an excess of testosterone, for every man has too much – that's his curse – and every woman doesn't have enough – that's hers. Even though bottles were flung and threats were made to see each other downstairs on the ground, men on both sides were offered water and lemonade, and as the sun itself was dipping back into the horizon and much of the literal heat of the day was dissipating, the men too calmed down, and as music was turned up (a natural mix of Desi and Western pop, hip-hop, r 'n' b, and the lately desired music, house) things went back to normal, or well as normal as they could be, considering the fact that now the police would definitely be on the way.

I was holding the stool, lazily looking at the sky and how as the sun dipped – or rather, the Earth rotated to an angle at which the sun was no longer at its zenith (depends on which way you wish to see the glass, as half-full or half-empty) – white light scattered itself all over the sky and all kinds of hues blended and mixed into each other all across the sky and reflected back into our eyes and into the visual sensory cortex and then, perhaps, into my aesthetic-sensitive neurons. So many colours spilling, blending, making the sky as full of vitality as the ground beneath it.

My cousin's friends came in and stood next to me and tried to strike up a conversation. I hated having my musings interrupted by useless talk, especially by men whom I did not know and who I knew would lead me into trouble later on from both my parents and my fiancé.

"So I heard you study at Harvard?"

"You heard right."

"How does that feel, to be going to Harvard?" *(Awkward sentence construction and misplaced modifiers are common in Pakistani English.)*

I shrugged my shoulders, still looking out at the sky, wondering how nature, even when silent, speaks volumes to the human heart and soul, and human beings will talk and yap and it will be nonsensical noise pollution meaning and signifying nothing.

"It feels just like it does going to any other university. Everything you learn is significant and valid no matter where it's learned from."

"Wow, that's spoken like a true scholar."

"*Not really, it just happens to be common sense, which is increasingly becoming uncommon.*" I smiled at my own *Mayaism.*

"*Yes, so I think the music is playing. Why don't you go dance with your fiancé?*"

Still not looking at him, Maya replied, "No, sorry, not interested in dancing." (*Especially*, she thought privately, *when it's in this drunken environment with all these drunk Pakistanis who, whether they are fourteen, forty, or sixty-five, are as inebriated and prone to getting literally 'wasted' as freshmen in college are.*)

"Ummmm, no thanks."

By the time she wondered why Arzoo hadn't come to this gathering to save her from her inevitable predicament, her cousin, hearing sirens in the distance, got spooked and recalled the kite; he really didn't want to go to the station, let alone give away any of his precious money as bribe money. Moreover, he was clearly feeling more than uncomfortable that his friend was trying to converse with his fiancé, and realising the tension in the air, the friend excused himself and left.

"What were you thinking?"

"What do you mean, what was I thinking?" she replied quizzically, staring at his face, hoping somewhere deep inside he would get in touch with his humanity and find a way to break through her fortress that didn't involve any form of accusation or defensive attack.

"Why were you talking to him?"

"Uhhhh, I wasn't talking to him. He was talking to me; I was merely replying."

"Well, I didn't like it."

"Well, then you shouldn't have introduced me to him. I mean, if someone comes and talks to me I can't just move out of the way; it's common social courtesy to reply, especially when he is such a good friend of yours."

"If you knew common social courtesy, you would've just walked away."

"You have to be kidding me. You did not just say that? Walk away? I am sorry, I can't do that! That's rude. I haven't been brought up to be rude. I mean, what is he going to think?" (Maya couldn't care less what he thought, but she knew that what people thought or said mattered unnecessarily to her cousin and so she delivered an argument that would be more tailored to the person she was talking to, and she was right!)

"Hmmm, yeah! So what did you talk about?"

"About how the music is on and how I should dance with you!"

"That's it? It took you ten minutes to say that?"

"Well, I don't exactly remember what we spoke about except that it was completely immaterial." (She felt slightly perturbed by what she had to go through while Arzoo was busy partying away the arrival of spring with other people their own age. Clearly telling her parents about Ali had brought about no significant change than her own freedom being constricted.)

"How can you not remember? I thought you had a photographic memory!"

"Perhaps I do, but with the wide array of information out there in the world, my mind selectively remembers information and throws unnecessary information out."

"Oh, please! Don't give me all this philosophical jargon. You just had a conversation with him; how could you so easily forget what it was about?"

"BECAUSE I WASN'T PAYING ATTENTION. GOD! Why do you have to continually question me?"

"If I am to marry you, can't I know what you are like?"

"Of course, of course you can, but you will never know what I am like if you constantly create situations that make me feel as if I am on inquisition all of the time. Then even when I feel like telling you things and sharing with you, I will only refrain from doing so simply because I constantly want to avoid these outbursts all the time. I am not a fighter; I like peace. I like being in a state of calm. I like being comfortable with my hormones in place and especially my adrenaline levels. Anger is not good for my body, just as much as it is not good for you." Maya heaved a sigh of relief, hoping that her words had somehow touched him, had somehow given him security. After all, she had finally shared her feelings with him; cautious and careful as she had always been around him, she had finally let down a bit of her guard, if for no other reason than to just be friends at least.

However, Maya was presuming something that potentially could not happen in this world. Sometimes we are so preoccupied with what our expectations and perceptions are of people that we fail to see the real person. Her cousin was used to this banter, used to this perception of her as closed, secretive, and reserved, so any attempts made by her to diffuse the situation would only naturally be misconstrued. It wasn't her fault or his – it never is anyone's – it was the constraints of the situation, and even though she tried to make an effort to rise above it, Maya did not proceed wholeheartedly to counter the effects of the seemingly fated misfortune they were both destined for.

All her cousin got out of her entire disclosure were the words 'I am a peace lover', and so he replied in kind: "So what you are trying to say is I am a fighter? God, why are you such a feminist? Why do you only think that all men want to do is control?"

"I never said that and I don't understand how feminism is related to my being peaceful. I never know how your logic works or how you draw in two seemingly unrelated events into one coherent argument. Where is your premise for drawing such conclusions? Of course, the majority of husbands in this country are staunch supporters of the feudal lord mentality, where they might have moved from their lands in the villages to the cities, but the majority of them cannot escape their ingrained desire to rule. So wives generally replace feuds, but I don't think our current generation is like that. I feel like the media is (usually) having quite a positive impact on curtailing this feudal husband from springing."

She tried to use as much of an analytical tone as possible so as not to be misconstrued, but being misunderstood was undoubtedly Maya's tragic fate. "So now I am a feudal husband?"

"WHAT IS WRONG WITH YOU?" she said sharply, her eyebrows furrowed in a grimace of anger. "What is it? Are you slow of comprehension or just inherently polemic that you must misconstrue everything I say! God! With all the thoughts that actually run through my head I don't have time for this. I want to think and talk about epistemology, about the inception of the universe, about epicureanism and Sufism. What I don't want to talk about is how useless my life has become to be boiled down to you said this and you said that. It's seriously pointless!"

"I know that you went to Harvard but are you trying to say that my feelings are pointless?"

"You know what? You're right and I am wrong. Why don't we just leave it at that!"

But at that exact same moment, her mother, sharp as a hawk, was contemplating whether to approach the two and intervene in the brawl or go on hearing the other women's pointless conversations and go on smiling. I believe she was more tired with all the chitchat than anything else, but she decided that it was maternal desire to protect her daughter from social scandal that made her leave the group of frolicking, laughing nonsense and make her way to the two. Of course with her mother being involved, one could no longer just leave things at that!

"Oh, hello, children! What's happening?" she said, with a huge smile to her son-in-law-to-be and evil eyes to her daughter.

And then her cousin did what Maya hated the most: he complained to her mother. "Nothing, aunty! We were just discussing how Maya goes to Harvard and is therefore more intellectually stimulated than the rest of us."

Her mother didn't even wait for her cousin to finish and openly pounced on Maya. "Being proud isn't becoming, Maya! You will get nowhere in life if you maintain this level of arrogance."

Her cousin smiled smugly; her mother berating her only served to enhance his perception that he was right. It was tragic that that only made him less flexible in trying to see the situation from another perspective and therefore arrive at a necessary solution. Moreover, when you end up pushing a certain personality type on someone who is nothing of that sort, they only end up behaving in the same manner that you claimed that they did, even if they aren't in essence like that. Maya wasn't proud, but everyone believing that she was only made her want to fulfil that expectancy bias.

Proud or not proud, she was even more adamant about fulfilling the resolve she had developed during her other-worldly state – about ending 'this' with her cousin and getting her parents to accept the man she wished to marry.

Is the world a delusional enjoyment? Or a miserable continuum? What about the world after? If there is one after, that is. As she looked between her mother and her cousin, she didn't know what worried her more: the demons that existed in between the worlds of sleeping and waking or those that inhabited the world of her conscious. She looked up at the sky, at this patch where surprisingly a sole kite still marked the sky – it was bright and yellow, standing alone yet shining bright. Her thoughts were interrupted by the police, who had just barged in.

THE QUEEN'S COURT

THE VOICE OF the 10pm peddler echoes throughout the neighbourhood – it's a scrambled, running, jarring sort of proclamation where words interlink with one another and become incoherent in much the same way as the repeated cries of an auctioneer as he shouts out a 'Going once, going twice, going three times.' Yet the auctioneer wishes merely to sell off another's possession for a commission, while the poor peddler cycles around the area in an attempt to barter off something, anything, in order to buy food to feed his family of six or eight.

Off on the dusty roadside a quadriplegic with amputated arms and legs snakes his torso along the main road while little ten-year-olds, permanently exempted from school due to their government-adjusted status as orphans, scurry about competing for the pity of each car that passes by. Yet not all these urchins are orphans; quite a few are possessed of living parents who find sending at least some of their brood out into the streets to swindle money off the guilt-ridden rich of more immediate use to the family than the intangible benefits of an education. After all, what good could schooling do for children when there are hardly any teachers, and those that exist are firm advocators of abusive techniques, and the classrooms are falling apart and government-led schools lack any sort of curriculum or an incentive to 'teach future peddlers how to count.' No, the streets are definitely more advantageous to their survival; the few rupees earned by the little doe-eyed felons will at least offset the cost of increasing inflation and the accompanying rise in wheat and sugar prices.

A beggar network primarily sustains itself on the occasional guilt of the rich. The networks are in effect an unofficial tax paid to keep one's conscience clean. The beggar networks earn their daily bread whenever the 'weakness of either a basic moral duty or a belief in society providing all with a shred of human dignity' afflicted the otherwise cold soul (due to air-conditioning, of course) safely ensconced within a Mercedes or Porsche. This emotional blackmail seemed a just tax for the usually indifferent multi-millionaire stuck in the same traffic and hot, muggy streets as countless rickshaw drivers and the multitudes of destitute urban poor, eager to make ends meet in a city that seem like a shrine to their suffering.

As a matter of principle, the wealthy would normally scoff at handing over the literally insignificant bit of loose change that the poor abused children asked for. After all, their precious invaluable money had been earned through 'hard work', never mind the corruption that went in to it. This most *haram* notion of meanness amongst the rich gave rise to a sort of cyclical knee-jerk mythmaking that conjured up horror stories of deliberately maimed children serving dark mafioso masters.

The shibboleth of the Mercedes- and Porsche-driving class held that in order to counter sentiments the wealthy might have against handing over their informal tithes and more efficiently awaken the upper classes' sense of virtuosity, the elusive heads of these beggar networks captured children and used acid to create burn wounds or, worse yet, amputated healthy arms and legs in order to generate 'more pity'. And so the belief held that these poor mutilated children who strive all day and night at intersections begging the rich for scraps of paper do so in order to enrich the devils who have physically and socially handicapped them.

To be sure, unfortunate children had been hurt and maimed in such unfathomably evil schemes, but it required a certain selfishness to conjure in one's mind a vast and intricate network that precluded every filthy and hungry urchin from the small change required to buy a bit of *naan*.* Charity can thus never be counted as a commodity. Human kindness never is a sure thing, but greed is.

Eunuchs, hermaphrodites and the gender indifferent add diversity and entertainment to these otherwise depressing intersections. Despite being the tragic and all-too-typical outliers of a patriarchal world, and thereby snubbed and ridiculed in virtually all spheres of the Pakistani society, the *Khusras*** earn their livelihood by brazenly dancing in front of red lights.

---

* Local cuisine bread made in an underground clay oven.
** Eunuchs.

Some onlookers will laugh, some scorn, some insult, yet all remain marvelled by the spectacular and impromptu break they provide from a busy day at the office or a taxing dinner with in-laws.

The *Khusras* are unafraid of rejection or ridicule, turning derision and jeers into smiles and sassy cheers. The fact that they sometimes stop traffic with elaborately choreographed routines matters little to the traffic control officers stationed nearby; after all, the officers get their cut of their corner's earnings at the end of the day just like a normal pay cheque.

But the spectacle of the intersection goes on! Frenzied mothers with covered heads holler at rickshaw drivers to halt and bid them to take them and their sick children to hospital, hoping that some doctor will take pity and offer treatment or medicines at a lower rate than the practitioners' self-created market price. However, the doctors, like everyone else, are much too preoccupied with the opulence and the infinite supply of paper that the rich possess; the oath to serve mankind and do no harm takes a backseat to the oath of the almighty rupee, Mercedes, and annual trips to Dubai and London.

The *Marassis** wear the same yellow garments day after day, driving the colour of spring and festivity to one of mockery in open defiance of the dirt, filth, and poverty crowning their existence. They sleep and stand at the roundabout, ready to commence playing as soon as they see a fancy car pass – especially one with green government number plates. Chance and sympathy form the bulk of their daily wage.

The bickering, brawling, sobbing, jeering, taunting, shouting – all the sounds of the desperate poor – loudly reverberate through this sole bustling street, yet there are places those sounds will never reach.

The sounds of the ever-increasing infliction and tribulation of the mendicants and the impoverished swerve past the main road and into the side alleys, just above where they die upon the barricades of army checkpoints meant to guard against the reality of poverty rather than terrorists. Yet even if the sounds could penetrate the barricades and travel into the affluent neighbourhoods above, they would hit the walls of 99 B and immediately bounce back. The high walls of 99 B, the Chief Minister's house, are heavily fortified against all intruders and are especially soundproof to the outside plight of the suffering classes.

---

* Beggars that sing and dance for entertainment.

Glasses clinked and the sound of pretentious hoary laughter filled the drawing room. Even though there is no gender segregation among the wealthy, in order to accommodate the large number of courtiers, the women – being no doubt more numerous in attendance as none would miss this occasion – occupied the huge drawing room on the first floor of the house, while the men relocated above until dinner was served. Yet this was only part of the reason for the segregation, for the men simply needed time away from their wives, and the wives – well, they needed time to scheme.

The men mostly stood in the upper lounge puffing cigars and drinking virgin cocktails, wishing for the hundredth time that there was alcohol in their beverages and that the Chief Minister – who was usually quite the host, as he was known to host events where 'dancing foreign girls', gin, and whisky would be abundant in supply – was not so keen on following the rules and airs of Islamic piety tonight. Sadly, the wives were in attendance this evening and such titillating shenanigans would have to wait until he summoned them over the next 'cabinet crisis'.

The unfortunate Mr B was indulging the poor Mr R in conversation. (He was poor, you see, because in spite of being a millionaire and a halfway decent human being, he had to contend day in and day out with a woman who was vicious, dominating, unrelenting, and sleeping with every foreigner in Lahore.)

Mr B thought that he'd like to have a go with Mrs R even as he addressed the poor old cuckold. "So tell me, old boy, why did you buy that godawful parcel for 3 *crores*?"*

R puffed up as he responded, "Why? Because the land was for that much and the poor fellow was bankrupt!"

"Ha ha ha ha," Mr B ruthlessly chuckled. "Wait, so are you trying to tell me that when in that man's state of desperation you could have bought the land for one-third the price, you chose instead to pay for its full market value?"

"Yes, I am saying just that," said the poor honourable Mr R. Such honour was of the most commendable sort because it entailed fairness for another that implied empathy, a trait most lacking among his peers.

"Well, my boy," chipped in the sixty-year-old Mr W, "you must look out for yourself in this world. If you were in that position no one would have

---

* Crore is a local monetary denomination. 1 crore = 10 million rupees.

wasted a second in taking advantage of you, and I mean no one. Trust me. I speak from experience."

I can't say that I agree with that, W, thought Mr R. But when it comes from the old Bengal Tiger I do not dare think the contrary, lest you glare those perfect teeth at my own holdings.

You see, it was common knowledge that Mr W had snared his wealth – he had seized large tracts of poor people's land and evicted them by force, only to cultivate the land into a housing scheme and sell off the properties for exorbitant prices. No one knew what happened to the homeless or which ditch they eventually found themselves in. All anyone knew was that Mr W was now one of the richest men in the country and no law, no court, nor any person was going to hold him responsible for his illegal actions. In fact, as long as he continued to rake in the millions, his social value increased accordingly. But these thoughts just passed into Mr R's head for a few seconds; only a fool would give them voice.

Instead, Mr R tactfully proclaimed, "Ah! Well, *sahib gee!** You may be right, but I like to be fair in my dealings! My mother always taught me that, and Allah, bless her soul, it has always benefited me."

"Ha! Fair," said Mr W, walking over to the other side of the room, "there is no fair, boy!"

Mr A, on other hand, was increasingly adamant about imparting a completely different set of values to Mr H. "I am telling you, she is amazing in bed! The way her body moves, by God, it's like she has no bones."

A horrified Mr H remarked, "By God, man! Do you have no shame? You have a wife and two beautiful children. If not for her, then at least for your children." However, H's reproach was lost on a man who was incapable of feeling responsibility in light of his own self-indulgence.

Mr A just shrugged his shoulders. "Nah! What they don't know can't hurt them!"

H continued, "It's not about what they do or don't; how can you kiss your children good night without feeling any remorse about the fact that you aren't just screwing someone other than their mother, but ruining their chances for a healthy home environment."

"Well, those twerps will be just fine nonetheless; I can't breathe if I am not true to myself."

---

* Respected sir.

"Well, then, you should never have married!"

"Oh come on, man. You know I had to – you know my mother never accepts a no!"

"You should have stuck to your guns and not given in if you were just going to cheat later on. Your children are innocent, they don't deserve this," replied H, whose naiveté was starting to unnerve the other men.

"Oh come on, man! My wife doesn't mind as long as I leave her huge wads of cash or a bag the night I won't be in. Can't a guy have a little fun?" Fun? Many married men in Lahore are using that word as a passage to their debauchery and (some) of their wives' sad fates. What is the woman's fault if her husband is a sex addict or alcoholic or, in many cases, even a homosexual? By all means, it is the man's (and sometimes even woman's) own choice what they want to do or who they want to be, but why drag another unsuspecting person down with them? And why, if the other spouse (usually the woman) finds out about the other's true self, must family and society force them to stay together for the sake of the children, who in most cases remain more tortured in an unhappy home than they would be had their parents agreed to a separation?

Mr U, on the other hand, sat smugly assessing Mr T, or rather, Minister of Education T. The latter had been shrewd enough to gain money from the government as well as many international nongovernmental organisations for building schools in his home province of Baluchistan. However, instead of opening more schools, he closed most of the existing ones, proclaiming they were unnecessary under the details of his new modernisation programme. The reality was, however, that the money had gone straight into his pocket, and as far as he was concerned that was a good place for it because education for the masses would create greater awareness and as a result would lead to them asking for dangerous things like 'greater accountability' and 'societal equity'.

Baluchistan and the greater Punjab were the stomping grounds of Pakistan's political mafia; despite the efforts of the international community, development in the area was pitifully slow and beset by corruption. If anything positive happened, it was usually just a means of pretence to keep voters pacified for the next time elections came around.

Believe it or not, there were conscious efforts to keep literacy as low as possible and even if sites for schools were occasionally established and the buildings, or what could sometimes be accounted for as makeshift buildings in villages, erected, teachers were absent or uneducated and often violent. The curriculum for eighth graders was the same as for second graders and often there were no grade-level distinctions between age groups and all the children were bundled together in a mass of heat, suffocation, and abuse, while Taliban fighters infiltrating from Afghanistan waited with bottles of acid for the few girls brave enough to want to learn how to read.

Speaking of girls, downstairs the women were engaged in no less corrupt discourse under their sumptuously-coloured lipsticks, fluttering lashes and designer gowns.

Mrs H raised her eyebrow as she saw both R and A light cigarettes. The air suddenly became even stuffier. *Young girls*, she thought. *They have no sense of propriety or respect of their gender. How indecent of them to smoke. Humph*!

With that she crinkled her nose, but Mrs R and Mrs A were too involved in malicious gossip as they leaned into each other, giggling and flirting with one another, to notice the elderly woman's discontent – she was fifty-two years old and clearly her opinion was no longer valid.

Mrs S and Mrs U sat discussing women's menstrual cycle and how not only did it bloat them but made them feel filthy; clearly the fact that it enabled them to bear children or even that it staved off the spectre of pregnancy following sex was pointless to them. Mrs W meanwhile continued to popularise her son's wealthy worthlessness to everyone who listened and the subtopic of today was his latest present. She listed the old cars she and her husband had purchased for him – a Jaguar, a Mercedes, a Rolls Royce and (to the jealous coos of the others) a McLaren.

The continuous screeching, high shrill voices of women blabbering about nothing but nonsense, lies, and untruths they fabricated to suit their own theories about the world would be enough to drive any sane person crazy. Only the plump Mrs J sat quietly, wisely observing this circus of feminine beauty and stupidity. She wasn't beautiful, appearance-wise, but her restraint, calm, and genuine heart made her have the most desirable soul.

For you see, babies are born with the same amount of soul in them and it is the good and the bad acts we do that either enlarge or shrink it; perhaps that is what the monotheistic faiths imply when they say our good deeds and bad will be weighed on Judgement Day. The universe watches and like an energy reserve, counts up the good and the bad you do in separate reactors and unleashes the one that fills up first back to you. This isn't to say that whatever bad or good happens to you is solely based on your actions alone. A great number of times accidents happen and whether they be in the guise of good or bad, these accidents are engineered to test the strength of our characters.

So as Mrs J sat and gulped her third virgin piña colada and grabbed a fistful of prawns from the waiters who went around the room, and as Mrs R and Mrs A burst into unabashed laughter once again, she purposefully ignored their ridicule and instead grabbed more condiments from the waiter as he passed by a second time. It wasn't by accident that Mrs J ate so much, but by chance she couldn't have children and by her will she coped with her pain through God's greatest blessing: food. Chocolates, pastries, baguettes, French fries – you name it and Mrs J ate it.

It is of course Mrs J's choice, and only hers, what she wishes to put in her body and I am perhaps as much of an epicurean as Mrs J, yet it is for the effects that this overindulgence would have on her body that I worry for this kindly and extremely persevering lady. She has, however, been very fortunate in another regard – she has a husband who truly loves her. He loved her the moment he laid eyes on her and continues to do so in spite of the fact that she could never bear children; even today her face still retains the spark and the finely curved features that still capture his heart. He had made a pact with God then to love her always and in spite of the pain he had of not having any kids, of his mother's incessant demands and jibes at her daughter-in-law, he remained steadfast in his support of her as his perfect and only life companion.

However, the lack of children pained Mrs J more than him and in spite of his continual attempts to appease her and make her believe that he was indeed completely okay with the fact that they didn't have any, she felt that she was torturing him and was so livid with the fact that she couldn't give him this one happiness that she actually asked him to marry a second wife, and she promised that she would love those children as much as her own. He, however, couldn't imagine sharing even a single iota of the primacy he afforded his dear wife with someone else and so denounced the idea as preposterous. In spite of their incredible companionship, this pain continued to grow between the two.

The chatter suddenly stopped and there was complete silence as the Chief Minister's wife approached the door. She was quite a formidable woman and one whose presence demanded immediate respect. She was decked out from head to toe in one of the most expensive designer *shalwar kameez*; many of the women made mental notes to ask her where she obtained the dress so that they could purchase the same one. Her diamond earrings touched her neck and it must have been quite worrisome for her earlobes to carry the formidable burden, and yet in spite of their stretched countenance, they somehow refused to tear. Matching diamond bracelets and a necklace accompanied the 'great' lady, but what was most captivating was the huge solitaire perched on her right hand. A flush of envy swept through the courtiers as they again made mental notes to force their husbands to get them diamonds at least half that size. A Chanel clutch of expensive crocodile skin was nestled within the solitaire-encrusted hand, and matching shoes graced her manly, but clearly demonstrative of her noble Kashmiri descent, feet.

Her homely face was done up professionally; thousands of rupees were spent in getting the makeup artist to illuminate her eyes, refine her lips, and contour her cheeks. Her mouth was set in a line of firm determination and her eyebrows, now calm and steady, were usually knitted together when she was furious; or even more terrifying to the secretaries, her servant, and her children was when she raised one solitary brow, inviting them to question their lack of good conduct. It wasn't just her opulence that would demand respect but her determined will in getting whatever she desired and her sheer strength in coping with the useless, philandering husband who now sat on one of the country's most prestigious thrones.

Like any competent 'monarch', she had her posse, her brood of courtiers – all the 'yes' people. They said yes to her follies, yes to her impossibilities, yes to her denials and to her ability to hide her fears, yes to her every wish, and yes to her every petulant request. They sought her and presented her with goods and bribes of all kinds from gold trinkets and cards, to even commissions on the business ventures they conducted that had nothing to do with her.

The moment of reverential silence passed as soon as the Queen smiled and the brood of courtiers rushed to say their *Salaams** – each woman wishing to be the first to pay her respects. They stealthily elbowed and stepped on toes, subtly shoved and nearly ran. Only Mrs J retained her

---

* Greetings.

160

dignity by remaining comfortably seated on her seat as if she were stuck on it with some natural adhesive.

After the Chief Minister's wife was done greeting everyone, she carried her exalted presence all the way to her 'throne' at the end of the drawing room beside a series of couches reserved for those whom she would select to temporarily entertain her with their presence on this glorious night. Along the way, her procession halted just before the self-respecting Mrs J. The heavyset woman gracefully got up to greet the first lady and, despite the fact they were meeting for the umpteenth time, the first lady was impressed by the calm demeanour and honest reserve of Mrs J. Both women had an unspoken yet high regard for the other. For a moment, the CM's wife was gripped by the thought of elevating Mrs J to be a part of her social cabinet. However, the enchantment ended as soon as Mrs J sat down and went right back to her snacks.

It is excruciatingly arduous to not lay the blame of corruption on the ever-eager laps, hands and mouths of the political figures of Pakistan. Yet they seem to be the most visible targets, easily held culpable for the country's economic and monetary dilapidation, while the ISI,* the army and its bureaucracy, shielded from public eye and media scrutiny, indulged in the most heinous forms of decline and crookedness. However, they are too stealthy, too criminal and much too powerful to be part of our story; I leave them to your own concern and attention and for now we look at the execution of the easiest target – the political immorality.

It should also be of interest to you, reader, that most illegal business deals and concessions are not initially executed by the politicians and businessmen in question but by their wives! They sit and gossip, flirt and twirl their hair, and humorously drop in their husband's desires to the Queen, who, as is the case with all queens, is the only one in absolute control of her husband's actions. Of course, he had two other secret wives, one in the capital and one in another province, and he had always indulged in whatever whim guided his lecherous spirit.

Had the first lady's father still been alive, he would have made her realise the folly of her choice of husband. Sadly, he was long gone before her husband had begun to show his true colours. Even if he were alive, perhaps he would have been blinded by the profound fondness the CM had for his

---

* Pakistani intelligence agency, like the CIA.

first legal (and publicly, only) wife. She might not be the sole beneficiary of his male potency, but she held all his other strings; he relied on her for the best judgment (or at least advice, which was better than his own foolish reasoning); he trusted her with his fears, occasionally literally using her as a shoulder to cry on; and he truly believed in her to do that which he could not.

In short, her meticulous running of both house and country relieved him from his children, to his personal staff and affairs, country crises, and international pressures. She in turn conducted her business with a calm practical outlook, focusing on the absolute power she wielded to keep herself from the growing pain in her heart every time she heard a rumour regarding her husband's indiscretions.

As she sat in the drawing room, she relished the euphoric thrill of being fawned over; some things just never got old.

"Oh my Allah, *Baji*!"* gushed Mrs A. "Your ring is just to die for."

"Well," said Mrs W, "I always say that it isn't the article of clothing or the accessory that is important but the wearer of the article in question, and by God your hands are so beautiful." She purred louder than a spoilt Persian cat and grabbed the first lady's huge masculine hands, twirling them around and eagerly staring as if the force of her vision would transfer their false eminence into her.

The Queen was quite aware of her hardy disposition (she was of Kashmiri stock, after all). Feeling mocked, she withdrew her hand and declaimed W's overboard compliment. "Oh please, W! One should learn the art of flattery from you. The words that flow out of your mouth – if I were to eat them, I would get diabetes."

Everyone laughed at the completely platitudinous little jest. In her head, Mrs W called the Queen a little tart and a bitch and proceeded to pretend to be affronted by the Queen's disregard for her 'honest' intentions.

"Oh please! What do you want, W?" she quipped at her same-age dependent.

"Oh, why nothing, *bibi*!" W had upped the ante by humbling herself further in the Queen's presence; the bitch really wanted something this time.

"Oh come, come! We all know that your brother is in dire straits and that your husband is a wise enough fool to not pull him out of his economic

---

* Term of endearment for 'elder sister'.

deprivation for the tenth time. He needs a loan, doesn't he, for some new idea that has caught his fancy?"

"Well, yes, *bibi*. He is…" W continued to purr on, apparently trailing off in an attempt to create both suspense and false shame.

"Speak up, woman! I can't hear you." The others giggled and Mrs W wrinkled her nose before continuing.

"Well, *bibi*! My heart bleeds, it bleeds to see my brother in the condition he is. Oh my poor parents! They did as much as they could for him, but alas, he is an unfortunate, unfortunate soul. He is a poor lamb always sacrificed by others." (Quite the other way round, and everyone indeed knew that his tenacious disregard for others was perhaps one of the reasons for his unfortunate circumstances.)

This level of attention being given to the notorious brother was increasingly annoying the Queen, whose absence was replacing her presence. "I didn't ask you to start your ceaseless ranting because I wish to know about your brother's misery; I wish to know how I can help!"

She had been successful in veering the conversation from the brother to herself. "Well, my gracious madam, I was wondering if you could arrange for a loan for him."

The selected courtiers hushed into a silence as they awaited a decision from their Queen. Her face was one of austere complacency and for a split second, as one eyebrow shot up, everyone held their breath; poor Mrs W was almost pissing in her *shalwar*. She was sure she had jeopardised her invitation to the next Chief Ministerial gathering with her outright grovelling. But then the eyebrow went down and a wry smile took its place. Diaphragms relaxed as everyone let out breaths of relief.

"Well, of course, W, you and your husband have been such loyal supporters of the Party. Why don't you come over tomorrow and we will work out the technicalities of the loan." The basic technicality that needed undue care and attention was of course the 20% share of the loan that would be paid to her before the cheque had even been issued. As the first lady saw it, she was the middle person and entitled to at least 20%; 10% was getting too obsolete way too fast.

"Oh! You are so gracious, madam," said Mrs B. For the first time, she was directing her cooing voice and doe eyes to someone other than Mrs R. R, being jealous of this sudden change in Mrs B's object of attention, rolled her eyes in disdain. Of course, Mrs B had ulterior motives. Sycophants, toadies, humbugs, what humorous words for such an evil trait, flattery, because flattery has the ability to delude, to confuse someone and make them oblivious to their reality, causing them to live in a reality that would soon be their demise and the flatterer's unfair benefit. In the case of the ministerial Queen, she wasn't deluded into believing in a false sense of beauty or in the sense of possessing traits that she didn't ever personalise; instead she was deluded into believing in her infallibility in the possession of power that can never be taken or repossessed. She did realise that Mrs B, like everyone else, sugar-coated her dependency on her and, unlike the elder Mrs W, whose shrill voice annoyed her, she let the soft young beauty flirt her way to getting what her husband had instructed her to.

"You look so beautiful too," Mrs B, continued, "you're the perfect embodiment of grace and elegance—"

"Yes, we all know that," interjected the Queen. "Tell me something we all don't know. Go on then?"

"Well…"

"Well, girl?"

"Well, you are… um… ah…"

"I am what? Speak up, child. Since you adore me so much, tell me something I haven't heard about myself this evening?"

"Well, ma'am, you are more kind to me than my mother." The nonsensical attribute obviously made no sense and Mrs R had to restrain herself from bursting out in laughter in front of the Queen, who by now had raised the proverbial eyebrow of disdain.

Mrs B burst out in tears instead, as the reference she had made to her mother had broken the charm she was trying to entrap the Queen in.

The enchantment broken, the Queen bellowed in a harsher tone, "Well, it seems like your mother didn't really teach you polite etiquette for approaching people of dignified standing. In any case," she said, relaxing her brow, "I am QUITE far from your mother's age!" she humped.

In between snivels, Mrs B managed an "I-I-I-I am so sorry, ma'am."

"Well, what you said is said; that's the beauty of time and words, ladies – once they pass along they pass along – we only keep going in a linear manner, girl. We DON'T go back. Right?"

"Ye-e-s, yes, ma'a-a-a-a-m." Mrs B gulped back an over-exaggerated snivel, and Mrs A, equally fond of theatricalities, fished in her Prada for a tissue and offered it to the woman, who dabbed away at the tears at the corners of her eyes. Mrs A stuck her lower lip out in an utterly disingenuous show of sympathy.

"*Acha Bachay!*" *Bibi* doesn't have all day, just tell her what you want," said a voice from nearly across the room. It was the all-knowing Mrs S, reduced from her usual position of power by the presence of the Chief Minister's wife. Mrs S required a private audience with the Queen and therefore wanted the frivolous requests to end as soon as possible so that her own more pertinent request could be acknowledged.

"I," said Mrs B, looking down at the floor, "want," and then she looked up with full force, pursing her lips and fluttering her lashes. "I want, actually my husband wants, to be able to retain control of his land. We heard that for the new railway expansion the government wants to enact eminent domain and take control of the area, and that would hinder our business. You know that our fitness club and spa profits so many customers every day" (And indeed its exclusive memberships brought the couple millions.) "Even you yourself frequent our club from time to time, *bibi*; it would be a pity to have the club shut down." With that, she looked at the floor again.

"Yes, yes, hmmmm, you're right, we can't have that!" The Queen was thinking about her favourite Filipino masseuse. "I will talk to the Chief Minister about asking the Minister of Transportation to revoke his bill."

Mrs B beamed. Of course the Queen would take 10% to 20% of the club's profits henceforth, and while the wealthy would continue flourishing within the walls of Mr and Mrs B's health club and spa, another vital government plan was blown to smithereens.

The Queen now turned her gaze to a little further off in the drawing room, where Mrs J sat alone, munching on the chips and dip that were conveniently placed on the side table next to her. She shook her head at this once beautiful woman – beauty, you see, can no longer be natural but must be maintained and enhanced with products and scalpels. Although the Queen would never admit it to herself, she found Mrs J the most beautiful woman in the room. She wished once again to call her within the inner circle but actually felt it would offend the grace of the other women, and so turned her ear to yet another sycophant's conversation.

Mrs U was informing the Queen that they (the company her husband was CEO of) wanted greater access to gas lines. For the third time that night,

---

* Okay, child.

the Queen surprisingly agreed. However, this time she had no intention of upholding her promise. She would, of course, undoubtedly take her commission for the deal but had no intention of upholding it because the gas lines were the prerogative of the interior minister, a powerful man who would not take lightly to his back being stabbed for a change. The first lady had no desire to create a rift within the party and lose the support of this distinguished minister. No, she was going to take the monetary offering from Mrs U without even attempting to fulfil her request.

The conversation leapt from woman to woman, appeal to appeal, until finally Mrs R, tired of all this fawning and knowing that her husband would die before ever instructing her to ask for a favour from the Queen, noticed a tall slender figure entering the door – it was Ariyana, the blonde half-caste. Late as she usually was, R grimaced at the entrance of her exotic competition.

By this time, the men, hungry and tired of tearing down each other's egos, were lingering about in the hallway outside the drawing room. Ariyana respectfully acknowledged them as she bid her husband goodbye and entered the women's gathering.

Mrs R felt a flush of envy as she watched all the men entranced by this tall, slender woman. She could also see her husband's mouth agape for a few seconds before he gained composure and turned to look the other way. She looked over to where the beautiful woman's husband, Mr Y, stood, and R was extremely happy to realise that his brow was knotted in a slight grimace; he was clearly disturbed by all the attention that his wife was getting. *Humph!* she thought. *What a little tart!*

Nevertheless, she could still feel her blood thickening, her heart beating. She wanted nothing more than to rip the strands of blonde hair from the half-caste bitch's head as she walked into the room. R wanted to tear her light-coloured eyes out as they glistened with warmth; she desired to slap that smile off her face. *What a disgusting smile*, she thought, *so innocent and oblivious of whom feels what toward her.*

Mrs R frostily smiled after a few minutes of ignoring and then finally acknowledging Ariyana's excited waving. She signalled to the girl, inviting her to the Queen's inner circle. The Queen, of course, had no objection because Mr Y, the white girl's husband, was clearly rich and would be a huge asset in funding her husband's campaign for next year's re-election.

Ariyana, exuberant at her inclusion into the inner circle, was much too happy to doubt Mrs R's intentions. I mean, after all, when we have no ill will toward anyone we forget that others don't think or feel the way that we do; each person has his or her own thoughts and our reasoning can never be attributed to the thoughts and perceptions of others.

As she walked over from one end of the drawing room to where the Queen and her courtiers sat, all the women in the room looked her up and down. She had just mascara and lip gloss on and yet looked more radiant than all the women in the room, who had applied layers and layers of foundation (three shades lighter than their own skin tones). Her long blondish hair hung loosely, forming natural curls at the tip that none of their irons and curling irons could possibly achieve. She was wearing a simple *shalwar kameez* by – *wait, wait, which designer?* – the women thought, searching, searching, reaching deep into the recesses of their parietal and temporal lobes – oh my Allah, was that a Khaadi?!*

These women usually wore *shalwar kameez* by Khaadi for a brunch or when they wanted to show off their simple elegance to all the other mothers as they would pick up their children from school, and she, she was wearing this *shalwar kameez* to such a grand dinner and looked utterly smashing in it. They would openly laugh if they weren't at the same time mesmerised by the way the clothes hugged her model-like body – a body that was naturally slender and not slender the way most of theirs was by gym, starving, and yes, even liposuction.

She wore no jewellery, no clutch, no purse, and had simple black shoes, which were in fact Dior, but did not have the Dior emblem on them. Then they noticed her hand and gasped as they saw the same rock as the Queen's on her hand – a hand that was white and flawless, smooth and slender. The ring naturally looked even more beautiful on her hand than it did on the Queen's.

At last, Ariyana had arrived.

I went and sat down next to the women; they were all so beautiful and mesmerising with their jewels and captivating huge eyes, fluttering lashes and shiny white teeth. I admit I was slightly giddy at the prospect of having Mrs R invite me to the select group in the discreet corner of the drawing room. I mean, did they want me there? I never really had very many girlfriends, mostly only guys, so I guess I had always been more of a tomboy. I didn't know the intricacies of fashion or makeup; thank God hubby's sister is an angel

---

* Local high-street brand.

and occasionally helped me decide what to wear to these dinner parties and luncheons, though I must admit she occasionally got frustrated at what she called my 'simple' selections.

Somehow, Pakistani girls didn't really like me. Since childhood, I had always tried to blend in. I would sit for hours in the sun trying to get tan but to no avail. I would keep dying my hair black, but that only made me look more pale. To make matters worse, I kept getting taller and taller and stuck out even more like a sore thumb, permanently quashing my desires for acceptance into Lahori society. I wished I was brown and beautiful like these women. Ironically, a combination of artificial and natural (staying inside all the time) means made them as white as I was, but the difference between us remained – I lacked the full flavour of the ancient beauty etched on so many of their faces. My facial features came across as too doe-eyed, too Mary Jane for Lahore, my husband said too trusting.

I had spent my entire life living in a juxtaposition of east and west and coveted nothing more than that people should accept me for who I am, not the person I was willing to be for them. I had only met these women twice, and as Mrs R signalled to me, I had an epiphany – I felt it was finally my chance to have friends. My husband was extremely adamant about me making friends with these women and I couldn't agree more. The very thought of having someone to call, to share my secrets with or discuss my sex life with, made me feel nervous and exhilarated all at the same time.

Mrs R, more out of the need to be polemic than to flatter Ariyana, spat out a half-assed compliment. "Oh my! Your ring is so beautiful."

"Oh, yes, yes, very!" Mrs B chipped in.

"You're so lucky! Magnificent ring! What a huge stone!" chimed in another sycophant.

Whoever said that was slightly immaterial as the crescendo of toady voices arose in unison, coming in the same wave and pitch of ugly flattery. What is important is what Mrs R said next.

"Why, it's the same ring as *bibi's*. What a coincidence!"

The Queen was highly conscious of her tanner, stringier-looking hands and had been resentfully glaring at Ariyana's slender white fingers, on which the ring took on another ethereal quality of beauty. The last thing she wanted was for everyone to compare their hands and yet here were all the women staring at hers. She had an impulse to withdraw her hand, to hide it from view behind her back and yet she knew if she did, it would create even greater amusement for these hungry vultures. The Queen could almost hear their snickering. And now suddenly this woman became part of a comic tragedy, where it was a great test of her endurance and strength of character that she kept her hand out in full view waiting for the scrutiny.

Mrs W (not having forgotten the earlier insult and prepared to repay the Queen that debt), said "Oh my! Really, is it the same one? Ariyana's seems a little bigger. Perhaps it's because her hand is smaller, no?"

Their eyes snickered as their earlier envy for the ring now had the opportunity of being vented out in the appropriate arena. The poor Queen felt herself slipping, losing control as she was indirectly ridiculed both in her eyes and others'. After all, it's only when we're afraid of our own selves and fear ridicule that we actually give power over ourselves to others. The Queen sought desperately to regain her composure and her momentary loss of dignity. She gripped at loose threads for whom to embarrass and make uncomfortable until she finally realised that the only person who was worthy and deserving of humiliation was none other than the girl who had brought about her own.

Everyone suddenly became aware of the sudden drift in the environment as the Queen lifted a brow and looked at Ariyana. However, before unleashing a torrent of jeers at her, she turned her gaze to Mrs W to put her back in her place first. "W, dear, clearly your eyes require aid; my ring is distinctly bigger. The jeweller made sure my diamond was the largest."

"Oh yes! Yes *bibi*," said Mrs R in an attempt to redeem herself. "It is conspicuously so much bigger." The others added their voices of agreed flattery. After all, suddenly they were all in agreement that they didn't want to be negated by the Queen. As a collective they had power, but when the Queen started ingeniously deploying her power of divide and insult, they started to unbuckle, losing the sense of false power in the majority, each trying to look out for herself.

"See, Mrs W, you must see an optician. And you, girl," said the Queen, turning to face Ariyana, "so tell me child, where did you get your ring?"

"Why, ma'am, my husband got it for our first anniversary! Our rings are so beautiful."

"Ours?" said the Queen, raising one thin eyebrow; everyone let out gasps of shock. "Ours?" she questioned again.

"Why, yes ma'am! Our rings!" said Ariyana with confused conviction.

"But, girl, they are not the same. I had my one made in Karachi by none other than Saki the jeweller. It is certified as authentic – and I am truly sorry to say only *one* of its kind."

Saki was a jeweller who charged exorbitant prices for diamonds and rubies that were for much less at other jewellers; but whether his ornaments had any differences, let alone any remarkable distinguishing features, is inconsequential. Saki charged the most for his wares and so all the women wanted their husbands to buy their jewellery from him.

The underlying insult of the Queen's statement was lost on Ariyana.

"I believe my husband bought mine from there too," said Ariyana, beaming at the coincidence, oblivious that the Queen, by deftly stating the ring was the only of its kind, had expertly laid the groundwork for all Ariyana's following honest pronouncements to seem like highly contrived or desperate lies.

"Really? Well, how much did your husband pay for yours?" growled the Queen in response.

Mrs B, fearing that the Queen's good mood would be spoilt and her previous promises to them, more specifically to her, would be ruined, stepped in to calm the Queen's rising ire. "Yes, yes, *bibi*, I am sure you paid more for yours! Your diamond looks like it's at least a carat more."

"Two carats bigger. And perhaps Saki is getting a bit greedy. Selling his castoffs as legitimately cut," said the Queen.

"But, but," said a flustered Ariyana, before Mrs R and Mrs B both nudged her to shut up.

"It is two carats bigger, isn't it, Ariyana?" the Queen questioned, looking at the younger woman.

Ariyana gulped down the truthful answer that was forming its way up her oesophagus back down to her chest (after all, the one thing her father taught her was to always tell the truth and it had always benefited her). Instead she spoke out the lie that they all, especially the Queen, wanted to hear from her.

"Yes, actually, ma'am," said Ariyana, learning her place among the group for the first time.

The Queen purred at her victory but still wanted Ariyana to capitulate further. "I'm sorry, Ariyana. What was that, child?"

Ariyana bit down on her pride and tried to fight the flush of red rushing into her cheeks. She was utterly ashamed of the situation and herself but she went on, "I was told by Saki himself that yours was the biggest he had ever sold, ma'am. Ever."

The women let out a sigh of relief that the Queen had been pacified; however, she was far from done. She was about to make a jibe at Ariyana's clothes when the Chief Minister and the other men walked in. Her husband took care to greet all the women in attendance and the Queen burnt with envy as he specifically paid close attention to Ariyana. He even bent down to pass her a tissue paper, manners that he had never imparted on any female company, including his wife.

The Queen leaned back on her sofa, seething. Mrs R took notice of the elder woman's disposition and realised she now had the perfect opportunity to direct the Queen's venom at Ariyana. R purposefully walked over to the Queen and plopped down on an armchair next to the Queen's sofa.

An onlooker would never have guessed what vitriol the women exchanged between them regarding Ariyana. To the untrained eye, their conversation seemed to be inconsequential as they giggled and whispered, but the sad truth was words of poison and malice and deviousness were being exchanged. A plan was being hatched between two eager conspirators to put the damned half-caste back in her place.

Behind the beautiful mask of Mrs R's face there lurked the most evil of liars and the best of politicians, whose wit, cunning, and soft deceit no one could match except perhaps the shrewd Mrs J, whose large size (relative to the other women, of course) befitted her sharp mind and magnanimous heart. Mrs R had decided her mission was to teach Ariyana a lesson for thinking that her damned white self was capable of stealing other women's husbands (or that is the way she put it in her own head as well as to those around her). To Mrs R, Ariyana's pale skin, Mary-Sue face and blonde-tinged locks were an obnoxious affront to her own Eastern beauty; she coveted the girl's beauty and hated her for the innocence she surely must feign. Mrs R vowed that Ariyana would be Lahore's tragic mulatto.

Mrs R scanned the room and found Ariyana's husband, Mr Y, staring at his wife from across the room. Yet something seemed wrong with Mr Y, and Mrs R focused intently on the man. His brows were pinched together and his body tensed with – what was it? – ah, yes, what most men like to call protective instinct, but most women know to be true jealousy. Mrs R was pleased when she saw this sudden new development and praised Allah and the PRK surgery she had in Vienna for granting her such sharp vision. She was even more pleased when the seeds of an idea began taking shape in her mind. As she sat thinking to herself, the devious plan in her head grew and expanded until finally, Mrs R couldn't contain herself. She coolly stood and walked over to Ariyana and whispered in her ear.

"Ariyana, dear, I am having a tea tomorrow evening. Would you like to come? It's just for us girls and not these old croaks." As she withdrew she gently brushed her cheek against Ariyana's but failed to excuse herself; she flashed a smile and looked her straight in the eye. The move was meant to show that R felt completely at home in her presence, a subtle gesture that would surely bring Ariyana's guard down.

"Why certainly, Mrs R," Ariyana said. "I would love to be there."

"Great! Be there by six." She smiled again, flashing her glistening white and frighteningly perfect teeth.

Ariyana was ecstatic that she had again been invited into the circle and by the über-elitist Mrs R, no less! Giddy with excitement, she thought of her husband out in the crowd of jabberers and headed over to tell him the news. As Ariyana walked over to her husband a large figure stepped in front of her, completely blocking her path.

"Dear! You really are so beautiful up close even! Well, I must say, all the other ladies must envy you indeed! A piece of advice, girl: don't be fool enough to trust everyone," said Mrs J, as she stood squarely in front of the taller woman and looked up into her face.

J seemed harmless enough, but Ariyana wondered what the plump woman was getting at. "I don't understand. What do you mean, Mrs J?"

"I don't mean anything, girl. Just some advice: around these women, you always be careful."

J stepped out of Ariyana's way, allowing the woman the freedom to pass her; she smiled at the taller woman and two perfect dimples grew out of her plump cheeks. "Now excuse me; those half-starved prawns and hors d'oeuvres weren't enough to satisfy this stomach."

Ariyana wished to question Mrs J further about her blunt and eccentric comments, but before she could, the other woman had vanished into the midst of the crowd lining up outside the dining area. As soon as Ariyana saw her husband's warm smile and clasped his hands she could only think of how happy he made her; together they stepped out into the garden and were greeted by the aroma of the dinner awaiting the guests.

The opulent spread set up in the gardens outside would have humbled the Great Gatsby and bankrupted a vizier. Meticulously arranged under five beautiful white tents was a feast for the ages. Each tent featured the food of a different continent, with an ethnically appropriate chef overseeing half a dozen servers at their stations. The guests oohed and ahhed as a Chinese chef flipped and caught food in his wok, followed by a Brazilian spinning and slicing meats off a churrasco, and a red-cheeked American pulled out several beef briskets from a custom-built Texas-style barbeque oven.

As Ariyana basked in the glow of the opulence surrounding her, Mrs J's advice was quickly forgotten.

ALL GONE WRONG

NO MATTER HOW bruised or battered an animal, how pained and abused, it will not lose hope. The lion bowing under the crack of the whip will feel the edges of the cage and will temporarily relent, but neither the whip nor the ringmaster will be able to separate the lion from its dreams of running free on the grasslands. The hamster in the small-boxed cage might realise the realities of its constraints but furiously runs on the wheel, dreaming of catching food and being free. Likewise, the cockatoo might be tied to a stand with her wings clipped, but she will never lose her honour. If you try and abuse it, it will fling its little yellow crown up and frighten you, no matter how frightened it is itself. Hope is a timeless certainty, a part of our nature, and it is something that we can never truly relinquish. Neither, for that matter, could Maya.

When Maya was sure that everyone had gone to sleep, she unlocked herself in the toilet. She stared at her reflection and could barely recognise herself. Her eyes and mouth were so puffy that her face looked like it belonged to another person. She didn't recognise herself, didn't recognise the senseless broken thing she was. She walked out and went straight to bed. As she lay there, she began to think again. She was too tired to feel and her mind, finally glad that her emotions and bawling had temporarily halted their joint assault on her body, began to plague her with ideas of getting out of this trench she had somehow dug up for herself. As idea after idea popped into her mind – from threatening to commit suicide to actually doing it to running away, none seemed like a substantial enough rope to tug her out. They would only facilitate her sinking into a forlorn decay. No. She had to think of a much more reasonable plan. How to get rid of her cousin-fiancé?

And how could she make her parents agree that he just wasn't the one for their daughter? Suddenly, like a flash of bright light, a rope of an idea fell from the heavens toward her and she carefully attached it onto herself.

If there *was* no cousin-fiancé, there could be no marriage to him. Of course, killing him had been a frequent figurative desire of Maya's lately. However, Maya being Maya, sending her dreaded suitor to meet his most undeserved fate with seventy-two virgins was just in the realm of the imagination. No, what she had in mind was much less morose and gory: she would just simply tell him the truth. Yes, she would meet him and pour out her soul to him, including the cruelty that she was being made to suffer. She would appeal to his humanity and if he had any heart or any genuine feelings for her, he would naturally acquiesce to pull out of the relationship calmly and silently without involving her parents – surely such a sentiment is the least to be expected from any courteous gentleman, even a smitten one. After all, thought Maya (clinging desperately to her growing delusion), they were flesh and blood, so he would surely find it in him to do the right thing. Yes, she was going to go see him tomorrow and sort everything right out...

A MOST RATIONAL CASE OF MANSLAUGHTER

MAYA SAT ON the couch, waiting for him to come out of the toilet. He was taking ages and with every second she was losing her nerve. The last time she had met with her cousin-fiancé in person was during the disastrous Harvard visit and then at the pyrrhic spring *basant* rooftop. Given how both those events went, she had no idea what to expect.

After about twenty minutes he opened the door, dressed head to toe in cologne; one likes cologne, but an extreme usage of it, just like anything else, is extremely unnerving. He wore jeans, blue Prada shoes, a Louis Vuitton belt, and a white button-down shirt that was open at the neck to reveal a recently waxed chest. He would be considered a handsome Pakistani man by many standards yet because Maya respected his more or less honourable intentions and the fact that another held her heart, she had naturally never attempted to understand or appreciate his attractiveness. Being as she was, highly empathetic, with high EQ, meant she would not broach that sort of moral duplicity. He smiled and Maya awkwardly returned half a smile. "Yo, dude!"

"Hey!" The way his eyes lit up sent a tinge of doubt to her stomach. Deep down she knew he was prepared to fight till the end to have her.

"How have you been? How was your trip to Cali, hanging out with what's-her-face? Oh yeah, Paki Rita Ora."

"Oh, it was fun! Arzoo was such a great host." She looked down at her hands to avoid any discussion of California; she couldn't bear to be reminded of her lover at this point. Moreover, her cousin and Arzoo had a deep-seated, mutually reciprocated hatred of one another and she didn't want to ruin his mood right now by responding to his verbal jive at her dearest friend.

"So what do you want to do?" he said, plopping down on the couch next to her, reaching for the remote, only to use the action as the perfect guise for holding her hand. For a second, she stiffened as an electric shock of 'don't touch me' went through her body, but knowing that she wanted to keep him in good spirits, she slightly loosened up.

"Ummm, anything!"

"Do you want to watch TV?"

"Sure."

"What do you want to watch?"

"How about *Penny Dreadful*?"

"Nah. How about *Curb Your Enthusiasm*? Larry David is classic, man. Turn to HBO, there's a re-run tonight, I'm sure."

"Sure," she replied, only internally rolling her eyes. I mean, he always did this; if he wanted to watch what he wanted to, why go through the formality of even asking her in the first place? This is why she never even answered any of his questions, but for now she needed to stay calm.

Just then, one of the servants knocked on the door, carrying a tray full of delicious foods that were as tasty as they were international. The tray had a mountain of fresh and crispy French fries, mouth-watering *chat masala*,* Buffalo chicken wings, *dahi bhalla*,** lamb kebabs and even an overtly cheesy lasagne. Her mother-in-law-to-be was determined to be quite a gracious host and determined to win her daughter-in-law's heart by any means necessary, including every honest woman's true weakness – good food. Maya wasn't famished but glad for the opportunity God had just granted her to focus on something besides the stagnant conversation with her cousin-fiancé. She used the servant's entrance to extract her hand from her cousin's tight grasp – it was throbbing with his intensity – and she went for the greasiest treat first.

Maya bent down and grabbed a bowl (first offering one to her cousin, not because, as her mother claimed, men must be served first, but out of genuine courtesy designed to return the mood to some sort of reasonable equilibrium). She filled her bowl with *dahi bhalla* over which she poured the spicy sauce, *chat masala* and *pappri*.*** She sat back, waiting for the wings to

---

* Local spice powder.
** Yoghurt based spicy snack that is made of fried chickpea batter, potatoes and vegetables.
*** Crunchy salty wafers that one puts on dahi bhalla.

slightly cool down before digging in – which really meant only a tiny bite or two of each item – because, after all, girls nowadays have banned themselves from the most pleasing of all endeavours, junk food, thanks to Instagram; at least the photos on Snapchat disappear, a bloated Instagram picture hangs around forever like a passive-aggressive jilted ex whom you kind of, sort of, don't want to block/delete all the way.

The food having been eaten and the green tea having been drunk (see how that works?), Maya sat in silence, moving from the couch to the armchair. She sat playing with her favourite Chobani strawberry yogurt, which her kind and extremely vigilant mother-in-law had specially ordered, knowing it to be Maya's favourite. She turned the spoon round and round in the frosty pink, wishing she could shrink herself and bathe in the cup. How was she going to approach him? Would he get really angry? Or would he be kind about it? Could she trust him? With each twist she made with the spoon, picking up the yogurt and dropping it back in the cup, these thoughts kept revolving around and around until she couldn't help it and, dropping the spoon, she looked up at him.

"Listen. There is something I need to confess to you."

"Yeah, I was going to ask you; you seem pretty upset and lost."

"Yeah, me and my family are not on good terms right now. They pretty much hate me and I really need your help."

"Sure. Tell me with what?"

"Can I trust you?"

"Of course. Whatever you say will not leave this room."

"Are you sure, because the last few times…"

"No, no, I won't tell your family, especially not your mother. Don't worry. Come on, dude, tell me."

"Well, the thing is I thought our relationship wasn't going that great; I mean, I am sure you felt the same way; there was too much of an emotional dissonance between us and I told my parents that I don't want to do this, but they are adamant about it. They've threatened to end my education, to take my phone away, to keep me locked up at home. I mean, apart from you I can't see anyone anymore, not my friends, no one."

"Shit, dude! That's pretty horrible… you're lying – they can't do that!"

"No, they can and they have! Why would I lie to you?" Maya said, slightly annoyed by his inability to comprehend the seriousness of the situation. "Anyways, there's more. Well, there's this guy that I really used to like and, well, before I was too scared to tell my parents and they pressured me to make this engagement with you; I was so young, so how they expected me to acquiesce to their judgement willingly and to not have problems later on really is incredulous on their part."

She didn't even realise that she had got off the armchair and was sitting on her knees in front of him, holding his hands. She teared up when she spoke of her parents, teared up even more when she spoke of her lover, Ali, but with a little optimistic glisten in her eye, a flush in her cheeks, and a faint smile. She was trusting her cousin-fiancé with this information. She was trusting the humanity, the goodness, that she knew lay in everyone, that had lain dormant in him, and she was imploring that kindness to aid her.

"And I really, really beg you to help me. I have no way out. Please. All you have to do is just say you don't want to go ahead with this relationship without mentioning anything that I have told you. I mean, can you just say that you aren't into me anymore… I'll be so grateful to you… what you would have done for me… for us… you'd give us life, cousin. Life."

He was silent through this entire interlude, trying his best to avoid her intent gaze, her beseeching eyes. She looked at his face, trying to read a reaction, afraid that she had hurt him or, much worse, angered him. He finally looked right into her eyes. "How about I tell them that I have found another girl?" And then he laughed.

She laughed too, wiping her tears. "How about you say you got her pregnant?" At that they both burst into a huge bout of laughter. So much so, the servants shuffled outside the door – perhaps running off to inform the lady of the house of the good news that her son had finally breached Mam Maya's emotional ramparts and made her genuinely laugh.

"Nah! I think that's pushing it a bit too far." He then grasped her hand really tightly and said the only thing he meant in the entire time that she was there. "Maya, I don't think I will be able to let you go. Ever. I'm not perfect but I am man enough to fight for what I believe in and for me that is *us*. Whether you're all in or not."

She started panicking and pulled her hands away, knowing that she had perhaps been too forward. "But I just told you I love someone else."

"Hmm," he said. "Exactly, and I can't let you go without a fight."

Why can't you? she thought. *Even if you cared about me, if you loved me, you would never impose yourself on me and I would respect you even more just for this restraint. Furthermore, just to satisfy this male ego, why must you* *try to bend something to your libido that doesn't wish to be yours?* She could feel that she had willingly stood on the gallows; the *pansi ka phanda*[*] was tightening around her neck. Was it so wrong to want a husband and not some alliance of convenience?

So aloud she remained quiet until he started laughing and said, "Gotcha! Ha! Ha! I was just kidding. Of course I am going to help you."

"Really?" Without a moment's thought she threw her arms around him and for the first time gave him a hug. Of course, had she truly thought about his words and paid attention to his facial expression as he told her that he'd help, it would've been easy to know his intentions. He smelt her hair and realised that he never wanted to attain her more than he did now, but first there was a lesson to be learned.

I suppose it wasn't Maya's cousin-fiancé's fault that he didn't know what love was, that he didn't understand it as being an unconstructed bounty with a promise of no return, that he didn't realise that its power was between souls, not flesh, that in its purest unconditional form it was conceptualised in the utter and irrational fearlessness of never, ever giving up on the cosmic righteousness of two entwined souls coming together. That even if love was offered and not returned – unrequited, to use an old term – that it was pointless to use coercion, guile or any sort of manipulation to attain it because in the end the result would only be an illusion, as ephemeral and artificial as a carefully constructed Snap or Insta profile, the cracks in the lining bleeding through in the soulless and empty quotes, poses and pictures leveraged to seize at the vapid notion of social *worthiness.*

No. It wasn't his fault. He was just persistent in acquiring her, in fulfilling the challenge she presented, not understanding that it was the lure he was in love with, for how could he be in love with her when he knew nothing about her, when their souls never had or ever would touch? It was his fault, though, to put his desire and his anger before the sight of those little hands begging him for mercy, making her lament even more the fact that she had trusted him. This sad little man would never know unconditional love if it hit him in the face with its ten-inch dick.

On the surface, however, they seemed to have an understanding. Maya felt more relieved than anything. It looked like they were going to work something out. As they finished watching the episode of *Curb Your Enthusiasm*, which

---

[*] Noose.

Maya actually thought was pretty funny, she received a sad-faced emoji message from her mother in the family WhatsApp group. This was highly unusual, given the fact her mother considered *any* time Maya spent with her cousin-fiancé to be an inviolate bonding event for the future husband and wife – so much so that she would refrain from texting even in group lists Maya belonged to during that time. Perplexed and a bit worried, Maya genuinely bid her cousin-fiancé good night and waited in the drawing room while her driver brought round her Porsche. As the driver opened the door and Maya stepped inside, her WhatsApp exploded in a torrent of sad and crying emojis sent by all of her aunts. Maya settled into the leather seat and, as she was all too accustomed to by now, she braced her emotions for impact.

When Maya reached home, there was a sombre mood. Her extended family members were all present and as she said her *salams* they barely looked up and mumbled *waleikum asalams* in return. Wondering what had caused not just this gathering but also this state of despair, Maya (afraid that another conference was under way) went up to her girl cousin and asked her secretively what was happening.

"Laila is at home," said the cousin, before retreating back into the drawing room and locking the door. Laila returning to the house under any circumstance was *not* a good thing. Her husband was an abusive asshole to say the least.

Laila's husband had a strict policy of never letting her visit her parents' home under any circumstances without him – heck, that was a strict *Pakistani* policy. So if Laila showed up without him it usually meant that whatever he was using to beat her with or whatever new and horrible sexual deviance he was trying on her had caused her to break yet again.

The sad reality of the situation, coupled with its increasing frequency, led their mother to keep a cocktail of pills ready for just these occasions. She kept them locked in her safe in a box morbidly marked 'Laila Emergencies'. The irony was that the strong fentanyl-based painkillers that made up part of the cocktail actually *were* for physical pain she had endured at his hands on more than one occasion. The other half of the cocktail consisted of a frightening mix of SSRIs and other anti-depressives as well as, most horrifically, inhibition-reducing drugs. The latter mix of pills was perhaps the most startling because they were having an effect on Laila's reproductive system – the women of the family had already had to take Laila abroad to abort two foetuses due to genetic markers for developmental disabilities showing up in routine screenings. Yet her mother persisted in the face of it; Laila had no shortage of eggs – one would work out, and above all she had more value as a *good wife* than a single divorced mother.

Maya went to look for her sister, who she knew needed her. She went for the drawing room, the one used for the most serious of family conferences, but found herself blocked by one of the servants.

"Mam Maya, Mam says you are to wait in your room." The heavyset and diabetic woman moved to block the door.

Maya was incensed. "Sarita, please get out of the way. I need to see my sister."

Sarita looked at the floor. "Mam Maya, Mam says please you are to go upstairs. Some things are only for married women to see. Best you leave, Mam Maya."

Maya bit her tongue. She knew whatever had happened to her sister this time was bad enough that her mother didn't want her to know about it. She knew her mother felt it would poison her mind against her cousin-fiancé and arranged marriages. Maya also knew that the number one reason her mother didn't want her in that room was because of what she represented – a *dissenting voice*.

Each time Laila fled home after she was severely beaten and battered by her husband, the women sequestered her and literally just patched her up like a boxer at ringside. Then, like a cult, the family (the women exclusively, as this is considered their domain) used peer-group pressure to convince Laila to go back to her husband and endure a fresh round of beatings. The lot of them were like the damn flying monkeys from the *Wizard of Oz*, a bunch of enablers. Why, as far as they were concerned, men sent their sons to die in Kashmir for honour and it was no less a woman's duty to do so in the name of the enduring institution of marriage. To her mother, Laila's sacrifice – if it came to that – was one for the noble cause of family honour.

The servant did not move. Maya took a few steps back; she was going to ram right through this damn aunty, if need be, to see her sister. Just then a knock was heard at the main door of the house. Someone answered and one of the family guards walked in escorting Doctor X, the family doctor, along with two of his nurses. The doctor barely looked at Maya and as the nurses passed she read the side of one of the special-purpose bags they carried; it said 'Burn Kit'.

MOTHER DEAREST

WORD HAD HIT the streets and soon spread like a wildfire: the family name was going to be ground into dust. Laila was home (her marriage status was naturally precarious) and the cousin-fiancé had had a nervous breakdown and had announced to all that would hear that Maya was in a relationship with someone else. This, folks, was the part where Maya's dad or brother were supposed to commence with the especially bloody honour-killing. The more brutal the killing, the more respect it would bring back to the family, sort of like grunts making ear necklaces in Vietnam.

Yet Maya's family weren't monsters. Sure, her mother felt she raised her daughters well enough to take a good beating from a man (though she had never *ever* endured one herself) but she wasn't about to see any of her children hurt seriously just to satisfy some provincial village-derived notion of what was right. So, partly to show everyone up and to show her daughters that, despite them despising her as some sort of armchair chicken hawk commander sending them off to physical torture by their spouses despite her never having seen a minute of relationship abuse, that yes, she indeed could take one for the team. *I*, Mrs K thought, as she ingested the lethal cocktail of pills, *can be a goddamned hero too.*

TO BE CARRIED BY SIX

"MAMA! MAMA! WHAT has happened to Mother?" Nile screamed and sobbed at the same time from the next room.

"It is okay! It is okay!" my aunt replied in a tone feigning calm, as there were clear overtones of panic. She barked orders to my cousins to carry my mother into the car and take her immediately into the hospital; she had taken what seemed like too many sleeping pills.

I sat there stunned into immobility, unable to get up, unable to help them, all the time cursing myself, feeling like my disgrace was bound to lead to such a tragedy. My mother, no, I thought. Please, please, God, please, please let her be okay.

Just then my mother's sister entered the room. She had always been just as passionate as my mom. There was a glass of water in her hands. "You bitch," she screamed. "This is because of you! This is all because of you." She flung the glass on my face and it hit my head, making quite an impact and a bump, which lasted about two weeks. Thankfully it shattered into pieces on the ground and not on my head. She walked up to me and grabbed me by the shoulders, her nails digging into my skin, and through clenched teeth said, "Get up, Maya! Get up! You HAVE to come and see what you have done." But my feet felt like jelly; I could barely stand. My mother was going to die because of me and there was nothing I could do to change that. No, no, no, no. I wanted the ground to open its jaws and ingest me in its earthen depths. I wanted to burn in the strongest of fires and scatter my ashes everywhere, but I did not wish to be here. I did not wish to be further blamed by everyone around me and by myself until there was absolutely nothing left in me to fight back. It is the worst thing to do to a child, to make them believe that not only are they a source of dishonour and disrespect for their parents but the catalyst for their supposed death. Please take me away from here, please take me away from here. "Move, Maya. Move."

Just then Nile also entered the room and, sobbing and wailing, passion overtaking his senses and without a moment's thought, he hurled himself at me, punching and kicking. I suddenly unfroze and snapped into motion; my ego's dying embers were inflamed with the thought that my younger brother had the audacity to attack me and for something that I had begun to refuse to believe was completely my fault. This was most uncharacteristic of Nile. He was a stoner whose mediocrity was only mitigated by his love for Arzoo. That was really the only redeemable trait he possessed.

My father, my poor, gentle, sweet father, hearing the commotion also entered the room and, trying unsuccessfully to pry us apart, first slapped my brother (primarily because I was his little girl and the enraged boy was senselessly just attacking me) and then lightly slapped me (just to show everyone that yes, he was going to hold me accountable for something too). "Stop it, you two. Stop it. Do you have no sense? Your mother is in the hospital with no one but your two cousins and we have to get there. Stop panicking and let's go." My burst of energy had now left me slightly powerless and, pushed and prodded, I was led into the hallway, when everyone noticed I had no shoes on and no coat to shelter me from the slightly chilly night wind, as if I needed any protection at this point. However, the maid rushed into the room and emerged with the suddenly much-needed clothing, and once I was fully covered, our crying and sobbing entourage made its way into the garage, where we were joined by another member of the household. My mother's mother, hearing the news from her other daughter (yes, the one that had hit my head with a glass) also pulled up in the driveway and, upon hearing that they had shifted her to the hospital, joined in the crying. My father's sister then got a call from her son at the hospital, who announced that it was probably too late. Everyone fell into a new bout of grief and loudly lamented the tragedy as they sat in the Range Rover and the Mercedes. I sat in the same car as one of my aunts, my grandmother, my father and my – now less furious and more upset – brother. My grandmother was actually hitting herself and, really understanding the idiocy of everyone's reactions and just how much they fed into the general pool of panic, my father called out and begged everyone to stop sounding like my mother was dead. She was still very much alive and our acting like this would only jinx her speedy recovery.

I did not ululate or loudly grieve, but that did not mean that I was any less moved. I kept all my anxiety inside myself and slowly and steadily it trickled out of my eyes and down my face; I could taste the salt, but I didn't even have the energy to brush the tears away. I have never been afraid of cats or dogs like most Lahori girls, or even of lizards and cockroaches; I have never been afraid of betrayal or failure, but for the first time I was feeling fear, real true fear – the fear of losing someone. I felt my eight-year-old nightmares of my mother dying (a consequence of Bambi) coming alive, and, like when I was eight, I did not know what to do except just pray that she would be okay.

We reached the hospital and I don't even know how I brought myself to get out of the car, but I did. We entered the emergency room and, like all hospitals in Pakistan, doctors were terrified of moving families outside operating rooms, especially when they seemed to be as passionate and hot-blooded as mine. People of brown skin are perhaps the most highly strung, impulsive, and easily excitable in the world. When you see a person with brown skin who is emotionally triggered, remember: extremely flammable.

Now back to the doctor, who, unfortunate little thing, tried to weave his way through the family and to my mom. The sobbing and the staunch immobility of the family around the bed was making it impossible for him to properly operate. To make matters worse, my brother got into another fit and started shouting. My father's sister, practically (at least in comparison to everyone else) understanding the doctor's plight, asked the other children to immediately evacuate the room and to take my brother with them. I was obviously a liability that no one wished to deal with at that moment and so no one objected to my staying. I was standing as petrified as humanly possible and so not a deterrent to the doctor. The doctor and the nurses now wished to clean my mother's stomach and proceeded to make her puke. They asked my drugged and almost passing out mother how many pills she had consumed. First she said five, then eight – she had actually taken fourteen! The doctor tried inserting the tube into her nose, but she started fighting and grappling with this superhuman strength that everyone was shocked at. My father proceeded to hold her hands, my aunt her legs, and realising that I was horrified, and the best way to get myself out of the shock was by making myself useful, I grabbed her feet. Even then she struggled and wouldn't let the tube perforate her nose. Suddenly feeling extremely angry at her, I started screaming, "Let him do it! Let him do it! OR I SWEAR TO GOD I WILL NEVER FORGIVE YOU! I SWEAR TO GOD I WILL

FOLLOW YOU so unless you don't want me to have my corpse join you in being gnawed away by maggots and ants, LET HIM DO IT!" I meant every word I said; I was actually thinking of how I might be looking down at my own funeral procession, my spirit perched up on a tree.

Somehow my frenzied orders made their way into some unconscious recess of her mind and she let her body momentarily relax, during which time the doctor, thanking God for listening to his prayers, inserted the tube and started pumping her stomach. Watching the remains of her stomach and the sleeping pills emerging out of the tube almost made my stomach turn and yet I stood firm, holding her feet and hoping that somehow my hands were magically transferring my love and strength into her. Once she had puked everything out, which ended up being quite a considerable amount for her tiny frame, and the doctor had informed us that she was out of danger but was going to be kept for observation for a few hours, the children entered the room and I stealthily crept outside. I suppose they didn't need to see my shamed face to ruin the moment of jubilation.

I sat outside in the waiting room. The sun was trudging along the horizon, as enshrouded among the clouds as I was in the corner chair. The room was empty and there was no sign of any movement but the sun's, which slowly and luminously brought forth all life with it. It was a new day. Never before had I been so grateful to see the onset of another little page in my life; never before was I so thankful to have the opportunity to breathe, to be able to sit, think, and feel. I took one deep breath, buried my face in my hands, and wept for the fact that I would have one of many more days (bitter or sweet) with my mother.

My heart released its anguish and only stopped when my mother's cousin shook me. They were taking my mother to another room on the third floor and wanted me to accompany them. We all sat there (me crying the whole time), shocked by my mother's act. The other children had left (even Nile did after profusely apologising to me for his bout of insanity. I forgave him; after all, he did seem genuinely upset over the matter), but I wanted to stay there till it was time to take her back. I saw my father leave to go out into the hall and saw as he leaned against the wall, that his calm broke and much the same way as I had, he cried and wept into the wall. I wanted to reach out and hold his hand and tell him that I was sorry that he was going through this, but I just stood there, hoping that somehow my love this time could get transferred without any physical contact. I wanted to go tell him how brave he was and how much

I wanted to wrap my arms around him, but for some reason, as we always do when we are needed the most, I held back.

At 10am we took my mother back home and at 11am I was in my room, lying on my bed, unable to go to sleep. I should have gone to sleep; I needed the rest to cope with everyone and my impending doom the next day, but at the moment I was happy that my mom was alive and well, even though I thought, with a streak of anger, how stupid could she be, ending her life because of one stupid boy and my decision to not marry that imbecile? I know she thought that, based on this action of hers, I was going to do what she wanted.

Poor Maya! She did know her mother and her family substantially well! The attempted suicide only made them more determined that Maya ought to be swayed by the harrowing experience into submission. Indeed, now they were sure of it.

BITCHES AND SLUTS

THEY SAY A person's room tells you of their personality, it is empirically proven so, I wonder what they would say of houses. I wonder what they would say of Mrs R's house in particular. The huge gates, once opened, led to a long driveway lined with palm trees, which were Mrs R's personal debutante instalment on her arrival as the young daughter-in-law. They were a consequence of her great admiration for the unchallenged tastes of the wealthy residing in Beverly Hills, whose homes and lifestyles had been replicated many a time within many Hollywood productions. L.A. of course wasn't her only inspiration; the front of the house was of a Romanesque style with high columns; the insides were decorated in both Mughal and Victorian styles (quite an eclectic mix of the epitome of luxury in both the East and West); huge gardens included a mini golf course, Spanish Moorish–style swimming pools, a colossal home theatre, and of course decorative pieces collected from Lalique, Lladro and other exotic places all over the world (objects that blatantly shouted out their origins to ensure that every visitor knew that Mrs R was a frequent traveller to the most unusual of places for Pakistanis). Even more so, the throng of another most essential display, the horde of servants, made Mrs R's opulence and taste extremely evident.

Yet what was also apparent to those sharp enough to observe were Mrs R's fickle inconsistencies; she couldn't decide on a unitary theme for her house. What was made evident to the trained eye was her superficiality, because on the surface everything looked spotless and clean, but if the keen observer in question were to move the consoles or the flower arrangements, they would see the dirt underneath. What was also eager for revelation was not only the lengths that Mrs R would go to to make obvious her imprint on the house and to make all aware that it was her space and domain, but also the lengths that she would go to to make everyone aware that her husband was a billionaire. Of course, such wealth meant that you were a frequent target for not just envy but also threats, kidnappings, and other atrocious fears, so besides the police van patrolling the immediate street outside her house and the guards posted at the gates, there were secret service spies posted in the bushes of the garden.

Evidently Mrs R failed to appreciate the fact that such a large amount of security could lead to a greater threat too, especially when many of the wealthy have been robbed and even murdered by their servants, in particular by those to whom they have been extremely abusive. Mrs R was anything but a pleasant boss; the great pharaohs themselves would have been pleased with her ill treatment. But she wasn't one for statistics; the 'tight-net' security only increased her own status in society as it created another web of illusion leading people to only guess how much wealth she possessed if she displayed this much around the house and had so much security. Mrs R was wealthy, but as is the case with most wealthy, not as much so as she led others to believe. The house belied certain very evident aspects of her personality, but clearly not enough for us, reader, to know her.

We now turn to another aspect of people's judgement of personality: they say that people can accurately make judgements based on other people's faces! I therefore further wonder what people would think of Mrs R based on her face, based on the high forehead, the perfect nose (personally I think it has had some time under the knife), the perfectly curved lips (again, I think they might have had a brief acquaintance with Botox), and yes, her eyes – the beautiful almond shape that is characteristic of most Pakistani women. They were big and wide with long lashes that fluttered in either scorn or as an expression of evident control over all those around her. Yet I suppose her eyes, untouched by anything, were the most evident indicators of who she really was. Her eyes were beautiful, yes, just like the rest of her, but they lacked conviction. They needed their beauty to wield power. They were light brown and where they should have encouraged warmth and loyalty, they were cold and all clammed up – never truly letting anything in. Yet as they moved to and fro, flickering from person to person, scene to scene, they were shrewd observers capable of understanding the exact nature of those around her – their strengths, and in particular their weaknesses.

I believe Mrs R's character strength – her evaluation, and especially that of failure – was in fact one of her greatest weaknesses. In searching for others' weaknesses, you make evident your fear of losing favour with others, your own desire to retain power and to be constantly surrounded by 'yes' people. Making other people aware of their shortcomings usually leads to them not trying to decipher yours. After all, they just get so caught up in concentrating on their failings that, flustered and confused, they usually tend to view you, the person aware of their faults, as a grander person. Moreover, if they know your fault then naturally you have a more inferior status in their eyes, for now they have social power over you. Of course, if any one person would make Mrs R aware of her own flaws, they would be surprised to find that she would be just as susceptible to crying, of feeling discomposed and even afraid. It was just because everyone was too afraid to speak out against her that her hold on all the socialites remained unchallenged. Of course, her malicious patterns were obvious to those who knew Mrs R and this unspoken hierarchy thus was firmly integrated in all the socialites' code of conduct during events and get-togethers. A stranger to all those unspoken realities and givens would probably be not as much influenced by Mrs R as she would hope.

She sat there sipping tea and as I looked at her, I was once again reminded of how beautiful and composed she was. Her every move was so carefully calculated, her every movement so full of balance and poise that just the way her hands moved and glided in the air would lead one to be mesmerised by the soft and dramatic gestures. I was once again moved to think of her as a big cat, a big black sleek feline whose yellow eyes flickered and moved, waiting, waiting…

"Ariyana…"

"Hmmmm – sorry, sorry! I don't know why I start daydreaming."

"Oh! It's okay, honey! You must not have had enough sleep last night."

I could feel all the other women snicker silently, but Mrs R's face had a sombre expression and I tried not to blush (quite an unfortunate result of having white skin).

"I was just asking you if you wanted more sugar with your tea."

"N-n-n-n-o, I am fine."

"Are you sure?"

"Y-y-yes. I am sure. I am so full. I ate so much. The food was delicious. Thank you so much. Everything was wonderful."

And indeed it had been. Mrs R had got the finest chefs to whip up the feast and the catering was from, of course, the most expensive of all caterers. Tea between four to five friends often involves sandwiches, scones, biscuits, and perhaps the actual tea. In Mrs R's realm, they implied everything from the most exquisite of Pakistani dishes to lobster and scallops. And how could I forget the desserts: chocolate pudding, lava molten cake, tiramisu, crème brûlée, chocolate pecan pie, fruit salad with whipped cream; the feast for a hundred was hardly touched by these five women – Mrs R, Ariyana, Mrs B, Mrs A, and another of their friends, Mrs L. They were all young, petite women in their twenties and could eat as much as they wanted, a luxury they wouldn't be able to afford a decade later. Even so, most of them did not eat much and even when both Ariyana and Mrs L ate their fill, there was still enough left over to feed the entire neighbourhood for a week. Of course, Mrs R would give some food as take-away to these women, some to her ungrateful dirty servants, and the rest to the neighbourhood. Of course it wasn't due to the kindness of her heart that she would dispense with the food but because she never, and I repeat never, kept leftovers; it was against both her prestige and her morals regarding health and food.

After the hearty meal, the women had an entire photo shoot for Facebook, as was natural for every get-together. They had to take pictures on the lawn, as Mrs R preferred natural lighting. They each then updated their status and their profile pictures to the pictures they had just taken and immediately got responses from all those who genuinely thought the women looked gorgeous and all those who were bitter about not being invited. Ariyana was new to this social media culture but felt pleased that both Mrs B and Mrs A had kept their profile picture with her, and even more so when everyone instant messaged her telling her that she was looking gorgeous in their profile pictures, a fact that clearly deeply infuriated Mrs R and that she quickly wanted to remedy.

Ariyana wasn't pleased about the flattery per se but about the fact that for the first time she was actually getting to do 'girl things' with 'girlfriends' and that everyone wasn't just turning away from her as they did in high school. What Ariyana didn't realise was that not all grown-ups are the same and that not everyone always deserves the benefit of the doubt, at least not after twenty times. When they are teenagers, bullies are open about their hostilities, but as they get older, like Mrs R, they get smarter about knowing how to channel those hostilities into more crafty and concealed means.

Nevertheless, after the pictures were taken and the comments were received, the women retired to the smaller study/drawing room for a more intimate sipping of tea and coffee with biscuits and macaroons that remained untouched, and as Mrs R glanced at them she sighed, realising that now that they were out, they would have to be consumed by the servants.

Ariyana hadn't known what to expect. After the dinner at the Chief Minister's house her husband had been a little edgy, but when she mentioned the fact that Mrs R had invited four or five women over to her house for tea, he was happy for her. And even though she had been slightly reluctant at first about accepting the invitation, he was so excited about the prospect that his wife would finally have friends and would be incorporated into his world that she found herself pulling up into the palm tree driveway with a servant dressed handsomely with a long *pagri.*ˎ She had been slightly jittery and had actually accepted her sister-in-law's attempts at dressing her up once again, and was wearing Chanel heels and carrying a Louis Vuitton and, as it was, the high-end accessories only succeeded in making her feel more awkward.

After all, if you aren't comfortable in what you are wearing, then irrespective of what you are wearing, you will feel out of place and uncomfortable. Mrs B, pea-brained Mrs B, much to Mrs R's disgust and Ariyana's embarrassment, couldn't help but tell the latter that she looked like a model in her hip-hugging leather pants and Chanel heels. The tea was affable enough and everyone had been all smiles and small talk, but somehow Ariyana could tell that something wasn't right. Nevertheless, she was determined to make the most of it and create a favourable impression. Poor girl, try as she might, her impression had already been set, and irrespective of how hard she tried, she might be able to impress the women but would not be able to change the staunch mistaken perception that these envious women, and especially the unwavering Mrs R, had of her.

Mrs A said, "Well, Ariyana, we heard that your husband's company has got a new contract with some company abroad and that your husband's net profits are now in billions."

Of course, trust Mrs A to discuss people's wealth as if it was the most decent thing to do over tea. Conversation decorum would be too new a concept to her. Within seconds, Ariyana was as red as the brim of the teacup she was holding, but managed to mumble, "Yes, I know that my husband

---

* A turban worn on the head the way the servants of the Nawabs and Maharajas in olden times had.

has a contract with this new company, but I don't know anything about his profits. I never know or pay attention to such things."

I am sure you don't, thought every woman there, especially Mrs L, whose husband was more of a millionaire than a billionaire, and who was wondering about how much Mr Y gave Ariyana monthly as her personal stipend for all the luxury that a woman of their society naturally required.

Perhaps Mrs R had picked up on Mrs L's envious musings, for aloud she said, "Ah well! That just means so many 'more nicer'" (most Pakistanis have an undoubtedly strange grammar issue with saying 'more taller' and 'more smarter', not realising that the 'er' already indicates comparison) "presents and shopping for you."

"Ummmm, yes," said Ariyana, smiling, shopping being the last thing on her mind.

"So," said Mrs R, leaning back and looking intently at Ariyana with that same glance that made Ariyana feel that she was actually the main course for the evening, "tell us more about you. All of us here are your friends." She smiled one of her icy unreal smiles, moving her hands to indicate that everyone else around her had the same opinion as she did. To show their support, all of them nodded their heads. Mrs R didn't like anyone else dominating the conversation and didn't appreciate anyone else bonding with Ariyana.

"Well, there's nothing much about me. I got a masters in psychology, met my husband in grad school at Princeton, and am actually waiting to settle down before I start working."

"You want to work?" interrupted Mrs B, her beautiful doe eyes shooting up in complete incredulous disbelief. There comes a moment when the 'alpha person' feels that they are losing power and when the underdog surprisingly is favoured by the masses – now comes one such a moment.

All shyness forgotten, Ariyana adopted a tone that unveiled the passion that sometimes sparkled in her eyes or glimmered in her warm smile. "Why, yes! I want to start a children's clinic. I think so many children in this country suffer from uncountable traumatic experiences and have no one to talk to. I want to start a clinic where there is a really friendly conducive environment that enables children to talk of their fears regarding peer pressure, family tensions, and even teacher abuse—"

However, Mrs R, who felt that her authority was challenged and that all the other women were starting to look at Ariyana with a degree of awe, which could not be permissible under the circumstances, rudely interrupted Ariyana's moment of heroism. After all, moments only last for a brief period and must end as soon as they begin.

"Mrs B, why must you ask Mrs Y about her goals in life? I am sure she doesn't wish to share them with us humble housewives."

"N-no."

"It's okay, Ariyana! We know how you feel about us."

"No, really I don't."

"What we want to know is more about you, more about what it is that makes all six feet…"

"I am not six feet! I am five eleven!" a hapless Ariyana mumbled to Mrs R, who naturally behaved as if her voice had been the only audible one in the room and consequently kept talking.

"…feet of you tick, more about what you do, but even more interestingly, about you and Y," she continued.

"Well, that's so much information. What specifically do you want to know?" Ariyana smiled.

"Everything," said Mrs R, lying back on the sofa, playing with her teaspoon before looking up at Ariyana as if giving the prey an elusive head start – enough time to run, to feel as if it were free to make a choice, but actually was completely hopping about in the panther's lair.

"Like how did you guys meet?" said Mrs B. She was actually warming up to Ariyana and genuinely wished to know about her.

"Well, we met in this seminar on the threats that stereotypes pose," she said, reminiscing as a smile curled up on the corners of her mouth, the way it does for people who are bringing forward a memory that is very precious to them.

"I suppose he was tired of the stereotype associated with being a Pakistani and what being both a Muslim and from this country meant in the eyes of a white person and wanted to understand that bias from a more analytical viewpoint and I… I just don't know why I went," even though she knew: having a foot in both worlds meant that she was viewed from a stereotypical perspective in both places. "I just found it interesting. We started talking after the conference; he was surprised to know that I knew how to speak Urdu, and even more so that I was Pakistani. We went out for coffee at the end of the street; our conversation was so pleasant, so full of the promise of the young who have a determination to change the world that we didn't even realise the time flying by. We ended up telling each other everything about ourselves. It was one of the most magical nights of my life. He dropped me off at my apartment, but I actually didn't hear from him again for another week."

"Really?" smiled Mrs R. "Perhaps you didn't make a good enough first impression."

"Well, no, he was extremely hesitant about approaching me, thinking that I didn't want anything to do with him, and I was so pleased when I went to answer the door to see him standing there with a bouquet of flowers. I loved him from that moment. No one had really ever accepted me the way he had. After that we did everything together; went on trips, shopped, had dinner, and studied at the library." Every single woman in the room, some hardly knowing their husband before marriage, some having married their cousins and some, men much older than them, felt a stab of envy at Mrs Y's account of her affair with her husband. "And then one year ago we got engaged, then married and," she concluded with a smile, "you all know the rest."

There was silence, a silence that Mrs R didn't like because she felt like Ariyana had made her first decisive victory over all the women in the room, and especially over her.

"Oh, yes, we do know, but come on, Ariyana, you didn't tell us any of the juicy details. This was so PG. Come on. We are all grown adults. Tell us the fun stuff," said Mrs R, WhatsApping Mrs A to ask Ariyana about the first night they slept together.

Like clockwork, a hesitant Mrs A pitched in, "Yeah, like the first time you guys slept together." She felt embarrassed the second she said that, but Mrs R was very pleased with her little posse member's handiwork and so she messaged her back with a smiley.

Ariyana coloured and started mumbling, "Umm… I didn't… I mean, I…"

"Oh, come on, sweetheart!" winked Mrs R. "Tell us."

Ariyana took a deep breath, calming herself and her nerves before proceeding again. "Well, we didn't sleep together till the night we got engaged." (*Of course!* thought Mrs R and the slightly less envious Mrs L. *She had to seal the deal.*) Unfortunately, Ariyana added something she immediately regretted. "I didn't have very many good experiences with men, but Y changed everything."

"How many?" said Mrs L this time; she was pretty sure that Ariyana, being white, was a complete tart.

"I'm sorry?" Ariyana definitely felt Mrs L snicker and was quite sure she was the one who snickered before. Mrs L, unlike the other women, including Mrs R, had just met Ariyana for the first time and so was undoubtedly being guided by her stereotypes.

"How many men?"

"I'm sorry! That's kind of private, but enough. Enough to make me know the kind of man I wanted, the kind of man who was worth my love, any woman's love."

"Really? So how many men would you say a woman has to sleep with in order for her to have an accurate appraisal of the man she wants? Just saying a rough estimate."

"I don't know! All I know is that I am the luckiest woman for having met Y."

"That you are," chipped in Mrs B, annoyed at Mrs L's treatment of the situation and, well, her new friend.

"The only problem, actually the only regret I have, is telling Y each and every thing about my past."

"Why?" said Mrs R, her eyes suddenly twinkling with the prospect of some private information. "Why would you regret it?"

"Why? Ha, because now, irrespective of what I do, he has these slivers of doubts and suspicions. I know he can't help it. He doesn't even say it outwardly to me but I know that men around me bother him, he tenses. I know it is because he loves me, but I don't know why he doesn't realise that all that was before and now I have him. I would never cheat on him, ever."

"Of course," said Mrs R, getting up and sitting next to Ariyana and placing her hand on hers. "Of course you won't. I am sure he will trust you. Don't worry. Just give it time."

"Yes," said Ariyana, smiling. "That's what everyone says."

"Yes, everyone is always right and what's more, we will always be here for you whenever you want to talk."

Ariyana didn't know why she did it, but she threw her arms around an extremely rigid Mrs R, who, in light of learning of this new weakness of her newest and most formidable enemy, was too pleased to not hug back. Over Ariyana's head, she winked at the others. B and A looked away, but she didn't care. A plan was formulating itself in her head.

WHEN YOU ARE CAUGHT SEXTING

SHE LAUGHED AS she glanced at her phone screen. Her iPhone was her best friend and to part with it would be synonymous with parting with her arm. She had been painting her nails a bright orange and (in spite of her parents' incessant pleading) had still been wearing booty shorts in Lahore. (There wouldn't have been a problem with wearing shorts in her room but Arzoo wasn't one to stay rooted to her room, floundering about the entire mansion, and as her mother had informed her countless times, numerous frustrated illiterate male servants roamed the house and they wouldn't look to Arzoo with respect. Arzoo was too involved in her new college Cali culture to care, but had she the maturity that accompanied a young woman, she would realise that there was a big difference between beach boys who thought shorts were normal and servants who had only seen such clothing in movies. But of course, to constrain a child, especially one like Arzoo, irrespective of how old they are, only means that you are encouraging the child to indulge in the contrary of what he or she is told.)

The WhatsApp message read, "I miss you, girl!"

"Oh really?"

"Really I swear there isn't a single girl in Scotland who can turn me on the way you do."

"Ha ha ha ha I am sure ;)"

"I mean it!"

"Well why don't you just come over, I am sure I can sneak you in."

"Well I want to come now. Send me a picture of your body, please, I want a preview before I come get the real thing."

"'Come get the real thing'? It's not yours to claim but mine to share."

"Oh boy! I am sorry, just send me a picture, please, I have been dreaming about your body since we went to college, it's been six months and all I have been looking forward to during this spring break was your body. Please, I have been pining every day for it."

She rolled her eyes and yet smiled, superficially flattered that her body was so wanted, but somewhere deep down inside she was also a little upset about the fact that it was her body that was desired and not her, and for now it pleased her to be needed. Being both slightly narcissistic and a secret feminist, it made her feel powerful, for she had the capability to control men's weaknesses, their desires. For her that was a high greater than anything else. Flirting and hooking up really wasn't just for bodily pleasure, but for being coveted, for that pleasure deep inside that you are wanted and that you have the power to give or not.

Moreover, she was pissed at Ian, pissed at the last girl she caught wound around his neck, and secretly wanted to get back at him even if he would never know; it was spring break and he was, of course, halfway across the world, so really it was for her own personal satisfaction. So she took off her shorts and her crop top and stood in front of her full-length mirror wearing black stilettos and a Victoria's Secret leopard print bombshell bra and matching thong. Her long dark hair touched her back and just for full effect, she had made her eyes ferociously beautiful with smouldering black eye shadow and liner and stood with one hand on her hip, the other taking pictures while holding the phone.

She then did a side squat and took another picture, after which she stood with her legs parted and took another one. Arzoo finally turned around and with one hand holding the camera turned slightly just to make sure that her entire back was captured. Completely satisfied with the model-like pictures that were now flooding her media library, she flopped onto the settee, anxious about sending them. She was so thrilled about the fact that she was pleasing another person that she didn't realise that she had fatally sent her mother the pictures.

Mrs N and the boy were right next to each other on her WhatsApp contact list and so, as is the case with most touch-screens, they fail to register the exact place your finger touches the screen, and she ended up selecting Mrs N's contact only to see the chat open and the picture already sent to her. Realising the grave blunder she had made she started swearing, but no matter how many times she said 'fuck' and 'shit' the deed had been done and the picture had been sent.

She looked toward her phone for the familiar ping of a message, but seconds passed and no infuriating ping arrived. She then got up and paced around the room, opening both her room door and her window to hear her mother scream, but nothing. The phone wasn't projecting her mother's ire, nor was there a primal scream of agony; there was just silence. And if you've all been in the place where Arzoo was right now, when you were expecting a dreadful outcome that was just delaying itself, you will recognise her perilous affliction in having to wait. However, her mother used the last mode of communication Arzoo thought she possibly would (or literally could); the laptop open on the bed beeped and her mother was requesting a Google Hangout.

She replied, telling her mom that she was busy doing work, and her mother immediately answered back saying, "We need to talk. Video NOW."

"What's it about?"

"These pictures, of course!"

Rolling her eyes, Arzoo got up, threw the shorts in the hamper in the bathroom, and opened her cupboard to take out the most conservative *shalwar kameez* she could find, or, as she claimed, those that even her servants wouldn't wear, but her mother had purposefully designed for her. She tied her hair, wiped off the red lipstick (literally making every conscious effort to appease her mother as much as she could) and locked her phone, keeping it hidden safely in the drawer away from her mother's prying eyes. Not that she would be able to open the phone, much less understand half of the colloquial phrases in there, but still, it is always better to be careful. She did this not in preparation of her online intervention but because she was afraid her mother might physically pop in at any point, and she rather preferred the virtual one. So in preparation for that chance surprise visit, she got up and locked the door so that, were her mother to suddenly come, she was prepared.

"Why did it take you so long to turn the video on? At least you're wearing the *shalwar kameez* I got stitched, it looks wonderful – I told you so. If only you would listen to me. What's that picture about? I am giving you five seconds to explain what was going on in that head of yours?"

"Ummm, Mom, I was basically telling my friend Sukaina that I have lost weight and she didn't believe me so I sent her the picture. I mean, I was trying to recommend her a diet and showing her that my plan worked, that's all!"

"Okay, fine! But you shouldn't be sending such pictures to other girls, what if they show it to other people? Or worse, what if some servant stole your phone and saw your picture?"

Arzoo saw her mother shuddering at the thought of a servant man being exposed to her daughter's precious body. Her mother always had this fear of male servants' dirty sexual prowess.

"Moreover it can be unhealthy for a young woman to fixate on her body image. We've talked about that. Today you send Sukaina half-naked pictures and tomorrow you're throwing up the food you just ate because you think you're fat; it's a slippery slope."

"Soooooooooo that's it? Can I go now? I was in the middle of a book."

"NO, that's not it! Arzoo, do I look daft to you? I KNOW you're not recreating Madonna's *Like a Virgin* album cover just to show Sukaina you lost weight! What are you thinking, making poses like that and in that lingerie, no less! You're objectifying yourself, Arzoo! I raised you to be above that. I AM so disappointed in you. I just don't get why you keep doing things like this. Do you think Maya does stuff like that?"

"Great! Now Dad's online. Can you never keep anything to yourself?"

"Oh my Allah! I wanted to raise a Benazir Bhutto and I instead have an Amy Winehouse."

"Mother, you know that they are both DEAD! Right?"

"Look here, young lady, don't be getting fresh with me here!"

Arzoo's dad came on the screen. "Arzoo, what's this that I am hearing about some unseemly pictures…"

Arzoo: "Dad, they aren't that bad, I was just showing Sukaina."

Dad: "Okay, she was just showing her friend, so what's the problem?"

Mom: "This is why she thinks she can get away with everything. She has you to back her up all the time."

Dad: "*Jaan*, my sweet little *jaan*, you never let me finish."

Mom: "So you think it's okay for her to dress like that?"

Dad: "Oh *bhae* (man)! I am always a fan of do in Rome what the Romans do. Remember when Maya's mother and you went to that beach in the south of France?" he said, the latter half in a humorous tone, making Arzoo giggle and her mother fume and turn to her iPhone.

The beach story involved, ahem, Mrs K and Mrs N having quite their bachelorette adventure. Mrs N was engaged and Mrs K was to be married in a fortnight, and yet for that one day Mr N of course is unaware of the particulars. Maya's mom forgot all her previous learned piousness and could not avert her eyes from a well-endowed Brazilian youth. Of course Arzoo's mom was chill about the whole affair and exfiltrated herself expertly but Maya's mom's repressed passions almost took a hold of her and till today that bitterness has transformed her soul into disbelieving the existence of love. For now, as annoyed as Mrs N was about the fact that her husband was using her exploits as examples in front of her child – Lord forbid he discuss his own – she was even angrier at the fact that her daughter wasn't turning out to be what she expected.

Arzoo: "Mom, what are you doing?"

Mom: "Something I should have done a long time ago, arggghh! Oh, my Allah, that's it, I'm calling in reinforcements."

Arzoo: "What? Who?"

Mrs N: "The whole family, the entire Mughal Army elephants and whatever it takes to get some sanity instilled in this house and especially in you."

Arzoo: "Wait – the entire family, Mom? You're overreacting!"

Mrs N: "The whole family needs to see your little one-person Agent Provocateur fashion show. We're putting a stop to this right now. Your aunts in any case want to tell us something about you. Allah only knows what they have found out about you now." She heaved a sigh of exaggerated despair.

Dad: "Oh! Come on, dear."

Mrs N: "Be strong, honey, be strong. She is the child, we can't let her win. I need a united front here."

Arzoo: "Mom!"

Beep! First aunt drops in. "Oh my Arzoo *beti*,* are you mad!"

Indeed, the aunt made her parents forget about the current pictures and made them aware of another more pressing factor that had instigated this trial of modesty and husband acquisition – Arzoo had created two Facebook accounts, one for her family and one for Stanford, but somehow somewhere one of the illegitimate good-for-nothings who wished to ask for her hand in marriage was an internet fanatic and had gained access to her

---

* Child.

secret profile and leaked it to his mother, and together the duo had passed the information on to her aunt, including pictures through WhatsApp, who had quite naturally, without any qualms, passed not just the information but the pictures to every member of the family. These pictures were perhaps even worse than the WhatsApp ones that Arzoo had accidentally sent her mom, because they were from frat beach events, Mardi Gras, and exotic erotic, so not only was Arzoo wearing just as scant clothing as possible but was also surrounded by her guy friends. Haram!

Within seconds, a number of messages appeared. Great! Her mother had called the entire cavalry. Forget the aunts – she had invited all the uncles, even those from her father's side. Taking a deep breath she opened the messages, and as her mother added them on one by one she clenched her fists to face inquisition.

God! she thought through gritted teeth. *How could I have been so stupid to teach them how to use the internet?* Yes, indeed at that point she was practically ecstatic about the fact that she had taught these archaic vessels who didn't even know what a keyboard was how to make effective use of modern-day communication. Oh, how we come to regret some of our actions later on.

There were six adults online – six, darn it – and she was only one. She looked over her list and saw that her father was still online too. She could actually picture him at that very moment in his office with his head bowed down. How she wished that he wouldn't suffer any embarrassment because of her.

Arzoo's aunt, her mother's sister and quite her little wannabe: "Arzoo, we really require you to have a husband; there is no way we can let you roam around free like this. We saw your pictures on Facebook and the *haram* clothes that you have been wearing and the boys that you have been hugging."

Arzoo's uncle (father's brother): "I don't even know if you will ever get a husband anymore. This is not the way of *shareef khandans** to conduct themselves. You are bringing disgrace and shame to this family."

Arzoo's mother's older brother, the Big Boss, added, "Yes. I am sorry, there is no way we can let you study anymore without a husband. Get married and then you can continue your education. We don't even care who it is as long as he is not a white guy."

---

* Respectable families.

Arzoo retaliated, "How can you say that? Have a husband and then go study? How am I to give my education my best with an incomplete asshole who will require constant pampering and taking care of. NO, NO, NO. Who are you all to tell me what to do? First try and control your own children, doing coke and heroin and God knows what."

Arzoo's mother's sister (offended by the reference to their children): "Well, who are we? We are your family, your blood. You little slut, you should have thought about that before spending your nights dressed in those heinous clothes with all those American boys."

Arzoo: "What are you talking about? I just took a picture, that doesn't mean anything. They are just hugging me and I just love dressing like that."

Arzoo's mother's obese cousin: "Where did get you outfits like this? Oh my Allah! And your mother just sent me the WhatsApp pic you sent her. Where is that from? Tell me, you harlot; was it at the one in the Burj Mall in Dubai or the Moda Mall in Bahrain? Come clean and be honest, girl!"

Arzoo: "It was from Victoria's Secret, the store in Union Square. Though I do prefer Agent Provocateur. It might just be conducive to your tastes too, Aunty."

Mother's obese cousin, pretending to ignore the last bit: "Aha, I see, Union Square San Francisco, eh. The belly of the beast. I am taking note of that den of wickedness."

Arzoo: "I bet you are, Aunty." (Laughing to herself.)

Arzoo's father (in a separate conversation to her): "Arzoo *beti*, why must you bring yourself to a point where all these hungry animals tear you apart! You are smart and beautiful and I trust you to make the right decision; please stop being unwise."

Arzoo: "Yes I know, Daddy, but I am only twenty-one and I want to enjoy life."

Arzoo's father: "Yes sweetheart, I get that, but you need to know how to be balanced and slightly more modest."

Arzoo's father in the global chat: "Everyone, please let's be calm and not abusive!"

Arzoo's mother: "Why? Her aunts and uncles are right!" To Arzoo: "How can you love dressing like that? How many times have I told you, you must be wise enough to know when to wear what and when to say what? I am tired of trying to make you understand that you aren't an island on its own; you will always have to live with other people, and what those people think or feel about you is important! It is reputation that makes you."

Arzoo: "I don't care about reputation; I just care about being happy."

Arzoo's mother: "Curse the day I read Dr Spock's books! This is all a result of my upbringing. I know it."

Arzoo's father's sister's husband (first to her mother): "No, no, *bhen*.* You mustn't think like that; children nowadays just have a brain of their own." To Arzoo: "You have no idea what we are, my child. We have given you unconstructed love and you have taken us for granted, but you have no idea what we are."

Arzoo's mother's brother's wife: "I always mention how girls shouldn't be let loose like this, and that too in America. *Taubah Taubah*.** Girls should be married off when they are sixteen, seventeen, and not a day above that. Really, Mr N, what is the point of keeping Fadhi close to this girl... tch tch. Though I always knew he wasn't much of an influence to begin with."

Arzoo (again to all): "I don't wish to marry." (She was angry at this non-blood family member's involvement in her personal life. Hell, she was furious at all of them trying to behave like they owned her.) "I don't wish to have a husband for another five years till I am at least twenty-six years old. I wish to travel and work and be my own person. I wish to be free and away from this claustrophobic house, and as far as Fadhi is concerned..."

Arzoo, as always conveniently interrupted by her mother: "Claustrophobic house! After all that your father and I have done to make this house full of love and understanding? We went out of our way to make sure you had the upbringing we never did. If your grandparents were here they would start digging graves for themselves if they didn't have one already."

Arzoo's mother's cousin (quite the fat little nosy rude woman and interrupting her mother): "So that we can leave you free to do your *luchpana*.*** Sorry, we will not leave you alone to sleep with all these white boys, you wrong girl."

Arzoo: "HOW DARE YOU? I haven't slept with anyone. How dare you try to imply what your illiterate mind knows nothing about?"

Arzoo's mother's cousin: "HOW DARE YOU EVEN ATTEMPT TO

---

*   Sister.
**   God forbid.
***   Corrupt activities.

RAISE YOUR VOICE AT ME YOU INCORRIGIBLE LOOSE WHORE? I am illiterate? I am happier being illiterate than your kind of un-Islamic literate. I am ashamed for your mother for the day she gave birth to you. You have exploited her and her trust."

Arzoo's father's brother's wife: "Have some remorse. You have slandered our name in society; at least have the decency to refrain from upsetting your elders anymore. Enough is enough! What kind of a daughter are you? Are you from our family?"

The further abasement of the one by the many went on and on. Arzoo sat on her round wrought-iron princess bed raised from the floor by a series of steps, her former glory and beauty crushed; her spirit felt like someone had dragged it out of her, beaten it for hours on end with whips and knives, bows, and yes, even spears, and thrown it back in. The taunts and insults had constricted her and her freedom (the most essential aspect to her existence). As a result, the more she felt them trying to constrain her, the more her body kept escaping into this danger mode where her defensiveness arose to unbounded levels.

The more the invasion of insults popped up and the more they attempted to violate her character, the more defiant she remained. She was no longer the pleasant girl who lived in the world of warm sun, shorts, and bikinis. She had been reduced to a sore broken animal who used the keyboard to holler and snarl to protect itself. The confrontation had completely changed her mood; how dare these random people who had no share in her life try to impose their ideas and values on her life just because they were connected through her blood?

She knew her father was the only one who saw her belittled and degraded; yet he was the reason that they had the right to even debase her. Had he wished to stop this onslaught, only he could have. However, he remained silent, neither interfering nor adding injury all he thought of was what happened to her and how he could protect his daughter now (particularly from herself).

It annoyed her sometimes, his goodness. Thank God her socially conscious mother had had enough and had the sense to not bring up the WhatsApp picture again. Hopefully she had forgotten! Her parents had never beaten her (as is a regular custom in Pakistani households) and she didn't like humiliating their much better method of parenting in front of these self-righteous toadies who had no control whatsoever over their own children, but because her parents were wealthier, these relatives just wanted to use every opportunity to degrade them. Well, it was her parents' own fault for including them. But somewhere deep inside her heart, even though she would never admit it, she felt that perhaps they weren't that mistaken after all – perhaps there was something wrong with her. After all, her parents were upset for a reason and they felt that *umrah*, religious pilgrimage to Mecca, would be the likely solution to it all.

Had all this unbounded, unrestricted freedom been truly good for her or was it not just the freedom but how she had placed herself within the situations, taking advantage of her parents' lenience?

Arzoo would have done a marvellous job as an actress in a Victorian melodrama. She, of course, didn't have it as bad as Maya. Her issue was one of mild discord where her family would eventually relent and where she would seek the path that she wanted to choose for herself. Right now, spurred on by the women's histrionics and theatrical displays, the men, and especially her parents, seemed more rational, even though they continued to type warnings, for they were merely frightening her because sometimes grown-ups had nothing better to do; but Maya, on the other hand, would lose all semblance of the life that she had.

DADDY'S LITTLE GIRL

NAMES ARE ANOMALOUS little affairs in most Eastern and Islamic cultures. I know I keep referring to the names of my characters only because I feel the meanings of their names have certain fatalistic tendencies. Arzoo knew her name meant desire, and she wished more than anything that her life wouldn't just be a series of ifs and what-could-have-beens but concrete actions executed by her will and her will alone. All she simultaneously wished was to not have her loved ones dragged along with her ceaseless contemplative assertions.

When Mr N returned from the office, he was a bit fatigued. He wasn't too pleased with the way the Google Hangout had panned out and he was sure neither was his wife. So he wasn't surprised to walk into the room to find her sitting on the couch, her little plump self enveloped in tissue paper. Her mascara streaked her cheeks and she looked extremely upset. He dropped his briefcase, forgetting his own worries, and tried to pacify her.

"What's wrong, *jaan*?"

"I worry for her, Mr N. I really, really do."

"Oh ho! So do I, Mrs N, but she's still young, she's still going to make the mistakes that she is destined to make. As parents we can only show her what we think is the right or the wrong path; the rest is up to her to eventually decide."

"I know you are right," she said, sobbing, "but the way all those people were talking to her. I didn't like it, Mr N. I didn't like them degrading our daughter like that, though I think she needed a taste of what our world is really like. All she lives in is that Cali bubble of hers. Will it ever burst?"

"Yes, yes, Mrs N, of course it will!"

"But what kind of a woman will she grow up into? Will she maintain her family values with her individual goals? I don't know if she will ever get married. She doesn't look like she will."

"Don't say such things, *jaan*. Have some faith in us, but even more in her. She will turn out just fine. You mark my words."

"Yes. I just hope going for *umrah* will be a good idea. I hope it reconciles her with her religion and tradition."

"It will, *jaan*, it will. Maybe I will go talk to her."

The doorway was open; unknown to her parents, Arzoo was listening and silently tiptoed back to her room, feeling both guilty and ungrateful but ever more in love with her father. She tiptoed back as fast as she could, availing both speed and slightness of her foot to get to her room before her father did. She plopped on the sofa and turned the flat screen on to make it appear as if she was engrossed in the latest chick flick playing on HBO.

She heard a knock on the door. "May I come in?"

"Of course, Daddy," she said, sitting up straighter from her feigned lounging position. "What's up?"

"Well, *beti*. I wish to talk to you about the events of earlier today."

"Yes! What about them?" said Arzoo, feeling angry with her nosy interfering relatives.

"*Beti*! I admit that they should not have treated you like that but," he said, turning to his daughter, "Arzoo, this is not the way. Dear, you must learn to be decent; I admit it's a novel notion to all you Westernised children, but decency will guarantee you respect in this community and I have told you multiple times to act wisely. I know it's hard for you to balance out the East and West, to realise how to maintain being true to yourself while at the same time fulfilling society's expectations of you. We have done the best we could to raise you into the intelligent, witty, beautiful young woman you are. You are my one and only child, and I am proud to call you my daughter." He paused for a bit, remembering his son who was no more. "But, *beti*, sometime along the line you will have to understand that you are no longer a child; you are growing up, and the older you grow, the more your responsibilities and troubles will increase, as do of course the joys. The scale of things just keeps on increasing, but your life will always be what you make of it. So if these people banter and gossip, just don't give them occasion to do so. Be the formidable force, the woman whom everyone respects, and you will make me even more proud. I want to tell all of them out there that my daughter is not just as good as all of their sons but better. So whatever you choose, Arzoo, just be smart about it, *beti*."

They were both smiling and weeping and Arzoo gave him the tightest hug imaginable.

"Your mother," he said over her head, "can be a little foolish and get carried away sometimes, swayed in the direction of what people think and say, but she loves you and will always want what's best for you, or as she perceives it to be."

"I know, Daddy, I know."

"Well, I am glad we got that over with," he said, kissing the top of his daughter's head. "I hope you are willing to join us for *umrah*; you know I don't like forcing you and leave it as your choice. Tell us when you have made a decision."

He left the room, but not without infusing Arzoo with his essence and his unspoken expectations.

I love him more than anything. I know for a fact that my soul was split from him and put inside me, for I don't know anyone who understands me better than he does. My every thought, my every sarcastic gesture, my every lie, my every truth, my every wish, my every darkest desire, my every step, my every laugh is known to him. I don't know how we have this bond, but I know my father and I are telepathically connected. He is the one and only person I know who wishes to take me into his arms and just suck out all my pain, replacing it with giddy joy. He has the softest heart – servants, businessmen, labourers, politicians, children and old men and women alike acknowledge the goodness in him, but none so much as me. He and only he knows how to unconditionally love, to take, take, take everyone's anger, deception, and at times hatred, and to give, give, give love. I see him often lost in a thoughtful, kind, but always a faraway look.

His hands are the most beautiful hands – he was going to be an artist and desired to paint or to help people as a doctor, but his father informed him that he had to earn money, and making money as the former was a rarity and the latter would take eons to get established, and without another word this kind man gave away his dreams and aspirations and NEVER complained. He didn't complain then or when his father asked him to marry my mother without asking him what he wanted, he didn't complain when his father sent him to college earlier than he was due, he didn't complain when his older brother was too much of an idealist to be practical enough for business and he had to step up to take the family business mantle, he didn't complain when he was asked to be a politician, nor was he complaining now, when I, his daughter, was unknowingly making his life a living hell. In Lahore, a daughter who didn't wish to wed was bound to make your life hell.

I didn't wish to marry anyone, no matter how rich or fabulous they were, how politically strong or socially desirable; I wished to be my own person. I wished to travel, to interact with people from all ethnicities, all walks of life, and take and permanently carry a part of their identities with me. I wished to be an amalgamation of all the peoples of the world. I wished to satisfy my palate with the richness of global foods, I desired to step out of the airport and breathe the air I breathe every day, but which would now contain a different whiff of the region. I yearned to be able to laugh with the same abandonment that my soul wished to seek. Through these travels, I wished to find myself and the one place that I can call home, for Lahore wasn't my home.

I didn't want to be constricted in a society so accustomed to hedonism and its negative impact that it becomes oblivious to the evils it routinely and perpetually has come to represent. I didn't want to be bound to one man, especially when my person didn't even know who she was. I wasn't Maya. We might have been born and bred in the same manner and we might have the same current battles to face: both our parents had currently become obsessed with the prospects of our marriage. Society had easily duped them to become blind adherents to the system and our Western education, which had, at one point, seemed to have made them so proud, was now the biggest blockage to a fruitful existence with our Lahori community. Yet, I wasn't like Maya. She was and always had been in love; she always yearned for her other half and for more than four years, I was a witness to the completeness they both gave each other. I could never fathom settling down, never imagine loving a man so much, even if he was as nice as Maya's lover, as to sacrifice everything for him.

No, I wished to sacrifice everything for myself. More than anything, I wished to accomplish my life's goals and dreams, to work, to live and most importantly to let live. My parents didn't exactly understand this – they were never going to be surrounded by their buffoon relatives either. I am so sure that Maya, being a part of an elaborate family system like myself, felt my plight. Yet, where her family was carrying on a charade of being modern with their fancy clothes and posh mannerisms, they could never shake off their constrictive mentality; my family had evolved more in spirit than in show (which was good, since they weren't exactly pressuring me to marry a guy of their choice, especially if

I already had someone in mind; consequently they were unmitigated in their persistence because I didn't).

These emergent family meetings in every house could be explained by the family reluctance for generational change and the family desire to remain in control and prevail as idempotent, irrespective of what was happening in the world outside. Maya didn't have a cell phone as her parents had confiscated it in order to prevent her from remaining in touch with her lover, ever since she told her cousin-fiancé the truth. (Perhaps I should reply to one of Nile's usual hundred texts and find out if she is okay, I thought.) If we had been directly in communication though, it would have been interesting for both of us to note that ironically we were experiencing similar discrepancies between family values and our newfound freedoms. Where did we fit in this conundrum of East and West, of the self as a unit and the family as the collective driving force? I suppose as best friends our fates were always more linked then we could have supposed.

Her mother, too, was a sweet soul and Arzoo did love her, almost just as much as her father. They really wanted her to accompany them. But would *umrah* actually cure her internal conflict? Would it bring peace to a heart that was unwavering, inconsistent, and unsatisfied? Would it disengage and liberate her free soul? I suppose she would soon find out.

Arzoo walked into her parents' room and, hugging them, informed them that she was very excited about going for *umrah*. In spite of her resolve about society and her future goals, she felt that she owed them at least enough respect to show them she was happy about their intentions when they, especially her father, had such blind trust and respect for her. It only made her want to be better, though; when that aspiration would actually culminate into her father's reality was still a little while from its self-achievement.

THE AGE OF LOSING INNOCENCE

MR S SAT in his drawing room. He was always finding ways and means to meet his goals. At the age of two, it was to do everything his parents didn't want, at five it was to gain his mother's undivided attention, at ten it was to be selected for the neighbourhood cricket team, at fifteen it was to get the latest Mercedes Benz, at twenty-four to marry the wealthiest girl, at twenty-nine to finally have his factories settle down, at forty-eight to expand more and buy off his brother's share, at fifty to open up new gas pipelines, and now at fifty it was to somehow attain the girl who had started haunting his dreams.

He was married to a woman whom his mother had been shrewd enough to arrange an alliance with; perhaps she had been too shrewd, for besides her affluent wealth, his wife possessed no love, no compassion, no empathy. All his wife did have was incredible access to her hands and she used them with ever-increasing frequency even on him (he was, after all, her husband!). She retained no shame for her children or even for him, slapping them as frequently as she did the servants. It is quite a turn of events when a wife physically abuses a man and slowly he ceases to be a man and starts existing only in the shadows of his former self. He is a reflection, no more to be taken seriously than a false image of reality where things are inverted. He had stopped thinking of his function as anything other than a robot at home, a machine engineered with the tact and the purpose to visit the factory that provided the millions that paid for the house, his wife's expensive tastes, his rotten children's excursions and frequent splurges at stores. How he hated the factory and didn't really understand why his wife didn't hire someone else to go show face as the CEO!

But lately, oh sweet, sweet dreams… every time he would close his eyes, he could picture her and slowly the dreams started creeping into his conscious life, waving their magic around into his office, his food, his study, even into his wife's face. He hadn't felt this way in a long, long time; the only time his body felt this excited was whenever he had achieved a goal, be it his wedding night or the day he got to play cricket, and lately there had been no triumphs so great or pursuits so complex that he felt elated when he accomplished them. There had just been trifles – unimportant, insignificant trifles.

He didn't remember how it was that she suddenly changed into such a beautiful woman, but he clearly remembered the day that he first noticed her passage to such an enchanting beauty. It was dinnertime and his wife needed her to put the baby back to sleep. Mrs S had been quite adamant about having a fourth child in her late thirties for the simple reason that committees and bags were not enough to occupy her anymore. She felt a surge of worthlessness as her other children were all teenagers and much too old to need their mother and too young to openly admit it, and so she decided to get pregnant; after all, she would finally have something that would be an engrossing, worthwhile pastime. The baby ended up taking after his father and not being too beautiful like the other four; she, tired of the child most of the time, left most of the responsibilities of the child to Fehranaz.

His wife had then required her to come back, after the baby was sound asleep, and clean the baby's vomit off of the floor – the food remains and bile were ruining the white carpet. When she came back with a *takki*, Fehranaz bent down to scrub the vomit as well as she could, but the carpet was white and thus more susceptible to staining. She vigorously rubbed the carpet while simultaneously making every possible attempt to not cast a harrowing gaze at Mrs S's drumming fingers or make contact with her intent glare at the remaining spot on the useless white carpet. Mr S had been at that moment going through his accounts in his head, and how to further maximise profits for his next gambling match, when his gaze suddenly fell on the soft, full swelling of her breasts. She was on her knees and as her body rocked back and forth he was incensed with the thought of being the one to shake her body, to hold those breasts as they bounced back and forth with each scrub.

He wanted those eyes to look at him with surprise and that mouth to scream with the pleasure of him owning her. But then he saw his wife's gaze drifting from the carpet to him, and to avoid any speculation and unwanted screaming, he calmly and quickly diverted his gaze to the clock on the mantelpiece and got up to retire to his study, with his dinner untouched and his mind on her delectable body.

The next few weeks were a game of cat and bird. Mr S sat like a cat, always staring at the little bird fluttering its wings, spreading life and energy, living contemporaneously on land and in the sky. He wanted so much to fly away with her on the wings of youth and yet he could not – he was old and wrinkly, white-haired and miserable. He was fat, a father and, worst of all, he was married. All he could do was crouch low in the shadows, in the corridors, and watch her hop about bouncing, cleaning, laughing. Her silk mane, hidden in the *dupatta* that his wife forced Fehranaz to keep on her head, would often become loose and fall out as she, not yet ripe in age, forgot to be a woman and instead remembered only how to be a girl. His mind wreaked havoc in his body as he desired nothing more than to possess her, to make her his, to implant himself in her and demarcate her as his. And yet he was tortured by his own conscientiousness – he had always played by the rules and always was a firm believer in the upkeep of civil and moral authority – well, at least superficially, of course.

What was more dangerous, of course, was that he worried about his wife finding out, and that would be the end of his existence as he knew it. A chill went down his back as he thought about her hand, but Mr S was a man now enchanted by not just lust, but the even more pleasing craving of breaking rules. Being a devout follower of rules, he was now suddenly gripped by the extreme folly of his ways and how gratifying it would be for him to no more indulge the moral ideals and principles of those who have no imagination, but now to only indulge his own fantasies.

There was a dinner at his house and he was at this moment standing in front of the mirror; all great matter of self-discovery materialises from the unconscious to the conscious in front of mirrors. As he looked in the mirror, he saw the image of a man who had never lived, who had constantly pleased others, but now that man knew he was going to please himself. He saw the man thrilled by an amorous encounter and by the fact that now he was the sole benefactor and master of himself. The man's white hair was now a symbol of power, his jaw set with conviction, his sparse wrinkles an indicator of wisdom. He was the reflection, and the inverted image he saw in the mirror was who he really was, who he wanted to be and now who he was going to be.

He heard a shrill shout awaken him from his trance, asking him to come down to greet the guests. He was going to be the man in the mirror, but for now he had to keep that fact hidden from the woman he had been unfortunately bound to for life. So he fixed his hair and decided to obey the shrieks and join his wife in welcoming the guests for dinner – what a laborious night it was going to be. But then he remembered that Fehranaz was going to be serving food and his heart skipped a beat at the thought of seeing her face and body again.

The first time he touched her was when she had been cleaning the flowerpot. He came and stood next to her and started commenting on the beauty of flowers and how as they bloomed and blossomed, their vibrant beauty became ever more omnipresent. Abashed by the thought that the older *sahib* actually thought that she was worthy enough to be spoken to, she glanced down at the floor at the black and white marble beneath the massive oak centre table and at her dilapidated hand-me-down sandals, seeming so out of place in all this elegance that it actually made her feel even more ashamed.

He seemed to follow her gaze and let out a sigh of feigned anguish. "What sad times we live in when such beautiful feet, which ought to grace the likes of Jimmy Choo and Dior, are placed within such broken and run-down worthless shoes. Really, where has my wife left her head these days? Tsk, tsk, tsk."

She didn't know what to feel – she was both flustered and flattered by the comment and made to feel extremely awkward by its direct tone. After all, why was he talking to her in this manner? She did what any respectable servant girl would do – she mumbled a 'yes' and looked down at the floor. She looked up just in time to catch him winking at her and hastily lowered her gaze to the flower arrangement. The crystal vase had no dirt on it, as at least every single decoration piece in the house was cleaned twice every day. Cleanliness was a prerequisite in the house and in spite of the knowledge that Fehranaz clearly had of the vase's spotless demeanour, she, nervous suddenly, stood with one hand on the table and the other wiping the crystal with a dust cloth over and over again as if every time she cleaned it a new layer of dust emerged.

He crept in on her slowly with increasingly shaky nerves and an infirm bravado – because it was after a long time that he had become acquainted with his libido. As he neared her he looked at the table, at the hand with the long fingers, and brushed his fingers lightly over her hand, almost as if he did it by accident, before conveniently reaching in the bouquet and extracting a long-stemmed red rose. A chilling shudder went down Fehranaz's back as she felt increasingly uncomfortable. She discounted the brushing as an accident; it just had to be one! Yet even her innocent little brain picked up on his wrong energy and as she looked up, Mr S was walking away and she could almost have sworn she saw him wink again.

The second time that Mr S approached Fehranaz was again at dinner while she was serving food for the husband and wife. As Fehranaz bent over his wife's plate to put out the curry, he couldn't help but keep his gaze, for a moment more than was cautious in his wife's presence, at the maid's neck and at the cleavage that enticingly popped up. After the moment of brazen rebelliousness, Mr S quickly diverted his intrepid stare to not be too obviously hung up on Fehranaz's welcoming chest. His wife caught his eyes leaving the girls' chest, but she was too preoccupied with where her yellow Fendi bag was to pay conscious attention to her. You see, the yellow bag would look perfect with what she was wearing tomorrow and nothing else would do.

As Fehranaz approached Mr S, he got more and more excited by her smell. It intoxicated his senses and made him impatient with the thought of owning her. But then, as Fehranaz stirred the ladle and scooped up some curry to pour onto Mr S's plate, the baby cried. Mrs S asked Fehranaz to go and quiet the baby, but upon realising that she was still serving and that it would take her a good amount of time to clean her (probably) dirty hands, an unwilling and irritated Mrs S grumbled a general dislike for servants and their point when one had to do all work themselves and got up to take care of HER baby HERself.

Mrs S, oblivious of, or rather unconsciously aloof about, her husband's designs, proceeded to go to the baby upstairs. Mr S could not believe his luck at this golden opportunity that had presented itself. He could feel Fehranaz bend down, he could feel her skin squish and pop out. Oh, how her smell, warmth and proximity to him was driving him frenzied with desire. She, on the other hand, felt extremely uncomfortable suddenly; she could feel Mr S's laboured breathing and his beaky eyes, but there was something about him that she couldn't quite put a finger on. All she knew was that the closer he leaned into her, the more improper she found his nearness to her and, before she could move away, he leaned over to pick up the bread on the other side of her, his arm and hand 'accidentally' brushing her breasts.

Mr S had conducted the grabbing of the bread at the most opportune time so that his purposeful encounter with her breasts would seem natural. Accident or not, Fehranaz was highly embarrassed by the situation, though Mr S kept looking at her with this odd smile. Blushing, she excused herself and scuttled into the kitchen at luckily the same time that Mrs S was walking down the stairs.

Only her moustache boy was in the kitchen and Fehranaz ran straight into his arms, weeping. However, this consoling embrace could only last a few minutes as the cook was entering from the side door.

Ironically, when their *bibi gee* had seen a blur of Fehranaz escape into the kitchen, she again commented on the general disinterest and commitment that Pakistani servants exhibited; perhaps, she claimed, it would be undoubtedly more prudent to not have so many as most other rich people do in the world as it created a diffusion of responsibility of sorts. Mrs S, though she thought that she was a pioneer of such wisdom, had hit upon the biggest fundamental rule about efficiency – if you want something done, you do it yourself.

The third time of all the times that Mr S tried to force himself onto Fehranaz was perhaps the most important one, for now Fehranaz was no longer suspicious but, much to her fear and anxiety, knew and wholly believed that Mr S had improper intentions. Mrs S was out for a committee lunch and the children were still in school. The rest of the servants had retired into the quarters, as Mr S had had an early lunch and only Fehranaz remained in the house, as she had to take care of the baby.

"*Meray ghar ayi ek nani pari,*"* Fehranaz rocked the baby in her arms and it softly cooed and eventually went to sleep. She stared down at the little fingers, the little feet and felt such a love for the child. It wasn't a beautiful baby like its other siblings but was more precious, and as she looked into its soft innocent face she could bet a hundred rupees that the baby was going to be the nicest and most courteous of them all. She wondered how such innocence could not move stern hearts; Mrs S, for instance, would hardly hold the baby, she would hardly show it any care or concern.

Fehranaz knew that the missus loved the baby perhaps more than the others and at least as much as her elder daughter. She would often catch

---

* 'A little angel came to my house.' It is a term of endearment for young children.

the woman staring at the baby, feeling this motherly need to hold, but then somehow managing to stop herself. The servant girl didn't understand the point of withholding love; after all, if you love someone then you should shower them with it, unafraid of rejection or loss of ego. And what ego is there between a mother and a baby? Yet Mrs S undoubtedly felt that the idea of fawning and showing love was uncouth and ill-mannered and, in spite of her body's natural desires, she let poise and society dictate her outward show of expressions. The baby would have been quite alone and neglected were it not for Fehranaz and her constant vigilant care and unbounded love for it.

Fehranaz herself could never forget her mother and the cold steel expression of her face as her father pried her away from the woman who gave birth to her, and even if Fehranaz didn't know the whole picture of her mother's love and broken heart, as this baby would grow up to unfortunately know neither, she felt bonded to the baby in this special pact of children with negligent mothers. So she was even more determined that this baby be treated properly and that she would fill the void that had haunted her for her thirteen to fourteen years of existence. Thus the baby got love from the illiterate and unhygienic servants, as the mother claimed they were, while she, literate and hygienic, was too much of a fool for loving that which was her own flesh and blood.

Fehranaz was sitting staring at the baby, having this whirlwind of emotion for the little helpless bundle of a thing, when the intercom in the nursery rang. The poor child would be kept away in the nursery/attic that its parents had constructed for it so that they wouldn't have to be disturbed by its crying in the middle of the night. Often Fehranaz would fall asleep on the floor next to the cradle, too fearful about leaving the little creature alone at night to fend for itself and cry out to a darkness that would never offer any condolence. No, she'd much rather fall asleep on the floor than leave the child alone. The arrangement obviously suited the family perfectly. She picked up the phone.

"*Aslam aleikum!*"

"*Waleikum Asalam.* Fehranaz *jaan*, is that you?"

"Y-y-yes sir." She was both overwhelmed by the tone of his voice and suspiciousness of his question – other than herself nobody entered the nursery, and since the baby didn't talk it couldn't be anyone other than she who answered the phone.

"Well! I am trying to call up the kitchen, but no one is answering and I have a slight headache. Would you be a little *jaan* and run up into the kitchen and fix me some *chai*?"*

"B-b-but I can't leave the baby alone."

"I said I have a headache." His tone went from all sugar and sweet and spring to a much harsher pitch and for a second Fehranaz gulped back a great deal of saliva; having a headstrong mule for a wife meant that Mr S didn't take too kindly to being contradicted by anyone else.

"Y-y-yes, I will be right down."

"That's a good girl. Now hurry on downstairs."

Mr S hung up, satisfied with his little charade of luring her into the study and Fehranaz stared at the phone, confounded by the change in her master. She ran into the kitchen, surprised to see that two of the cooks and one of the cleaning women were sitting chatting at the round table. On being questioned if they had received any intercom calls from the boss, they replied in the negative. Even more perplexed, but shrugging off her natural warning instincts, Fehranaz quickly made the tea and, carefully balancing the pot along with a plate of biscuits, made her way to the study, which was on the other side of the house, in quite a secluded corner save for the fact that it faced the garden. She almost spilt the milk as she tried to intricately balance the tray on one hand. Realising that it would be an epic failure, she placed the tray on the floor and knocked on the door.

As Mr S opened the door, he stood dumbfounded for seconds as he looked into her green cat eyes. He had never had the opportunity of looking directly into her eyes or even at the rest of her face – her pursed full lips, her small perfectly shaped nose, her ruddy cheeks, and impeccable complexion. He stood entranced by her and she stood afraid and confused by his enchantment and oblivious to the fact that she was the underlying cause of it. He broke the trance, which had been awkward to her and magically energising for him, by stepping back and asking her to place the tray on his desk.

As she walked over to the beautifully carved mahogany desk, that Mrs S had ordered from one of the most famous furniture stores in London, he rushed to clear off some papers to make room for her before sitting on the chair inside the table. She placed the tray on the table and commenced in creating the perfect cup of tea that Mr S claimed was only possible with her

---

* Black tea.

hands. She was extremely nervous and could feel her heart beat rapidly and steadily increase. Her hands trembled as she removed the tea cosy and picked up the pot, having placed the strainer over the teacup. Having fortunately been successful in pouring the tea, she progressed to pour the milk into the cup. However, her hands were so uncontrollably jittery that she ended up spilling the entire pot of milk into the cup, out in the saucer, and even onto the tray. That only succeeded in upsetting her nerves even more and before even cleaning up the mess, she was about to press her hands into a ball of healing calm to prevent them from being so shaky.

However, before she could use her own hands to calm her nervous trembling, a pair of hands shot up and placed her hands in theirs. She was so shocked by Mr S's actions that she couldn't even draw her hands back; afraid of what he could be capable of, she remained frozen – her hands now too upset to even tremble. He pressed her hands and said, "Come on, my dear, nothing to worry about! Calm down. You have nothing to fear." His voice was soft yet heavy with something Fehranaz had never felt and so wouldn't know for what it was – unfiltered adulterous, detestable lust. So in spite of his calm smiling demeanour, when he stopped rubbing and looking at her hands and instead looked up into her eyes, she thought that at this point there was nothing she feared more – not even Mrs S's hand. Having realised that her beating heart, jelly legs and sweating were products of fear, she was suddenly gripped by the inalienable need to extricate herself from this situation and so she removed her hands from his grasp and back into her own ownership.

As she turned around to leave the room, he, recovering from the setback of her defiance, grabbed her wrist again and simultaneously got up from his chair. "Hold on there," he suddenly bellowed; again his anger being directed not at her but at the general aversion he had developed toward being defied in general. Her heart started beating faster than wild horses galloping across the moor, but she obeyed his command – she stopped.

Her obedience immediately calmed him down and he transformed back into the even more fearful silk-smooth man who was craving intimacy and striving for it through sweet words and a façade of calm. "Come here," he whispered hoarsely and pulled her back into his arms, holding her from behind. He placed one hand between her legs and one on her breasts and whispered softly, "Shhhhh! It's okay. Don't struggle. There is nothing to be fearful of!" His voice continued to belie a false sense of calm, yet his hands were frenzied with desire and he prodded and rubbed and clutched and shook her privacy. Fehranaz hated what his hands were doing; she didn't know why he was touching her. All she knew was that she didn't like it. No one told her that a man wasn't supposed to touch you, but in spite of the lack of this formalised education, she knew that what was happening was wrong. Before she knew what was happening, Fehranaz felt something hard on her back and was much too afraid to turn around to see what it was and only stood still as Mr S, clutching her, moved up and down against her back. She could feel his breathing getting more and more laboured and before she could contrive a plan to go, he, panting, heard the door open and Mrs S bark out to the cook to get her *chai*.

He let go of Fehranaz as if suddenly she was as hot as molten lava; she, in turn, fell to her knees. Having regained composure from being touched and wrongly abused, she got up and ran out of the room as fast as her feet could carry her. Panting, Mr S retired on the chair, content with the progress of the day. Fehranaz was now aware of his intentions, and yet he was still dissatisfied with the lack of an actual culmination. Well, he would just bang his wife later that night, picturing Fehranaz in her place, but for now his hand would do. He locked the study and set about his business.

At the same time that Mr S possessed Fehranaz in his imagination and his hand, Fehranaz ran into his wife. The latter woman had had a taxing day at the luncheon, where her new clothing style wasn't much appreciated by Mrs R and her younger clan; she could have sworn she saw a sense of derision in their eyes. She almost reprimanded them for using her, an elder, as a target. They should keep their insulting sarcasm for unsuspecting fools their own age, the primary example being Ariyana. The poor girl was too innocent and clearly had no idea of the evil the other girls bore her. In any case, how dare they feel that she, Mrs S, was at the same level as that simpleton? She was adamant about proving them wrong next time and giving them a lesson, but for now all she needed was a nice cup of tea, and only Fehranaz made the best kind.

She kept hollering her name, only to see the girl, completely dishevelled and shocked, running from the other side of the house. "Where were you, you stupid girl?" She gave her a slap on the back. For the first time since Fehranaz had entered the house, she did not flinch when the woman hit her; she just continued looking with wide eyes that were not blinking. "Why are you looking at me as if you just saw a ghost and what were you doing in that part of the house? Who told you to leave the baby?"

Fear glued Fehranaz's lips and proved to be a successful adhesive against truth and in favour of Mr S's illicit immoral actions and the later demise of her innocence. If only she had been able to tell the truth, but she feared being called a liar, feared being thrown out into the streets, feared both the master and the mistress. Fehranaz remained unresponsive to Mrs S's screams and her slaps, erroneously believing that suffering now would be better than the suffering she would have to feel later on. Fear has the ability of tarnishing our rational thought process and there is nothing more heart-wrenching than a young girl's pertinent fears, especially when that girl has nothing but herself to rely on. Must we be critical of the cause of that fear and the perpetrator of the loss of the child's innocence or must we be content with the fact that perhaps the perpetrator is merely human, as much a victim as his victim, or must we realise that there is no justification for the destruction of innocence, as innocence, being a normative ideal, is bound to be eventually destroyed? Were they both wronged by fate and, if so, once you are wronged are you justified in creating more wrong or must we analyse that, irrespective of how much a temptress the unsuspecting Fehranaz was to Mr S, that he willingly gave up his innocence and forcibly claimed hers?

Mr S continued to pursue his desire to see Fehranaz whenever Mrs S was out of the house and opportune circumstances clearly presented themselves on numerous occasions. He moved from touching her on top of her clothes to under her clothes and from breathing on her neck to kissing, sucking, and biting her skin. However, there was never enough time to actually encourage her to repay him in kind until that unfortunate long weekend that Mrs S took the children to her parents' house. Had the baby gone, Fehranaz too would have been lucky enough to escape Mr S's clutches. Unfortunately the baby fell sick and the weather was much too cold to transfer her. Therefore, under the pretext that the baby would catch a further chill, and secretly pleased that she had got rid of both child and maid for a weekend, Mrs S proceeded to leave the duo at home, much to the chagrin of Fehranaz, who begged and pleaded her madam to take her with them, but of course her pleas fell on deaf ears.

Harrowed with fear and impatience, Fehranaz spent her days as close as possible to her kitchen boy lover, who served as shadow, helper, and friend (she hadn't even told him of Mr S's commands to present herself at least three times a week to him and his carnal desires for her). At night she would clutch the baby and try to hold on to as much of her innocence as she could by breathing in the baby's untainted scent.

The first two days went passively enough, as on Friday Mr S himself had to go to work at the factory site out of town and returned home fatigued, desiring nothing more than a warm bed to sleep on. The next day, his equally despondent friends, tired of their wives and pleased with the fact that one of their buddies had an empty house, all migrated for food and drinks, a great deal way too many drinks, to Mr S's house. Many Pakistani 'drinkers' have no grown-up etiquette that is synonymous with social drinking and, having gained more than what would be considered as successful inebriation, Mr S was too busy in his alcohol stupor to actually remember about making his way to Fehranaz and her beautiful face and equally enchanting body. But the next night, the next night there were no hapless chances in fate that could save Fehranaz.

At about midnight, when all the servants had left to their respective servant quarters in the adjacent house, Mr S decided to use the intercom to call Fehranaz into the study. Rocking the baby, Fehranaz had dozed off while still sitting on the floor, one hand on the baby's cradle. Her momentary dreaming was halted as she was jolted awake by the ringing on the intercom. However, irrespective of the lapse in time, she remained much too terrified to pick up any of the ten calls that ensued.

Mr S placed the receiver back on its base and was livid with anger. How dare she not pick up the phone? He would have to go teach her a lesson. He ran up the stairs. Hearing his impatient footsteps, Fehranaz, drenched in sweat, locked the door. He pounded on the door and then tried to control his impatience with a subtler and encouraging tone. "Fehranaz, my dear, my *jaan*, open the door. Please dear, open the door... open the door." His incessant knocking on the door had only served to exasperate her growing apathy and now, in spite of his luring sweetness, a trick she had become all too familiar with, she remained apprehensive and wisely wouldn't move toward the door. When he said, "Won't you open the door, dear?" she got the courage to blurt out, "No!"

That was enough to send him back to his id, his true wild self, and he banged and banged on the door. "Open the door, you bitch! Open the door right now! You little slut, you either open the door or I will teach you a lesson you will never forget." By now the baby had woken up and was incessantly crying, the noise being too much for her fragile ears. Fehranaz picked the baby up and forgot the tears on her own face as she tried to soothe it. Irrespective of the wails, the knocking continued and continued till it became a part of the forgotten background for Fehranaz and the baby until even more suddenly than when it started, the knocking stopped.

The head cook, who was Mrs S's tattletale and had a huge grudge against Fehranaz for no other reason than the fact that she was beautiful, unbeknown to Mr S had been following him. Upon hearing the loud banging on the door, she stood in the hallway, maliciously pleased with her master's plight and the reason for it. After what seemed like hours but was in fact minutes, she coughed to draw attention and Mr S, embarrassed, stood still and then regained his composure and a new authoritative tone, which even frightened the cook. "What do you want? WHO asked YOU to be here? Were you stealing some of my wife's jewellery, eh?"

"No, no sir!"

"Well, if I hear anyone asking me about this incident, I will know it's from you and I will tell the police that you stole my wife's diamond jewellery, which will conveniently be missing from her safe at that time."

The cook, never having witnessed this concealed anger of her master before, stood gaping for seconds and said quite truthfully, "No, no sir, no one will find out about this, ever."

Mr S nodded his head when the cook called out and stopped him. "If you must get in, sir, there is a spare key that the madam keeps in her room. I know where it is!" She grinned slyly, every ounce of her vixen self dripping out of her sharp teeth as she smiled.

"Where is it?"

"Well, sir, you see, I need a little help remembering."

"How much do you want?"

"Well, sir, my daughter's getting married and I need to prepare for her *jahaiz*."*

"How much?"

"Umm... umm," she said, twirling the end of her *dupatta*. Her yellow broken teeth were hidden from view as her rough lips tightened in a scared grimace, and then her sharp hawk eyes looked straight at him as if throwing the dice and challenging fate to accept her gamble.

Mr S smiled a very crooked smile and said, "How about you take two lakhs and bring me the keys as fast as your fat legs can carry you."

---

* Dowry.

"Oh sir! You are kind, so, so kind!" She almost kissed his hand, but then realised what his sick mind was possibly attempting to do; the servant viewed the master's flesh as filth. Recoiling, she continued down the hall, buttering him as much as she possibly could until she was out of earshot and then she started cursing his sick state of mind, coming to the conclusion that all wealthy people were immoral and lewd and that hell will be brimming with the rich, for, after all, what vice could the poor do that could land them in hell? She failed to recognise her own sin in aiding her master, for to her, Fehranaz deserved what was coming her way; she had no right to be so poor and so beautiful. In light of her own greed and material wealth, she had been the clinching factor in the loss of a child's innocence. She herself had daughters, two near to Fehranaz's age, and instead of protecting her the way a mother should have, she had not just thrown Fehranaz to the molestation of her body and soul but had actually contrived to make it possible.

Fehranaz sat clutching the baby. She was glad that the persistent knocking had stopped. After about twenty minutes, when she was confident enough that Mr S must have retired to his room, she heard a rattling of keys and the handle turned, the door flung open and in walked Mr S as the devil incarnate. Fehranaz was still on the floor and clutched the baby with an ever-increasing fervour. Mr S shut the door behind him and walked ever so slowly towards her. Fehranaz slid further and further back on the floor until her back lay against the wall, the baby still in her arms.

"Oh, my dear, you should have listened to me," he whispered as softly as he could. "You should have listened to me because now you have made me really, really angry. I don't really like being disobeyed and I am just going to have to teach you a lesson."

Her eyes were wide with fear and her mouth was so dry. Yet she managed to hoarsely whisper, "Please, please, sir. Please forgive me."

"Oh no, girl! I am not going to forgive you. You know once I decide on something, nothing can deter me from my decision. Come here, dear," he said.

"No," she whispered.

"No? What did you say, eh?"

"Please sir, no, please…"

"Put that infernal baby away," he shouted, grabbing one of her arms and dragging her on the floor. Fehranaz was crying quite profusely now. "NOOOOOO," she cried.

"Put that baby AWAY before I throw it away and crack its skull." Fehranaz let the sperm giver – for after all, the term 'father' deserves a level of respect – take the baby and place it back in the cot. She was still on the floor crying and whimpering and as he approached her he grabbed her *dupatta* and threw it off.

"Take off your *kameez*."

She just continued crying and clutching herself, intermittently whispering 'please' and 'no'. He commanded again through gritted teeth, "Take your *kameez* off!" But Fehranaz was too lost in herself, too caught up in escaping from reality to realise what reality was demanding of her. Realising that his commands were falling on a very shocked little girl, Mr S proceeded to take her *kameez* off and, being unsuccessful, frustrated with the delay in his immediate gratification and annoyed by Fehranaz's whimpering, he tore her *kameez*, leaving her torso bare and ready for his taking.

She sat there with her breasts hanging; her perfect pink nipples and areolas were causing his blood to scream and made him reach out and grope them. His hands fondled her breasts; she had stopped crying at this point, only sniffling. Her face had a blank look as if she was no longer present in the world but existing in some other world where Mr S was still her master and her body was still conserved from perverted gazes and touches. Fehranaz was in a world that would never exist, but it was only in her mind, not in the physical present of her being. After a while, it stopped existing even in her head.

Mr S had now started biting and licking her neck and moved on to sucking and biting her nipples. Fehranaz felt so disgusted by him; all she wanted was to take his head and jam it against the wall the same way that he had claimed he would do to his own child. Before she knew it, the Gucci belt was off, and the Armani pants. Mr S stood with his organ all awake and ready to devour. Fehranaz was terrified at the sight of this other thing; she had seen other boys' private parts, but they were mostly children's and were small and not pointing the way Mr S's was. He took two of his fingers and put them down her throat. "Don't use your teeth," he said. "Otherwise I will beat you." He made her open her mouth and stuffed his most prized possession, the cause of all his sleepless nights, into her mouth and let out a sigh of relief, only to bark again, "Open your mouth fully; take it down your throat." Fehranaz felt like puking; this weird third arm smelt and he was stuffing all of it down her throat. She kept gagging but he didn't care; he just held her by her head and forced more and more down her throat.

He finally took it out and shouted, "Did you enjoy that?" Fehranaz sat quietly, completely embarrassed about the fact that she was naked in front of a man and started crying all over again. "Do you want to continue this?" She didn't reply so he shouted again, pulling the hair he was holding onto, twisting her neck sideways. "TELL ME!" She shook her head to a no. He stopped pulling her hair. "So you didn't enjoy that, you beautiful, beautiful girl? Let's try something I know you will like." He smiled his crooked, twisted smile again and reached for her *shalwar*.

By this point, Fehranaz felt herself coming back to life; she could feel control coming back in her shaky jelly legs and arms and she pushed back. He held onto her wrists. "Stop struggling, you little tart." But it was hard pulling down her *shalwar* when she continued kicking and screaming. She ended up kicking his stomach and before he knew it, she was out of his clutches and running toward the door. But the cook was standing watch outside.

Upon seeing her, Fehranaz momentarily relaxed and between sobs said, "Cook, Cook, do you know what sir is trying to do to me? He made me completely naked and is touching me and…"

"I know."

"Please help me, *maa*."* The word seemed lost on this ironclad woman.

"Oh! I will." Being a hefty woman, it wasn't hard for her to take a hold of Fehranaz's wrists and drag her back before throwing her inside. "Stay in and please your master, you little whore."

"Sir." The cook smiled at Mr S and slammed the door. Even when she heard Fehranaz scream later on, it didn't change her heart; she merely shrugged, believing once again that she got what she deserved.

Fehranaz felt so betrayed by a woman whom she had viewed as her mother for most of her life. All she kept on thinking was how she had always loved and taken care of that woman and never thought ill of her in spite of the number of times that the woman had shouted at her or complained to Mrs S about her, but now, now she had not just turned on someone who was like a daughter, but had triple-crossed both her class and her gender too. So Fehranaz, so upset about the betrayal, stopped struggling when Mr

---

* Mother.

S removed her shalwar, stopped crying when he grabbed her by her behind and using his body weight pinned her on the floor. She just screamed when he entered her and kept on screaming even when he had stopped.

The baby had woken up again and cried and screamed with her. But she still didn't shed a tear, feeling that the baby, innocent and pure, was the only one who felt and cried for her injustice. She just whimpered when he finally got off her, pulled up his pants, and said, "Now, wasn't that fun? I'll make sure we have more of these fun times." She winced when she heard the word more and lay there naked on the floor for hours after he left. When she finally came to terms with what had happened, she wept and wept, hugging herself, praying to Allah, wondering why this had happened to her. After all, she was only thirteen, but after tonight no longer a child.

A GOSSIP STEW

WHEN ONE RECEIVED a visit from Mrs S, and that too an impromptu one, it generally meant one thing: somewhere in Lahori society an event had transpired of such temerity and ferocity, of such salaciousness, that it was deemed worthy of passage from Mrs S's ears to her lips and her iPhone, thereby becoming the latest titbit of local gossip marked 'Immediate Circulation, Wide Broadcast'.

Now, like any good tabloid journalist, Mrs S would always seek a comment from the concerned party before proceeding to verbal publication. Thus, if she showed up at your house one morning unannounced it meant *you* were her chosen victim. It was also of imminent significance that you realised that somewhere in her choice to make whatever issue you faced gossip-worthy there was a purpose, indeed always a plan, behind Mrs S's actions. So when Mrs N (Arzoo's mother) was busy putting her face on, as she heard her maid walk in, she was a bit piqued at being disturbed, which incidentally made her face look naturally radiant (oh the small wonders).

"Sugra! How many times have I told you to knock on the door before prancing in my room as if it were your God-given right; I assure you it isn't, you know, girl."

Sugra, the servant girl, was one of the sharp cunning ones that most masters characterise as being the caricature of people in the lower classes. Despite her being a thief, 'Bibi Gee Tax' as she called it, and a bit of a promiscuous nineteen-year-old, Sugra was extremely energetic in dealing with the children that accompanied the relatives or any other social visit and even more so in running the house according to the way Mrs N desired, and so, being so vital to the latter, it wouldn't have been wise to fire her over a missing few thousand rupees or whatever driver or servant boy had caught the girl's eye and been arranged to spend extra time in the house this week. "*Bibi gee*, there is a woman here to see you!"

"Okay! Relax, Sugra! What's the state of emergency? Just tell whoever it is that I am still sleeping."

"*Bibi gee*, she seems very anxious; she keeps switching her legs, crossing the right one over the left before switching it again."

"Well, hmmm, what is she wearing?"

"She's dressed very nicely and she is carrying the same bag as your turquoise one except that it's orange."

"My Birkin?" said Mrs N, more to herself than Sugra. "Who has an orange Birkin? Hmm… what shoes was she wearing?"

"These really nice orange ones. I think they have an LV on them." Sugra was one of the lucky servants who had education till at least third or fourth grade and could read the English alphabet.

"Was she relatively older?" (Old in Pakistan meant anything over thirty years.)

"Why, yes, yes, much, much old! About your age."

Mrs N, offended, wrinkled her nose at the nineteen-year-old and got lost in thought, adding a natural sheen to her cheeks and wondering whom it could possibly be.

"Oh wait, *bibi gee*! I just remembered. She asked me to tell you that Mrs S is eagerly waiting to have breakfast with you."

Mrs N dropped her brush on her dressing table and looked at Sugra crossly, remarking, "You extremely clever girl, I just wasted five minutes in asking you what she was wearing and you couldn't tell me what her name was." Slapping her forehead, she tied her robe around her and said, "I am just going to brush my teeth. You run down and tell Mrs S that I was asleep and I will be right down. Get her a glass of orange juice, right? Please not from the box, that's for other guests; get freshly squeezed for her and tell the cook to start preparing a breakfast trolley, cheese omelettes, scrambled eggs and boiled, and ask the driver to get croissants and pastries from the bakery. Actually, you go give the juice and deal with the cook, I will deal with the driver. Make sure to put out the new cutlery that we bought, perhaps the Royal Albert set."

Sugra had a remarkable gift for remembering details, from the number of diamonds that Mrs N possessed to the number of handbags that ought to be hung on the rack to the number of shoes, and, yes, even the combination of the safe (from which she borrowed a little bit, justifying herself with the fact that the woman was a millionaire and a few missing hundreds would be of no significance; the aforementioned Bibi Gee tax). So it wasn't hard for her to remember the details of all that Mrs N had mentioned and all that she hadn't – the butter, jam and marmalade and the actual tea – just a mere mention of but a few foodstuffs forgotten by the suddenly very anxious Mrs N.

Sugra rushed to provide the freshly squeezed orange juice while Mrs N tried to make herself look as natural as possible and, giving up on making her lips a naturally red rouge, rubbed the lipstick off and was content with the stain it left behind. Moments after Mrs S sipped her orange juice and switched her legs for the hundredth time, Mrs N, quite the cute plump little woman, emerged in her lavish silken robe. Mrs S got up and the two women said their salaams; they kissed the air more than each other's cheeks. Before Mrs N sat down she undid her robe, only to tie it tighter so that Mrs S would notice the fact that she had lost weight – a move which of course did not go unnoticed by Mrs S's keen gaze.

"Oh, Mrs N, you sure have lost weight!"

"Really?" she replied, appearing as ambivalent as she could because it was very hard to muster the restraint to contain her excitement. "I really didn't notice!"

"No, no, you have!"

"Well, thank you," said a beaming Mrs N, but then the lily-livered woman remembered that Mrs S had shown up to her house without informing her and she was suddenly extremely anxious again. She fidgeted with her hands when she was feeling intimidated and of course she started mumbling and talking unnecessarily. "Your shoes, they are so beautiful."

"Oh! I know," said Mrs S. "I know!"

"Are they Louis Vuitton?" As if the huge LV wasn't visible enough.

"Yes, yes," she added with a smile.

Another awkward moment of silence, during which Mrs N shouted out to Sugra's sister Mina to set the breakfast trolley.

"Your robe is so graceful too, such a luminous purple." At this point she actually reached out to touch the silk to make sure that it was pure silk.

"Yes, my husband had it specifically tailored and fitted for me. It even has my initials at the back!"

"Wow! That's so sweet of him."

By this point, the driver, having driven as fast as his poor life allowed him and afraid of losing his salary bonus for the month, had come back with the breakfast carbs, and the *behra,** was putting them together on the trolley with the help of two of the cooks.

"Well, let's cut the story short. I came to tell you" (Mrs N held her breath) "about Maya." (Mrs N let out a sigh of relief.) "Have you heard what's been happening?"

"No, no, I don't know," replied Mrs N, her handsome features furrowed in an expression of confusion. "Actually, wait, I remember Arzoo being upset about something regarding Maya, but never got around to asking her."

"Well," said Mrs S, adopting her renowned haughty and self-centred tone, "I came to you because I thought, you and Mrs K being close, you would have known – not many people do." In fact, now, apart from these two ladies and Maya's immediate family and those involved, no one else did.

"Hmm." Mrs N got a little bit offended at the fact that Mrs S knew about some secret regarding Maya that she, her mother's childhood best friend, did not. Then she remembered something and smiled. "I am sure Mrs K would have told me. In fact, you know she has been calling me for the past two days, but I have been busy dealing with some of my own issues and haven't been able to get in touch with her again."

"Well, yes, I am sure, otherwise I would never have come to you," spoke she who is too self-righteous for the rest of society. "I too wouldn't have known except that I went over to see her father. I needed support for the irrigation project I have told you about. Anyway, I walked in and heard a great deal of shouting and banging of doors; I even heard the crashing of a *calque,*" shuddered Mrs S. "Mr and Mrs K seemed very agitated when they walked in. They looked like they hadn't slept in days. It seemed like they had literally aged overnight." Mrs S was using her latterly-gained knowledge to form a more compelling narrative, though I do believe at that point she wasn't concerned with the couple's appearance but with the sounds she had heard. "Of course they tried their best to hide the truth from me, but you know me, nothing escapes these wise eyes. I know I may not be highly educated in England, but I am sharp, Mrs N. Books are not necessary for gaining smarts. I knew something was wrong, who wouldn't after hearing the screams? But I proceeded to ask Mr K if he wished to be on board my

---

* Waiter or bearer.

project. Of course, all business talk done and over with, I asked Mrs K if she was well. I am sorry – I couldn't help it – and she just stared at Mr K and within seconds started bawling. I mean, I have *never* seen a grown woman cry like that."

Getting more and more flustered by Mrs S's slow narrative, Mrs N lost her patience.

"Well, why was she crying?"

"Patience, my dear, I was just getting to that. Well, they both told me that Maya refuses to marry her cousin. Apparently there is some other boy involved who she has been in love with from some point."

"Really?" said an incredulous Mrs N. "Maya, sweet, dear, quiet little Maya?"

"Yes! Yes! I know. SHOCKING, isn't it? I couldn't believe it either and I am afraid neither can her parents. The poor dears are in such shock."

The *behra* and the maid brought in the trolley, and Mrs S broke off her narrative, having been distracted by the smell of the freshly baked croissants and the cheese dripping out of the omelette. Mrs N was perhaps even more befuddled than Mrs S, as she was on a diet, but recovering from the sight of the delicious food, she got up to serve the woman, along with her servants. Making sure that Mrs S's plate was full of each kind of pastry, Mrs N sat back down to her breakfast of black tea, half a slice of brown bread, and a boiled egg. If you ever go to a Pakistani gathering or dinner or have Pakistani friends, you will understand how much they will make you eat, and not eating is seen as an outright offence. Mrs S, always being a petite and slender woman, could afford to eat as much as she wanted; even though she had just had a baby, it hardly showed. An envious Mrs N looked at her slender body and munched on the tasteless boiled egg.

"Mrs N, I know you aren't much of a sugar fan, but won't you at least try the croissant? It is scrumptious."

Mrs N nodded her head and to distract attention from her diet, she said, "No, Mrs S, I am not in much mood to eat." (Even though she was speaking through mouthfuls.) "I am thinking of my poor friend Mrs K. I didn't expect this from Maya. How could she? I mean, I could've expected this from my Arzoo, even, but not Maya."

"Yes, I know Mrs N, the very best of us can sometimes be inflicted with sin. This is why I told you. You have to keep your daughters constrained; otherwise they will cease to be in your control. I told you and I told Mrs

K not to send your daughters abroad for studying, but both of you were so adamant about sending them to Harvard and Stanford. I wasn't against your interests; I am not your enemy. I was looking out for the girls' best interests. Both of them are very dear to me. All this education does is give all these young girls such monstrous ideas about men and women being equal, and how their life is theirs and they must fight for their rights – so American. They forget about their family, their duty; they become so career oriented and it unfortunately makes it so hard for them to adjust themselves in society after that. I warned you."

"I am sorry, Mrs S, but one girl's mistake cannot be sufficient to hold all educated young women accountable for all the vices in the world. In fact, I don't even think it's a sin to marry whom one wants to. I mean, it's not like she wants to marry a white man! Lord forbid! I just feel bad for her mother because I know how full of principles my dear friend is, and how hard it will be for her to balance this incident with her own values. She is very stubborn and runs her whole house with an iron fist. She has raised her children as if they were in military camp. Everything is scripted, timed, and based on her commands. Any deviation and it makes her furious. Now this, this is truly going to test her grasp on reality."

"Yes, well, Mrs S, you still fail to see my point. Girls are getting so modern these days, the kind of people they hang out with, the kind of clothes they wear, and then the pictures they put on Facebook and the SnapaGram…" At this point she gave Mrs N a meaningful glance and the other, being of a lighter skin colour, blushed furiously. "I mean, my son's always on that goddamn laptop MacBook Air of his, always on Facebook or Xbox or on his iPod – I swear technology will enslave our children. Anyway, Facebook seems to be his biggest pastime and the other day I just sneaked up on him, and the kind of pictures I saw, what the girls were wearing and the way they were hugging all these white boys…" Mrs S clearly used the plural but as her expression turned to one of smug egocentrism and Mrs N blushed even more, it became even more apparent what 'girls' she were referring to.

"Well, Mrs S, you mistake me. I am not for girls running around naked and partying the way white girls do." Mrs S shuddered, and just to make sure that Mrs S realised that she wasn't a bad mother, Mrs N looked directly into Mrs S's eyes and said, "I believe in women's education and liberation, but not at the expense of Islamic values. In fact, I feel my Arzoo is getting too Westernised and to remind her of her Islamic heritage, her father and I have thought of chartering a plane and taking the whole family on pilgrimage." She ended her speech with a tiny little humph and instead of being offended, Mrs S was so pleased she reached over and gave Mrs N a big hug.

"You have no idea how pleased I am with your decision, Mrs N, so, so delighted! Are you seriously chartering a plane for *umrah*?"

"Oh yes, yes! My husband thought it was high time that we had a family bonding experience, and what better way to bond than over an authentic Islamic spiritual experience in Holy Mecca itself?"

"Oh yes, yes, most definitely. Your husband is a wise man. We spend so much money the wrong way rather than spending it in the way of Islam – so, so commendable. I am sure pilgrimage will do wonders for Arzoo. I only wish we could help Mrs K, poor, poor woman. What face will she show to society, especially when she is backstabbed by her own daughter – tsk, tsk."

A little offended by the way Maya was being discussed, Mrs N snapped at the woman, "Don't worry, I am on the case now. I will try and work out a solution. And Maya didn't backstab her mother. The poor girl is just a little conflicted."

Mrs S seemed even more pleased with this decision than she did about the pilgrimage. It only made one question her motives. After all, did she truly wish to help Maya or did she actually want to curry favour with her father for the project? Whatever the case, she left Mrs N in a state of extreme contemplation. The woman was so lost in thought that she didn't even remember to ask the servants to remove the trolley and the rest of the food. She didn't even notice the cup that was left on the wooden table without a coaster that was leaving quite the stain.

THE MOULIN ROUGE EFFECT

Slavery ended well over a century ago, yet the roots of it remain a firm foundation for the very many female relationships in my part of the world. Whether you are a daughter, a mother, a sister, or a wife, your gender-ascribed roles in consistency to those around you are the only functions that you are expected to fulfil. There is never a 'you', never any thought or reflection given to the desires of the individual. You are but a part of the 'we', part of the family, the society that you belong to, and any attempt at aspiring to get rid of the 'we' and, while establishing cordial relationships with the 'we', ascertaining the necessity of the 'me' is seen as nothing short of the grossest kind of treason.

And so this was Maya's downfall. As you had no doubt ascertained from Mrs S's latest tabloid endeavour and her visit to the best friend of Maya's mother, her cousin-fiancé had surreptitiously released selective information designed to ruin Maya while making himself look like the victim. In her earnestness and belief in humanity, Maya had been completely honest with her cousin-fiancé, something that from the dawn of time all good men have wished, hoped and prayed women are. Yet tragically, he took her honesty and her belief and trust in him and twisted her confession into a means for him to secure what he felt was ordained to be his, rather than earned: his possession of Maya.

Maya's mother screamed, "What kind of a daughter are you? You have lied and CHEATED and are *badmash*."*

Maya responded, "I did not tell you any fibs, nor did I delude you into

---

* Trouble-maker, corrupt, immoral.

believing in a reality that neither existed nor ever will. I did not betray you into believing in a 'me'; that was nothing more than a portrayal of your own expectations. Moreover, I am not *badmash* because I do not wish to marry your and father's cousin's son, and have been in love with someone else for the past *five* years!"

Mrs S: "Shameless, shameless girl! Have some respect for the fact that your elders are in the same room, and you are going on and on about love – so un-Islamic."

Maya: "Firstly, you are no one to force your view on religion. I have my own and am well acquainted with my creator, thank you. Secondly, even my darling grandparents had a love marriage so I don't understand what the taboo about the word love is in here."

Maya's mother's sister: "Shut up! That time was different. Look at yourself and your family's status and how you are embroiling it in filth."

Maya: "Status? What was our status two generations back? Both my grandfathers lived in a squatter shack at the side of the road. They didn't even have money to eat, and now, when we all have money, you want to presume that that money is indicative of a status you might not have been fortunate enough to have fallen into."

Maya's brother-in-law, and Laila's infamous husband, sat leaning forward with an arm cocked on his thigh; he exuded all the haughtiness and sleaze of a 70s porn producer. "My, my! Look at the way your tongue is darting back and forth, darting venom for us, your family, and for what? That useless bastard? Someone ought to give you a good hiding and teach you the proper manners of a Lahori family of status."

Maya decided to remain quiet. Her hurt and betrayal was mounting to a point where she thought she was going to lose her calm and belie her internal pain and disappointment. Her family, including the other conspirators – Laila, her husband, Mrs S and Mrs N, who had finally called Mrs K and confronted her about why she was left out and was eagerly welcomed back in the fold – had moved to London for a week to deal with this unfortunate new calamity that had afflicted them, and the day before, her brother-in-law had taken her for a run around Hyde Park, only to inform her that he was the 'cool brother', the friend in the family who not only understood her sentiments but would advocate them onto the family platform. BULL FUCKING SHIT! He had attempted to extract information from her only to have greater proof to be used against her.

The most important rule of Lahori society: beware of the wolf in Louis Vuitton clothing!

Maya's brother-in-law (again, his tone, attitude and abuse both shocked her and made her question who everyone in her family really was): "Someone call that motherfucking gigolo and tell him to get to us if he is interested. After all, we aren't going to be going around all day waiting on his lowly parents to ask for our daughter's hand in marriage. She's already signed up to be one of his house girls anyway." She wasn't his daughter but Maya's mother nodded her head in approval.

Maya's cousin: "Oh no, gee! I called him yesterday and told him to get his father to call in twenty-four hours or sever all connections, and it's been more than a day."

Call or sever all ties. This was the great game of *Desi* wedding brinksmanship. It was the ultimate bluff used to secure a higher or lower dowry or even to just run a margin call on a family's intent of finances. The challenged party had twenty-four hours to call and accede to all outstanding demands or they had to completely and permanently back away from the proposed marriage negotiations (as well as certain social events for a time).

Humph, Maya thought. *Of course my beloved and his poor frightened father are thinking of the most respectable manner to approach such unrelenting men who think they are their own version of the Pakistani mafia.*

Mrs N: "Maya, dear, look where you have brought yourself. I don't care about anyone else; I don't like how you're being degraded for one boy."

Maya's mother: "Leave it, Mrs N! This girl is beyond repair now." *No child ever is,* thought Mrs N, as would any sane parent. "But he, he shouldn't be able to get away with it! This girl doesn't know what we are capable of. We can get his entire family fixed to the point where he will come begging us and telling her he doesn't wish to marry her."

Maya's brother-in-law chimed in: "Yes! I have connections. We can get his mother and sister fucked the same way that he had our daughter. An eye for an eye and then some. You're pathetic, Maya – to give your body up like that. And if we were to honour-kill you it still wouldn't clear our name. No, we need to make *their* women bleed too."

Maya: "WHAT IS WRONG WITH YOU? You all sound like primitive village feudal lords. WHAT IS WRONG WITH YOUR MENTALITY?"

Maya's brother-in-law shot back: "Look at her. Look at the way she is defending him. Oh my God! He has her so completely under his influence. She's this fucking loser's whore and nothing more."

Nile had refused to be part of this gathering. To him, this constant attack on Maya was both insane and inhumane and he, for one, had had enough. Being a boy, he could at least extract himself from the gathering. According to social and familial hierarchy, he still didn't have the power to contradict the elders just yet, but Laila, poor Laila didn't have an option. She silently watched her husband upbraiding her sister and finally found the courage to speak. Her words were, if anything, a half-measured comment aimed to deflect at least some of the verbal blows being levied at her kid sister.

"We must act with propriety and decency. Let's remember Maya is the victim here."

Maya's father's sister: "Are you sure you are not pregnant? Because if you are, we can take care of it, and if you have slept with him, we can take care of that too where your second cousin won't even know."

"No, no," Maya whispered. She had now broken into tears. She clearly wasn't fool enough to get pregnant and she wasn't even sure how her family would be the one to question her and her honour like that. What is wrong with all of them? Why must love for them be material either in terms of money or sex? Who she gave her virginity to wasn't their choice or their honour, but hers! God had given her a mind to control her body. Her virginity was hers to give away without it being discussed in such flippant patriarchal tones as if it, like her, was but a thing to be thrown around.

Maya's mother's brother: "Well, you should call him and tell him that this is his last chance."

Her father, like Arzoo's, did not intervene and remained silent – though this conference was much more grave than mere pictures – as did Laila. They really did look like father and daughter, watching quietly as Maya was being cheapened and abused. She kept looking at them, helplessly hoping that one of them would get up and say 'enough', but neither did.

Before they could say anything, her dad's phone rang and it was Ali's father.

Her father did not deem it appropriate to discuss his daughter's marriage and assumed that he would get too personally involved.

"*Asalam Aleikum*," the boy's father said, in a combination of hesitant politeness and exaggerated forcefulness that was a direct consequence of the reluctance at approaching this touchy topic.

"Gee," her darling brother-in-law replied, with an even more authoritative vigour indicating both his seniority and social prestige.

"My son said that you people have consented to this relationship and if you people have consented, then so have we."

"Well, we have not consented, nor will we ever."

"But my son led me to believe that your family is interested in the matter."

"If you have this girl married to your son in the next month, then yes; otherwise, no."

"Gee, sir! Look here! My son is still in college; there is no way he can get married in a month!"

Everyone in the room knew that that was the only reason why Laila's husband mentioned that. Having acquired the means not only to gain just the upper hand but also to make the other party's conversation appear foolish to the highest degree, Laila's darling husband then attempted to move on to the next level of intimidation.

"Do you know who I am? I am..." the list went on to explain his very remarkable social, business and political achievements, which really had made him a notable figure within Pakistan. However, honestly or in order to avoid further confrontation, the man replied that he had not heard of Maya's brother-in-law. This only served to exasperate the tension.

"Well, if you don't know who I am, then know this. In a month either you ask your son to marry our daughter," since when Maya had become his daughter she didn't know, "or we will fix your son."

The threat had achieved its intended purpose.

"We are sorry. There is no way my son is capable of marrying your daughter at this point."

"Well, if he is not capable of marrying her, then tell him not to call her, because he doesn't know what he is getting himself into. We come from a *shareef** household and don't take kindly to the violation of our *izzat*.** Do you understand me?"

"Then you also please make sure that Maya *beti* doesn't contact my son either." With that, the phone was hung up and Maya felt her entire world collapse. She was silent for a good five minutes, during which she contemplated the recent unfolding of events. How had she been such a fool? She had never in her most deranged fantasies imagined that her family

---

*   Well-respected, noble.
** Respect.

would not appreciate her and her choice. When they rejected him, they were rejecting the most important part of her! Didn't they see this wasn't just about the fact that she loved him and not her cousin, but this was her means of breaking away from a system that had constantly suffocated and imprisoned her? She wanted to revolutionise her life based on her terms and not fall into the pattern of what society expected from her and what she was meant to deliver. Her own family had failed to live up to her expectations.

You grow up in extremely peaceful and happy surroundings and naturally suppose that those around you are infallible, that they are gods who do no wrong and protect you from all wrong. She had always looked up to them and they cared for her – each and every one of them. Every time she prayed she would pray for their long life. In spite of all the heaps of wealth and luxury, her family, and her parents in particular, had instilled in the children the desire to remain modest and charitable. Maya did love all of them (except for her brother-in-law) and they all did love her. It is most painful to realise that the gods you erect as children are but mere humans capable of as much flaw and vice as you are. I fear that is the hardest part of growing up.

Screaming at her mother (for she expected her mother to understand the most) she ran into the toilet and wept all night. It is pitiful to hear a woman cry and scream – they heard her laments but her bestial wails aroused no compassion; there was no move by them to knock on the door. They were too petrified and hurt that Maya still didn't see any sense to make any attempt. It's always the hardest to tell people you love that you love them when you think they are wrong, but that is when they need it the most. The only heart that was determined into any sort of resolution that night was Laila's; she could almost hear Maya's pain.

It is the worst feeling in the world to feel alone, to feel as if the entire world is but a means of berating you into a vegetative state of existence because without others – as man is the paragon of social interaction – one truly feels to exist. My family, my friends, everyone had forsaken me, and now, I was pretty sure, so had the boy I loved; after all, after such blatant disrespect, why would he wish to wed someone who was the cause of it? My family, oh God, the tears knew no end. How could they betray me like this? How? Didn't they love me? Didn't they wish for my happiness? Why were they so constrained by society, so embroiled in the web of tea parties and luncheons?

She wanted to curl up in a ball and dive into herself, never to come out. She lay on the bathroom floor sobbing and gasping, wishing so desperately that she had someone, anyone, to talk to. But she had no one, just God, and perhaps even God wasn't listening. She wept and wept, begging Allah to help her.

I wanted to live a life where, at the end of the day, I knew I was honest to myself; I wanted to die knowing that I was truly, truly happy. Of course there would be days where I would fight both with myself and those around me, where I would be miserable, where I would pull my hair and regret my decision. We all have those days. But mostly, it would be bliss because I would have achieved what most spend their entire life without; I would have gained a life that would root itself into the core essence of man, of love, of humanity. I would have lived a life where I did not have superficial joy wrapped around 'things', around paraphernalia that was just good to look at, but would be inanimate, dead, and lifeless. I would live life on my own terms and on the basis of a marriage that was not between two families, or two social equals, but between two hearts. Why didn't everyone see that? Why must my pure intentions be denigrated to nothing but 'fantasy'? I wasn't a fool as they called me and I wasn't blinded by love; for the first time in my life I had an outlet for being myself and not the tailored perfect woman that society required me to be.

Whatever is one's reality will always be another's fantasy. And her friends had been there throughout, supporting her to have the courage to fight for her right to relinquish her status as a trophy wife, but come the storm and they had all moved their ships to safety. Her mother had called them to inquire about the affair and had unleashed quite a deal of hail at them. They were supposed to be her support system and yet they had flinched, they had abandoned her when she needed them the most and the majority of them had cut off all communication with her.

One of her friends had actually unbuckled her true self when her mother had called, and told her that she had never been on board, never supported Maya's love, and told her that she had always advised Maya to always listen to her parents. The fury she felt at this betrayal and at her friends' lies was nothing compared to the hurt. What's more, they had been friends for over fifteen years! One call, one text saying 'I am sorry' and Maya would have forgiven her, but the friend didn't even find all those moments in those fifteen years worthwhile. Everyone is entitled to their own opinion, and Maya wished her friend had told her of her real perceptions before, and even if she thought that Maya was wrong in her search to acquire her beloved, so what? That's what friends are for – to disagree with you every step of the way.

Maya would always forgive her because she thought about the days they would sit on swings and play quest for Camelot, how they would eat French fries with *chat masala,* how they would sit for hours discussing Shakespeare, how when her friend's father died she was the one who felt that she would infiltrate her friend's life with so much love that she would cease feeling the need for a father, she was the one who left another friend when she stole this friend's crush and she was the only one who never laughed at her friend and her eccentricities like everyone else did and had embraced them and respected her all the more for them. No, Maya wasn't upset about the betrayal as much as the fact that her friend hadn't even once bothered to text to find out how her life had been going along.

Even Arzoo had forgotten her for now. Arzoo had her own demons to fight, but all she had to do was call Maya and Maya would have been there for her just as she had been every step of the way ever since they were born seconds apart of each other. Arzoo had, according to Maya, bigger and better things to move onto. One decision, one fight had changed her entire world; it had made friends strangers and families enemies. It had warped her perception of reality to a point where she did not know what the past twenty-one years of her life were or who really truly cared for her.

Why must the world be so cruel? Why must they be so unrelenting? One mistake and no one was willing to listen to me, let alone forgive me. If they wish not to forgive, then why condemn me to a life I didn't want? I might as well be dead. Overnight I had not just fallen from grace, but from the honour I had had and the respect I had for myself. I was humiliated beyond words but knew that respect was fickle; what affected me more were all the relationships I had lost. I had been what many jealous people had called a princess – one flick of my finger and my family made sure I had grasped my heart's desire to my heart's content. One mistake and now I was to truly live like a princess, trapped and suffocated for a life I was meant to live not for my own sake, but for the 'common good'. Was this fight really worth it? I thought again about how it wasn't just about love and how I could never be happy with anyone else; it was about me and how for the first time I had found agency in a world of cluttered materialism. I had said yes to the ballet and swimming lessons, yes to the tea parties and dinners, yes to the clothes I was supposed to wear and the people I was to meet, yes to the college I was to go to and the 'A's I was to get so... No, I was no longer going to be a social toy to be manipulated at the others' will.

God had finally helped her. She was Maya and she had now met herself.

Maya's little voice: "What do you want to do?"

Maya: "I don't know."

The little voice: "Yes you do."

Maya: "No I don't."

The little voice: "You do. You're just scared."

Of course, we all fancy ideas that are impossible from time to time, but the secret is that nothing is impossible. Nothing is beyond our reach. All you have to do is believe in yourself, believe in your capability of reaching out and grabbing what you desire. No one tells you how long you have to wait, or how perilous the journey, how if you attain your goal whether it still carries the same charm or has the same power that it had over you when you sought it. Most importantly, no one tells you the number of times you have to fail in order to succeed or how you might lose yourself along the way or even how many people you hurt along the way. It is the greatest hurdle to assess the grief you give others over a goal you may not be certain about. So always, always believe, because what you desire is the greatest reflection of your soul; just don't stop believing in yourself.

AND EVERY LEVEE BREAKS

LAILA LEFT THE 'conference' much in the same way that Maya had been feeling as she lay on the toilet floor. She saw her little sister berated and abused in ways that she wouldn't wish on even an enemy. The entire way back to her husband's Knightsbridge apartment, in the First Class seat on Emirates, in the car ride from the airport to her Lahore house, she sat in silence and occasionally glanced at her husband, feeling even more disgusted with his duplicity than she was with his absurd fetishes and disregard for her body and soul. How dare he interfere in her sister's life? How dare he try to ruin Maya's life like he had ruined hers? How could she have been such a fool as to fall for her family's and his emotional manipulations and go back to him?

And what's more, she thought with a shudder, she had never ever seen her family members behave the way they had. Was Maya no more than a chattel – a cow like her to be sold to the highest bidder? How could their mother allow such an extreme disrespect of her daughter's honour for the sake of social expectations? What mother could sacrifice her natural motherly instincts for the sake of what people would think and say? She had come to the conference with the belief that she would be saving Maya from a fate similar to hers. Her father had no more courage in him to face his wife than Laila had to face her mother and she was more than disappointed with his continual lack of balls. He could face all the most twisted corrupt politicians in Pakistan, but not his wife. And Mrs S and the relatives, she thought with mounting anger, they just needed an excuse to tarnish her beautiful sister, just a reason to pick on someone with their self-conceited righteousness. Even Mrs N stood silent and watched. But her husband – oh, how she wanted to rip his throat out at this very point.

How he sat there all suave in his Armani suit jacket with his overconfident (for once) sober self, issuing commands and barking out platitudes as if he ran the show, ran their family. How dare he? No, she wasn't going to let Maya be abused anymore. She hadn't been too close to her sister; they had been four years apart in age and always in different phases in their lives, but that didn't mean she didn't love Maya as if she were her own daughter. She would protect Maya, she would save her from this demonic society. Like a sweeping light, courage electrified her body; it thrilled her to know that finally, she – and only she – would be in control of her fate. After all, in light of what she would do, marrying who you love would not be deemed as horrible and Maya would be free to live the life she wanted without scrutiny, without force, without any judgment of any kind. She wiped the tear that trickled down her cheek; she was ready to make the sacrifice to ensure that at least one of them would live the life that they deserved.

She thought of her wedding night again.

"And why are you so quiet? I took care of the business caused by that whore-sister of yours. You should be thanking me." His words fell on the ears of a woman whose soul was soon to be liberated. What she had planned for him would reverberate in its finality.

"I just asked you a question." Upon not receiving an answer the second time, Laila's husband kept one hand on the steering wheel and lightly smacked her face with the other. Even though the driver had come to fetch them (with two other cars) at the Lahore airport and taken them home, her husband was adamant about driving his Ferrari himself and asked the driver to follow behind in one of the other BMWs.

"Are you hard of hearing? Seems like you are thinking of some new clever scheme. Why? What is it? Are you planning to murder me?" He laughed as if her even having such thoughts were ludicrous.

"Nothing, nothing, I am just tired." (*I promise you, in my mind, I am roasting you alive on the biggest fire you can imagine right now. Too bad I have a conscience, unlike you.*)

"Ha ha ha ha ha. Yes, Laila, my poor stupid little wife," he said, playing with her cheeks. She tried her best not to recoil at his touch, even if it was friendly. His proximity nauseated her. So she stopped feeling his touch and concentrated on what she had to do and how she had to execute it.

It was only when the engine stopped that she realised that they had reached home. She stepped out of the car and went straight to her room, knowing that the man would follow suit – when he arrived, she would be ready. She would execute the plan. He did. He locked the door, obviously still not satisfied with the power high he got from Maya's public execution. He smiled, reaching in to touch her, and for the first time she smiled back. He instantly realised this as a challenge to his dominance.

Confused, he looked at her.

"Don't. Touch. Me," she said.

"What?" he said, completely bewildered.

"Don't touch me!" she repeated. "Are you hard of hearing?" Laila knew now more than ever that it was time for her to strike. She coiled back, like a cornered viper. She slid her hand on the bedroom dresser.

Getting over his initial shock, he laughed and said, "Seems like all the girls in your family have gone mad. Seems like I need to teach you some manners." He reached in and grabbed her hair.

Now! Laila thought. *Now! Just as he's in close.* She hid her hand and let him pull her in, let him leer in her face, sniff her hair. Her hair always brought him a moment of weakness. She readied herself to do what was a righteous justice.

She looked him squarely in the eye and said very firmly, "I want a divorce."

Her husband looked like he didn't know what had hit him (there really is a first time for everything). He sat crouching on the bed for a few minutes while she got up like a robot and packed just the essentials. She had no need for anything else – well, anything other than what was already in the packed suitcase from London.

It was funny. After all the beatings and the rapes, those four words careened into his heart like the dangerously pointed end of a hairbrush that had been sharpened quietly and secretly over months like a prison shiv.

Laila had opened the lock of the front door (the servants wisely disappeared whenever they had any problems) and was about to turn the handle when her husband finally spoke. "You know I won't give you one. Try as much as you want, you can *never* leave me. It will be just like the separation. You will come back. They will make you."

She turned around and looked at his handsome face, only now noticing how ugly it was. "Funny, I thought you were going to say that. You'll be hearing from my lawyers soon enough."

"You're going to drag this to court?" He laughed. "YOU STUPID BITCH. I will disclaim you as a whore. Every person in the court, society, everyone will call you a whore. You know what happens to women who bring divorce to court here. Just last week Mohamed Asad the lawyer had to clean the brains of an uppity Chinyoti bitch off his shoes."

She smiled. "And you think I care?"

He was quiet for a few seconds before he spoke again. "YOU WHORE, YOUR ENTIRE FAMILY'S A WHO—"

She opened the door and shut it on his screaming hateful voice for the last time. She walked outside the house and before opening the gate, turned and looked at the house again. She thought about what people say, that sometimes you get attached to places, and that homes are a part of us. No, she wouldn't miss this prison. It was never her home.

It was 1am. Laila didn't know how to drive, didn't even know if she was going to her parents. No, perhaps she'd see them in the morning and go to her friend's right now, she lived nearby anyway.

It was 1.05am as Laila shut the gate. She didn't know where she was going or what she was going to do (well, after tomorrow). All she knew was that she was never going back. As a child, she had been told never to venture out alone in the dark. It was pitch black and she was a woman walking the streets of Lahore alone, but for the first time she was unafraid.

MISFITS AND MISTAKES

IT HAD BEEN at least a fortnight since they had made love. Perhaps when husbands have business issues even they don't suffer as much as their wives! Ariyana had known that Y was in some kind of an ordeal since the moment he had come home Monday evening. He hadn't smiled, he hadn't kissed her or given her a friendly pat; in fact, he had hardly even spoken to her. When she had asked him to pass the *ghobi*,* for instance, he merely nodded for a few minutes before waking up from his zombie-like slumber and asking her if she had said something. Upon repeating herself for the third time, he finally passed her the vegetable. Ariyana initially felt that perhaps it was something she had said or done. After all, it had only been a month since she had found out that they were pregnant and she had originally received the treatment she had expected – he had showered her with presents, with love. Even her mother-in-law had stopped making jabs at her for being half-white and started behaving as excitedly as she could for the arrival of a grandchild.

But now it was like she had ceased to exist for him and, try as she did to bring him back, he was too engrossed in whatever was bothering him to give her any attention. There was only one satisfaction that she got from his behaviour; her mother-in-law got a taste of it. It wasn't that she felt good that her mother-in-law got what she deserved, especially for the way that she made Ariyana feel all day – a useless, worthless, gold-digging whore, but that if Y treated his mother the same way that he was treating her, then she could rightfully believe that she wasn't to be blamed for his actions. Her mother-in-law, too, after repeatedly referring to Ariyana as the ill omen that

---

* Cauliflower curry.

had finally affected her son, had enough 'house politics' acumen to realise that her son was in trouble. She also knew that her daughter-in-law was too earnest in her love for her husband, and in order to be the perfect wife would not even dream of jeopardising their relationship by asking him what was on his mind until he didn't confide in her and so the mother fulfilled the role that most wives should: became the nosy inquisitor, and hounded her son, hoping for some response, until he did relinquish to his mother's onslaught of care and gave up the story of his melancholic mood. Of course, one could only conclude that the only thing that could have sufficient consequence to drive him to this mood of apathy and dejection would be none other than a business failure.

So when fourteen days after dealing with a sullen Y in the house, Mrs Y (the elder) called Ariyana for tea outside in the lounge, the latter wasn't surprised that it had to do with her son.

"You know I don't know what your mother taught you; I mean, I didn't know that white women have no idea how to take care of their husbands."

Ariyana just bit her lip, taking in this insult of a mother she hardly remembered, and even though it pained her to know that her half-white lineage would constantly be discussed in the manner that it was, she had come to develop negative associations with the matter. Moreover, the more she answered back, the more it would prod her mother-in-law into greater retaliation and their verbal battle would never end. It was more to conserve her energy, something the elder Mrs Y never seemed to lack, that Ariyana kept quiet and listened.

"I mean your husband has been so upset and needs comfort and attention and you have just been gliding along, becoming even more silent in his silence. You haven't even bothered to ask him what's been bothering him. You white women think that you know how to do everything, you're so educated and liberated that you shouldn't even get married!"

That was it. "I am not white," she mumbled.

"Excuse me. Did you say something?"

"I said I am not white. I have as much Pakistani blood in me as I do white. And if I am such a bad wife to your son, if you're such a great mother, why didn't you just solve his problem?"

Of course, the sarcasm was lost on Mrs Y, who grinned and said, "Of course! Only I truly love my son and know how to take care of him." Ariyana rolled her eyes. "You must learn from me how to treat my grandson."

This instinctively brought forth Ariyana's protective streak, leaking adrenaline in her blood, causing her heart to beat faster so she couldn't help but snap back, "It can be a granddaughter as much as it will be a son, and I really feel you need to stop saying 'grandson' because both Y and I don't care."

"Oh my! Look at you. Stop saying such things. I pray to Allah every day that my son has a son. We have never had firstborns who are girls in our family and I pray that that tradition never breaks."

For the first time Ariyana wanted to punch this woman for her completely illiterate thoughts. She was the only person that made Ariyana want to abandon her cool calm psychologist's mind and adopt a personal stance that mirrored her passion. Of course, one would have to wonder whether Mrs Y was that illiterate after all – she had the capability of unnerving such a collected young woman, and her point about sons, as ignorant a notion as it seemed to be, did have a point. If her family had to compete with the rest of society, then society valued sons more. It was only through having mothers like Ariyana that any form of positive change in society could be expected and women could have the footing and the respect that they deserved. After all, it's the matriarchal household that upholds the values of a patriarchal world. Even if we are influenced by culture, we are the ones who create it and thereby we are the only ones who can bring about a change to it.

"I am telling you, Ariyana, don't anger Allah." Ariyana was even quieter, mentally beating this woman to a pulp. "Nevertheless, I went to my poor little Y and he told me that it's regarding his business project. You know, it's the one his poor dear late father had attempted to do right before he died, and Y has been fighting with all his paternal uncles and their sons that this project is sensible and that they will all make profits out of it. Frankly, I think his father wasn't in his right mind when he was drafting the blueprints for this project, but there is no telling Y that. He has taken upon himself to make his father's last wish a reality and nothing will deter him."

Ariyana stopped being angry; she was feeling a fresh, new wave of admiration for her husband. "Why, that's so admirable!"

"Admirable? It's foolishness, is what it is. Squandering our family money on useless projects; well, his uncles feel the same way that I do and even though Y has the biggest share in the family business, the board still voted against him so he has been upset, trying to find funds for this project and meeting with failure everywhere."

"Well, why are people not enthusiastic about this?"

"It's because it's some alternative energy project; I mean, who would want to invest in such risky work as that?"

Moments after her mother-in-law had left, Ariyana was possessed with the idea of helping her husband. She thought of the one person who would know whom to contact. With a smile on her face, she picked up the phone and dialled Mrs S's number. She told her the details of the situation and the importance of finding an investor. Mrs S was more than pleased at not just being contacted but also in being given this grave task. Spurred on more by her need to be in control than her Good Samaritan values, she searched her mind for the most likely person. She went to the file cabinet of businessmen and opened drawer after drawer of known investors or people who had some kind of connection with big investment projects until she came to Mr J. Just nine months ago he had signed a contract with an American company that specialised in energy.

Smiling, she called Mrs J, only to find out that Mr J did not retain the contact information (his phone had been stolen). Mrs S was completely disappointed at the fact that it had, until Mrs J told her that Mr R had signed a contract more recently, about two months ago, with the same company. Extremely pleased with her social contacts and methods of discerning information, Mrs S called Mrs R.

"*Asalam aleikum.*"

"*Waleikum*, Mrs S, how may I help you today?"

"Well, I was wondering if you could arrange a meeting with the CEO of the American energy company that your husband signed on to."

"Oh! Meeting for whom?"

"Well, Ariyana, she wants it for her husband."

The rest of Mrs S's conversation was lost on Mrs R. All she thought of was Ariyana and the plan that was formulating inside her head to teach the girl some respect for others in society, especially when she and her hierarchy of power were under threat.

"Well, Mrs S, I can never turn you down. You are in luck; the man is in town. He is staying at the Pearl Continental. Should I arrange a meeting for, let's say, Friday noon?"

Mrs R couldn't believe her luck; her plan was going to be more successful than she could ever have hoped for.

As Mrs S hung up and called Ariyana, there was a moment when the latter felt suspicious about Mrs R's involvement. The woman had been nothing but amiable, inviting her to her house for tea and treating her with warmth and affection, but somehow, somewhere, all of that extra congeniality directed toward her, especially when it didn't exist for anyone else, made it feel slightly forced, slightly pretentious. Moreover, Ariyana couldn't think of anything that Mrs R could want from her or that she needed help with. Ariyana forgot that sometimes people aren't nice because they wish to bribe you with their sweet words and elaborate gestures, but sometimes they are nice when they wish to mask darker, deeper-seated emotions. The momentary doubt was just that – it existed for a span of seconds and then she felt so excited about for once being helpful to her darling husband, and how finally she would actually have done enough to make her mother-in-law respect her for being pro-active, that all else was forgotten.

When Friday afternoon came around, Ariyana was a familiar combination of both an excitable ardency and volatile emotionality – she was adamant about doing something right for a change. Even her husband perceived her jitteriness. As he had not been making many perceptions recently, the fact that he noticed something must have meant that it was of enough of a demonstrative degree for him to make a comment. She couldn't eat much breakfast, though her mother-in-law forced her to chug a glass of full-fat milk in order for her son's son to be white-skinned. For all her belittling about white skin, the elder Mrs Y was adamant about her grand 'son' being white and, as she believed, consuming lighter-looking foods would aid in producing the child's lighter skin.

After her husband left for work and her mother-in-law started dressing for an early committee brunch that she had to attend, Ariyana too started on the mission to find the perfect outfit. She wanted it to be simple enough so that it represented her, but lavish enough to create a good first impression on the CEO and make him aware that her husband was affluent enough and not some fraudulent man on a mission to swindle the man's money.

Ariyana finally came across this really suave *shalwar kameez* that her sister-in-law had tailored for her. She loved the woman – too bad her sister through marriage was already married and couldn't visit as often. She applied makeup, wore one of the pairs of designer heels that were naturally, not too high and that her sister-in-law had purchased with her brother, Y's, money. She carried a matching Prada tote and, glancing in the mirror, was actually quite pleased with the way that she looked. Tiptoeing outside, or as much as one could tiptoe in heels, Ariyana peeked out. Thankfully, her mother-in-law had already left. Upon leaving her room she did wonder if she should take the driver, but then decided against it. She wanted to surprise Y with the initiative that she had taken for him, and the driver had a loud mouth. Moreover, she wasn't very comfortable sitting in the car with him, having caught him staring at her numerous times in the mirror, but, worrying for his eleven children, never complained to her own husband. No, she was going to drive herself.

The car ride to the hotel wasn't that long, since their house was already on the Mall Road and the majority of people were at mosques for Friday prayers. She was glad, as she wanted this over and done with as soon as possible. Upon reaching the hotel, Ariyana called the number that Mrs S had given her.

"*Asalam aleikum.*"

"Oh, hello there! You must be Ariyana?"

"Yes, yes I am!"

"Well, come on up! I am in room 403."

"All right! See you in a bit."

Ariyana hung up, feeling a little sceptical about going to the man's room as opposed to meeting in a coffee shop in the lobby, but decided against feeling too demanding. Unknown to poor ignorant Ariyana, Mrs R had contrived the meeting in the room. She had told the executive that Ariyana was shy and did not wish to have her husband's business plans discussed publicly. Of course, that was a thought that could never possibly have entered Ariyana's unsuspecting mind.

Ariyana walked over to the elevator. Her stomach was a concoction of fear and anxiety now, the excitement at helping her husband kept vanishing with each floor that the elevator whizzed by. The doors flung open and she stepped out onto the fourth floor and proceeded to room 403. Having detected the room in the maze of the turning corridors, she stood outside for a few minutes debating whether to go inside or just walk away. After what seemed like a century, she finally got the courage to knock on the door. A smiling pleasant face greeted her. He wasn't yet fifty – perhaps in his mid or late forties – and was the proud proprietor of a full head of hair that was mostly dark black but streaked with a bit of white. His blue eyes were surprisingly warm yet calculating – after all, he didn't make millions by simply being affable, though, like every wealthy American businessman, he realised the importance of hospitable and compatible mannerisms.

"Well, hello there! My, you're very young!"

"Yes, I am twenty-four."

"And are you Pakistani?"

"Yes, half."

"Oh! That's great! Where is your American parent from?"

"My mother, she is from Chicago."

"It's very nice to meet a fellow American in these parts, even if it's just half of one," he added with a wink, which made Ariyana stop feeling nervous. She finally relaxed and smiled back.

"Well, where are my manners? I haven't even properly introduced myself, I got so carried away with the disparity between what you actually look like and what I imagined. My name is Mr Lawrence and I am very pleased to meet you." He stuck out a hand, urging her to shake it, and as she returned the handshake, she made sure that it was firm and did not betray the jitteriness she had been feeling a while back.

"Well, come on in to my humble abode. It's not much, but it sure is comfortable."

The rest of the conversation is not of much importance except that the man, intrigued by Ariyana, made every effort to make her feel comfortable and ultimately, and as was quite evident by his welcoming actions, agreed to the proposal. He claimed, and I quote, "It was an ingenious idea for solving at least part of Pakistan's energy crisis."

Unfortunately, at about the same time that Ariyana was initially shaking the American CEO's hand, her husband returned from Friday prayers to find his wife not at home. After having inquired of the servants of her whereabouts and finding out that they surprisingly had no idea, he was even more baffled to learn that she hadn't taken the driver with her.

Y sat with a knitted eyebrow, musing about where his beautiful wife was; she never left for anywhere without telling him where she was headed off to, but thinking that perhaps she had a doctor's appointment or that some friend had come and taken her for a drive, he tried calling her to inquire where she was, but he was even more worried because he couldn't find his file. He was sure he had left it in the car and had actually come back home instead of to the office in pursuit of it.

Ariyana didn't pick up. Her phone was on silent, carefully nestled in her Prada while she was enthusiastically showing the contents of the file to a very interested Mr Lawrence. Mr Y would have forgotten his wife's temporary disappearance as an occurrence not worth pondering over for more than the ten minutes that he had already dedicated to it until, that is, his phone rang. He stared at the screen. It was an unknown number and, thinking that it was perhaps an international call, he picked up to the sound of the strange voice.

"Is this Mr Y?"

"Yes. Who is this?"

"Your wife's in PC room 403 with an American."

"What? WHO IS THIS?" but before he could receive a reply from the anonymous tipper, the phone clicked off.

It took Mr Y a good five minutes to register what was happening and after that, from the moment he sat in the car to his maniacal driving on the roads to his almost colliding with the truck carrying sugar cane to his arrival at the Pearl Continental hotel and then his subsequent hiding in the corner of the corridor, away from the view of both the elevator and anyone leaving 403, Mr Y's actions were particularly a special case of testosterone on overdrive as opposed to a man relying on reason.

Once the initial onslaught of the hormone wore off and as minutes passed, roughly about half an hour, and he was beginning to think that the call had been a hoax, the door of 403 opened and out stepped a beaming Ariyana, with a handsome, slightly older American man. Y clenched his fists and his teeth as she reached over to give him a flying kiss on the cheek. Oh, how he wanted the man's cheekbone to taste his knuckles. How he hated the woman that he had loved so dearly until only moments ago. He didn't wish to see her face ever again after today. He wanted to beat her too, but he knew he would never bring himself to do that. He wanted to shout and scream at her right now and tell her that he knew what she was up to. How could she have betrayed him like this? Her engaging eyes were repellent to him, her slender graceful body sinful, her warm smiles a signature of falsehood – even the baby (which probably wasn't his) a disgraceful abuse.

No, he was going to wait till she got home. He didn't wish to create a scene in the hotel.

Y made his decision, but he never once thought of the repercussions of that decision. He didn't seek to delve into the fact that seeing isn't always believing, especially when you have been preconditioned to see that something. He never thought to ask her about her exploit, nor did he think that it was anything but an illicit affair behind his back. After all, we usually trust strangers more than people we love, especially because sometimes, like Y, we are insecure about our own involvement in that relationship and thus readily believe someone else over people we know and love. No one questions an anonymous tip. Would you?

SAFA, MARWA, AND LOVE

"ALLAH O AKBAR Allah," (Allah is Great!) the muezzin's voice reverberated through the long corridors, around the men and women standing with their hands placed one above another over their hearts, into the ears of these worshippers and out of their lips in a synchronised, 'Ameen', the English equivalent of Amen. The thousands of Muslims congregated around the Ka'bah now bent over to prostrate over the ground in a symbol of abandonment and humility. *I too bent down and felt not just unified with these multitudes of strangers who had nothing more in common with me than our faith, but felt harmony and embraced this peace I hadn't felt in the longest time. I bent down in front of my God, in front of the energy that created the universe, created me or, as Newton says, can never be created or destroyed. I don't believe in God because my mother told me He existed when I was five, nor do I pray five times a day as part of the same humdrum routine that everyone has restored the obligatory namaz (prayer) to. I pray because when I feel like the world is spinning out of control, when I feel stressed to a point where I would gladly rip out my hair, when nothing makes sense and when, as had happened recently, my reality crumbles and evaporates into the thin air of nonexistence, I acquiesce to the soothing calm that accompanies consigning my troubles to an entity other than myself.*

Whether you dispute the existence of my God, whether you call Him by different names or have split His attributes to numerous other spiritual beings, it is immaterial. Still, there are times when from one moment to the next you feel like you are slipping away and you need to have something to grasp onto; it is faith that not only gets you through but also gives the impossible trimmings to a shapeless, hopeless future and makes plausible that which just yesterday seemed inconceivable and unattainable. So I give myself time off from this tempestuous and frenzied world and for just ten minutes a day disperse myself into a contemplative meditation where nothing exists but me, my God, and the opening up of my heart to Him the way I do to no one. For me, praying is as important as having three meals a day or sleeping nine to ten hours a day; it is a part of my life, not as a means of exhibition or to satisfy a duty that is just forcefully a part of my schedule, but because it is as essential and natural to my survival as the air I breathe.

I have seen people in my society, not to be either fastidious or priggish, but 'people' indicating mostly women, who pray as a means of materialising a faith that is non-existent. They will start praying the moment guests appear on their doorstep or when they want to indicate a counterfeiting piety in order to gain supremacy in discussions; no one wishes to publicly discount a devout person, irrespective of how self-righteous. I have on numerous accounts been a witness to these women praying and then diverting their gaze or their ear to some delicious gossip brewing down the hall. Most of these women are godless and irreverent to the highest degree and start praying as soon as they enter old age.

No, to me God exists in the smiles on people's faces, in the way people sometimes salaam and acknowledge the goodness that exists in us all and do a deed for other people and want nothing in return. They say if you do some good deed from one hand then even the other hand should not know of the kindness that the first has successfully pursued. God does not lead man astray until and unless man forgets to be true to his true self, true to this good that is the part of us that is a part of God. It is through this link with Allah that we all are connected to one another and to the universe, the chain of all the happenings.

I sit in the hypostyle mosque – in the vast courtyard surrounding the Ka'bah. It is one of those places where people never stop congregating, and during hajj period millions are accommodated in these high-columned structures. The Quran does not specifically demarcate separate praying areas for men and women, and so the Ka'bah, unlike other areas, does not uphold gender segregation. It is truly magnificent and delightful to see people of every hue and colour, every gender, every ethnicity and race, performing circumambulations around this black cube, signifying their devotion and humble oblation to Allah. More than even praying, it is this blissful union between Muslims that makes me so happy. For the hundredth time since I arrived in Mecca, I felt so agitated about the fact that no non-Muslims were allowed into the vicinity. If only they were allowed, they would recognise and begin to associate Muslims with events other than 9/11 or the political, not religious, objectives of groups like the al-Qaeda.

I only wish with all my heart that they could come and see how pure Islam is, much like pure Christianity or pure Judaism or even Buddhism and Baha'i. It is tragic that the horrific mistake of a few comes to define the existence and the identity of millions. Hatred only presides over more hatred until, much like Palestine and Israel, it becomes impossible to reach a peaceful compromise. Whyever get to a point from which returning seems impossible? Masked rage and contempt is dangerous, but even more so are those people who like instigating fear and malice just out of a polemic nature that is sightless of good. If only the world would one day realise that it is much harder keeping on a track where one has to be more mindful of others than the self, but doing so always leads to a path where there may be winding roads and dead ends, but always respect of the self.

"Arzoo, Arzoo," my father calls, "where are you?"

I stop thinking of the peaceful world that I was conjuring up amid the harsh cruel realities of everyday life and realise that all I can do is hope and pray. I wish someone would make a poster of greed 2012 instead of Kony 2012, for Kony is just one of the many hundreds and thousands who go unpunished, unnoticed, whose lust ranges from money, power, land, resources to human bodies and whose corruption remains unchecked, reprehensible, and unbounded, fostering and breeding greater vice and degeneration of the human race. I get up to perform umrah with my family.

The circumambulation or *tawaf* around the Ka'bah can be weary, especially because the greater the brood of worshippers, the larger the rotations. It is not that Muslims worship the black box, but they offer fealty and homage to the symbolism behind the cube; it is reminiscent of the faithful, of the prophets from Adam to Abraham, Jesus to Muhammad, and most of all it is a highly enigmatic space denoting Allah (though in Islam, Allah is present everywhere at all times as the infallible, omnipotent energy of the universe). It is quite an epicentre of all the good possibly present in the Muslim world; women remain untainted by acquisitive desiring gazes, during prayer times people leave their shops open unafraid of their goods being robbed, there are the occasional beggars who will hassle you to no end, and most people are generally on their best behaviour as they, both encouraged by the aura of Muslim morality and their pilgrim status, are fearful of Allah, who they suddenly realise is closer to them – though in Islam this apprehension to offend should be forever present. In fact, Islam openly states the altruistic spirit of mankind, informing its followers that Allah treats you the way you treat others, and before most everything a Muslim says, 'Bismillah ar-Rehman ar-Rahim' ('In (or with) the name of Allah, the Beneficent, the Merciful'), evoking qualities of generosity and forgiveness from the energy of this universe.

If only Muslims, quite the popular yet perhaps erroneous modern-day picture of intolerance, would practise what they expect, they would receive what they themselves are fundamentally required to imbibe. Yet few believers of the faith remain touched by this equitable unsullied nature of Islam, which in and of it is used to mean peace and purity. It is only when they visit the Ka'bah that the otherwise non-existent virtuousness toward God and his people becomes visible. Ignorance of Islam is merely a symptom, not a cause, of many Muslims' callous outlook toward humanity.

I felt a tug at the core of my being as I made rotations around the Ka'bah and tears trickled down my cheeks, disappearing down my neck as softly and stealthily as they had emerged. I decided to make each circle mean something, each prayer to support a theme, and so in each consecutive circumambulation I prayed for the usual – first for my family, for health, for success, for forgiveness, for greater tolerance, and then when I nearly got bumped by a blind person, I had something new to pray for. I prayed for those that cannot see, not just those who have been literally devoid of sight, but also those who, in spite of being given the blessing of sight, remain impervious to truth and justice. I prayed for the state of mankind and the desire to make it better and, lastly, but most importantly, I prayed for love, love that has the ability to eradicate corroded seals of ironclad hearts and love that seeks union and forgiveness. I prayed for the spirit of love and that sometime, somewhere, all of us are caressed by its pressing lightness and that when we are, we don't shiver and forget, but smile and always remember, enabling it to enlighten our humanity and us.

It is a simultaneous exercise for Muslims, though perhaps lost on some, to utilise their empathy and ignite an implacable and resolute faith in their creator and in the belief that all adversity must be combated with determination and an unrelenting conviction that it will turn out okay. They, women and men, young and old, and, yes, even those handicapped in wheelchairs, forget that as they run between the areas marked by green-lighted tubes on the ceiling, they celebrate the love of a woman and her unshakable trust in Allah and his ability to grant her water in the middle of a desert by not just sitting around waiting for water to emerge, but actually running, making the effort before being granted the material blessing.

I looked at the young boy walking somewhat slowly next to me; I looked down at his feet – he has a prosthetic leg. Touched by his faith, I admonished myself for the lack of mine. Thinking of Ian, I urged myself to understand that I am was love and needed nothing further. I closed my eyes, praying to Allah to aid me in my quest for the fulfilment of both my love and my self-discovery as true and honest ventures, as the love for all that wishes to seek prudence in the culmination of its discourse and the strength to face it if it does not. Helpless and yet invigorated, I walked on the same path as the woman who had trodden it in an attempt to seek Allah's assistance for her love as I did now for the love both within me and for all of mankind.

MARHABA DUBAI

THE ESSENTIAL CULMINATION of pilgrimage, as you all know from before, isn't just in Mecca, but a couple of thousand miles away on the little island of United Arab Emirates, or more specifically, Dubai. It can be extremely tiring to live in minimal case scenarios, especially for the N family, and spiritually striving to attain oneness with Allah or at least trying to publicly cleanse one's 'sins'; though if half of the pilgrims merely even knew what their sins were, Allah would perhaps be more pleased than with the sometimes pretentious display of charity, which upon leaving Mecca evaporates. Naturally such trying conditions must be met with relaxation and a recuperating of one's strength, and what better way to achieve such strength than in the midst of the luxury, the opulence, the outer world experience that Dubai could afford. Even more of a plus, Dubai was a more convenient mid-point than London or Paris and such a stark difference in the Arab traditions between the pious and the transformed desert cum entertainment hub was refreshing.

Arzoo's family, and in particular her mother and her aunt, were adherents to this theory. So the family flew First Class via Emirates for a grand shopping spree in Dubai. Arzoo, possessing quite the libertarian soul, wasn't too much in the mood to shop, the pilgrimage still affecting her sense of her identity and her growing unease with the horrors that humans are capable of, but Maya's parents had also decided to join the Ns in their stay in Dubai, and Arzoo was ecstatic about being able to finally meet her best friend. There would be no Fadhi or Nile this time, as the former was on break in Mexico and Nile had exams, but she was happy that it would be just her and Maya. The Ks' basic purpose for the travel was to give Maya a change in environment, especially one that had complete proximity to them, so that she would become more susceptible to their wishes, not realising that, whereas that might have been the case with them, the opposite could be true in Maya's case.

Arzoo called Maya's room at the Burj al Arab, where she, too, was staying, and Mrs K picked up. Arzoo had to do a great deal of pleading to get permission to meet Maya for lunch at the bar next to the beach. In much the same way that Mrs N had a soft spot for Maya, Mrs K had one for Arzoo and eventually relented. Excited, Arzoo put on her bikini and covered it with a sarong and her shawl, just so that her own mother wouldn't create a scene. She really didn't understand how clothing was to affect her inner morality – it was just a means of expression. Her relationship to God had nothing to do with how she dressed, but being grateful about the fact that she was in Dubai and about to reconnect with her true sister, she was in no mood to strike up an argument with her mother on the merits of 'proper' dressing. She wished for the hundredth time that her mother had been to college abroad and understood Arzoo's liberal spirit more – it wasn't Westernisation, just a more unimposing outlook on life.

Glancing around the room to make sure she had everything, Arzoo rushed into the elevator, threw the shawl into her Gucci beach bag and put on shades, ready for a fun day in the sun with Maya. She went straight to the bar and ordered a Diet Coke – she wasn't about to get inebriated with so many Pakistanis around, especially after pilgrimage. A number of boys passing by stopped to stare at Arzoo's wonderful body and her beautiful face, but she paid no attention. For once she was worried about things other than flirting, which to her was and always had been more a mental conquest than a question about physical or sexual attraction. She was worried about Maya and, falling into an unfamiliar state of contemplative worry, thought about the world, again disappointed with how cruel and unforgiving people can be, vowing that she would live her life to the fullest. After all, she had a ceaseless list of wants and she wasn't about to wait for their attainment. One of her favourite platitudes was 'only dead fish go with the flow' and to be quite honest, she wasn't dead; as far as she knew, you only die once. The wind was blowing her hair, the cold Diet Coke cooled her insides on this hot day, the smell of hamburgers and French fries filled the room, and the sounds of people laughing and being happy were weaving their way into her cochlea. She'd never felt more alive. Why do people go around in endless circles trying to attain money, power, property, when all they're looking for is this need to feel alive? As for life, it is right there, right under our noses, right in between the inhalation and exhalation of a breath or the fluttering of an eyelid. Life exists in the plateau of unconscious and conscious experiences we forget to appreciate every day...

"ARZOOOO."

Arzoo halted her current strain of harrowing, bombarding thoughts, turned around, and without a word, hugged her best friend in one eager assuring embrace. Maya's face was streaked with tears and it wasn't until she tasted the salt that Arzoo realised that she herself had been crying as well.

"Oh my God! Look at us, Maya." She reached up and played with her friend's hair, lovingly pushing it behind her ears. "Seriously, today is about both of us having fun. No tears, no crying, let's make the most of this day – we won't ever get it again."

Maya smiled. "Yes, you are right!"

"So tell me, have you done any shopping?"

"Not too much, we just reached here yesterday! But mother went straight to BurJuman. Bought these white Christian Dior wedges."

"Oh yeah! I saw them too! I bought them in turquoise, though."

"Yeah, you would!" said Maya, laughing. "I love how I am just a black and white melodrama and you are one colourful creature."

She gave her best friend's hand a squeeze, loving how their contrasting personalities somehow culminated into one.

"The new Christian Louboutins are pretty nice, but I mean, once you buy one it becomes redundant to have the same red sole over and over again."

"Oh! I completely agree. Did you see the new Roberto Cavalli bags? The new green ostrich-skin one is divine."

"No," Arzoo replied with a smile, "but I am sure you and I could go later on today. Let's go to the Mall of the Emirates. Cavalli or no, I just feel like going to open spaces after all these restrictions!"

Just then the waiter came around; he was an extremely handsome man, probably Lebanese, with hazel eyes, a strong jaw, and wavy gold-brown hair. He first approached Maya, not because she was more attractive, because any passer-by would agree that the duo were equally gorgeous, but because she was nearer. Failing to get Maya's attention, he tried to make conversation with Arzoo and was pleased to find his flirting met with not just approval there but quite an enthusiastic reciprocation.

"Oh, my Allah! I haven't seen such beautiful eyes – where are you from?"

She giggled and replied, "Why, from Lahore." She winked and Maya rolled her eyes at Arzoo's typical corny jokes that, for some reason, men found highly amusing. They were too busy staring at her captivating eyes and bulging cleavage and too happy with the prospect to care about the words that came out of her mouth. After all, isn't that what flirting is, the reassurance that you find someone attractive and the false illusion of a sort of promise to reach a sort of 'culmination'? It is the potential of a promise that perhaps drives men to a frenzy that is greater than if the promise were actually upheld. To be fair to Arzoo, she really hadn't been in the mood to flirt and was merely providing entertainment to cheer Maya out of her dejected state; perhaps just pretending to be happy would be positively correlated with her own affective appraisal.

"Well, you really are beautiful! And what can I get you?"

"How about some sex?" she asked coyly. "Some sex on the beach?"

The distressed waiter was quite a sight to behold as he stuttered and, knocking things around, made his way to the male restroom while the two girls burst out in laughter.

"Arzoo, rely on you to send the waiter away; I am so hungry. I want a burger and fries. God, all that food in the restaurant upstairs is so bad. I never know why people pay so much for food that tastes so… I mean, you definitely need to have a distinct flavour to approve the kinds of food my parents are eating up there."

"That makes two of us. Hold on!"

Arzoo signalled to another waiter – a much older, more mature one – and ordered two hamburgers with sweet potato fries for herself and regular ones for Maya. As she did so, she didn't notice Maya's faraway look until a few seconds after.

A LOVE SQUARE

To love someone, to truly love them, means to truly rise above all human-made constructs from a mélange of society, from religion to economics, yes, even to those that bind you and your ego together.

I don't know what the meaning of love is, nor do I ever suppose that anyone will ever find out its true essence, because like reality, love is multifaceted. But uncertainty with love, that is an extremely unimaginable and common pain. It stabs and stabs away at you – one would rather be killed once than to feel the pangs of what could be, and that too in an intermittent cycle. I feel so blessed to have felt love but equally cursed in doubting its reciprocity. If there are infinite possibilities for every instance, then why not just as many causes for deception? If you give someone your heart, body, and, even more, your soul, what guarantee do you have that they will honour it, treasure it, and never give you occasion to regret the very act of loving them in the first place?

I gave you my everything, didn't I, Ali? I lost everyone, my family, my friends, my respect, my freedom. I don't want to hold this as a plausible excuse to bind you to me unwillingly. I really am merely stating the facts.

Maya is going through his Facebook, such a glorious evolution in communication, and yet such a wretched tool of invasion into privacy.

I wish more than anything that I never desired to venture into this forbidden territory and that the idea of streaming through it had never taken seed in the epicentre of my stubborn will. I go through it and realise that I am in love with a stranger. The pictures are of another person; they aren't scandalous per se, just belong to a different person. Then I get to the inbox messages and they are swarming with little inconsequential lies: S gave me the petition while it was

T, I went to school yesterday for three hours, as your Facebook inbox friends attested you never did.

Little inconsequential lies and yet they are sufficient to make me ask, have you hooked up with any of these girls? If there is nothing between you and them, why would you blatantly lie? And other than the matter of these girls, who are you? I don't know! I don't know who you are. I feel like tearing my hair and wondering which quicksand I have willingly plunged into. More than anything, I too am bewildered by my ability to ask the next question (I wish I could just stop my thoughts but thoughts are thoughts and will first think of the last thing that you want to): were you worth the fight I fought with everyone? If I don't know you, how can I love you? Whatever you would've thrown my way – other women, drugs, yes, even immature satirical fights, moods, fits – I could have taken it if you had told me. If you had confided in me about anything in the world I would never let you succumb to your suffering but would have been the soothing calm you so desperately desired.

These might seem frivolous reasons to you, my reader, and yet they are enough to make one in love doubt, and doubt is truly the biggest pain of all. When you love someone more than yourself you forget the very 'I' that suddenly starts existing when the 'you' threatens to separate itself from the 'I'.

If you love me then how can you stand by and watch me deal with so much misery? If you are my other half, how can I feel at this moment that I am broken and permanently split into a two that was never a one?

Maya was going through what we all go through from time to time: a nervous breakdown. It was a product of her parents' didactic reasoning, hinting to her that the same behaviour pattern fits all prototypes of young men – deceitful, non-serious, irascible under a false eager countenance, liars, and above all fortune and 'booty' seekers. Of course that is not the case, but it is very hard to disbelieve something as false, especially when your parents and family are so earnestly trying day in and day out to make you see what their parochial minds deem fit as reason. But true love is ethereal – it doesn't comprehend human laws or human stereotypes for behaviour; it just exists above that.

She had been secretly huddled on the toilet, scanning her iPad away from her mother's prying eyes, and upon hearing her mother's knocks had quickly wiped away the tears and turned on the shower so as to not arouse any suspicions. She was grateful to hear of the fact that her mother had granted her permission to meet Arzoo – the first time she would be seeing her since her visit to San Francisco and in fact, the first time she would be seeing any other person who wasn't a part of her family. And yet, tired as she was, Ali and his apparent 'deceit' continued to haunt her thoughts.

"Maya, Maya."

"Hmmm. Sorry, Arzoo, I was just thinking!"

"About what?"

"Nothing, nothing." She smiled so as to not burden her friend too much. After all, they were here to catch up and have a good time.

"Oh, come on! Look at me. What's wrong? Is it your parents? Are they giving you a hard time?"

"Yes, but – but that's not it."

"What is it, then?"

"He doesn't love me anymore." Arzoo embraced a crying Maya, who just kept on crying – well, more like howling out her pain – and whenever she had enough breath to, she would blurt out huge chunks of whining words. "I just tried to guess his password, wasn't very hard, it was my name, and when I went on Facebook there were all these pictures and you know I am fighting with everyone for him and it just hurt me so much to see that he isn't what he is."

"Maya, Maya, look at me, okay? Look at me. Please stop crying and look at me. There, there's a good girl, Maya, stop being a fool. He loves you. Everyone knows that. You are letting your parents get to your head. Please stay strong! You're creating stories in your head based on pictures and you, more than anyone, should know how to create doubt through false images." At this Arzoo slyly smiled.

"You think so?" she sniffled, moving away from Arzoo's embrace to look directly at her.

"Maya, I have known you for twenty-one years. I know so. Why don't you just call him?"

Maya's beautiful eyes widened in terror. She shook her head. "My parents will check my phone."

"So, silly, here, use mine."

So Maya did what she wasn't supposed to do: she called him. After much tears and shouting the two resolved the misunderstanding. They were merely vessels of the brawls that always arise out of long distance, and in this case, the Capulet and the Montagu family types (I will put the families into stereotypes) that had made it their life's mission to keep the two apart. Perhaps we believe people we love because we want to, but I think it's more than that – we know we sometimes have faith in them when they don't have it in themselves. It is this unyielding, irrefutable certainty that love has for another that allows the world to call love blind. But it is only the blind who see the world as it truly is, who don't rely on deceptive eyes that are trained by the mind to be easily duped into picking out edges and contours and be oblivious of what really is out there.

In fact, as many illusions have demonstrated, it is the very heuristics or means of survival by which the eyes are trained that actually make it so easy to deceive them. There are no colours in the world and yet we see them every day in the dresses we wear or the flowers that bloom out into the garden or, even more so, in the skins of the people we encounter; they aren't coloured (our mind just interprets the light reflecting off them as colour). People have similarly developed heuristics about other people's characters, which shock them or confuse them when people don't behave the way they expect them too. Love doesn't blind; it lets the other be free, and only when you keep the highest esteem about someone (and keep in mind that they are human and may falter on your expectations), slowly and steadily they will start fulfilling the image you have of them. Love is blind, but only because it refuses to fit into the world of false sight.

She hung up, knowing that she had executed the forbidden (for which her own execution would be highly probable), but nonetheless her soul felt calm, at ease. Maya closed her eyes and reminisced about him, dreaming and living the days since the second she laid eyes on him.

Maya remembered the first time she saw him; she was seventeen and had been running down the stairs behind his best friend, whom she had been friends with, trying to convince him to not just create a new Facebook account, but one with slightly raunchy pictures to make her crush all the way in London jealous of her interactions with her new bestie. (The crush in London is a pointless story and one of no consequence, other than that it made Maya feel that she was in love, the false type where it's more of an obsessive desire that makes one feel depleted and useless [there is no point in love if it demeans you – I am not saying love should always be reciprocated, but at the end of the day, even if it doesn't make you a better human being, it should give you the strength to be able to harness that passion into a more beneficial you and respect yourself for it].)

Ali was leaning against the banister, waiting for the best friend alongside his brother. As she ran down the stairs she stopped for a brief moment to look at him (she never stopped to look at anyone); till this day she doesn't know why she stopped or why when he looked at her and looked down at the floor out of respect, her heart skipped a beat. He had eyes of such a green that it made her think of deep thickets inside the forest, full of peace and purity. Maya texted her friend later on, asking him who he was, only to find out that he was Arzoo's friend's brother (they were poles apart in nature, even more so than in physical appearance, hence the inability to recognise the similar genetic code the two shared). The next time they all met was when her friends and his friends were trying to avoid aunty's judgmental gaze and sat in the coffeehouse. Maya, sometimes being too confident, a necessary factor to have rubbed off from Arzoo, couldn't help informing him that he had really nice eyes; he looked at her for a brief moment (too brief, she felt) and mumbled about how beautiful her eyes were too.

He looked down again and her heart did that funny skip again. Everyone laughed, making fun of his shy demeanour, but she quietly looked at him. She knew she was in love and it wasn't because her hormones were no longer in her control, but because, for the first time, she knew she could trust someone with all her heart. It was that moment between doubt and belief (she probably wasn't even aware of the fact that she was fighting this battle in her mind) and he looked at her again and she just knew that at that moment, even if he asked her to run millions of miles away with him she would. She smiled. So did he. The next few days were the most exhilarating days in making her a sure, refined, poised woman (even more so than when she would make love to him many years later). They went through a process of seeking and being sought as both the *ashiq* (the one seeking) and the *mashooq* (the object of the longing) entrapped by *ishq* (the highest degree of love) until it made them senseless of everything else except the growing of their own selves through possession of the other.

She remembered the first time they kissed (she was his first but, shhhh, don't tell anyone, I am sure he will be mad at me right now for telling you). He didn't know how to move his mouth or what to do with his tongue, but he was the fastest learner alive and started loving her mouth the way she wanted him to. He even asked her if he could see 'it' in the most innocent and politest manner so that instead of being affronted, she was humoured by his flustered frustration (to be sure he was the first guy to see her 'it' and the only one to have 'it'). He moulded himself to be the most perfect lover imaginable, but in this path of self-discovery Maya forgot that she had to discover both of them as one and not as separate entities, still understanding their own concepts of self. They were on completely different planes and, as is usual with young love, misunderstandings and apprehension took over the innocence they had founded together.

Misguided insecurities led to him withdrawing and her to resort to something that was inconsistent with her own self. She started flirting with other boys, all other boys, to get his attention, not comprehending that her shallow behaviour only made him doubt her more. It is one of life's greatest tragedies when two people, vulnerable both in terms of their years and to each other, actually grow into, amidst and around each other, and form who they will be for the rest of their lives with that someone else, but don't know beforehand that they will never be able to let go of that person because that person usually knows them better than they will even know themselves. They were made for each other; no two people completed each other the way they did, but the world thought that they weren't ready and, influenced by others, they decided to stop dating.

I suppose they were happier before they had officially started dating, when it wasn't expectations that bound them but the ability to surpass such levels because none were set. Just the terms 'boyfriend' and 'girlfriend' sometimes lead people to assumptions that may not be what they need or should want in their relationship, but are what eventually drives them apart. Whether you are dating or married, treat each day as if it's the first time you met the person you want to spend the rest of your life with. They knew they wanted to be with each other forever. (At least, Maya did – out of all the boys who had ever wanted her, he was the only one who did not make her shudder at the thought of marriage. In fact, two months into dating and she had an epiphany of their wedding day; she saw the image as clearly as she could see her hands in front of her and held onto it every day that they weren't together.)

Society thought they weren't ready and so they, being extremely young and not possessing the intrepid spirit of the dreamer in their twenties, came to believe that they weren't. And then of course there was college and everyone tells you that it's 'stupid' to have a relationship in your freshman year of fun, frolicking endeavours and one night stands. He bided his time and his emptiness with distance from Maya by indulging in drinking, smoking pot, and of course, bro bonding on PlayStation and Xbox. (Not to say I am not a gaming fanatic myself; back in the day when I wasn't yet thirteen and wasn't yet made to realise that gaming is usually a strictly male-monopolised pastime, I was pretty versatile with my fingers and my mind, and of course the essential coordination between the two.) She, on the other hand, tried to distract herself from the pain of feeling like she was half a person through her studies, secretly hoping that he would be the first to break, his ego proportionate to the Empire State, and hers an equal Burj Khalifa.

When her constant phone and even more persistent Facebook interaction with him led to no further resolution, hurt and disappointed, she sought other ways to achieve her purposes. To attract his attention, she was no longer the courteous, elegant, awe-inspiring and honourable princess who had inspired his love but became everything that he despised. It started with pictures and clothes (the sluttiest that she could find, skirts that barely covered her ass and tops with necks so low they barely had a front, not to mention the constant bare midriff); then it was the outrageous flirting and occasional making out (never sex of course). The more outrageous her means of getting a reaction from him, the more withdrawn and distant he kept on getting. They did try to get over each other, but sometimes the harder you try to get over things that are just meant to be, the more they haunt you and bind you to them. They spent many sleepless nights thinking about each other. Even though Maya was clearly cheating on him, she would have nightmares at least once a fortnight where she would wake up having dreamt of his indiscretions (which we may never know, but as he later claimed, were never real actualities except for an inebriated kiss or two at the club, which in the face of Maya's own transgressions ought to most necessarily be discounted). No matter how hard she tried, the fact was there wasn't a day that she wouldn't think about him, not one boy that she didn't close her eyes and imagine was him, not one night that she spent not crying for him. He too was miserable, but in order to hide his misery remained aloof and unreachable (his line of defence against her slutty behaviour).

The only relief the two had was the breaks between semesters where one would seek the other, usually the man the woman, though occasionally these roles were reversed, and everything else would be forgotten except for the need they had for each other. I am by no means trying to imply a physical need, nor am I trying to state that they used each other (for we all use everyone for one purpose or the other). They constantly needed to rekindle the images they had for each other in their minds out into the physical world; they, simply put, made each other complete. All they had eyes for was each other and everyone started seeing and understanding how she gave him the strength and the confidence to be the man that he would end up being, and how he gave her the purpose, the endurance, the temperament to make her his other half. Slowly and steadily, he became the human hand that tamed the wild black panther that he had created in her.

They both loved each other, but because they were young and immature, they still had doubts. They did not have doubts when they met on breaks in Lahore, when they visited each other back and forth from one part of the great United States of America to another, when they would spend all day as one person completing each other's words and actions and even at night when, away from the prying eyes of family and friends, they would spend all night in each other's arms (they had secretly promised each other never to make love till they got married, wanting to make that night as special as possible). Yet it was the in between, the not being here and there, the distance created and the human mind's imagination of supposing the worst, thereby allowing them to misinterpret even the most basic of actions to create the doubt that the other did not love. Resigning to the fact that she loved him more than anyone else, something happened inside Maya; she wished to be selfless and free him from this oath of fealty she felt she had made him swear to. Quite an error on her part, because she never tried to ask him or inquire what his intentions were but just assumed that was what he actually wanted.

So what happened next was nothing short of Maya's own hamartia and her inability to rise to the situation and act according to what her heart told her: she was afraid of herself and thus unable to act toward the best of all her potential destinies. Poor girl.

"Maya!"

"Hmmm, Arzoo."

"I know you're thinking of him and love him very much, but please pay a little attention to me too."

"I am sorry, I am sorry. Tell me, what's up?"

"Maya, I have made up my mind that I am not going to return to Pakistan after I go back this fall. I have had it with our society and I just don't belong there. I never have. You've always been the perfect dutiful one, the one who all the parents loved, all the teachers. You know, no one ever got me except for you, no one ever accepted who or what I am."

"Do your parents know?"

"No, no they don't. I mean, I am doing the quarter abroad and then when I go back to Stanford that's it, no more. I have had it with this society and with my family. I have had it with this constant popular consensus that a woman is inferior to a man. I just can't stomach such horrendous notions anymore. I will come back when I find myself. I don't think it's possible to find yourself amidst all the social expectations and pressure in Pakistan. Every time I come back, I feel like my soul is being caged. That's not home for me anymore, Maya."

"What am I going to do without you, Arzoo?"

"Awww, you can come visit me! You know your mother will never say no and before the summer, the grown-ups don't even have to know of my decision. I wish you could stay back with me in the US, but your parents aren't letting you go back this time, are they? If it weren't for your goddamn cousin – he has ruined your life. Why did you ever get engaged, Maya?" She looked so furiously at Maya, but the other wasn't even looking her way. Arzoo played with her Diet Coke (the waiter had never returned with her sex on the beach).

Maya didn't have a concrete answer to that one and this time they were both lost in thought. This time they both were reminiscing on Maya's past.

★

Two years ago.

"We all give him nine out of ten," said her aunt.

Maya had been plagued with proposals from high-strung impetuous youths and their persistent mothers since the tender age of sixteen. Yet, recognising the genius of her intellect, her capability to mould her strength to gains (both academic and social), and the sheer force of her will, her parents had initially decided upon –and were quite excited by – the prospect of her pursuing her dream of higher education. After all, wealth in terms of money does not assure one's inclusion into the crème de la crème anywhere; education is a means of metamorphosing the millions in the bank to the social status that permanently marks you as belonging to the 'upper class'.

Maya, with her evanescent charm and her qualms for creating a better world, had the sufficient capability of changing her family's perception from feudal lords and tractor owners (extremely wealthy, but still not intellectually stimulated) to the revered orders of society (the way that for generations Arzoo's family had established itself, through both their troves of endless wealth and the pursuit of well-educated individuals amid the family). Her parents were evidently right; Maya's acceptance into Harvard was the single most joyous occasion for her household. She had been ecstatic about being a source of pride and prestige to her family by being the first woman ever to go to college outside Pakistan and the sole member to have been admitted into an Ivy League school.

The Pakistani, especially the Lahori, obsession with the Ivies, has led many unfortunate sons and daughters to be wrongly and forcefully pushed by their parents, obviously leading to greater failure than success. It is for the sake of most of these hapless frustrated youths in Lahore that I feel I ought to mention this little tidbit to make parents realise that children ought to go to the school or college that correlates with their level of intellect and with the environment that best caters to their emotional internal needs, where they invariably feel like they belong, and where they haven't been prodded and nudged, beaten and screamed at to get to. Children are not only under the most insane kind of stress from the time they enter first grade to achieve this Ivy League end goal, but in the interim most parents forget that they are children and forget to cater to their emotional and physical needs, making them more puppet – and robot-like as opposed to actual flesh and blood that breathes and feels. No wonder clinical depression is common among the youth (especially the ones that have testosterone to already deal with). But Maya had attained Harvard on her parents' actual encouragement, as well as mostly her own merit. Thereby, even if her parents entertained virtually all the prospective courtiers, her mother and father remained unmoved on their resolution to support their daughter.

However, unknown to Maya, after her freshman year, within the span of eight to nine months, society had cast its web and caught her parents in the mesh; they had come to 'realise' a number of crucial facts. Firstly, that it would be too late for her to get proposals – after all, anyone over nineteen is much too old. Secondly, she might become too headstrong and therefore incapable of adapting to a man, for after all, all the expectations of most compromises and adaptation were naturally endowed to the woman. Lastly, but most importantly, there was a high probability that Maya might run away with a white man, for Emerson and Kant no longer held any value and she had nothing better to do at Harvard than to make herself available to white dick for matrimony nonetheless. Her morals, her ethical standing, her love for education, and most of all her right to make the decision that was hers to make, were left unacknowledged by her parents' haste and panic in getting her hitched as soon as possible.

So when her parents' second cousin had proposed on behalf of her son, it had been the clinching factor to drive them into the state of frenzied excitement at getting Maya to agree. After all, he was RICH, okay enough to look at, capable of belying a false sense of confidence and charm that was absent internally, and they were family, no matter how distant or how little communication they had had with them in recent years; they were of good social repute and the alliance would be beneficial to both sets of parents, especially in terms of monetary advancement for the guys and social for hers. No one bothered wondering if Maya would be pleased or even partial toward this decision because the parents made most decisions, though the boy was already privy to the deal, since he was successfully established and ready to settle down.

Maya was a freshman, and irrespective of the fact that she was in love with someone else, she was unwilling under any circumstance to get hitched when her life had just begun, when she had just found herself outside the protective field of her parents and her restrictive society; she could just feel the first lining of her cocoon barely giving way. As always, when her parents asked her to take a look at her second cousin as a new 'prospect', she relented, believing that it was only a social necessity, an act she was conducting out of good will and one in which her parents weren't invested. However, she had no inkling that, this time, things would be different. Their meeting in her drawing room was cordial and relaxed because Maya was viewing him as nothing more than an acquaintance that she was just being made to meet, and as always when Maya met strangers, her self rushed out to greet them (it got excited with the prospect of meeting yet another of its kind and was intrigued always with how unique yet another specimen of mankind is).

If you do realise, reader, it is often easier to talk to complete strangers than people you know and have loved for years, for strangers don't judge you or expect from you, and are not disappointed by you; there is no reciprocity of hurt, just the joy in the encounter of another. Maya thought that just because she viewed this as a meeting designed as a formality, he felt the same way. After all, she had never really spoken to her second cousin, always being forbidden to interact with any boy in the family. But often when we assume that others feel or think the way we do, we are creating and imbibing a parochial viewpoint that only makes our reality plausible to us while all other possibilities are blocked out. People usually tend not to think or feel the way we do, and as humans our entire social interaction unfortunately depends on mere hunches, guesses into others' internal workings. Like Maya, we are often wrong and, like Maya, when we forget to remember that there is a theory of mind, a realisation that others act and are motivated to act by different causes, we find ourselves with unexpected consequences.

She failed to acknowledge the nervousness of his laughter, the repeated licking of his lips, and the intent gaze with which he looked at her. She just laughed, charmed and thrilled with the prospect of having made yet another new human encounter. So when he asked if he was to meet her father, out of polite courtesy she agreed to his request and acquiesced to their meeting. Unknowingly she had sealed her fate. Her parents and their second cousin took the act as a sign that Maya was interested. Perhaps it is because when we really want something we feel that every sign is a hint from fate and, ignoring the alarm bells, we proceed to include all chance fortuities as part of our plan. Signs are interpretable in multiple ways and each interpretation is indicative of a potential destiny. To but believe that each one is imperative of the potential destiny we want to make an actuality is nothing short of foolishness.

Yet her family and his were deterministic to the extent of buffoonery and were adamant for this to work, so when her father asked her what she thought of him in front of the whole family, she gave him a six out of ten. (It is indelibly wrong to rate people as if they are being auctioned, yet sometimes the simpler the means of assessing something, the easier it is to convey the message. Even though each member of the family might have different characteristics that supported a five or an eight, the number ascribed gave one a clear indication of the level that the family member held that person in.) So when Maya gave the cousin a six, it should have been clear to everyone that she found him affable enough but not enough to marry him.

"Yes, but I believe he is a six."

"Hmmmmm," said her father, "but he's so dashing and brilliant. Look, all your cousins and aunts and uncles and we, your parents, gave him a nine."

"Hmmmm! Yes he had certain redeemable qualities; he seems punctual and hardworking but still – I don't know."

"Well, there is no harm in meeting again. His family wants to invite you for dinner."

"But…"

"But when an opportunity awaits you, you mustn't stall it. Allah will think you have been ungrateful for his blessings," said her mother. Yes, one mustn't waste opportunities yet one must have the tact of differentiating the elusive ones from the one that correlates to the internal workings of one's naturally inclining destiny.

"*Acha*." Maya's thoughts were far away with the man she loved.

"Why don't you go talk to your grandfather?" said her aunt.

The most significant thing that her grandfather told her was that she ought to go with the flow, but she ought to know, like Arzoo, that dead fish go with the flow. After all, he said, even if they say yes temporarily, they could say no later and she could take the next three months to truly think over this decision. Completely relieved, this advice from the head of the family made her feel like she had complete control over her own fate, and thrilled by this concession, she misinterpreted the political motivation behind this allowance; the more free that Maya was led to believe she was, the more she would be inclined to the desires of her family. This carrot-and-stick tactic is what the British applied to dupe the Indian rulers and what is still currently used by families in Pakistan to disillusion their children.

Maya thought of the boy she loved more than herself once again and thought that it was her fault that she had constricted and restricted his prospects and so she thought of the most selfless thing she could do – she decided to let him go free. However, her most selfless act turned out to be the most selfish, as she made this decision for both their lives on her own and had failed to include him in her calculations.

A week later, when she boarded the plane for Harvard, she thought that not only did she have the sufficient freedom to conduct her own fate but that were she to incline to her parents' wishes, she would not only make them incredibly happy and proud, but she would also finally make her lover happy. In her attempts to please all those around her, Maya had failed to realise what she herself wanted. One moment to another, our lives continue on a road to their final destination, and yet before we reach this world to be discovered we forget to live for ourselves. The pleasure to please others was so paramount that Maya was continually discounting both her need to tell Ali of what her parents had planned and how in her heart, how truly uncomfortable and unhappy she was. When her father would ask her three months later if there was anyone in her life, for she seemed unenthusiastic about this new 'fortunate' turn of events, she failed to tell him. She failed to speak up. That was the opportunity she lost.

The next three months were supposed to be Maya's time to think about the decision and yet her parents were constantly forcing her cousin on her; he would incessantly call and all of them remained oblivious of her class times or the workload that being at Harvard meant she would be subjected to. He would be petulant were she too busy to pick up his calls, and her parents, particularly her mother, would side with him, and between them they made Maya's life the inferno that Dante wrote about. Her aunts and mother continued to set the date for the engagement ceremony (the date of which had been set in spite of the fact that Maya had never said yes) and preparations were being made for the big day on the grandest scale. The most expensive caterers were inquired for, the most lavish of decorators, and presents for her fiancé and his family were acquired for millions of dollars. Between what colour dress she wanted to wear and what watch she officially wished to give him and how many carats she wanted the in-between interlocutor to ask the boy's mother to get and even how many guests were to be called on the occasion, Maya remained aloof.

She hated pink yet that's what she would wear. She couldn't care less if she gave him a Cartier or a Patek Phillippe; she couldn't even give less of a shit about the diamond she would receive on her fourth finger, and even though she informed them that she wished to keep the number of guests to a minimum because not only did she not want her lover to find out, but she also didn't want too many people to know, as she was fast approaching the realisation that she was going to have to say no, the guests were thousands in number. All she thought about was the significance of the ring on the fourth finger, the fact that they said it was the artery or vein that went straight to the heart and permanently sealed a bond of love. What had she done?

A MOMENT OF TRUTH

SHE WAS FEELING sick again. It was the third time this week. Perhaps Allah was punishing her or, even better, perhaps he was helping her and she would soon be dead and forever deprived of her torturous existence. She clung to the sides of the toilet and let out the contents of whatever she had eaten the night before; it never feels nice to puke but it's especially painful to do so when the food you consumed had high spice content, which I assure you is quite the norm of most Pakistani food. She had just wiped the corners of her mouth when the cook knocked on the door of the servant lavatory. She tried to flush, but it wouldn't.

Thud. Thud. Thud. "Hurry up, you good-for-nothing miscreant! *Bibi gee* is calling you."

Since that night, she hadn't been able to look at Cook's face, nor Cook at hers. Fehranaz still thought of that night and the many other nights that followed as a horrible nightmare, one she didn't share with Mrs S or any of the other servants. The only person who could help her was the one who would secretly teach Fehranaz in between committee party events, but as Mrs S had stopped taking Fehranaz, there was no way of contacting them either.

Fehranaz tried flushing her vomit again; it didn't work again. Ah, well, just a pleasant remnant she would leave for Cook. Without another word she opened the door and walked out, making sure as to not touch Cook, nor look at her, and to completely deny Cook's opulent dirty presence as if doing so would blot out her deception.

Cook too made a grimace of filth and annoyance as Fehranaz walked by only to step in, stare at the toilet and cover her nose and mouth with her *dupatta*. "Filthy girl, just look at her manners, as if we, her servants, will look after her." After several attempts to flush the vomit, Cook was finally successful. As she lowered her shalwar and sat down to relieve herself, she thought of Fehranaz's vomit and being a shrewd woman, understood the cause of it, a cause that would never have been known to Fehranaz herself.

"Yes, Mrs S?"

"Where were you?"

"In the toilet. Why, *bibi gee*?"

"Don't give me smart answers, young girl, or I will give you a boxing you will remember. Now, run up and iron my clothes. I am late for the brunch I had to go to and you know none of these useless servants knows how to iron my clothes without burning them except for unfortunately you. Why, girl, what are you still doing here staring at my face? I won't even make it to tomorrow's brunch at this rate. HURRY UP!"

Fehranaz ran as fast as her long slender legs could carry her, and being long and slender, they did enable her to run at quite the pace. She opened Mrs S's room, crossed the dressing table, and went to the walk-in closet next to the toilet. Most people didn't have access to Mrs S's private room; if they did they would be even more awed by her collection and articles of clothing and their meticulous upkeep than even her room!

The closet, or shall I dare to say room, was circular with a white marble-topped console in the centre. Skilful woodwork, glass and marble were the main building blocks of this secret room, which contained drawers for socks, hair clips, watches, sunglasses, and at least six different ones on two sides for jewellery, from the 'casual' Louis Vuitton and Gucci designer items to the diamonds and rubies. Clothes hung on railings in at least fifteen rows all around the room and there were eight separate racks and open cupboards for shoes. There were also open shelves of nail polish, lipstick, hair products, and one must not be sinful in forgetting the handbags. Some were again kept in the open on marble shelves, and to prevent ruin to the most expensive ones, special glass cabinets were constructed to ensure that the handbags received the perfect amount of lighting and were away from ordinary oxygenated air. Of course, upon entering the room, one felt that one was in the boutique store of one's dreams, but being an everyday visitor to this room, it was unable to retain any of its charms for Fehranaz. To her, it was just work, work, work and search, search, search for the correct article or she would suffer the consequences.

She rushed into the room to find that Mrs S had left at least five different outfits at the top of the marble counter; I mean, if Mrs S still hadn't decided on what to wear, then it would be because of her own indecisiveness as opposed to Fehranaz's being in the toilet that she would be late. She picked up the clothes and took them into the laundry room to iron. She was still on the second one when she heard Mrs S's shouts – they were louder than usual and pierced the air with a greater degree of foreboding and, as it was, they were calling out her name.

Fehranaz's first instinct was to shut the laundry room door and pretend that she hadn't heard Mrs S screaming at the top of her lungs, but then, realising that as she would have to face her sooner or later, sooner would be better, since Mrs S hated delays, she sighed and turned the iron off, putting the cashmere shawl as far away from it as possible.

Fehranaz walked back to the living room to see Mrs S flushed and livid with anger. She could see her hands tremble, ready to strike out at the first thing that came in their path; Cook stood next to her with a deviant little smile on her face.

"I AM GOING TO ASK YOU THESE QUESTIONS ONE TIME AND ONE TIME ONLY AND I WILL EXPECT YOU TO TELL ME THE TRUTH. IN FACT, HERE IS THE QURAN. HOLD IT SO THAT I CAN MAKE YOU SWEAR ON IT AND KNOW IF YOU ARE A LIAR ALONG WITH OTHER THINGS."

Fehranaz gulped back a great deal of saliva, afraid of what information Cook had told *bibi gee*; she was sure today would be her last day on this Earth. Nevertheless, her trembling hands managed to hold the Quran. Having done so, she managed to gather enough courage to face her ultimate trial, where the court, plaintiff and judge were all one woman. She looked right into Mrs S's eyes.

"Oh no, no, no! Don't look into my eyes. HOW DARE YOU HAVE THE AUDACITY TO LOOK AT ME SO BOLDLY AFTER EVERYTHING THAT YOU HAVE DONE. Now tell me, have you been getting sick every morning?"

Fehranaz let out a sigh of relief, slightly confused as to why Mrs S would care about her being sick. "Y-y-yes ma'am."

Both Cook and Mrs S exchanged glances. Cook's said 'I told you so' and Mrs S's was more like 'Great! I just can't believe my luck.'

"Well, then, have you been a fool to let that boy touch you? Cook told me that you and him have been up to things not permissible."

Misunderstanding Mrs S's meaning of the word 'touch', or rather the exact intensity associated with the word, Fehranaz looked down at the floor and blushed.

Mrs S stared at her with a gaping mouth for a second and then reached over and smacked her, causing Cook to smile even more.

"Well, you fool! You have got yourself pregnant."

Fehranaz was so shocked that she of course started crying.

"NOW YOU'RE CRYING. YOU SHOULD HAVE THOUGHT ABOUT THIS BEFORE YOU CONSUMMATED YOUR LUST, BEFORE ALL THAT FUN YOU HAD. YOU DIRTY WHORE."

Not taking her eyes off of Fehranaz, she said to the cook, "Tell the boy that his services are no longer required and that if I see him on my premises by afternoon I will call the police. And as for you, young lady, I want you out of my sight! I don't care where you go or what you do, I just want you OUT of this house! After all the time that I have clothed you and fed you and done so much for you. This is what I get in return for bringing you up. I don't forgive such big mistakes, Fehranaz, be they yours or be they mine, so out you go. I will give you a day to pack your things, then I want you gone. I don't want such lewd behaviour to persist under my roof. I don't want you to set an example for my other children, and yet by kicking you out I hope that they will learn I don't tolerate any kind of nonsense."

Fehranaz just kept on weeping; she wanted to protest, wanted to tell the truth, and yet she just couldn't. Fear once again glued her lips firmer than before so she just stood there weeping.

"And please stop this incessant crying, and if you must cry then do it away from my presence." She finally turned to the cook. "I am presuming you will take care of things. I am already late for my brunch." She ran into her room and emerged moments later in an outfit that wasn't among any of the five that she had given Fehranaz to iron.

After her clicking heels could be heard down the hall and outside, Cook, still standing there relishing Fehranaz's moment of misery, turned to her and said, "Serves you right, you little whore." Before leaving the room, she spat on Fehranaz's feet and laughed.

Fehranaz sat there for several minutes contemplating the events of the morning. *Oh Allah! Why are you doing this to me? Why?* Again and again she turned to the skies, in this case the roof, because nothing made sense, and kept weeping. She thought about the devil's spawn growing inside her, of how she was going to take care of herself out on the streets. She thought of her love and how she would never see him again; perhaps when he learned of her condition he would never even want to. She wept and wept, her thoughts oscillating between the baby and the boy with the moustache who she loved until she realised that the only way out was to kill the baby and the only way to kill it was to kill herself. Strangely at peace, she wiped away her tears and thought about getting up.

Cook, unaware what Fehranaz had silently decided, again walked into the drawing room and forcibly lifted Fehranaz.

"Get up, you whore, Mr S is calling you in his study."

"No," screamed Fehranaz, "NOOOOOOOO, I WON'T GO!"

"Ahhh! Even your slut mother will go." Pushing, prodding and dragging Fehranaz, the cook shoved her inside the study, for poor slender Fehranaz was no match for the woman's masculine brute strength.

Mr S sat on his mahogany desk, his glasses perched on his nose, looking like he had just made another deal with the devil.

"Well, good morning beautiful. I haven't seen you in so many days." (Silence.) "I have been waiting for such a long time for the perfect opportunity." (Silence.)

He got off his desk and made his way to Fehranaz. Her eyes were wide with fear and she shook her head, screaming and retreating against the wall, "Nooooooo, nooooo, please, please, NOOOOOOO. I am pregnant."

"I don't care," he said, grabbing her by the throat and forcing her on her knees. "Gently now. We can't afford any tearing of clothes; my wife will be back shortly." He breathed in her hair, relishing her scent.

At that very moment, unknown to the trio (Fehranaz, Mr S, and Cook) Mrs S was just opening the front door. In her angry haste, she had forgotten her wallet. She was about to climb the stairs and would have gone and sat back in the car and driven away had her eye not caught Cook awkwardly hovering outside the study. The large smelly woman kept pacing back and forth in front of the door, scratching her head and muttering about being a secret keeper. Of course, Mrs S couldn't hear the muttering; she just looked on with furrowed eyebrows at Cook and proceeded to walk over to her.

Seeing Mrs S, Cook broke out in a sweat and a very nervous smile. "Mrs S... what are you doing back here so early?"

"Who are you to ask me what I am doing here in my own house? But I will assuredly ask you a question: what are you doing here?"

"I, ummmm…"

"Perhaps it was a bit hard for you to comprehend the first time. What are you doing here?"

Before Cook could answer, Mrs S heard a girl screaming from inside the study. Extremely perplexed now, she proceeded to open the door, when Cook came in between her and the handle and said, "No, *bibi gee*, don't go inside, don't!"

"How dare you? Move out of the way." Without another word, Cook ran into the kitchen as fast as her stout and chubby legs could carry her.

As Mr S was on his knees with his back to the door and had a screaming, crying Fehranaz half-naked in front of him, he didn't hear the door open or his wife's exasperated gasp; he didn't see her grimace of horror so he didn't feel the decoration piece as it went flying over and hit his head. When he eventually came around, boy, how he wished he hadn't.

As soon as Mr S was out cold, Mrs S rushed toward Fehranaz, covered her with her clothes and embraced her, holding her tightly. Fehranaz was too shocked and scared to realise how much of a comfort Mrs S was trying to be; her words were soft, almost soothing. Fehranaz just clutched onto the woman as she had onto her mother at the age of five, and bawled.

Fehranaz was also oblivious of the heaving chest that she held onto and the tears that fell down onto her hair. For what seemed like an hour, both women sat huddled on the study floor, an unconscious Mr S lying in front of them.

They heard his muttering, his nonsensical jabber as he opened his eyes, but neither of the two women assisted him. After all, why would they?

"Whaaa, what happened? My head. OWWWW, MY HEAD."

It took Mr S a couple of minutes to recover from his mild concussion, make a correct assessment of his surroundings and register as reality that his wife was looking at him sternly. Tears streaked down her face, but she was no longer crying; she was merely holding onto a snivelling Fehranaz. He didn't take his wife for the comforting sort, especially the kind who would console the servant girl he had been doing. Yet he had never thought that she would ever find out or that he would even ever do such a thing – letting his lower organ think for his upper 'more' masterful one. He looked at his wife's face for a brief second and the panicking began.

Mrs S disengaged Fehranaz from herself and, holding her wrists, gently looked at her, saying, "Fehranaz, dear, go up and lie in my bed; I will be up shortly. Off you go."

Sense finally took over Fehranaz and without another word or snivel she ran out of the room, leaving the Mr to fend alone against his Mrs. They both stood up; she kept glaring at him with a fiery gaze that would have burnt through a heart of lead and he kept looking down at his shoes, only to realise that his pants were still not drawn up and his member (the object of his shame) lay bare and visible.

He proceeded to pull up his pants and cover his shame when his wife interrupted him; her voice was sharp, cold, and biting. "Oh no, no! Why pull up your pants? Let them be."

Without looking at her, he still continued pulling up the pants, when she interrupted him again. "I said LET THEM BE! After all, we have all been a witness to the sickness that resides in your soul. I always knew you were a sick, demented little man. Did you have no shame? A POOR INNOCENT GIRL YOUNGER THAN YOUR OWN DAUGHTER! I feel filthy even being in the same room as you."

He wanted to protest, but wisely thought to remain silent and dropped his pants again.

"There… much better! I want the world to see your shame… leave it like that."

He wished he was dead rather than going through this, but then realised that he had brought it upon himself and remained silent, as did she.

She thought long and hard before breaking the deathly silence. "You have two choices, Mr S. Either you go outside without your pants and I tell the world what you've done and you remain in society as you are, a shameful horrible man, or you leave home this second without a penny to your person and I still tell people of what you have done. You just won't have to hear what they have to say about you. Oh, yes! And there is a third option. Should you not wish to comply I will call the police and they will arrest your raping disgusting self. You should be glad I gave you three when your disgusting filth doesn't even deserve one."

With that she walked out of the room. Mrs S was standing outside long enough to hear the study door lock and one of the drawers open. Mr S chose the fourth option. Everyone heard the gunshot.

Mrs S paid no heed to it. She just walked up the stairs, into her room, and, weeping, asked Fehranaz to forgive her for not being vigilant enough.

TABLES TURNED?

It was Mrs W's annual garden party; at the rate that these women held parties and consumed tea, you would think that they would be able to fund entire villages, furnish actual schools, and lift hundreds out of poverty, but that's just what you would think. They were just too caught up in their way of life to ever dream of parting with it. Oh, don't get me wrong: they were plenty charitable, but their charity was more like someone throwing off a little of their thickly earned cream as if it was refuse that just needed flicking away. Where the money went, if it was put to good use – in fact, if it was even put to any use – was quite unnecessary! They had done their part and got rid of their share.

The garden party at Mrs W's was one of the most awaited events of the year. Women would have jewellery and outfits made months in advance; some would even travel specifically to Europe to buy the perfectly matching shoes and bag. Everyone who was anyone was invited to the event and if you weren't, well, you just weren't anyone worthy of the circle. Her 'garden' to the rear of the house was more like acres of cultivated land, including a mini golf course, two swimming pools, a maze, a barbeque hub, a tennis court, rows of trees and flowers of every kind, including the imported Japanese cherry blossom trees, rather than a garden. Beautiful white lights lined the trees and the walls, giving an ethereal quality to the flora and fauna. Round tables were laid out, where the name of each guest was carefully and meticulously placed on every table. A stage was erected next to the artificial waterfall and fountain (yes, they were also present in this nightly wonderland) so that the sweet melody playing in the air could be heard in conjunction with the soft flow of water.

At least fifteen buffet tables were laid out and Pakistani, Oriental, and Western food was in abundance. There were at least six different kinds of salads apart from the salad bar, ten different kinds of chicken – grilled, fried, steamed – lamb chops, kebabs, as well as every combination of pasta, vegetables, and Pakistani curry you could imagine. Mrs W would ensure that anything her guests could possibly desire was available.

The food was as much of an attraction to the women as the men, but they were drawn to the event for two other extremely crucial reasons. Firstly, they wanted to make sure that everyone knew they were somebody. Identities in this circle exist only in the eyes of others; the self had no need of self-appreciating. Secondly, and decidedly the more important of the two reasons, they didn't want to be left out of any new gossip that had come around, as everyone knew a great deal of news was always shared at Mrs W's party. After all, just last year everyone found out that Mr E had a second wife and the year before that, that Mrs O's daughter had become pregnant out of wedlock (and I clearly want to point out how everyone referred to the daughter as Mrs O's and not Mr O's offspring, as if only the mother was to blame for her daughter's illegitimate child). Every single female entity was delirious to inquire about this year's breaking news save one person. For once, she sat quietly at the head table, unwilling to create a ruckus or be the centre of all that was happening.

"Why, did you hear she broke off her engagement for the third time?" said Mrs B.

"Tsk, tsk," said Mrs A. "Her poor parents – where are they going to find her a boy the fourth time around!"

"I know!"

"Well, that's why I say girls nowadays need to be taught their cultural values; all this television is getting to their heads," said a piqued up Mrs W; it seemed she was taking up someone else's role of self-righteous affront. "What do you think, Mrs S?"

The oddly quiet woman twirled her glass and licked her lips before replying, still looking at her glass. "Let the damn girl do as she pleases. What's it to me?"

Every single woman exchanged glances; given the circumstances, they had all been surprised that she had actually shown up. Old habits die hard even in the face of disaster and death, and irrespective of how much Mrs S tried to not come to the garden party, she couldn't help herself.

"Hmmm, well, perhaps you're right!" Mrs W was perhaps a little too bashful about involving Mrs S in the conversation.

"Has anyone heard from Ariyana?" asked the kind Mrs J, trying her level best to help Mrs S out of her moment of social scrutiny.

"No," said Mrs B.

"Neither have I," said Mrs A.

"I tried calling her a couple of times. Her phone's off!"

"That's odd," said Mrs J. "Wonder where the poor girl is."

"I spoke to her," interrupted Mrs S, still looking at the cup before looking up at everyone. "I spoke to her a few days back. She wanted to get in touch with some American CEO for her husband. Mrs R knows all about it."

"Oh yes, yes! Well, I never spoke to her directly, Mrs S. I mean, you gave her his number!" Only Mrs J, astute, sensitive Mrs J, noticed Mrs R's flushed colour and made a note of it; she was surprised, in the face of everything else, that Mrs R wasn't her usual biting self. In the wake of Mrs S's tragedy, no one was trying to notice anything else.

"Yes, I did!"

The table broke into an awkward silence after Mrs S's definitive yes. Well, it did until Mrs R could return to her blunt uncontrollable self and break the uncomfortable quiet. "They say they found your husband's body in the water in the sewerage canal. They say it washed up on the side of the banks and even though the face was hideously distorted they could still tell he was your husband."

Mrs S winced slightly; she was still looking at the cup. Mrs J scowled at Mrs R, who merely shrugged her shoulders and haughtily replied, "Don't look at me like that. All of you were dying to bring it up."

"Have some respect for the dead, if not the living," Mrs J tried to rebuke her, but was cut short by Mrs S. The woman had an eerie look on her face that was even less like herself than her uncanny silence. Some people would afterwards say she looked devastated, others that she was almost happy – they each made their assumptions based on the words she said.

"No, it's okay, Mrs J," she said sweetly. "Let her bark. After all, that's what bitches do." She smiled, only to have Mrs R wince this time. Mrs R was in turn almost about to reply when Mrs S raised her hand to silence her. "I assure you I don't care. And as for my husband, if that's what you wish to call him, I have no agony for his departing from this world. I hope he has his soul burnt in the deepest fires of hell. Oh, don't look at me like that! I mean every word I say. I am quiet because I am thinking about my poor thirteen-year-old maid who is pregnant with my husband's child. Yes, he raped her, not once, multiple times. And I hope no one worries for me. I know how to fend for myself. Even if my husband hadn't earned a dime, my father left me a great deal of wealth and, as for that worthless dead man's factories, I have been practically running them, so actually he was an unfortunate worthless weight that had been pulling me down for years. I will be just fine without a rapist under my roof. Does that answer all your questions, ladies? Well, I must say, I want some dessert. Anyone care to join me?"

It took everyone quite a long time to get over the shock of the news, but Mrs J, really a very jolly, empathetic woman, smiled, got up, and said, "You know wherever there is dessert, there I am."

Mrs S hadn't answered all the unspoken questions at the table. How did she find out? What did she do? But most importantly, how did he die and how did the body get into the canal in the first place? One thing is for sure: no one dared to ask Mrs S ever again or to challenge her in a game of words, not even Mrs R.

WINE AND CHEESE

AND SO THERE came that point in the year when the 'sisters' loaded their cars with their belongings and journeyed over to their President's vineyard in Temecula. Arzoo sat in the convertible with the President, hair flowing and skin tanned under the warm Californian sun. They had become unlikely friends, both quite different in their unique approaches and etiquettes of life and yet attracted to each other due to the magnetism within and beauty without; they established a bond of recognising an equal in the other.

Arzoo's other best girlfriend, Charlotte, didn't like this sudden shift in affiliations and felt that the President, with her luxurious lifestyle and extravagant ways, was luring Arzoo into the same superficial material trap that Arzoo had been trying to desperately rid herself of. Yet, Arzoo was never one to listen to her; to her, her best friend was envious because she couldn't let loose as she was too constricted by her insipid lacklustre paradigm of life.

"How is the boyfriend?"

"I am sorry. I can't hear you?"

"I said how is Ian?"

"Oh! He is great!" She smiled. It was hard to hear each other over the wind that rapped up against their eardrums, cancelling out all other noise except for its roar, and as it was getting chilly, Arzoo shouted out to her associate, requesting her to close the roof.

The President was exiting the freeway and, also feeling the 7pm wind, readily acquiesced to Arzoo's appeal. They were pulling up into Temecula and, to be quite honest, Arzoo was greatly disappointed. Napa Valley, the artificial replica of the real wine country, did not impress her, and yet she

293

knew it mattered not where you were but who you were with and with the company that she was with, things were bound to get electrifying.

"Water polo players really are great," said the President, winking. Of course she was having a little covert shenanigan with the captain of the team. "Such perfect abs, no?"

"Oh, definitely!" replied Arzoo, though she would've loved to have pointed out that other than having the flawlessly crunched six pack, the immaculately lifted biceps, and the exemplary tight little ass, Ian, with his blue eyes and unkempt long blond hair, also had the most pristine face. Arzoo bit her lip and failed to bring forth what was obvious to most of her sorority's female population because she did not wish to incur any disfavour with the President (especially by comparing their men), having just recently been brought into the elite girl fold.

"Well," said the President, playing on her iPhone while trying to maintain an eye on the road – a fact that most texters on the road fail to understand is one of those things that can never be possible until and unless they devise a way for people to have two sets of eyes – "I believe they might be joining us for an after-dinner party." She now turned to Arzoo and winked again.

Considerably roused, Arzoo smirked back. "Who are 'they'?"

"Chi Omega Lambda Pi Sigma."

"Oooooooo, yes," replied Arzoo, "it would make the trip so much more fabulous." Arzoo was indeed looking forward to a weekend retreat with the girls but believed that an excess of testosterone was the only viable ingredient to calm down the inverse reaction between an abundant proliferation of oestrogen and vice versa.

"But shhhh, don't tell the other girls. You know how they get much too self-conscious or try and act overly drunk and stupid, knowing that boys will be coming over. I want them to be themselves when the boys magically emerge – smart, witty, and thoroughly attractive, not slobbering drunks just waiting to get laid." Arzoo knew exactly what she meant and could never appreciate a woman who thought that belittling herself by trying to appear dumb was attractive to a man. "Let's just surprise them."

The second they pulled up at the vineyard, a number of cars were already parked and girls stood outside in shorts and cute tops taking pictures on their iPhones. Arzoo and the President joined them and, baring the 'skinny arm', half of them did the sorority squat and took a big group picture. "TUMECULA!" Quite their sorority's Kodak moment – too bad Arzoo's best girlfriend condescendingly thought that she was too above everyone else to be a part of the festivities. She ought to get off of her high palm tree and come down where the shade was!

The girls made their way into the house for a deliciously prepared meal and, of course, wine. Being a red wine girl, Arzoo drank some of the finest of the President's fairly recently-established vineyard. She did mix it up with some cheese and bread, always having a voracious appetite for cheese. She never liked to admit it but in an odd way it made her think of home: wholesome and dairy.

As the girls were still eating and conversation started getting louder and falsely happier as the escalation in the drinking got greater, getting woozy and still a bit tired from the drive, Arzoo decided to take a short little nap and went up to her assigned room, as the President's roommate, and flung herself on the bed, unconscious in the dreamless sleep that wine can conjure.

She woke up to the sound of clatter. It took her a minute to familiarise herself with her strange environment and recall that the reason she wasn't back in her room at Stanford was because she was at a winery. Arzoo then attempted to make out the source of the noise and opened the bathroom door to find the President standing in a gold shimmery dress, her long legs looking resplendent standing over the counter – a dollar bill lay scrolled up in her hand and she appeared to be snorting a line of white stuff, evidently cocaine, into her nose. Perhaps Charlotte wasn't too far off.

Arzoo stood at the door for about thirty seconds before coughing in order to draw attention to herself. The President pushed back her blonde hair, awkward about the fact that Arzoo had caught her, and then said with a smile, "Oh! You are awake. Well, that was just some Adderall. Gives a kick with the wine."

"Sure," replied Arzoo, taking her clothes off and walking straight to the shower. The President looked at Arzoo, distracted momentarily by the way her body curved around the edges in a way she had never seen a white body do, and then exclaimed, "Arzoo." Arzoo shut off the shower. "Okay, I am sorry. It was coke and I know I shouldn't be doing it, but it's so hard to deal with my parents' divorce and—" The President burst out crying and Arzoo, naked and wet, leapt out of the shower to give her a hug. The President did indeed realise that the curves were as much fun to hold as they were to look at and after Arzoo broke off the hug, she wiped away the tears that had formed so as not to ruin the rest of her mascara and whispered, "Just please don't tell anyone."

Arzoo nodded. "I would never," she said, and went back into the shower. She emerged moments later downstairs in a short fitted red dress that hugged those admirable curves and accentuated her equally long gorgeous legs. She slowly crept downstairs in her Jimmy Choos and was welcomed into the world of chaos; as the Greeks would say, "What a shit show!"

The immaculately clean house was now converted to Satan's den with all the furniture turned upside down. Clearly the boys had arrived and, other than the bar, where the alcohol bottles, like pillars and sacraments of worship, were kept whole in spite of their brittle nature, everything else just seemed to have deteriorated in the two or three hours she had napped and showered. People were grinding up against walls and seemed to be drunk to the third degree of drunk – that of a fool.

Well, she thought, with a shudder at the crass and uncouth manners of the so-called Greeks, *if the boys are here then that means so is Ian.* She was scanning the room and saw him perched against a counter, drinking his beer, warding off all the girls that approached him until he too spotted his queen bee and smiled.

They walked over to each other, grinning, the rest of the world becoming a background to their assessment of each other. Eyes, ears, bodies were attuned to nothing but each other's passionate frequencies and then they were in each other's arms and mouths.

"Hello, beautiful!"

She blushed and spoke through fluttered lashes, "Hi."

He twirled her before kissing her again, biting her juicy lower lip.

"Do you want to get out of here?"

"Sure," she smiled.

He practically picked her up and walked out into the back garden. The noise and suffocation evaporated as the calm serene night welcomed them. He ran back in and came back with another bottle of wine, red of course, and two glasses.

"Beautiful night, isn't it?"

"Ah yes! The moon looks so big. I wonder why that always seems to happen in California."

"It's a special world."

"Yes. It is."

"So you never told me if you were planning on staying here after school was over or if you were going back. I mean, it is senior year."

"I am staying." She turned toward him. "I am probably never going to go back. I never fitted in that world, try as hard as I would. I don't belong there. I mean how can I, when all I am expected to do is change?"

"Hmmmm." He kissed her. "Wine?"

"Yes!"

He poured her a glass and Arzoo was drinking before she felt something in her mouth. It felt like some small metallic little thingamajig in the cup. Well, she was right, she thought, upon visually surveying the glass. It was small and metallic but it was a ring!

Ian got down on one knee. Arzoo felt everything happen in slow motion, from the moment she found the ring to the moment she finally had the courage to look him in the eye – him on one knee on the ground. It was as if time had unwound its stringent adherence to being punctual and instead decided to lag and prolong the moment till Arzoo felt she would go crazy.

He, on the other hand, smiled and said, "I love you, Arzoo. Would you want to belong here with me?"

In that one minute he had said the magical words, the words that she had wanted to hear, and time once again picked up its pace, along with the beating of her heart, and without thinking her mouth opened, her tongue rolled back and she whispered, "Yes."

Everything was silent before he leapt up and, picking her up in his arms, took her inside. He placed her on the counter and stood on top of it, announcing his recent victory to the world. "Ladies and gentlemen. I have an announcement to make. Arzoo and I just got engaged." For a split second, the seniors all stared at each other, unable to grasp the possibility of such a young engaged couple at Stanford; but social expectations quickly overcome shock and as they all plastered on fake smiles and ran over to give their drunken congratulations, they never got to tell Arzoo how young she was and how unprepared for a life with Ian – well, especially with someone like Ian.

That night, after the most passionate lovemaking ever, as Arzoo lay in bed, a troubling thought entered her head. Was she really doing what was right? In her attempt to escape a society of falsehood and deceit, was she merely accepting a lie just in the desperation for her soul to belong somewhere, anywhere? But then Ian woke up and as he snuggled next to her, she could feel his smooth chest, feel his eyes poring down on her with an intensity that implied he still wasn't done and as she sat on top of him this time, straddling him with a smirk, all practical thoughts were lobotomised.

WORDS MAKETH A WOMAN

THERE COMES A point in your life when you come to find out that all that you know and hold to be true isn't – most of it is a sham and your mind, the little trickster, has been shamelessly lying to convince you and, above all, repeatedly affirming to you that your reality is the only reality. But then that point comes when you realise that people actually think and feel differently than you do. They are not an extension of the thoughts and the actions that you ascribe to them but the welders of an entirely new construction. Mrs S, for instance, had no idea that her husband, the biggest portion of her identity, wasn't as she had thought he was. He wasn't the quiet, demure man who continuously erred and who let his wife berate him into being whole and good again. Perhaps he had always been the frustrated, angry, sly man who could rape a thirteen-year-old right under her nose, for he was intermittently frugal with her money and had a poor head for both business and company, and perhaps these errors, which she would attribute to an unresolved childhood, were products of a darker, sinister soul. She had misjudged, irrespective of the fact that everyone would mould themselves to her wishes and commands (it was only superficially, for not just her husband but her children and the other servants always did as they pleased in hiding). Time would not even artificially lend itself to be manipulated; what was done was done and could never be undone – no, not even by her. So Mrs S made a resolution to amend the sin that her husband had committed by assuring the receiver of that injustice, Fehranaz, every sort of consolation that was imaginable. For the first time, Mrs S's motives arose out of a truly conscientious and kind spirit, one whose motives weren't blurred and tainted by her bigoted self-view but were truly capable of providing

299

Fehranaz any sort of comfort and maternal love that the latter needed. Granted, there was one thing Mrs S still didn't know about.

Mrs S had stopped the wagging tongues, she had increased her respect in society by tenfold, she was now the chair of the company (which invariably now meant an increase in productivity and profits for not only her but all the shareholders), she had even prevented her children from knowing the truth about their father, and even if they would blame her and her austere hand for it, she still managed to gather the strength to withstand their doubt and hurt. Mrs S bore all this and Fehranaz, no matter how much of a victim, still had been the perpetrator of the greater change in Mrs S's life. However, there was a catch – Mrs S would not let Fehranaz abort the baby. Of course, many people had suggested it, but she was going to refuse. The child was on its way to inception and even if it was in the process of being created, she felt that it was already alive, and life, like death, mustn't be taken for granted.

Gradually Mrs S became quite maniacally obsessed with keeping Fehranaz under her eye – afraid that some wrong would come to her and the baby by either the other servants or her own neglected and outraged children. She consented to Fehranaz still taking care of Mrs S's own youngest baby and even agreed to the cook's boy coming back for work as long as Fehranaz would accompany her, Mrs S, to each and every committee party. The cook's boy had been initially outraged by Fehranaz's showing belly and would refuse to speak to her, but on learning the truth felt a passion so dear that it ripped at his soul, gnawed at his heart, brought forth tears in his eyes; and if Mr S hadn't already been dead, he would have made sure that the old lecher was. Thus, Fehranaz and the cook's boy resumed their romance, never really talking and embracing, just looking and loving.

Yet, embarrassed by the child growing inside her, Fehranaz started wearing extremely loose clothes, a sight that was quite comical, since except for her belly, nothing else was protruding or had lost any of its perfection, and even if she assented to accompanying Mrs S, she would bring the baby and would stand or sit in the corner or retreat to where the servants of the house were. Of course, such evasion wouldn't have kept the slithering tongues from gossiping, but Mrs S's calm demeanour and meaningful glances surely did. Party after party passed with no important change to be noted except at Fehranaz's tenth committee party at, surprisingly, Maya's Lahore house.

"Mrs K, you have done such a good job!"

"Oh, yes, so refined and... simple." Mrs W was highly envious of the fact that Mrs K's summer Lahore house was more elaborate than her actual house and to belie her envy she used the word 'simple', which was perhaps the biggest insult any Pakistani woman can give another.

Mrs K ignored this atrocity – this blatant disregard of her interior décor – and instead turned to her best friend, Mrs N, and softly whispered, "Have you heard from Arzoo yet?"

"No. Not yet. It has been days since she's called us and she won't return our calls. I am really worried."

"I told you we made a mistake in letting our daughters go abroad to study. I told you. That's why my husband and I aren't sending Maya back. She doesn't deserve it."

"I don't know," replied Mrs N, still unaware that education could be the root of rebellion and wilful spirits, "I don't know."

Everyone's attention was at this moment diverted as Maya entered the room – she looked exceptionally beautiful in the long spring dress she was wearing. Parental pressure and abuse had caused her to lose weight and none of the observers, save Mrs S and Mrs N, could tell why they found her so alluring all of a sudden. She pulled off grief really well, with style, grace, and a head held high. She came in and sat next to her mother-in-law; her mother's eye, ever watchful and stern, rooted itself on her, making sure that she behaved with decency and propriety. Even when she would be talking to all those around her, that one eye would rotate 360 degrees, never fixating on anything but Maya and her mother-in-law's facial expression. I do assure you, the eye was also apt and skilled in lip reading and midway during the tea party Mrs K was satisfied with Maya's dutiful performance, after which she could finally devote all her attention and, yes, both her eyes to the guests and their needs.

After what seemed like an immeasurable lapse of time between pouring her mother-in-law tea, bringing food from the table for the elder woman for the fifth time, and chatting nonstop about how lovely her son was – Maya did this not because of her parents, but because she found the older lady quite a jovial, simple soul – she felt like she would suffocate and faint in between the jarring laughter and screeches of the women. She was anxious to retreat into her world – into the world of knowledge and higher ideals, not pettiness and catty games of social fitness. Luckily, the eating part was over and as the women retired into the drawing room, Maya could tell from her mother's slightly less brusque stance that she was pleased with the evening's turnout and she excused herself from the 'chitchat festivities' to her room. She was preoccupied with a memory, a memory that went a long way back and one that had recently been her only consolation in all this madness.

"Were you trying to read?" said Maya, pushing back her pigtails. Arzoo was running out in the mud with Nile, his friends, and all the guests' sons. Maya, being the only girl (Arzoo with her short hair and dungarees didn't quite qualify), just couldn't understand the point of getting dirty when one could just snuggle indoors and let one's mind escape. So, distraught with the possibility of mud smearing her new dress, little ten- almost eleven-year-old Maya came to her bookshelf to find a little five-year-old staring at the cover of Harry Potter and the Chamber of Secrets, trying to make sense of the words.

The little girl nodded.

"Really? You can read English?" said Maya, amazed.

"Yes ma'am, yes I can a little bit know the alphabet and Mrs S sends me to school sometimes, but then I couldn't."

"Oh, that's okay," said Maya.

"Yes, but I always watch TV with the children and read their homework books when they are asleep and sit with their tutors, hearing what they have to say. I am not great, but I can pass, I can understand a fair amount."

Maya looked at her with an odd curiosity. "Do you like to read?"

"Yes, Maya bibi," replied Fehranaz, nodding her head, flushed and smiling, "I do very much."

Maya thought for a second, just a split second, and being one of those who did not let contentment or class frown upon an ailing hand, leapt at the chance of passing on love, happiness, and above all, knowledge. Since that day, whenever Fehranaz accompanied Mrs S to her frequent skirmishes around town, she and Maya would sneak around and hide in a corner, indulging their guilty pleasures in many kinds of knowledge. But stories, they were always Fehranaz's favourite part. As they entered worlds with men with antlers and some with pointy teeth, women on brooms and soldiers with arrows, their own world with its Mr S's, cousin-fiancés, strict parents, and unapproachable employers was always forgotten.

Maya thought for a split second about how even though she couldn't return to the scholastic walls of her beloved Harvard, she had used her already gained knowledge to help someone else, even if that person was just one little, now pregnant girl. Knowledge is supposed to be shared and in that brief moment, Maya had found the perfect time utiliser of most of her locked-up pre-planned existence at the mansion. Her life was verbatim of her mother's desires; each movement from school to piano lessons and biking required the following of and adherence to a strict rulebook, which undoubtedly always must be obeyed. Fehranaz was the only little secret that she would keep. So when little ten-year-old Maya said to Fehranaz, "I believe I will teach you whenever it is possible – I will teach you all that I know," and both girls smiled, finding a friend in the strangest of circumstances, Maya would never truly know whom she would help more.

Maya was in such a rush to get to her room that she almost missed Fehranaz standing next to the bookshelf outside her room. Fehranaz was holding an English novel, *The Chronicles of Narnia: The Voyage of the Dawn Treader,* and straining over one of the pages, running her finger under the lines and trying desperately to read.

"Hey," said Maya. "I am sorry if I kept you waiting."

Fehranaz got so afraid that it was Mrs S or one of the committee women that in her moment of panic she dropped the book, nearly knocking over a shelf and then, flustered and even more upset, strived to pick up the books, accidentally knocking down another shelf.

She would have perhaps knocked down the entire case had Maya not reached out and, touching Fehranaz's shoulders, calmed her, saying, "Oh my God! No, please don't worry about it. No, seriously, Fehranaz, here, I will do it. Oh my God, and you are pregnant. Don't bend too much. I don't know if one can when one is in this child-bearing state." After she had convinced Fehranaz to stand up, Maya put the books back and got up, smiling at the girl, remembering her the way she always did – a dedicated pupil of knowledge.

"No matter how many times I read it, C. S. Lewis makes me feel so enchanted."

"Yes. He does engross you, doesn't he?" Maya lost her thought and instead thought of the pain and humiliation that Fehranaz would go through every day; she was Maya's pupil and, as every good educator knows, her teacher as well. Being a generous soul, she wished to ease some of her grief and so was thinking of the best possible way to do so. "Hmmm. Fehranaz, I was wondering, perhaps we should..." It had been quite a while since she had seen Fehranaz and what Maya was going to say was that perhaps they should enlighten Mrs S about their veiled pact and make Fehranaz's meetings a regular matter. Well, as is the case of those with long lives (or so they say in sub-continental proverbial terms: you mention them and there they are), Mrs S arrived right on cue.

"There you are, Fehranaz. I have been looking all over for you. You had me worried sick and the baby won't stop crying" (And then she noticed Maya.) "Oh, hello dear! You look lovely in that dress. I must say, everyone found you looking even more unbelievably gorgeous than usual. Is that designer or your mother's tailor? *Jaan*, why are you looking at me like that?"

"It is because I must tell you something," said Maya, with such an air of regal importance that Mrs S stopped her jabbering and said, "Yes, please do go on!"

Fehranaz, terrified that she would lose all favour with Mrs S once she found out that she too had been conducting secret meetings behind her back, stared at Maya with a harrowed expression of dread, begging her to not disclose the truth, but Maya ignored her, knowing that Fehranaz needed support now more than ever.

"Aunty, I think we should confess something. I have been secretly teaching Fehranaz for more than ten years now and I forced her to undertake an oath to not disclose it to anyone, for you know how my mother is about disturbed schedules; well, I think it is time that we come clean with it. My mother no longer cares about such a minor deviation from the course she has set for me and so you remain our only obstacle. No. No. Please let me finish. Before you interrupt me I will tell you that Fehranaz is an avid reader, has close to a photographic memory, quickly remedies her mistakes, does more work than I ask her, and what is most important, she listens, and her capabilities are equal to a ninth grader right now. Pretty soon she will be a lawyer or a dentist and—"

"So that's how you knew how to select the DVDs and put the children's books in order. I always wondered." Fehranaz was looking at the floor – she was too devastated to look up. To Maya, "Of course I agree, child, in fact, thank you! You are a magnanimous person. May Allah bless you always. I wonder why I didn't think of this before. It would both benefit Fehranaz and reduce her loneliness, and quite frankly her dependence on me."

Yes. I suppose anyone can have a change of heart and the day that Fehranaz became a woman, she had no notion that the woman whose hand haunted her dreams would be the one to lift her up and out of the trench that had ensnared her, let alone be the one who would be the ultimate means of her deliverance.

As she trailed off, both girls looked at each other, thankful, eyes shining and hearts fluttering with new strings of hope, ready to embark on the mysteries of words and companionship.

THE VILLAGE SOLACE

IN A STORY full of people not possessing the prized male paraphernalia, it would be only fair if one such individual monopolising the asset was given a voice. His name is Nile. He is twenty years old, the sole brother of Laila and Maya and, unlike them, very much still a virgin – in terms of not just the body but in his understanding of himself. You might remember him playing FIFA, high out of his mind, and as both his sisters perceived falsely, without a care in the world.

Lahore is a city emanating life, culture, and history, but sometimes, like the River Ravi, which runs in the heart of it, Lahore too becomes inundated with the babble and hubbub that can, for a while, be a part of its charm. The hustle and bustle of the crowds, the bartering shrieks of the hawkers, the cries of the children straddled on the hips of the women zigzagging in between the vehicles, the profanities barked out of the rickshaw and toward the donkey cart, whose owner lashes his anger out on the poor beast, the clash of fists striking air and vibrating empty threats, the honks of the horns honking away, creating a most jarring synchronised pitch, the pleas of the mendicants – the heroin addicts, the crazies, and the ones who was genuinely maimed and marred. Noise, noise, clamour, clamour. Yes, Lahore was teeming with 'life' and also pollution and chaos and a general neglect of humanity. Yet it was home.

I had grown up in the city amid all this clamour and clatter. It was what I knew, what I had always known. Why, then, did I feel so lost as I drove through these busy streets? I had everything – friends, family, and everything any twenty-year-old could want or possibly need since they were sixteen: a PlayStation, a car, a flat-screen TV. Really, the people squabbling and arguing on the streets would peacefully accept and reside within my life were they given the chance to exchange my person with theirs. The only thing I had that kept me alive throughout my teen years was my music, and yet my parents thought that that was a waste of time, a blatant abuse of the 'time', 'energy', and 'MONEY' they had invested in my future and me. Music, they thought, was for the weak, and I had to take on the family business, and in order to do so I must do well in my school (that was by far the first and most crucial step in the formation of a profitable future).

Straight As in O levels was now the parents' broken fantasy – actually even mostly Bs would have sufficed, since a practical worldly man should not get too obliterated in books and the fantasy they present – good enough grades in A levels, a wonderful résumé of college, football captain, cricket team co-captain, official school debating team member (the list of extracurricular activities can be variably elongated based on his parents' (Mr and Mrs K's) expectations so we move on to the next item in the list of expectations)*, a good school – preferably an Ivy and if not the top three, then the esteemed UPENN – marriage to a society elitist daughter, and of course taking on the mantle of the family business and being trapped in an endless cycle of others' expectations and demands.*

I wanted to scream and ask them, what about me? What about what I want? Where was my say in the formulation of this perfect existence? The more I convinced myself that this was what my destiny was – it had been foretold by my parents before my birth – the less I believed in it. I had every 'thing' any of these squatters and beggars desired. I suppose the pollution is always darker where you are standing. I did have everything, but why then did I still feel as if in between all this pandemonium of city life, my voice ceased to be?

Nile was the youngest and perhaps most spoilt of the three siblings and yet, contrary to what his sisters believed, he clearly wasn't without his share of predicaments and parental expectations – perhaps some of the very few troubles with being a part of a family that valued society above all. All the women in the house were slowly beginning to corrode; their grievances were beginning to take a hold of the atmosphere in the house until it became too claustrophobic for Nile to even breathe. No. He wanted life and not to be dragged down with them on their path to complete annihilation. It wasn't that he was selfish; he wasn't. Other than that outburst that he had had on Maya upon fearing that his mother had died, he cared deeply about his sisters and was disgusted to his core with what was happening to them.

That's perhaps why he wanted to leave so desperately; he couldn't stand it all anymore. When he packed up his bags and left, Mr and Mrs K hardly paid note; they were too busy in other endeavours, primarily the regret of having daughters.

November 15, 2008, was an extremely significant day, for it's the day that I finally decided I had to leave Lahore. My family had broken apart and had lost any semblance of sanity that they had retained; my mother had recently tried to kill herself, my older sister was about to kill herself (or, God forbid, I was going to be actually asked to kill her), and my eldest sister was just plain missing. In short, I had to get the hell out of Lahore; I wasn't about to stagnate in the mental institution of our walled fortress. My parents had too much on their hands to be worried about me for once, and even if they were disappointed, unlike how they treated my sisters, they couldn't stop me from what I desired to do. So I decided to travel to the little village where my cook had been brought up, up in the north of Pakistan. That village may be my cook's home town today, but three generations ago, it is where my grandfather came from and where our huge family 'haveli', or home, still stands. He left the bliss and peace of the natural state of man for the deceptive promise of wealth and power in the city and now I, tired of the latter, was retracing his steps to go back to where I actually belonged.

It was a tiny remote village with hardly any cell coverage. Being the SMS enthusiast that I was, my fingers were paradoxically keen to not be drumming away on the keypad of the phone. For once, I desired to be free of the innate human reaction, or at least mine, to immediately respond to a text.

My cook's family had been generous to take me in while we opened up the family home and in spite of my constant offers of paying them a handsome sum for their hospitality, their decision remained unmoved. It was good to find somewhere in this increasingly homogenous world where the prospect of money had not yet overcome the ancient mores and proprieties. After all, he was Maya's dai gee's brother and upon leaving our employment, she too had come to the village and our reunion was a sweet one.

I arrived when it was still light and after having a fulfilling meal of 'desi', or unprocessed foods, which my hosts (mostly Dai gee) had generously prepared, I went outside and sat down with a cup of warm milk, trying to contemplate what I had to do next as the sun started its long evening dance with the Hindu Kush. Nothing. The word reverberated inside my head. It touched the tip of my tongue but silently rolled and floated through my mouth and echoed in my ears. *The delicious sweetness of having nothing to do sent a jolt of excitement through me. There was no TV, so no movie that I had to see in order to kill time, there wasn't anyone that I had to meet to fulfil my social obligations, there was no game lying around that would keep my body in a state of anxiety without any actual exercise. In short, there was nothing that I 'had' to do. In fact, there wasn't even an air conditioner, quite an essential luxury within a Pakistani home environment; there was just the cool November breeze that was blowing through my hair.*

As I lay there on the grass, I closed my eyes, shutting out some of the light from the sun. I felt the blades of grass brushing against my fingers and I listened to the crickets, birds rustling in the trees and even the wind brushing as it travelled over the distant mountains and into the valley. We rely so much on our eyes, our deceitful eyes, which show us beauty, but always from a distance as onlookers, not as part of an organic whole. For the first time, I wasn't merely seeing but I was also feeling life. I realised that that's why I had always been pulled to Arzoo as a child; she was a force of nature so full of life that like a hurricane, her being, unbridled and free, took up all in its path, much like it had me.

The thought dawned on me that I might have found peace, but still no purpose. I remembered what Mother had done just two days before. How could she possibly have such an inherent disrespect for life? I then thought of Maya. (Nile wasn't yet aware of Laila's impending divorce.) I wish I hadn't let my temper take control and physically hurt her. In the heat of the moment the thought of losing my mother was blinding me and Maya seemed like the most susceptible target of my despondent fury. I still didn't mean to hurt her, and it was only while I lay in the grass that I felt the emotional pain my blows must have wrought upon her. She was already going through the hardest ordeal in her life, a predicament that no twenty-one-year-old should go through, which her parents should protect her from, not further aggravate. I felt ashamed at giving her more pain and had been still too ashamed to apologise.

My apology may not have given her much condolence and yet at least it would have been significant in letting her know that I was emotionally with her. I was a coward before I left, but perhaps I might find the courage here to do so.

Thinking about my family was too painful so I instead pondered over the issues I passively perceived every day: the din of the beggars, the neglected and the abused in Lahore, and in my reverie I realised that I was meant to make a difference. I opened my eyes. The sun was slowly creeping up, spilling colour into the sky just as hope was slowly spilling into me. I was going to be my people's future. In between the silence of the village, I had acknowledged their pleas and their cries and I knew I was going to start by rebuilding this village. I found my voice. It was no longer the sounds of my parents' commands, of society's laughter and wagging fingers, of the haughty temperaments of my high-achieving sisters and the jeering taunts of my friends. It was the sound of my heart that was determined to stay in this village and give to the people an equal opportunity to survive. I knew that the villagers were already happier than those who had the opportunities, but must be at least introduced to the basic rights of education and freedom to choose who their local politician was. It was the sound of my soul that had finally understood the meaning of its existence and had realised what it had missed. It is perhaps the most lyrical sound, the sound of yourself as it reaches into you and reassures you, harmonising you with you.

I thought of Maya again; perhaps it was Dai gee constantly asking me about her or perhaps it was my own guilt, and then I thought of calling my father and telling him what I had decided.

WHY DAUGHTERS?

IT HAD BEEN almost eight days since Laila had left her husband – well, it would be eight if you counted the hours she walked around in a shocked daze that night, surprisingly unmolested, with her two Louis Vuitton suitcases in tow. When she had been standing there telling her husband it was over, she had never felt more powerful in her life. The walk had reduced some of the initial exhilaration and as she walked along quiet streets and streets full of men smoking heroin or hashish, she would shudder and wonder if she had done the right thing. There was even a moment when she actually thought she should turn around. And yet doubt is an interesting emotion – it can either make you regret your decision or only give you further faith in it. The more doubt Laila had, the more she kept thinking about the reasons for her decision and the more she contemplated her own abuse, and even more so, the abuse and the demeaning treatment that Maya was going through just because she didn't want to marry someone that she thought wouldn't be a suitable life partner. It was Maya's choice; it was her life, her parents weren't going to live with the cousin, Maya would! And if she just didn't see happiness there then why couldn't they just all wish for her happiness? Just because of what society would say? Just because she was a girl and she and the family reputation would be tarnished because, in spite of the fact that men make all the rules, it is a woman's actions only that have an effect on the family honour, no? Just because they thought he was a better match and because they were older, their experience trumped Maya's own knowledge of herself? NO. NO. NO. Maya would not have to suffer; she, Laila, would give her a way out. At least one of them would have the chance for happiness.

Laila had finally reached her friend's house. She stood outside, staring at the modest house. Her friend wasn't as wealthy but had the most prosperous mind and opulent soul that she knew of. In art school, when her own family would be busy in the preparation of dinners and committees and political rallies, she would come to her friend's house and listen to her grandmother talk of how great the world was before the British partitioned India and Pakistan; they would spend hours eating, talking, and most of all, painting. Her friend, perhaps not as skilled as Laila, was the only other person who understood the kind of silence required when the brush is in one's hand. Naturally, Laila's parents never understood what art was or how one must pay one's due respect when riding the wave of creation. As long as their daughter smiled, looked pretty, and had made a handsome match, that's all that they cared for. After all, a daughter's most prevalent role was to marry well and make her parents proud in front of society. When you see parents in Lahore with their heads held high, you are right in assuming that their daughters have rich husbands to whom they are good wives.

Laila picked up her phone and dialled her friend's number. She didn't pick up. Laila called again but she didn't pick up again. The third time her friend didn't pick up, Laila started panicking, remembering that her friend was an excruciatingly annoying deep sleeper. However, by about the thirty-first call, her friend picked up and Laila heard a groggy voice on the other end of the receiver.

"H-H-H-HELLOOOO…"

"Hi!"

"Laila, is that you?"

"No, it's death from your painting; I am calling to tell you that you did such a horrible job at depicting me that I am here to collect you."

"Don't be stupid. What's up? Are you okay? What time is it?"

"I am fine! It's 5.30!"

"Are you okay? How come you called me so late? Wait, is that a car I just heard?"

"Yeah."

"Wait, where are you, Laila?"

"I have been standing outside your house for thirty minutes. I left my husband."

I don't know if it was out of shock or pure joy, but Laila's friend screamed so loud that not only did Laila's eardrum almost break and she consequently put the phone down, but also the entire house woke up. Her friend ran down the stairs to open the gate and find Laila standing with two LV suitcases in her hand and with a mixture of amusement, relief, and slight anxiety on her face, looking more magnificent than ever.

Laila ended up staying at her friend's house for two days. She had initially planned on calling her parents the next day but realised that her decision had left her emotionally vulnerable and she needed to collect her strength and fortify her emotional base around the newly empowered woman that she had recently come in touch with. Her friend's loving family was more than supportive, pleased with Laila's decision and applauding her courage. They shut themselves off from the world for those two days and the entire family focused on helping Laila. Her friend's grandmother's cooking did more than give her stability; it was the necessary sustenance of the soul to make her feel like she could stand on her own two feet. The love she got in that humble house among those truly God-fearing people in a week, she had never even received from her mother in her own house, let alone her husband's, and over time the happiness that her soul was being nourished with made Laila realise that she had indeed made the right decision. She had listened to her heart and soul and fought for herself; the universe was undoubtedly going to reward her for her unnecessarily elongated suffering and consequent patience. Honeymoons, like all moments, must end too. And after those two days of healing and isolation from the outside world, Laila was beginning to feel that she was infringing too much upon their kind generosity and support; she realised it was time to go home.

In spite of their incessant pleas that she stay longer, she waved them goodbye and asked them for one last favour – to take her to her parents' house. Her friend's father offered to do so and it was only when she was nearing her own cold, unwelcoming yet grand mansion that Laila remembered she had left her husband in the midst of a family crisis, that those two days would have been an eternity for Maya, given her predicament. Yet Laila knew she could not have showed up at her family house on the very night they were reeling from disappointment with Maya. Laila knew they would have only hardened their resolve against Maya's lover, thinking that Maya's intransigence had motivated Laila to up and leave her husband.

Her friend's father interrupted Laila's thoughts. He had stopped the car a little further away from the house and turned to speak to her.

"Laila, *beti*, what I am going to say to you is because I actually think of you as my daughter."

"*Gee gee* uncle, you are like my father. Whatever you say, I hold it as very dear to myself."

"Well, *beta*! I don't know exactly how to say this, but the decision you made was one that involved a great deal of courage and true honour. Now I don't know if it was the right one, for I don't know how your life events will pan out, but I know you followed your heart and that's something many people much older than you don't have the fortitude to grasp or the resolve to carry through. To me, *beti*, you are right."

"*Shuk—*"

"I am not done yet. I have seen you since you were a wee little thing to this remarkable, beautiful young woman. That means I also know your family. I know what they're like and I know they won't take kindly to your action. In fact, they'll be horrified; they will use every means possible to coerce you, dear, and more than that they will make you go back and I know that your husband, as socially conscious as them, will take you back. I am not saying your parents don't love you, Laila, all parents do, their instincts and love are just too manipulated by society and people's expectations, but," he said, turning around to pat her head, "but you must stay strong. Don't give in. You are above this. You have always been above this. Know that when you set about such a laudable change, you can't turn back. Good luck, *beti*. Our prayers are with you."

Tears trickled down Laila's cheeks and as she realised that it wasn't appropriate to hug him, she gave him a very meaningful glance and said, "*Shukriya** uncle, I can't even begin to tell you how much in your debt I am. I am so ashamed."

"Oh no, no! Laila, you are our *beti*. Don't embarrass me by thanking me. We are always here for you."

With that he drove up to the massive iron gates and honked, waiting for the security to verify the car and let it in. He drove up to the driveway and said *khuda hafiz*. She replied with a *khuda hafiz* and, heaving a deep sigh, gathered her nerves, ready to deliver the news that would forever change her relations with her parents.

Laila opened the big mahogany doors and stepped into the grand

---

* Thank you.

entrance; her house was even more hushed and uninviting than usual. It almost seemed as if all life was muffled and deliberately prevented from existing. There was just an uneasy gloom that had shadowed the marble floors, the Persian rugs, the wooden consoles, and the grand twin stairs. There wasn't even any sound of the servants gossiping. Where was everyone?

Just then, one of the maids emerged from the kitchen carrying a tray of *kichri** and 7Up.

"Hey, hey! Who is this for?"

"Oh! *Asalam aleikum choti, bibi gee*! This is for your mother."

"What? Why? What happened?"

The girl bent forward and whispered in the most sombre tone imaginable, as if she was giving Laila the codes for Pakistani nukes, "They are for your mother, *haan!*"** She repeated the same thing as if it should have been evident to Laila what that should mean.

"Why?"

"Oh," said the maid, "didn't you hear? Ah well!" She shrugged her shoulders in an extremely sassy Punjabi way. "*Chado gee,*"*** the other *choti bibi* just has no limits."

Angered by the maid's aberrant representation of Maya, Laila snapped at the maid, "Go on! Do your work. You don't have any need to gossip about things that you have no idea of."

"Humph," said the haughty maid, flicking her *dupatta* and walking up the stairs with a nod of her head that said, "Rich spoilt brats, they're all the same."

Laila shook her head. She was in complete favour of treating servants equally but not the way her mother had run her house, where arrogance, snitching, and backbiting was rewarded.

She took a few minutes before following her up the stairs into her mother's room. Her mother was lying on the bed, surrounded by all the aunts. One or two of the uncles were seated in the separate lounge section of the room, while her father was standing in a morose mood leaning against the wall, his fingers holding his temples. When she walked in, she could see his eyes twinkle with warmth and his mother exclaimed loudly in a voice

---

*   Lentil and rice cooked together, usually prepared for individuals suffering from an upset stomach.

**   Yes.

***   Let it go.

that already ought to be croaky, but which was also deeply exaggerated, "Oh, there comes Laila, Mama's *jaan*, Mama's love. My *jaan*, how did you know about this? I strictly told everyone not to tell you, I didn't want you to be unnecessarily disturbed."

"Mother, why are you in bed? What happened?"

"Ohhhhh! Oh! What should I tell you of—"

"What can your poor mother do when she has such disobedient *ulad*?* What can she do about her poor *kismet*?" her aunt interrupted, reaching over and squeezing her mother's hand.

"Okay, I guess you're referring to Maya," said Laila through gritted teeth, her anger tweaking the sides of her jaw. "But what exactly happened?"

"She tried to commit suicide, fifteen pills..." her dad stepped in calmly and without any melodrama answered her question. As relieved as she was that there was one practical person in the room, she was horrified to know the esteem with which her mother viewed life.

"What?" she said, her eyes widening and her jaw tightening. "WHY WOULD YOU DO SUCH A THING? ARE YOU CRAZY?

"No, no, my *beti*," she replied, making her voice as quiet as she could. "What can I do when I have a daughter who is hell bent on destroying this family?"

"Destroying this family? How? By disagreeing to marry someone. Is that so wrong?"

All the other aunts tsk-tsk-ed their disfavour. One or two of the eight actually even put their hands on their open mouths to display their outrage at Laila's support for the miscreant.

Laila ignored them and said, "Where are Maya and Nile?"

"Maya's in her room and Nile has gone to the village."

"Which village?"

"*Dada's*.**"

"Well, I am heading over there too."

Mrs K sat up straight now. "What are you talking about? Do you also want to embarrass me in the face of everyone? Go ahead. You do too..." Her lips quivered and a couple of hands went forward to squeeze her hand to console her.

---

* Children, offspring.
** Paternal grandfather's.

"You know what, Mother, I am tired of all of your hypocrisy. Let the girl marry who she wants to; she is not murdering anyone. Let her love when all of you are envious that you were forced into marriages and wish to force her too. Do you want her to have the same fate as all of you? Do you want her to have the same fate as me? Hell no! I pray to God no one has a husband even remotely like mine. A sick, perverted, violent son of a bitch like that one whom it sickens me to say is my husband.

"And as for you, Mother, I am disappointed to even say that you are my mother right now. If you are as God-fearing as you claim, do you not know that literally every religion in the world denounces suicide? Your life is the biggest gift that you have been given and instead of making the most of it, you wish to throw it away, not comprehending its infinite worth. Get out of this diamond cage for once and walk on the streets, you don't even have to go far; just walk a block and see all the poverty and the filth and even amidst all that, see the way that they embrace life, the way they appreciate the very chance to breathe, the fact that every new day is another blessing, not a chance to be further suffocated by this infernal society."

"Laila," her father said, lightly touching her arm and shaking his head, asking her to stop.

"No, Dad! I won't be quiet today. They all need to hear the truth. In fact, you know what? Maybe you're right. Nile was right to leave this madhouse. These people aren't worth the truth. Even if truth rounds them up and lights them up with gasoline, they will not know that it is they and their corrupt flesh that are burning. None of you are worth my time."

"*Haw hai*! Mrs K. This daughter of yours has an even sharper tongue."

"She even said we should be set on fire."

"My point exactly! You are so embroiled in your parochial viewpoints, so blinded with greed and envy and lust for money that you cannot see happiness and true honour."

They looked pretty comical with mouths open, eyes disbelieving, and minds comprehending her words as true, but their small minds were fighting a vehemently furious battle to kick her words out. She knew that her words would never win this battle. She turned around to look at her father and even before she did she knew he was going to be a quiet mixture of both pride and humiliation. She opened the door and before she went out, she turned around and said very calmly, "Oh, and by the way, I left that asshole husband of mine," and quickly shut the door on the face of all the gasps of shock, her mother's wailing and beating her chest, cursing the day she gave birth to daughters, her father becoming an even more rigid and sterner figure, as if he were made of cardboard, and the general reactions that one would expect at the announcement of divorce. It seemed she was doing a lot of opening and closing of doors and finding herself in the midst of it all.

LAILA JOINS NILE IN THE VILLAGE

ANOTHER WEEK PASSED and Laila grew agitated with her sequestration in the family house. The corridors were full of malicious gossip, her parents had practically disowned her and would refuse to speak to her, every single relative came to offer their condolences as if Laila had passed away; even the servants looked at her with pity, averting their eyes as if she were an uncovered leper begging for succour.

The only person who Laila shared any degree of love and comfort with was Maya, and yet Maya was no more a pillar of support than an errant Indian or Pakistani nuke in ensuring peace on the sub-continent. Maya would latch onto Laila and would need her for being her peace and comfort in her time of turmoil, but she was prone to detonate at times. For Laila, the hard times were over – her parents seemed to accept that no amount of coercion would convince her. But Maya they were sure they could eventually work on enough to convince her to return from her wayward path. Especially now, with Laila's little episode adding to the family's woes, they were ever more determined to keep Maya in their control. Somehow her parents had to keep things from falling apart.

And so, just as Laila feared, her parents mounted greater and greater pressure on Maya until she gave in. Mentally Laila could tell that her sister had pulled away and retreated to some well-fortified redoubt inside the recesses of her mind. Maya had wilfully given up ground so as to create for her an easier piece of terrain to defend. Laila watched as she moved with litheness, malleability, as she produced wan smiles that seemed unforced yet

319

to a sibling, and only a truly close sibling at that, seemed somehow wrong. Maya marched to the tune set by her parents as a member of the Red Army marched in front of their commissar, acquiescing in body and most, but not the entire, mind.

Her parents were methodical in their plan to *save* the family from certain social disaster. While her father was nominally a just man, he carried fears that his soft heart and love for his children would one day be the source of the family downfall in some cruel twist of faith. It was this concern, this deep and irrational and existential fear that haunts all just men who are leaders, that his wife used to tell him it would not hurt to 'mix it up a little' by being firm on the kids. He had no choice but to take her advice because this weakness was the kind of fear that one would only reveal to their dearest love. And so Maya's mother convinced her father that no real damage was being done to their daughter and if there was any true issue with correcting her in this manner, then surely there would have been some sort of grand societal collapse within the three thousand years of civilisation that modern Pakistani culture rested on.

And so they began their grand plan to right the family ship beginning with Maya, forcing her to first beg her cousin for mercy, to plead with him to take her back and to offer to go on regular dates with him. They monitored her phone, her messages to him, made her put his calls on speaker, and if she objected even to that excessive level of micromanagement, they would rein her in using either physical or verbal abuse, or emotional blackmail. It was in this manner that Maya's family confidently set about enslaving her to an existence of the drudgery associated with a loveless relationship borne only out of arbitrarily constructed social necessity.

The more Laila thought about it, the more she couldn't stand either what her parents were doing to Maya or the fact that they were the reasons she remained married to her twisted freak of a husband. She desperately wanted to be rid of him already. Despite the initial liberation and rebirth Laila experienced when she found the courage to walk out of the house for good, until she had a signed, sealed and delivered divorce she still felt empty and unsteady inside. She needed to get out of the house, to put *more* distance between herself and her scumbag of a husband, but also to give Maya space to formulate her next move. Laila knew her little sister wasn't fully broken but she also knew that her own marital failure fuelled her parents' desire to bend their youngest daughter to their will. So Laila figured she was best out of sight and out of mind. If she made herself unavailable to them then they would perhaps take it that her episode of flight from her husband was temporary and fixable, albeit a lower priority than Maya, since she was after all *already* married. Laila reckoned her absence would lull her parents into a false sense of security and give Maya that essential breathing room she so desperately needed.

Perhaps she should have stayed and been the constant support that Maya also needed and desperately required, but more importantly, Laila knew she could be a catalyst for further trouble coming her sister's way. She also just needed to get the hell out of that house and its stifling humidity of damp dirty urban air and judgement. And so, much to Maya's disappointment, Laila too left her filial prison and followed her brother on a planned week's trip to the birthplace of their grandfather, seeking solace.

SPICES AND BULLETS

"HELLO, MAYA! MAYA!" The voice on the other line seemed frantic but Maya made it out as being that of Pashmina, a cousin of Ali's.

"Pashmina! Pashmina! Hi dear, what's going on?" She shut the door; even though no one was near the kitchen, she didn't want to take chances by getting caught being on the phone. The answer to Maya's question came in sobs and wails from the other end of the line.

"Pash! What is wrong?"

"Maya, I don't know how to tell you this… but Ali's been shot!"

I didn't even have any space to breathe; I felt like my world had ended. I didn't even hear my phone hit the floor. I didn't even know that I had opened the door and had walked into my parents' room. I didn't even know that I was punching my father with the wildest blindest rage, screaming "HOW COULD YOU? HOW COULD YOU?" until my mother, getting over her shock, wrenched me back by my hair, yanking me off of him.

She gave me a tight slap across the face and it was only then that I stopped fighting, kicking, and screaming. "HAVE YOU LOST YOUR MIND OR HAS THE DEVIL POSSESSED YOU?"

The anger dissipating, grief took over and I sank to my knees howling, "How could you? How could you? Don't you know how much he means to me? He is my life! My other half! Don't you know that if he's gone then I am gone?"

My father, recovering from the pounding fists of a crazed person hitting his chest, shook my arms and said, "What are you talking about, you crazy girl? WHAT?"

"Don't touch me!" I screamed, flinging his hand aside. "Don't touch me. YOU HAD HIM SHOT, YOU HAD HIM SHOT!"

322

My mother slapped me again. "How dare you say such a thing as that to your own father! How dare you?"

"Maya," her father said, grabbing her by the shoulders. "Take a hold of yourself. Why would I, your father, even resort to that?"

Maya looked up to her father and saw how earnest he was; beyond that, through her tears she saw what made him such a great and just man. She saw in his eyes pain, sadness and empathy.

"Maya, look. I hate the boy, and have been anxious to see him disposed of for doing this to our family, but if murder was ever going to be the case I definitely would have been the one to pull the trigger, if only to face you and hope you would forgive me. We are not cowards in this family, my daughter. Lahore may think of us as many lowly things, but cowardice will not be one of them."

"Wait, wait, wait! Hold on a moment! How do you even know this?" interrupted her mother, ever to rent any moment of true connection her daughter had with her father.

"His cousin, Pashmina, told me!" sobbed Maya.

"What?" Another slap. "That's just great. You swore on the Quran that you wouldn't be in touch with that damn family. You swore on it. Now you just wait and see the destruction that God will send your way."

"I did not talk to *him*," she said through gritted teeth, simultaneously rising and realising that her parents were of no use. "You are just a closeted *Kafir** who worships upon the altar of money, jewellery and what society thinks of you, those are your gods. You have no sense of Allah or what his blessed essence entails, so what Allah will or won't do isn't a matter for you to decide," she said, and before they could say another thing she ran out of the room to grab her phone from the kitchen and find out what actually happened.

She ran all the way into her room, locked it, walked over to her toilet and shut herself in before calling the friend, and between sobs and muffled tones said, "H-hello. I am sorry about before. What happened?"

"Well, no issue, he had some robber encounter and you know how he is, he gave them everything but started to question them about the reasons for picking their particular profession; one of the robbers, probably drunk, shot him in the leg. He is in the OR right now; the doctor said that nearby

---

* An immoral heathen.

bystanders got him in on time. It was just a minor flesh wound so he will be fine. I am sorry if I panicked you before. I didn't know the details myself. His father called me and I called you on the way to the hospital; I hope it didn't cause more problems with your family."

"No. No. It's fine. I couldn't possibly have any more problems. Thanks for calling. And, listen, can you tell him one thing from me: tell him that I love him and that no matter what, I always will. Please, please tell him that, and, listen, keep updating me on his recovery, even if my parents take my phone away I will find a way of getting in touch with you."

"Good luck, Maya! And may Allah bless you for all the courage and strength that you have been exhibiting throughout this ordeal and for all the sacrifices you have made. Ali really loves you too and we all pray for you both."

"*Shukriya! Khuda hafiz.*"

"*Khuda hafiz.*"

By the time Maya had managed to end the conversation, her parents had managed to open her room door. They had asked the servant to find the duplicate keys in the basement and were now pounding away at the bathroom door. "Open the door, open the door, before I break it down."

Of course, she couldn't. It was securely bolted. "Break it down then!" screamed Maya.

Her father, being much more in control of his emotions, calmly told his wife to step aside. "Maya, open the door. You know you have to come out at some point and we have made a decision that we think you ought to hear."

She unlocked the door and flung it open. "What new scheme have you engendered now to ruin my life?"

"Well, your mother and I, actually I, have decided that it isn't right for all three of us to live under the same roof." (The thought had occurred to her father, but really it was after Nile's hundred phone calls that he had relented to this conclusion.) "I feel that this way we are just running around in circles. You need to come to terms with the fact that you are marrying your cousin: he is the best match for you and for this family. After what Laila did with this divorce business, at least one of you should have the decency to make your parents proud after all that they have done for you – sweated, bled for you. But I suppose ungratefulness runs in your blood; as the eldest does, the rest follow suit. But I will not let this sibling domino effect ruin this family and I will stop it at you. I repeat, you are to wed your cousin; there are no two ways about it. After you are married, you may continue your education and resume your other activities as well. Nevertheless, we have realised that this house isn't conducive to helping you come to terms with your reality so I suggest you pack your bags and join your brother and your sister in the village."

"But," protested her mother, "she will find a way to communicate with him again if we don't keep her under watch." Her father held out a hand to silence her.

"It doesn't matter. She can even have her phone if she pleases and communicate with that bastard as much as she wants, I don't care. I will make sure the servants and the villagers know what he looks like so that if he were to enter the premises, or you leave, they will beat both of you thoroughly with sticks, you rather soundly and him probably to death for dishonouring you and attempting what they most certainly will consider to be a grievously injurious assault upon their most cherished resource – that is, their pride. And so it will be just as it was in Papa's time. I assure you, the federal government's rules and laws don't apply in the tribal system. Communicate as much as you want. You will marry your cousin in the end."

"But," protested her mother again, "what will people say?"

"People are already saying what they are. I am doing this to stop their wagging tongues and to stop her cousin from declining this proposal. If people ask, tell them all three of the siblings have gone for a vacation together. If they want to be in exile, let them be in exile together and I will at least have some peace in this house finally. Elections are right around the corner so, Maya, will you pack your bags?"

Maya stood there calmly letting the information sink in, pleased with at least the convenience of escaping her restraints, no matter where her temporary freedom was leading her. She smiled sarcastically. "Are you asking me, or is that an order?"

"You know whenever a father asks, especially on the rare occasions that someone like I do, it is an order. Be packed and ready to leave by morning. Your flight to Peshawar is at six. You reach there around ten, and from there I have asked one of our Peshawar drivers to pick you up and take you to the village, okay?"

"Okay." And that was how all three of the K children found themselves on different paths, at different points in their lives, but ironically winding up at the same destination – the same grimy, squalid luxury-less little village that to each was a haven of different proportions and yet of imminent consequence.

Maya was going north, to the mountainous tribal areas interspersed amongst the interminable heights of the Hindu Kush. To the ungovernable primordial place the Americans called Al-Qaeda's last redoubt. To the place that the British and the Raj called the *frontier* but to her family for a hundred generations had been just *home*.

THE CALL

WE CAME BACK *to the apartment at the crack of dawn, both of us too tired after a night out at the Love & Propaganda to do anything but cuddle and sleep. He was asleep within seconds, quite inebriated and thus snoring and panting down my neck. Hours passed and even though sunlight was pouring into the room, I couldn't sleep. I kept thinking about my parents. I missed hearing my father's jovial laughter and my mother, my plump little mother's squeaky disapproval. I hadn't called them in months and, truth told, even if I was busy, one phone call wouldn't have taken too long. I guess I just felt that the more I distanced myself from them, the more I would be distancing myself from the unnecessary impediments of Pakistan and the society of the wealthy dissemblers who had it as their immediate agenda to curb the freedom of others that they so desperately desired. Yet I didn't realise that in distancing myself from these sycophants, I too was a hypocrite in wanting to cut off my roots, wanting to disengage myself from the most essential core of my reality.*

I thought about my dear American friend, always the same worldly, wise one, and the first thing she would say to me every time I met her at our sorority events: "Call your parents, Arzoo!" It was 6pm there. I picked up the phone and called the house.

"Asalam aleikum, Mama."

"Arzoo? ARZOOO BETI! Sugra, go call sahib gee – it's Arzoo's phone! Arzoo beti, how are you? Where have you been? Your father and I have been so worried about you, where have you been?"

Arzoo felt a flush of warmth, a desire to get on the first plane out and straight into her mother's plump soft arms. She controlled that impulse; it was hard for her to, but she had to for now. "Mama, that's two times you asked me where I have been. I have been right here, in the Bay Area. I have just been so busy every time that whenever I think about calling you and Dad back something or the other always comes up."

"Yes, Arzoo *beta*, I understand that you have been busy, but, *beta*, one call to your parents... we have been wrecked; we didn't even know whether you were dead or alive. Thank God that we had the number of that nice American friend of yours who told us that you were really busy doing some thesis and were always at the library and that we shouldn't feel exceptionally bad about being side-lined like this and that you were treating everyone..."

I smiled as I heard my mother ramble; the desire to see her was so great I had to physically control the tears that were coming. He stirred. I moved toward the toilet so that my mother wouldn't hear his grunts.

"Mama, yes, I know. I am sorry, I—"

"SUGRA. Did you not tell Sahib? Yes, well, tell him to pick up the other extension from the library. YES, HURRY. She is calling from America, you daft woman, not Rawalpindi. Arzoo *beti*, sorry. You know how irritating these servants purposely try to be."

"Hello..."

"DADDYYYY. *Asalam aleikum.* How are you?" As soon as she heard her father's voice, no self-control could possibly contain the tears that were overflowing from their ducts and down the whole length of her face.

"Arzoo, my *jaan*, how have you been? Your mother and I have been worried sick, please don't do this to us again."

"I am sorry, Daddy, I am sorry! I have missed you so much! Both of you, I just..."

"We have too, *beti*, we have too. Your mother doesn't sleep at night, she cries all the time, missing you."

I felt a stab of guilt for putting my parents through this ordeal, for making them feel insignificant in my life and for sacrificing their peace and calm in search of my own identity. So much of me was a part of them. How could I have forgotten that? Why had I let this physical distance erect itself, thinking it would automatically generate an emotional apathy between us? Why did I even wish to separate myself from my parents? I thought of the day that they found my pictures on Facebook and how disappointed I had made them. I suppose it was to avoid making them feel shame that I wished to break all connections with them. In my own selfish way maybe I was protecting them.

Maybe I was thinking all these things now to avoid the rising guilt that I felt at my own doing. They didn't deserve more pain from me. I know I wished to protect them from me, but I couldn't for much longer. They deserved to know the truth.

"When do you come back, *beti*?" said her mother. "This summer?"

"No, Mom, I…"

"What, I thought your school ends this summer. We even got tickets to come for your graduation before we go on a Euro tour together as a family and head back home."

"Yes, it does end then, Mother, but I am not coming back."

My father interrupted, "Oh, summer research again, Arzoo, or more volunteering with the DNC? Why didn't you consult with us before making this decision? We were looking forward to seeing you, my dear."

"You're right!"

"Of course he's right, Arzoo, you didn't even think of us as being meaningful enough to you. I mean, we have been pining for over a year now. We haven't seen you since Dubai and you…" Mrs N was almost crying now and that naturally upset both Mr N and Arzoo.

"Arzoo *beta*, I didn't expect this from you. Honestly, I know you go to Stanford and I trust you to always make the right decisions, but to exclude your parents like this is extremely unbecoming; it's been almost a *year*. I have a right to see my daughter, you know."

"Wait, Dad, there is more."

My parents were quiet and it made me extremely uneasy to know that they were silent because they were afraid of what news I would unleash their way. They already had begun to expect the worst from me.

"The reason I'm not coming back… the reason is because I am engaged."

"WHATTTT!" screamed her mother. "Arzoo, Arzoo, I don't, I can't… Arzoo. What?"

Her father remained quiet and that made her even more discontented with herself.

"His name's Ian. He is a water polo player. He is a real gentleman."

"A *GORA*? YOU WANT TO MARRY A *GORA*? OH, ALLAH SAVE ME. OH, WHY DID YOU MAKE ME LIVE FOR THIS DAY?"

Her mother wailed and cried, as expected, but for the first time Arzoo didn't roll her eyes. She felt her mother's desperation at being alienated by her daughter, of permanently being relocated to the status of an unknown within a matter of days. The shock had elicited opposing reactions in her parents – while her mother screamed and hollered her father remained quiet. Yet Arzoo could hear his suddenly laboured breathing and when he spoke, it was with such an eerie decisive authority that, being an alien to his tone, even her mother fell silent, whimpering softly.

"Arzoo, I am only going to say this once and I hope that I make myself extremely clear. You are no longer going to be financially dependent on us." She was going to interrupt and say that she had found a job in San Francisco and didn't need to be but decided for the better that it wouldn't be wise to talk now. "I will pay for your last quarter and then that's it."

"But—" interrupted Mrs N.

"No, Mrs N, no. Not this time. She made her decision and I will not try and dissuade her from it because I know it is fruitless, but this decision, this is mine. I no longer have a daughter. She made her decision, Mrs N. She made it and when she did, she didn't once think of us. I suppose that is America, it always finds a way to take what you have loved and cherished and grown. America always reaps what you have sown."

"Dad…"

"Enough, Arzoo. I don't wish to speak to you anymore." There was a pain in his chest. "Enough! Good luck on the path that you have chosen."

"*Khuda hafiz.*" But no one was on the other line; her parents had hung up.

She cried and cried, sitting huddled on the toilet floor. I suppose she had taken for granted that her parents would understand her mistake this time as they had always understood and forgiven. But there is a limit to everything, even a parent's unconditional love. She had tested those boundaries constantly and now she had made them helpless in their decision to part ways – for now. Her father had made clear that were she to abandon the fiancé, she would be welcomed back, but she wasn't about to give up Ian. She had planned to spend her life with him and her parents would just have to come to terms with it. They always did. The thought of this situation being a bit of an outlier did strike her as possible, but as she went and lay back in bed, at least one burden was lifted from her: she had told the truth. He woke up as soon as she snuggled back into the covers.

"Why are you crying?"

"I just spoke to my parents."

"And…"

"And, well, they are upset."

"No kidding," he said sarcastically. "They don't approve of me now but hey, dude! They will. They are your parents and if they don't, who cares? You got me."

"Yeah," Arzoo replied, a bit miffed by his indifference or ignorance of the situation, but then again perhaps his perspective on the situation was different from hers. Perhaps that is what attracted her most to him. This was love, right? And even if it wasn't, she had chosen her path herself for once, without anyone or anything urging her on, without any fear or hindrance. She was doing the right thing, right?

UNLIKELY HELPING HANDS

FINDING HERSELF STILL under its throes more than a week since her visit to Mrs W's grand event, Mrs J knew that it was high time that she dealt with this affliction – that since that event something just wasn't right within her psyche. What could possibly have been out of the ordinary that would have warranted such an emotional and mental lag? After all, Mrs J had quite a number of very pressing issues that she had to deal with on a regular basis, such as the fact that, irrespective of how desperately she wished to be a mother, she was very likely destined to leave this world with no issue of her own. And no matter the goodness of his heart and the depth of his love for her, Mrs J knew that this would weigh heavily upon her marriage when the time came.

So Mrs J sat down on her couch after her husband had left for the office and her mother-in-law had retired into her room for an afternoon of 'prayer', which consisted of nothing more than repeating phrases in Arabic that were complete gibberish to the old woman but were recited eagerly so as to enable her to exhibit the image of a woman that was as sufficiently religious and pious as society demanded for her age. What she actually did in the locked room is another matter; personally, I believe she watched Indian soaps on mute and as soon as someone knocked on the door she rushed over to the prayer mat to start her ceaseless repetition of phrases she did not understand or clearly put the effort into living by.

Mrs J sat on the sofa to try and reflect on the events of that night. She remembered Mrs S's momentous remark, she surely remembered the pudding and sumptuous snacks, she remembered Mrs W's awfully spoilt son, but something kept evading her and it wasn't until she gave up and turned the TV on that she suddenly realised what it was. Geo TV, a Pakistani news channel, was on and the newscaster was announcing the latest businessmen who were going to be standing for office in the upcoming election. Such things were of no appeal to Mrs J and she was about to flip the channel to BBC Food when one of the candidates' names caught her eye – none other than Mr Y himself. Mr Y was indeed running for parliament, a decision that had just been recently made and the media had been quick to broadcast.

And just like that, Mrs J remembered that she hadn't seen Ariyana at *any* event for a long time, and surely if her husband was running for office it would be natural – nay, even obligatory – for her to be present at these gatherings, to garner support from all the other socialites and their respective villages that voted as a singular bloc according to the stated desires of their more fiscally evolved city-dwelling relatives-cum-benefactors. Mrs J thought again about Mrs W's dinner and recalled that everyone claimed that they had tried to call Ariyana but had been unable to reach her. This was what had been bothering her this entire time! Where the hell was Ariyana?

Now that Mrs J had discovered the root of her anxiety, she was determined to satisfy her piqued thoughts. So she did the only thing that all these women did when they wanted a reasonable solution to their problems : she called Mrs S.

"*Asalam aleikum.*"

"*Walaikum*, Mrs J." Mrs S, like everyone else, valued the honest integrity and untainted humanity of this simple, kind woman and was always glad to receive a call from her, more than ever ready to aid her in any way possible. She had unsuccessfully suggested many dieticians, gym instructors, and fertility doctors and even though Mrs J did go to many of the latter, she remained unresolved in her desire to conform to the one size that fits all that everyone wished to be a proponent of, and Mrs S, though outwardly disappointed that her free advice wasn't accepted, secretly respected the woman for her unfailing adherence to her values. Moreover, Mrs S knew that, unlike the rest of the malicious chatty brood, Mrs J's intentions toward Mrs S would be nothing but genuine. "And how are you today?"

"Oh, well, fine, Mrs S, just fine. How about yourself?"

"Ha ha ha! For once in my life I actually know where my money is going off to, the house is in better order than ever before, the company is doing marvellously well, it's making more profits then it has in the past ten years, and the children are doing well in school. My son is just applying to college. Fehranaz is healthy."

"That's all good, Mrs S, but how are you?"

"Ah, Mrs J! I know you mean no harm so I guess you deserve the truth: I survive and live. I am a hardy little woman, I will survive through pretty much anything." She laughed again.

"I know, Mrs S… I am sorry for all that you have been through and I have told you a number of times that I don't really have much to do. There isn't much in this house other than me, the husband, and his mother, so I would be more than obliged to help you out."

"Yes, Mrs J, I know but I just have this very uncontrollable need to take control of things. If I could only delegate responsibilities to others – for the thing is, when I do, it stresses me out more, for I have to first be vigilant of what they are doing and then end up doing it myself. I appreciate your offer, though."

"Anytime, Mrs S. I…"

"What's wrong, Mrs J? Something upsetting you?"

"Well, yes… it's not about me, it's about Ariyana. I just… I don't know, Mrs S. I don't feel right about her just vanishing like this."

"You know, you're right, Mrs J. I probably would have noticed earlier had I not had all these problems to take care of, but you're right. It's not natural for her to have just faded away from the social scene like this."

"Yeah."

"I— I am sorry, go on, Mrs J."

"I was just going to say that all everyone said at Mrs W's party was that they have been receiving no response from her and then Mrs R, the way her face was all flushed…"

"Hmmm. When does that little intrusive, disrespectful, uncivilised, uncouth woman have anything better to do than just be polemical, impertinent, and vulgar? Let her be, Mrs J. The last time I spoke to her was when I asked her for that American CEO's number… in fact, hold on, that's when I last spoke to Ariyana as well – why she needed that number for her husband's business project, as I recall."

"Whatever it is, Mrs S, I don't like it, and I think we should…"

"My sentiments exactly. We should go to Ariyana's house and find out if she is okay."

"Y-ye—"

"I am just going to drop Fehranaz at Maya's for one of her tutorial sessions. Lovely girl, isn't that Maya? I can't believe she already graduated so early. Well, I am going to go drop her over there and then come pick you up. Does that sound good?"

"Oh yes! Yes, indeed," said Mrs J, finally glad to be able to get in a word.

Mrs S was clearly excited about this new investigative project Allah had thrown her way and arrived within thirty minutes, in a mood of great seriousness and with an energised self-righteousness. She talked the entire way, telling Mrs J about the significance of their mission and how they must approach the situation with delicacy.

"Mrs J," she said, right before they reached Ariyana's house, "please let me do the talking. You are a kind, simple woman and don't understand the tricks that people deploy to hide facts."

"Hmm," replied Mrs J in assent, as she had for much of the entire journey, realising that the quieter she was, the more she could hear.

"This is an extremely dubious matter. I don't know about you, but it has definitely made me very suspicious of the whole affair. What do you think?" said Mrs S.

"Hmmm, I really don't know." But in fact Mrs J's thoughts were bordering on the unpleasant and when her imagination began to fantasise about the unthinkable, perhaps something terrible had befallen Ariyana, she shuddered, praying that they would reach the house quickly and allay all fears.

When Mrs S's driver, himself a Pathan from her village, announced in his slightly uncouth Urdu accent that they had reached the house, Mrs J leapt from the car at roughly the same speed as Mrs S, which, given the latter's vigour and tiny frame, was quite a profound accomplishment. Having been ushered into the parlour, the maid informed them that Ariyana wasn't at home (at which point the women exchanged looks) and informed them that she would get the older *bibi*.

When she walked in the room to see a plump woman, who had once been extremely good-looking, and another tiny handsome one dressed in the most nuanced of fashions, inquiring about her hateful half-white daughter-in-law, she was extremely riled by their audacity and was anything but pleasant. "My daughter-in-law is in the States. What business is it of yours?" She quickly dismissed them and bid the servants show them the door.

Mrs S and Mrs J were still within earshot when they started discussing the mother-in-law's peculiar and inhospitable behaviour.

"I tell you, Mrs J, that is the worst kind of a woman, Allah only save such a house from such a woman… no concept of hospitality."

"Mrs S, for once I am in complete agreement with you. "

"I fear that this was most unbecoming and that my fear only deepens my suspicion that our dear friend has suffered some unmentionable fate."

"Yes," interrupted Mrs J for once, "I too feel that her behaviour was exaggerated to intentionally prevent us from asking too many questions. I mean, did you see the way her eyes twitched every time we mentioned Ariyana? I am telling you, she was definitely withholding information."

Mrs S remained quiet for some time, deeply engrossed in some thought before speaking again. "Hmmm, Mrs J, I believe that Mother Y was deliberately cold to us; I know she was lying to us about Ariyana."

Mrs J rolled her eyes and was about to tell Mrs S that her ingenious insight was a rewording of the same statement Mrs J had made only moments ago. However, she refrained from doing so, giving Mrs S satisfaction of her prowess.

"I think," she said instead, "we should question her husband."

"Driver," said Mrs S, raising her index finger, "I think it would be worthwhile to go pay a visit to Mr Y, wouldn't you agree, Mrs J?"

"Yes, yes," mumbled Mrs J as they sat in the car.

Within another twenty minutes the two amateur sleuths had reached the headquarters of the firm, the nest of the multimillion-dollar empire that Y's grandfather had built from scratch and that Y's father had elevated to incredible heights. The security guards stopped them outside at the checkpoint and as soon as they crossed the barbed wire-walled fences and entered the plush welcoming area, their initial excitement returned.

After a few minutes, an attractive Western-dressed secretary sporting a stylish bun and a warm smile spoke in hushed tones into the receiver. However, within seconds, clicking her heels, she walked over to the society women and, abandoning her scepticism, adopted the most artificial smile she could muster and said, "Ladies, this way please."

The sarcasm was evident in her voice and as she turned around, Mrs S nudged Mrs J, loudly whispering how secretaries are practically half-wives – a joke that didn't sit well with the secretary, clearly, and she had to think of her fat pay cheque to prevent her from turning around and slapping Mrs S!

Heels still clicking, she haughtily tossed her hips over to a private elevator located at a concealed angle near her desk and indicated that they should follow her. After three floors, the women found themselves seated opposite the handsome and enigmatic personality of Mr Y.

"Well, Mr Y," said Mrs S, just as he lit a cigar opposite them, "we demand to know the whereabouts of your wife."

Great, thought Mrs J. *Great way to handle the situation's delicacy.*

If Mr Y hadn't been shocked at the woman's audacity and the fact that she was already beyond the bounds of decency by trying to inquire – much less demand – information about matters that were his own personal affair, he would have actually been amused at the way she threw her tiny frame into his office.

"Now pray, Mrs S, tell me who you are to demand such a thing from me? Do tell me your grounds for such a line of talk! That I demand from you? Just what are you implying, woman?"

"Well, Mr Y, your wife has been missing and we have reason – no, we know that your mother is withholding information and that—"

"What she means to say, Y, dear," interrupted Mrs J, seeing the blood rush up into Y's ears and afraid that the large vein in his neck that was pulsing would burst, or worse, he would send them to the same fate that her imagination thought had befallen Ariyana, "was that we would just like to know where Ariyana is, please. We would like to speak to her. We have just been worried, that's all."

Y relaxed at the plump woman's gentle non-accusatory voice. His posture was less rigid as he leaned back before replying, one eyebrow raised. "I applaud you for your Good Samaritan endeavours, but I am afraid my wife has left for America to finish her schooling and won't be back for a while."

"You mean until your election is over? Her white skin and blonde hair not playing so well in Gujranwala, eh?"

The charm had been broken and Mrs S had succeeded in ruining Y's mood beyond repair. "Mrs S, I am afraid that that was completely out of line and I am going to have to ask you to go."

"Well," jeered Mrs S, "two can play this game," and, placing her Gucci firmly on his table, she said, "I will not budge till I know the truth about where your wife is."

Losing all patience and decency now, Y replied in an exasperated tone, "Oh, for the sake of Allah, woman! I don't have the time or the mental sanity to deal with you today. I have meetings all day, both business related and for my political career, and I won't let some, some, some housewife ruin that for me."

Mrs S's mouth dropped open at the insult of being called a housewife when she was managing perhaps as large a business as Y, and after branding him with a bunch of names, one of which was a 'girlish' wife-beater, she succeeded in enraging him enough to call security.

He had barely said the word 'security' when Mrs S, realising that he was serious, threw the chair back and got up. "*Khuda hafiz*, Mr Y, and this is the treatment I get, ten years your senior. Humph." And then she said perhaps the wisest thing that she had said that entire day: "And especially when I got that dear sweet poor wife of yours the number for that American CEO and actually arranged for Ariyana to even meet him, to help you! You devious lout! I mean, the nerve of you men to be…"

She turned around just in time to catch the look on Mr Y's face. The man looked like someone had reached into his pants and snatched out his entire manhood. "Mrs— Mrs S. W-w-wait. What were you saying about the American man?"

"Apart from being uncouth and obnoxious like your mother, are you daft and hard of hearing as well?"

"Mrs S," said Mrs J, observing the ashen look on Y's face and how he was almost sinking to the floor in disbelief, "I think the young man is being serious. Tell him what he wants to hear," she said quietly.

"Well, I told him what I had to already, that I gave Ariyana the number for the American CEO and arranged for them to meet at PC because the poor girl was adamant about helping this witless ungrateful husband of hers."

It took a while for Y to actually sink back into his chair, to feel the leather cushion, and after asking the women to take their seats again he resolved their confusion by telling them the events of the day – that he received the call and found his wife with a strange American man in the hotel and drew the only natural conclusion that the caller was directing him to.

"How could you doubt your own wife, Mr Y?" said Mrs J.

"What a fool, what an arrogant fool you are. You could have at least asked her once; you could have at least confirmed with her before so foolishly kicking her out, what a fool, what a ******* and a *******." Mrs J grabbed Mrs S by the shoulders to calm her down and to prevent her from further aggravating Mr Y's plight, but Mr Y held his hand out.

"Let her say whatever she is saying." He was shaking now. "I deserve it, I deserve it. I am such a blind bastard, such a weak man. I destroyed and doubted the one person who meant the most to me in this world. How could I have been such a fool? What did I do? Oh God! What did I do?" And he wept as Mrs J, kind lady, walked over to him. She laid a hand on his shoulder and said quite simply, "Come on, Y, dear, what is done is done, there is nothing that you can undo now; but what you can do is be a man now and ask your wife for forgiveness."

"B-but," said Y, "I don't know where she is, I just... Oh God, how could I? I just kicked her out, like she was trash. I mean, I thought..."

Well, thought Mrs S as she exchanged a disdainful look with Mrs J, not particularly impressed by the compassion she was showing the man, *let's just hope it's not too late.*

Mrs S had been silently watching the man and finally decided to take control of the situation. "Mrs J, step away from this man, there isn't a sight I detest more than a man crying, especially one crying over his own egotistical folly. Well, sir, now that I have your attention, I would recommend you get your act together. We have a great deal of searching to do. Please desist from this snivelling. You treated your wife as little more than a possession that suddenly lost all its worth and you made the choice to discard her as your will – and not propriety – directed. No, Mr Y, you don't even deserve to cry." Mrs S finally calmed down, after which she said in a really professional tone to Mr Y, "It's great that you have stopped crying; now we have to look for this poor discarded wife of yours."

"But I have no clue where she is, Mrs S. None whatsoever."

"Don't worry, dear Mrs S and I will help you, and as for the phone call, I have a really good idea as to who it was. Don't you worry. We will help you."

"I assure you now that I am on your side to help Ariyana, though clearly for her sake and in no way yours; consider the matter as good as solved." Mrs S stood up at this point with an air of dignified wisdom, signalling the end of their conversation.

MASSAGES AND ENDINGS

THE FILIPINA WAS out of town; of course, that had put quite a glaring dent in Mrs R's otherwise chirpy mood. Life was going great for her at this particular moment in the journey, and this being in a life that was particularly free of challenges. Mrs R's husband worshipped her, she had no mother-in-law to contend with, her children were at the top of their class, she was 45kgs, finally, all the women adored her, and what's more, that meddling, good-for-nothing white woman was finally out of the picture. The only little wrinkle that was forming on her perfectly smooth porcelain yet just slightly tanned forehead (the *slight* made all the difference, for a peasant was too dark and a foreigner was too white) was due to her favourite Filipina masseuse being out of town. Ah, well! The local Pakistani woman would just have to do.

"*Nahi nahi,** Mariam. Jesus, the nerve of these Christian women," she said, more to herself than poor Mariam, who barely understood English. "A hot stone massage implies there being a hot stone, not one that will freeze the hair off my skin."

"Sorry, sorry, ma'am," said poor Mariam, who dropped the hot oil on Mrs R's arm, clearly more out of her nervous disposition than the fact that she wanted to further aggravate her plight, along with the probability of whether she would keep this job.

Bitch, thought Mrs R, *now I will only have to teach you a lesson*. But she sweetly smiled the smile that the predator does right when it has the prey in its clutches and is contemplating whether the jugular vein is ripe for the taking. "May I please speak to the spa manager, love?"

---

* No, no.

340

"Why, Mrs R?" said Mariam, terrified that she would lose her new job; she thought of her mother's leukaemia, the siblings she had to feed, and the little child growing in her stomach, and her hands shook even more.

"Oh, dear, dear girl, no worries. I just want to have a word about my next appointment."

"Yes, yes ma'am, right away, ma'am."

A few minutes later Mrs Sherry, the wife of the owner and therefore quite naturally the manager of the spa, tapped on Mrs R's bare bony shoulder.

"Oh, Mrs R. *Asalam Aleikum!* My my, your skin looks all the more radiant every time I see you."

"Ah, Mrs Sherry, *Waleikum*. Well, you know what they say, beauty keeps magnifying." Mrs R was aware of the intense flattery that Mrs Sherry was using to soften Mrs R's staunchly irate disposition and her usual tantrums of displeasure and yet was equally thrilled by the remark on her skin, one which she indeed thoroughly agreed with, and so she managed to genuinely smile at the woman. She was still, however, not dissuaded from her burning desire to complain and, without a vestige of sympathy, that is exactly what she proceeded to do.

"You know, Mrs R, the other day this overweight woman – I am sure you know who I am referring to – came in and I promise you, with our recommended skin tightening she has lost a few inches."

"Yes, well, your establishment is of good repute, but lately... Ah, no matter."

"Oh no! Please, Mrs R, you are one of our most valued customers, please tell us what has ailed you on this wonderful day today."

"Well, Mrs Sherry, to this day I have never had such an awful massage. This girl is practically inexperienced and has absolutely no knowledge of how to relax my nerves; I came in with less knots than how many I am leaving with now."

The woman's body tensed and a look of wounded pride shadowed the contours around her opulent face. "Well... I do apologise."

"Yes, well, Mrs Sherry, I am afraid that if things go on like this your extremely worthy establishment will suffer a reduction in clientele, a *severe* reduction." She looked meaningfully at the woman and the latter knew and appreciated the other's threat enough to nod her head and exclaim, "Well, you have nothing to worry about. Ming Su is almost done with her other appointment and I will send her over to you, free of charge, of course."

"Well, that could brighten my day. I am always a fan of the Asian hands, locals… ha… they don't even know the concept of various kinds of pressure or…"

"Not to worry, Mrs R, you will never have to worry about that again. I hope you enjoy the massage." She did leave that room, only to instantly fire the poor unsuspecting Mariam.

Gleefully high with the negative energy of the day's power trip, Mrs R flung herself back on the massage bed and smirked; she was never more pleased or in love with herself than at that moment. Humming the latest Bollywood movie tunes to herself, she opened her Snapchat, going over everyone's updates, a venture she never publicly admitted to partaking in, and amused herself with the barrage of women showing off their various branded shoes and bags in their constant passive-aggressive game of one-upmanship.

She was laughing at a certain woman's unsuccessful endeavour to make her wrists seem anything but enormous by sporting a Hermes Apple watch when her phone started vibrating at about the same time that Ming Su walked into the room. 'Hubby calling' furiously flashed on the screen, urging her to pick up. She rolled her eyes, annoyed that her back massage would be further delayed and, waving at Ming Su to give her a few more minutes, picked up her husband's call.

"Yes, dear."

"Are you alone? I have to talk to you."

"Yes, but I am having a back massage. Please make it short."

"Oh, it is. Will you tell me where Ariyana is?"

Mrs R felt a flash of anger, followed by complete annoyance that the white bitch had yet to cease besmirching her perfect world. "No, I really don't know and, frankly speaking, I don't care. Why it should be of importance to you is beyond me."

"Ah, well! It is of paramount importance to me. I am giving you one chance to explain yourself."

"Dear, I have no idea what you are referring to. If you don't mind, I am hanging up to enjoy my time at the spa…"

"Damn it, woman! Will you for once take something I say seriously? Where is Ariyana?"

She was a bit scared by the harshness in his tone, but hid any such fear in her own voice. "I told you already, I don't know, nor do I care."

"Fine, have it your way! Mrs S and Mrs J came over today and I know everything. I gave you a chance to explain yourself, so I am going to tell you right damn now. Get dressed and get back to the house this minute, woman."

The line clicked dead on the other end. A sense of dread began to envelop Mrs R. It was the sort of feeling you'd get as a child when you got into severe trouble in school yet still had to sit through the entire day knowing that your angry disappointed parents awaited you at home. Mrs R was one of those who had the particular skill to have never been directly implicated in a scheme – she always had an exit strategy or a scapegoat – yet this time she was caught red-handed. Perhaps she had grown complacent with age and failed to plan accordingly. Perhaps it was the fact that her WhatsApp messages to the American businessman assuring him of Ariyana's romantic interest had been screenshotted and forwarded to her husband.

As she readied herself and moved to the car she was surprised at how numb she felt. She droned everything out and moved on autopilot to the car. She sat in the back, trying to grasp the situation she now found herself in. She could not find a way out. She was going to face the music one way or another. Her perfect life was going to be shattered – that white bitch had got the better of her, just like they always did. R could not deal with this, she could not deal with the shame, and she could not deal with the anger of her husband, the loss of face to him, her friends and her children, the months of gossip and speculation interchanged amongst the servants in every household in Lahore. No, she could not subject herself to this, she had to do something. It occurred to R that whenever a crisis struck someone she knew, they would go social media 'dark'. They would erase all their accounts and then suddenly reappear months later after whatever crisis had happened had passed.

It was this particular behaviour that motivated her to take things one step further. She directed the driver to head towards the airport. When he arrived, Mrs R took the remaining rupees she had in her purse and told him to go and see a woman or do whatever the hell he wished as long as he did not answer his phone nor return to the house until late evening. She was still numb when she walked up to the Emirates counter and gave them her Platinum status ID. When the attendant asked her where she wished to fly to, it took her a moment to consider. Dubai, of course, was too close – it was to be Istanbul or Kuala Lumpur. She considered that Istanbul was on the way to London and the West and afforded those who genuinely considered themselves to be her friends too much of an opportunity to stop by and visit once they had deduced she had gone into a self-imposed exile.

And so it was that Mrs R left Pakistan within two hours of her husband's call on a first-class flight to Kuala Lumpur. The way she saw it, the effect her disappearance would have on her husband, friends and family was secondary to the effect that the judgement of her actions would have on her. She would slowly fade out of their lives only to re-emerge, free of judgement and pain, just as others faded out of her Snapchat, Instagram, and Facebook feeds.

TO BE MARRIED TO MYSELF

SOMETIMES IN LIFE *you are faced with the worst possible outcome of a situation – you made a bad decision. Perhaps the path wasn't yours to choose. Perhaps it wasn't the one that you were intended for; perhaps in the long run that path may actually prove to be a blessing because weaknesses are often strengths and strengths weaknesses, or anyway, that's what they say, but when you look at the kitchen sink and see the unclean plates with last night's food grimily nestled and sloshed all over them, when you look at the unmade beds with the comforter thrown over the floor and the bedcovers haphazardly shoved behind the bed, when you look at the closets with the clothes hurled all over, practically on every inch of the floor, and when you look at the already germ-infested carpets infused with prolific stains and spills, the magazine and book shelves empty for their constituents are spewed all over the apartment, and then when you think back on the first day you bought the apartment, the way the furniture was impeccably placed in order, the way cleanliness was the norm, the way that the small two-bedroomed space was welcoming and not rotting with the stench of despair as it was now, then the smile you had then, beaming with hopes and dreams, turns to a frown such asd that which I had when I surveyed the place.*

What's more, when you stare at what used to be the most proficient and attractive water polo player, full of vitality, spunk, charisma, whose blonde hair and blue eyes melted many a heart, as they did mine, and then stare at the same blonde hair, which was now unkempt, the same six-pack abs and now see the first outpouring of mass that is soon to be converted to a pot belly, when you reminisce about the same man full of promise and vivacious energy and see this drunken couch potato, like me, you would wonder if buying the

345

apartment was just as bad a decision as being engaged to this man. But then
you do what I did; you shrug your shoulders and without a word, proceed to
go about cleaning the apartment until those that are inebriated in the room
acknowledge your presence and call out to you, "Arzoo, Arzoo…"

"Why are you yelling? I am right here. This apartment isn't big enough to withstand the force of your voice or to contain the gusto in your demands, so please, a little softly."

"Softly? WHY ARE YOU TELLING ME WHAT TO DO?" he bellowed.

"I just said softly; if you cannot talk softly then I am just going to go into the bedroom, shut the door, and drown myself in loud music so that I hear everything but your noise; am I making myself clear, Ian?"

With that she proceeded to the door, but he grabbed onto her hand and in a pitiful whining voice said, "You make all the money, don't you? Which is why you think I don't have feelings, thoughts… I do, I do have feelings. All I want all day is love."

"Really? And what do you think I want, huh? I come back from a hard day at the office only to deal with a slum of an apartment. If you don't work, at least try and keep the place clean so that when I come home at seven, I don't have to clean the house and cook food and cater to you after I come from work."

"Okay, I see, I see. So now you want to make me into a glorified nanny; that's it, isn't it? Well, I got news for you – you're the woman, and guess what? Unlike you, I actually have a legitimate Stanford degree and not one in fem lit!"

As always when noise escalation reached a point that her cochlea did not want to analyse, Arzoo put her hands over her ears and started humming a tune; music seemed to be the ever-present element of sanity in her life, both those lyrics that she found out in the world and those within herself.

"Listen to me when I am talking to you, listen, LISTEN TO ME!"

She let him scream, let him vent out his frustration; her own inner irritations appeased as if he vented for both of them. When he was through, she very calmly walked over to the table, picked up her Alexander McQueen (obviously her own purchase with her own pay cheque) and the car keys and informed him that she would be running to the grocery store to buy groceries. The fridge was already stocked but as it was a Sunday and as she had no office, she just wanted an excuse to leave home and not have to deal with her husband's constant self-imposed bipolar disorder.

As she was walking out the door, she could hear his whimpered muttering, "All I want is love; I wait all day, all day, and all I am is emasculated and made to feel like… Fuck this shit! I am the man, she should respect me, love me. I am the man. I love her. Why won't she love me back? Why? And on top of that she says don't drink beyond your limits. Which fool ever drinks to stay within his limits?" And then he cried the way he had never before in his life till, well, about eight months ago, when such crying had first become the norm.

He didn't cry the way that he did when he wanted a lollipop when he was six, when his father left with another man when he was eight, when he drove back after losing from a water polo tournament, and when his frat lost their housing. No, he cried the way he made all those girls cry when he wouldn't reply to their texts, when he refused to acknowledge the fact that they had given up their virginity to him, when he ended up getting with their friends, cousins, and, yes, even sisters. He cried with the joint hurt of all those girls he had given infinite amounts of pain to.

Once upon a time, she would do anything to run back with her arms stretched around him as the source of comfort and strength that he needed, but that was once upon a time and after a while, vampire-like people have such a knack for sucking all the strength and zeal from your being that you have none left to give them – well, none that is extra. All that still remains is for you to maintain enough zeal to get you from day to day. Did she still love him? She didn't know. All she knew was that somehow she had to maintain order and cleanliness in their apartment and lives, albeit even if it was for selfish reasons such as to prevent her own self from being checked into a mental facility. She knew venting out anger and frustration at someone to whom it wouldn't bring about a change would have no purpose other than to further aggravate the negativity prevalent in their little abode.

I shut the door on my fiancé, on his whining, compulsive self-pity, on my own failure at not realising the depths of despair that college glory can fall into and my failure at not being able to move away from that initial shock and bring both of us out of it. I suppose if I were to look back at this moment later on, I would firstly wonder how I ever became this person and I would know that I should have been strong enough to bring both of us out of this intermittent state of depression and neglect, but I was complacent with being a victim, and as long as I was a survivor, I had no need to help the one person who was the cause of it. I suppose I shouldn't have been selfish, especially because often when we attempt not doing what we know to be just and fair, karma has a way of sneaking up right behind us and screaming our senses back to reality. But it is so hard to be selfless when your hopes and dreams are crushed under the weight of one person and when you gave up everything to share your life with that person. It is so hard to forgive. When someone does us wrong, we usually lie to ourselves when we say that, sure, we forgive what X did to us or how Y treated us or how Z broke our heart. But do we really forget?

I suppose we only do when we have something else, something of much more corpulent proportions to gnaw away at our everyday thoughts. So we repress that hurt, letting it leak out time and time again to disturb nothing, mostly, other than our own peace of mind. If to err is human, to forgive divine, then how did Alexander Pope, devoid of most of life's pleasantries by birth, believe in such a human sentiment. He perhaps had more cause of misery than I had, but unlike him, I know I am only human, so how can I aspire to be divine? I know I should have tried for both our sakes. I should have forgiven him for all that he did, but I just couldn't. I will put the food on the table however I can, I will be the glorified maid cleaning and dusting till my knuckles and knees, bruised and battered, give way, I will clean and iron, shop for groceries and supplies, but I will never forgive this man, and I will never get pregnant with this man's child again. Sometimes you can forgive people on the basis that they, like you, are human too and capable of making mistakes, but when you don't want to forgive, then you, like me, would try to ease your conscience by not repeating mistakes, because you as a whole have become reproachful of them.

When all the angels of heaven and devils of hell came together, they indeed made man.

I drove to the supermarket and walked through aisle after aisle, not seeing the good, the quality, or the quantity, just the price. A whole plethora of numbers just ran around my head – 3 for 10, 2 for 40 – I had never had to deal with numbers; as a child, I hated the prospect of maths. My parents took care of the monetary aspects always. Being a passionate person and constantly driven by my inner id, I was never attracted to immobile, immovable, rigid numbers. Now, when I no longer had the luxury of too much money and the solace of a parental shadow, numbers had taken on a life of their own. The more I squirmed and protested against their assaulting stampede inside my head, the more they infiltrated my calm, my peace, my composure, till I thought that the numbers would be all that I would know and make sense of.

I could actually picture myself tossing down the cereal boxes, throwing the jars of pickles, flinging my arms about, crying and screaming the whole time. But all I did instead was take a deep breath and calmly walk out of the supermarket, empty-handed of course. I suppose belying an external state of calm isn't healthy, though many psychologists have proven that an over-exaggeration of stress actually causes greater health problems than denial of it; perhaps knowing that problems will go by is what makes people able to get over their internal and external strife.

But Arzoo's denial and calm were just as unhealthy, especially for public safety reasons, for those of you who have seen a woman suddenly lose her mind. On a not so humorous note, I once heard of a white woman who had four to five children very similar in age who picked her children up from school, practice or wherever they were distributed, brought them food, and then shot them and herself. The gory and extremely harrowing details of the event and the extremely disarraying thoughts that led her to kill her children are of too vital importance to be discussed here. Instead, I'd like to highlight the most important moral of the story: don't get so stressed to a point from which, like Arzoo, you find no return. Please, realise and understand your problems and find ways to encourage yourself to rise above them. Arzoo had the ability to rise above her problems, but in order to do so she had to identify what they were.

I walked over to the car, feeling dejected and depleted by the numbers still exploding in my head. I sat in the driver's seat and spent fifteen minutes looking for the keys, only to figure out that they were under me on the seat the entire time. I don't know why it was that I started bawling so much at that point; perhaps it was the realisation that sometimes things are literally right under you and you spend so much of your time just finding them. Completely dejected, my shoulders heaved, and clutching the steering wheel, I cried into the leather, as one would do in the arms of a dear friend. I don't know for how long I cried or how much or even why I was crying; it had never been my forte. I just know that tide of grief was sweeping out of the shores of my eyes and into the sands/skin of my face and I had no control over how it took control of me. I just knew that, as always, I was feeling something and I let it conquer me. I wept and wept, my body convulsing as each new wave of grief vanquished the mask of calm it had been deluding itself into.

I was so lost in feeling numb with the relief of crying that it took me a few minutes to register the fact that the faint thud, thud I had been hearing was someone knocking on my car window. I quickly wiped my tears away (as if my swollen lips, red cheeks, and puffy eyes wouldn't be enough of an indicator of the fact that I had been weeping). I was surprised to find our old Mexican housekeeper standing outside the car. She had been the help in making our apartment a home when we could afford her; she even took care of our apartment when we went to London. I always had a soft spot for this kind lady, but when Ian lost his job at the bank, it broke my heart to tell her that her services were no longer required. She was extremely upset at the news and I remember how she wept for a good two hours outside our door.

Ian obviously couldn't be more preoccupied with anything except himself and took no note of the soft crying, but I couldn't stand the small snivels of this poor woman, so I got out of the car bearing water and chocolates and held her hand as she wept and stuffed the candy down her throat. I realised then that she had been illegal and was worried about getting another job; I referred her to some people but realised that many were hesitant about employing an illegal woman and, well, after that I never knew or had time to find out what became of her.

It seems that life really doesn't wait to pay you back for what you did (good or bad) because the next thing I knew, I saw a bottle of water and chocolates making their way through the window and into my lap. In between sobs and smiles, I accepted the offering, and as I gulped down the sweets and the water, I looked up to see my prior housekeeper looking good. She seemed like she was doing well enough (she looked healthy and jolly, but then she usually was); the recession was perhaps not as detrimental to everyone.

"Arzoo, ma'am, how you? How you?"

"Oh! I am good, Isabella! How are you?"

"No cry! No cry! Beautiful eyes. No cry."

I suppose at this point I should've have pointed out that I knew as many words in Spanish as Isabella did in English. Well, to be quite honest, though, my vocabulary consisted of the five basic Spanish words that everyone knows, while Isabella was slightly more proficient in English than I clearly was in Spanish. That's the reason why we would always choose to communicate in English, irrespective of how poor hers was.

"Yes, yes, Isabella. I won't. How are you?"

"I good, good, yes! I make money but mucho problemo. My two brother ci ci, one to God, one uhuhuh pairenata cut gone," she said, signalling her thigh. In about the next fifteen minutes, Isabella finally successfully

conveyed to me that two of her three brothers got into an accident and one had passed away, the other was maimed for life, and her mother, out of grief, was extremely mentally unstable. To make matters worse, they were in Mexico and had no form of income and relied on the bulk of the meagre amount of money that she, their only sister, earned in the United States.

"Mucho, mucho problemo, money, money send Mexico." (Or as she said it, Mehico.)

I thought about Isabella's own five sons and her only daughter's children. (One daughter in the midst of many sons seems to be a common theme in Mexican genes and family planning, quite like the Pakistani people.) I wonder not only how she made ends meet, but how she even began formulating those ends. I looked at her eagerness, her unstoppable commitment to life, and happiness, and then for a second I glanced at my own reflection in the rearview mirror; at this dark, brooding, pathetic, depressed, angry woman. I looked at her insurmountable joy, at the purity of it, and realised my self needed to regenerate, to grow, to germinate hope and the fervour to actually be patient and wait for the culmination of dreams. This woman in my reflection really wasn't me.

Arzoo naturally gave the huggable woman a hug and asked her to visit. She thanked God for sending her Isabella – a chance connection can surprisingly help bring the strength that we thought was depleted within us.

I felt like I could take on the world again, I could get Ian a job, I could fix our apartment, work longer hours. I could make us happy again. It wasn't money that had constrained us and created the gap between us, for one just needs enough money to be comfortable; it was the dejection of our dreams and our hopes and the ensuing reactions we had to the changing elements within our own personalities. It wasn't money that would give us happiness again but respect and belief in ourselves and the us that somehow had lost its way in all the I's; I suppose Isabella had been vital to my thoughts in that she had made me realise that there are problems in everyone's life, and it is ultimately these problems, this bad, that makes us value the times that are good. We had been reminiscing so much about the good times we had had that we failed to create good today.

There is never any point in looking back, just moving forward. I reversed the car and as I drove it out into the main road, I reached into the glove compartment for my sunglasses, as the sun was still very bright and at its zenith, making it hard for my already puffy eyes to see. Keeping one hand on the wheel and the other in the compartment and, eyes constantly shifting between the wheel and the compartment, I was bound to be uncoordinated in my endeavours. The next thing I knew, a whole heap of papers fell out of the compartment and, cursing, I parked the car on the side of the street.

I was putting the papers back in when my eyes fell on the topmost paper and at the right corner of that paper, where the hospital's name was printed on the sheet, and then further down the paper, where the doctor's name and my name were printed. I held the paper and brought it closer to me, clinging to it, tears streaming down my face. All the momentary ecstasy of hope vanished as I thought about the contents of the paper and the horrible day that I walked into the hospital. Why didn't God give me a sign then? Why did he leave me to suffer at the consequence of my own decisions? I was alone, all alone, forsaken and forgotten by everyone I loved.

She went back to the apartment, overwhelmed and tired with all the crying and depression after venting in the car. He was sitting right where she left him, in front of the television screen, beer bottles and cans scattered all over the floor. He had one arm up, smelling his skin and sweat; funny thing, smell is – we unconsciously like or dislike other people's smells and are thereby consciously or unconsciously drawn to them based on their smell (no, not the smell of Gucci Guilty or Dior Addict, but their natural smell). However, our own smell is unquestionably the most superior. It has the ability to calm us, to soothe us, to make us more able to slightly adjust to outside changes by this familiarity with the constant inner self that prevails through our smell. You will often catch people touching their bodies and trying to rub their lips as a guise to bring their fingers closer to their nose and familiarise it with their smell.

Arzoo looked at him, smelling himself, so engrossed in NFL football (God only knows why Americans like to be unique in calling a game that hardly makes use of the foot, football, and actual football, soccer) that he neither realised his need to smell himself nor the fact that her eyes were puffy and her face streaked with makeup, let alone the fact that his fiancée had even returned home. If he needed her love, then he should have given some to her. Love is like respect; if you want respect, not only do you have to give it, but also you first have to respect yourself. Ian did love himself. He felt extreme mounds of pity and empathy for himself, but he didn't love himself enough, enough to be able to love another, to love her the way she wanted to be and should have been loved. His youthful narcissistic self-devotion had diminished (as had his looks) to just a whining demand for being taken care of. He had always told himself that he would never be like his father, a drunken alcoholic who had driven his mother away and ultimately himself into the arms of another man. But we are sometimes so used to a certain kind of injustice that we start imbibing and perpetuating the very injustice we were afraid of. In Arab or Pakistani culture, timid daughters-in-law assume the same role of domineering mothers-in-law, while daughters become the very nagging mothers that disturbed their own childhood development, and sons too start imbibing the same slothful or womanising ways that their fathers had adopted.

Heredity may be a vital factor in the adoption of biological traits, but biology, like your circumstances, is just an excuse. Where is the 'you' in all that is happening around you? Where is your self in your ability to take control of and change your victim status? We are all victims; it is up to us if we want to stay as such. Ian was a victim of his father's alcoholism and mother's ultimate abandonment and lack of interest in her son, but he had no right to use those same handicaps and apply them to his own life, bringing down another person with him. When all the angels in heaven and devils in hell come together, they truly make man and, like the discursive rhetoric, man has the capacity to both love and hate, to feel both pain and joy, to be both right and wrong, revengeful and forgiving. As we come across the fork in the road, the slightly more elusive fork in our own natures starts to take effect. Are you the blindly good angel or the incorrigible devil or simply human? Arzoo sat there staring at men run around, tackling each other, trying to get balls over to their home base. He had the choice to rise above every bad card that life dealt him and shock fate's dealer by not behaving in the way that fate expected him to, but he didn't.

She stood staring at him from the room, wishing that he would turn around, grab her, apologise, and tell her that he would fix all the wrong that he had done her. She waited for a few seconds and because she was human, she remembered that he was incapable of knowing and feeling for her at this point. Her lack of belief in him actually contributed to his persistence in being a slothful couch potato and to their intermittent cycle of hope and despair. She shut the door and locked it, turning the music on. She had rather sleep to the voices of Coldplay and Adele than the shouts and whimpers of her fiancé demanding attention she couldn't give, disrespecting her for her hard work, emasculating himself by first creating the situation where she had to be the breadwinner and then making her feel despondent for it. Most of all, she didn't want to hear him ask her for love when he had forgotten what that was himself.

For a split second, she almost got out of bed and had the desire to go out and scream at him, scream out all the hurt and pain that he had given her, but then she delved deeper in the covers. Shouting at him would imply there being a movement toward forgiving him and she had made up her mind to not forgive him, irrespective of what it would cost both of them. No, she could forgive his lazy, alcoholic, useless, pitiful self, but she could never forgive him for what he had done. Not even if they were born in infinite lifetimes and would be trapped again and again in those lifetimes like they were in their apartment and the only way out would be for her to forgive him. She still wouldn't forgive.

Arzoo shut her eyes, but the visions of that day kept obscuring her ability to sleep and her attempts at creating an artificial sense of calm. She remembered the fight with her fiancé, his insistence that she sleep with the VC so that he would get funds for his worthless start-up, the VC showing up for the dinner, her feeling groggy and unable to sit up straight and then finding herself the next morning in bed with him. Ian, shameless man, had drugged his future wife to sleep with a man in order to gain money. The VC, as fate would have it, turned out to be a fraud and Ian lost both his dignity and his fiancée all in one night. To make matters worse, when Arzoo, feeling sick, went to the hospital a couple of weeks later she found out that she was pregnant, whether with Ian or the fraudulent VC, she had no idea. All she knew was that she wanted to rid herself of this heinous child and the memory of the day where her honour was of no more significance than a few thousand that Ian wanted to obtain. In the East, a hymen's worth is often a life; here, her abstract female honour wasn't worth anything – no, not even a moment's consideration.

She wanted to tear out his throat. She felt frustrated at her own self for not getting rid of the child and resentful of the unborn child for being the sole reason that she still hadn't left. The fact that she had silently immersed herself in this humdrum existence to avoid answering the one question that was hounding at her was obvious – what was she going to do? She grabbed the pillow next to her and threw it against the door.

It was never the hapless child's fault for its inception. Arzoo lay unnecessary blame on that which still wasn't because it was better than acknowledging the fact that all this was inherently her fault. It was a colossal chain of events that had been instigated by a petulant and obstinate will that chose to not listen to any internal sanity but just the ferocity of its impulsiveness. Now look where she was – pregnant, unmarried, engaged to an abusive bum and no parents to back her up; just a job that brought enough money to get her through the month without any drastic worry, but that had created a freedom that hadn't been worth selling her soul over. She picked up the lamp and flung it at the door, wishing so much to hit Ian, but she too had had enough. Perhaps it was Rosa and finally acknowledging her grief, seeing Charlotte leading a happy normal life on Instagram or one of Nile's continuous persistent texts that she hadn't replied to in years but had remained a permanent one-way fixture in her life, but Arzoo knew she had finally had enough.

When she woke up the next morning, she was sure of one thing. She was getting out of here. There were plenty of people who she had completely cut out of her life, but Fadhi wasn't one of them. She called him and within minutes she had packed and left a crying, whining, pathetic Ian with just one thing to remember her by: the deathly ring that had caught her in such a fierce grip that it made her shudder wondering how she had become the real life visualisation of a Pakistani melodrama. As she saw Fadhi and hugged him, she began to feel a little more like herself. But then she thought of the baby growing inside her, and another cloud of unhappiness cast its shade on her thoughts.

EIGENWELT (ALL ALONE – WHEN YOU LOSE AND FIND YOURSELF)

I SAT IN *the pitch-black room staring at the walls, staring at the ceilings, staring at the floor. The darkness whispered to me, called out to me. I wanted to reach out, touch it, and own it. Yet man is a creature of the light. It fears the dark both within and external to the self. I am not elucidating a generalisation and unnecessarily imposing it on everyone, but merely portraying how man feels toward all that is not light. So I sat huddled within myself, too wrapped in the layers of Arzoo and what Arzoo was and is to shake off in one go all the trappings that had bound me experientially as one whole. Arzoo. Wish, desire, my entire life had been just desiring, wishing, covering, hungering, pining, never attaining, never feeling like a whole with anything or anyone. No contentment, never any satisfaction, just this unhealthy euphoria to desire, to be inflamed by want and even more aggravated by the incessant turmoil of waiting for the culmination of those wants.*

Why has my life, short as it is, always been structured around this incessant need to have desires for half the time and for the rest of the time receive no respite in their tardy culmination and often lack of motivation in being fulfilled? I searched and searched again and again for something, anything, to retard my series of hapless thoughts, but nothing. The word reverberated around the empty room, ricocheting and bouncing around the walls and entering my ears again with greater force.

Our mind is the most baffling part of our existence, for its adherence to experience and awareness can never ever be empirically tested or denied. It is the one absolute truth that we all acknowledge. In today's world, the mind remains the only decisive factor between man and machine because it is the mind, potentially the seat of the soul, the link to the universe, which has the power of self-reflexivity, to think of itself in all three time dimensions (if you believe that time only has three) and be capable of forming a construal about reality that is unique to that one person. Does the mind lead one astray, does consciousness ever err, or do we, incapable of helping ourselves with what thoughts we think, ever have a choice?

I had been a rock, I had been mud, I had been an unmovable, impenetrable mess that had sought bodily pleasure, forgetting the essence of me; of the 'us' that drives the collective man. And life had only begun to remind me of what I had neglected and forgotten. My poor dear parents, my friends. I had just relied on Ian, perhaps not even because I loved him, but because I derived a sadistic satisfaction from the fact that he was an open disregard of all that I despised, even if he himself hadn't been as conducive to my heart and even more so, my soul. I had known that since the beginning but discounted my soul's advice in light of the body's excitement. I had been obstinate, unyielding, and neglectful of all those that crossed my path, and now I was being taught the lesson that I wish I had been taught long before. The reality of what I had done was much too morose, too raw and curt to face. Yet I knew I was going to face it before ending it forever.

My mind took on yet another route to suffice its growing unease. Why did I exist? Whatever for? To be a failure to this space of mind and matter? To be a failure of all that is human? The rising despair took a hold of me again and the darkness was now just too unbearable. The eye can never see itself but through a reflection, both a physical and a social one, and yet here I was, seeing myself clearly, seeing the monster that I had created and who had just followed basic twenty-first-century instincts, denying my soul the compassion and courage to rise above hedonistic pleasures. What was wrong with me? What had I been thinking? Why had my thoughts, traitorous, traitorous thoughts, not listened to the mind? Why had I not? Was the reality that I had willingly generated so elusive, so unbreakable that the soul of the universe couldn't even reach through? I had everything that anyone could ever desire and yet all I had desired was MORE. Why can't man understand that the root of happiness is contentment, that self-actualisation only comes with pleasing the soul, mind (brain), and body, not just the body? Perhaps I had to set my soul free to enable it to reach its higher state of being. My body just deserved to break down and become one with the mud that it had been undoubtedly living as. My body didn't deserve to live.

Fadhi was out getting us dinner. The thought of him and the constant support he had been almost dissuaded me, but he wouldn't wake up, I knew that. I also knew that he had tried his best to reassure me, but I had never been one to believe another's words. I opened the drawer and took out the revolver; it had only two bullets in it. I chose to keep it that way – still too much of a coward to know of the exact moment I stopped existing. I closed my eyes and put it next to my head (next to the seat of that which ought to be freed first) and fired. Nothing. I fired again. Nothing. I looked at the revolver.

Why was death eluding me the same way that life had? Had I not achieved the lowest level of the self, the part that is the most animalistic and most unrefined? Why must I live and waste resources that another rightfully deserved? The thought that the universe had another plan for me – one that I was yet unaware of – thrilled me, but no, why would the universe? I was worthless. Even the air I breathed was a waste. The darkness had flung itself around me and like a shroud guided my hand, guided it to pick up the revolver and place it next to my eyes. I shut my eyes and felt a tear trickle down. I could hear a dog barking outside, the splat, splat of water as it fell somewhere, perhaps the toilet? I could hear the neighbours next door arguing over some meaningless point of disapproval, which at that exact moment was all that they cared about, and then I heard a baby cry and I stopped.

The light was returning. I thought of life. It was no one's fault but mine that mine had turned the way it had. I and only I needed to muster the will to make it better, to make it one that had true purpose. I fired on the wall; the bullet whizzed past me and hit the wall with a loud explosion. I breathed a sigh of relief, tears streaming down ever more reverently. I wanted to hear the dog bark, the water splatter, and couples argue. I had been wrong on so many counts, but I had no right to deny myself the gift of life. Who would have thought that sometimes being cowardly would have been more rewarding than being courageous? Whatever predicaments arose, whatever problems I was going to face, they could always be worse, and they would never be without my capacity to fix them. Did it matter what I did if now I had the capability to change what I was going to do?

Life had given me another chance, and chances, as everyone knows, are few. Perhaps it was I, myself, who was also giving life and myself a chance too. I wasn't going to let this opportunity fly by as I had the past twenty-three years *of wishing wishes for the body's realm. It was time to make things right, or right as my essence saw them to be. I thought of my parents, the core and reason of my existence, and felt the familiar tug at my heart. This time I was going to listen. I picked up the phone and called my mother.*

"Mama."

"Who is this? Arzoo?"

"Mama, I have left the American man." Well, it's not like she had a choice, but she wasn't about to burden her mother with another shocking detail of death just yet. She sniffled, thinking of his untimely demise just then, of the cops that she had to deal with, the burial... but she didn't want her mother to know, so she tried controlling as best as she could. "And I realise I have been so wrong and you and father have been so patient with me; you really are saints and I realise what I am meant to do in life now."

"*Beti*, we need you!" she sniffled. "You don't know what's been happening; there is chaos everywhere. We need you. Your father had two heart attacks and the K family... ah, *beti*... I, your dad, we need you. Your home is waiting."

"Mama, that's what I called to tell you. I am coming home."

They are lucky in life, those who realise at a young age the meaning of their existence. Arzoo was only twenty-three and her problems weren't as severe as those born into poverty and misery, they were self-created ones, and yet the issues had caused her to answer the puzzle of her existence and come to terms with herself. She had escaped incredible psychological conflict to arrive at her truth. What she didn't realise was that had there been no conflict, there would have been no desire to seek the truth. She would come to realise that some day in the future when she was perhaps older and wiser. But for now she was just glad to love, glad to be able to breathe, oh, sweet, sweet breath, and discount her stream of worldly desires for the higher states of being – eudemonia and the compassion, courage, and common sense admired in all but existing in few.

As she was urged further on to her path, she thought about how roundabout it had been but how now it was finally taking her to its destination. Her destination would have perhaps always been the same, but the particular path she chose was the hardest. All the more courage, compassion, and common sense to her, for the harder the path, the more the challenge and the greater the joy at eventual success. Existing is but always the means to an end; the harder you strive in your existing, the more you create meaning, and the more readily you can accept even death when it comes actually knocking on your door. As Arzoo found out, death never comes at one's bidding. It doesn't answer to your half-hearted knocking. But life, it leaps out at even a sliver of hope. If it doesn't give up on you, why do you give up on it?

MULTIFACETED LOVE

I LOOKED AT *her again – at the tall skinny body, at the white hands that stirred the milk in the pot, at the big beautiful doe eyes slightly perturbed by the prospect of mixing the perfect blend of tea and, most of all, at the dark blonde tresses that slightly brushed and touched the small of her back. Her hair wasn't nearly as long as mine had been, but it was perhaps the only type of hair I had seen that was nearly as captivating. I don't presume to be arrogant in my appreciation of the hair I had, but nonetheless I know, based on wide opinion, that it had been quite a resplendent picture of feminine beauty and grace. I traced my fingers through the short stubs that remained, still not quite used to the remains of nature's architecture. Like Ozymandias, all that remained were the roots, but unlike him, I had been the one who brought about their demise and was intrinsically pleased with the achievement of destruction as it was. At least I was no more an ornamental display to be gawked at.* (Though, reader, Laila had more going for her than just her hair; but to her it was not just a display to attract, but the ensnaring trap of her own torture.) *Maybe it was the fact that somewhere deep inside I did miss having my own hair or the fact that I was so used to the bounces, waves, and curls that fell from a head that I couldn't help but stare at hers. After all, that was the only reason that I was staring at it, right?*

"Do you want any more tea?"

"Hmmmmm." (Pause.) "I'm sorry. I don't know where my head is. I'm so sorry."

"No, no, it's okay." (Pause.) "I just asked you if you would like some more tea."

"Oh, yes." (Pause.) "That would be great." (Pause.) "You don't exactly have to do this. I could just make it myself, and you're pregnant. Seriously! Let me take care of you."

Ariyana smiled, her warm beaming innocent smile – a smile that would make one's heart skip a beat, a smile she hadn't smiled in some time – and then laughed, breaking their awkward exchange. "I am pregnant, not disabled. You, Nile, and Maya have been taking so much care of me and even the staff, Dai gee and Cook's family. You all have been such gracious hosts. I knew nothing about you and yet you took me in and have been taking care of me ever since. I—" (and she stopped for a brief moment, her voice cracking before she regained herself) "My child and I will be forever indebted to you."

I don't know what got a hold of me, but I felt this woman's indelible pain more sharply than my own. I wanted to go over to her and give her a hug and in between seconds where I debated what to do, I decided to go with my first instinct, and with arms hesitant to open, embraced her. She started weeping in my arms and before I knew it, I was weeping too. She hugged me with a purer need than I had felt in anyone before; it didn't require anything from me other than honest comfort. I, on the other hand, had never been wanted in such a way, and unexpected to even my own self, I was more than empathetic to her plight and was ever more eager to rise up to meet her need.

We held each other as if we were the last people left on this planet and as if the world had betrayed and abandoned us, which I suppose it pretty much had, but, being human, we never learned and still wanted nothing more than acceptance and company. When she stopped crying, my kameez was drenched in her tears and splotches of her hair were wet with mine. She turned away and when she moved back, she looked up into my face and smiled. After perhaps the longest time ever, I could feel my own muscles twitching and forming an expression that was something more than a blank withdrawal from the world. I could feel my soul energising, being called out by her smile, and I smiled back in response.

They say dialogue leads to peace, to breaking down barriers between enmities, hate, anger, betrayal, but to me, I know that sometimes between people there are no words required, just a realisation of the other and reciprocity in this realisation of the other. This strange fusion of white and brown, of woman and girl, had made me needed, me – not as a dutiful family member, a conscientious citizen or an object to be used and reused as one pleased, but me, Laila. She needed a companion, a friend, someone to console her and be there for her in her time of trial. I was more than happy to be the engineer of her solace for, in being so, I could feel my own stability returning. My work in the village had of course been successful in aiding my external self, in making me feel concrete, as if I had a purpose, but there was this hole that had continually got wider and wider inside me.

But since I had seen Ariyana a fortnight ago, standing helplessly at the side of the village (a protruding stomach not being the only thing gauging every man's interest) and had invited her to lodge with us, I could feel that gap saliently and increasingly becoming smaller.

"Thank you," she whispered.

I was about to respond with a 'no problem' when I both heard and saw the milk gurgling and spluttering out of the top of the steel pot. (Pakistani people always boil milk in pots on the stove.) I rushed to lower the heat, but Ariyana, beating me to it, turned around and said, "I am sorry, I am so sorry! I was so busy crying that I forgot all about the milk."

Reprimanding herself, she reached into the drawer, got a cloth and attempted to clean away the milk off the stove. "Ariyana, for God's sake, can you please stop acting like we are going to shoot you every time you do something wrong. Please, all we want from you is for you to rest and not worry. Stress is not good for you in this condition." *We finally got our second cups of black tea and I can assure you, there is nothing I love more than the smell of a fresh cup of black tea. The English may have ruled over us for hundreds of years and yet they left behind the most delightful of all legacies – black tea. I don't even like too much milk in mine as many people do, just a drop of it to add to the flavour and not take away from the natural essence of it. The smell of steaming hot tea swirled its way out from the cup and floated into my mouth, leaving a lingering, satisfying warmth. The aroma was enough to calm my nerves and my throbbing head (quite an unfortunate effect of profusely crying) and I could feel that instant soothing calm as soon as I put my lips to the cup and let the hot liquid enter my mouth and work its magic.*

I got up to retire into my room; it was midnight and in the village, unlike Lahore or Karachi, particularly if you had to aid in the running of a self-created NGO, not the time when you took dinner, but actually quite late to even go to bed. I got up to walk into the room and saw Ariyana sitting at the kitchen table fiddling with her thumbs, looking nervous and lost again. I took a deep breath and walked back over to the table.

"You know you can tell me about it!"

"About what?" she said, sweetly smiling as if I had just asked her if she wanted Nutella on bread.

"About why you are here? About why you are upset? About…"

"I am fine. Just completely fine."

"You sure?"

"Yes, yes," she said, nodding her head and smiling as if the smile would cover the sadness in her eye.

"Okay," I said. My conscience had only demanded me to inquire once; more than that would only seem intrusive, and I did not wish to appear as either coercive or meddlesome. I started to turn away when I suppose she changed her mind.

"Actually, there is something on my mind."

I turned around for the second time and went and sat on the stool opposite her. I believe that it's always easier talking to people when you are sitting opposite them rather than next to them, even if sitting next to them would allow you to tangibly be nearer (in the instance you want to pat or stroke). Ah, well! Just one of the countless trade-offs we make every day.

"Sure. Tell me what it is." I smiled, hoping that my newfound discovery of learning how to smile again would be enough to encourage her.

"Well," she said, twiddling her thumb, *"I really miss my husband."* A single tear trickled down her face and she brushed it away.

I didn't like the way she quickly tried to hide her emotion from me; I had thought that our exchange of tears would have been enough to further open us toward each other. I didn't even like the fact that she had started our moment of sharing by talking about her husband. I felt a stab of something I didn't know the origin of or have the genetic code for and just as hurriedly as she brushed the tear, I brushed away this unbalance in my emotional equilibrium.

"Oh dear! So why don't you just call him?"

I could feel my voice not being as level as I wished it to be, but we are our own worst critics and not everyone notices that about ourselves that we ourselves do, and Ariyana, already struggling with sharing her inner dilemmas, was oblivious of the slight, very slight, change in my tone.

She continued staring at her hands, nervously rubbing them, drumming her fingers on the table, and in my own mind, I wondered what she had been through to make her even more nervous than I was. Aloud, I said, *"Ariyana."*

"I can't call him," she whispered and cried at the same time. "I can't. I love him so much, but I won't call him. He kicked me out of the house. And I have no one, literally no one else in the world." She was bawling now, and not knowing what to do, I reached over and touched her hand, hoping that some certain human contact would be a means of assurance.

"Why would he do that?" I whispered, shocked and suddenly disgusted with yet another man I had never met.

"Because he thinks I cheated on him."

"Did you?"

"I would never; I love him so much. He doesn't even think that this baby is his. He called me a whore and kicked me out without hearing any explanation and all because of Mrs R and her posse, but especially Mrs R (I know she was the mysterious caller who tipped my husband off because only she and Mrs S knew and I know only Mrs R is capable of doing this). All she wanted to do was ruin me and I was such a fool to feel that she wanted to be my friend when, like a cobra, all that she was trying to do was wrap herself around me – and wait for the perfect moment to suffocate all life from me and I never did anything to her, never. All I ever wanted was for her to like me, for them all to like me. All I have ever wanted is to be accepted and loved for who I am. What's so wrong in that? You tell me, Laila. I have never hurt anything in my life, why should I suffer? He didn't even ask me what I wanted. He didn't even think twice; he just slapped me and discounted our child as illegitimate. He used to love me so much. Why did he just throw me out and in front of the whole house, in front of all the servants, in front of my mother-in-law. And she just stood there smirking as my husband threw me, his wife, out of the house with no money, no shelter, nothing, out in the middle of the night, and when I have no one, no mother – she abandoned me when I was a child – and a father who – no matter how hard I try, continually disowns me –.what have I ever done to deserve this?"

For a second I wish I hadn't asked Ariyana. Words interlinked with words as a desperate pain became the main theme of her storytelling. I barely made out what she was trying to tell me in between her tears and her fury; coherence was replaced with raw emotion. But I got the gist of it: this beautiful kind girl had been wronged by society, as are most beautiful kind people. It made me so upset to feel that another had been wronged for no reason than the very factors that should be raising her to greatness and blossoming her growth in an ideally welcoming society. Her husband had horribly wronged her. I suppose *it hurts more when someone you love infringes upon your rights, but unlike mine, at least he didn't do it out of some malicious need for a twisted form of self-pleasure. At that moment, though, I didn't care much about society and abusive husbands but about this delicate creature who was carrying the potential for another life within her, and I wanted nothing more than to love and protect her.*

"Ariyana, shhhh, shhhhh, sweetheart. Get a grip on yourself. It isn't good for your child."

She sniffled and unsuccessfully triedf to breathe and talk at the same time, only to slightly hiccup and break out in laughter. I joined her and as soon as she started, she stopped. Clearly, being pregnant wasn't the only thing that was affecting her erratic mood swings and I was determined to help her as much as I could.

"So you see, I can't call him."

"I agree, but think about it. Just the fact that you want to call him and the fact that you miss him implies that somewhere deep down inside you know that he is capable of forgiveness, that your husband isn't as bad as the action that you are defining and remembering him by."

"Yes," she said with one of her true smiles. "Yes, he had always been wonderful, so caring and loving. He is the only person – well, man – that I have ever met with whom I had no qualms until, well, he threw me out." Her smile turned into a frown again. "I suppose he was hurt that after giving me so much love I would betray him, but I didn't. How could he be so impulsive? How could he think that I would be foolish enough to throw away the one connection in my life that was of any consequence to me? He was my whole world – how could he doubt me? Eyes are so deceitful. I can't believe he let his eyes falsely deceive his heart. And you know something? she said. "I would have not cared about my own ego. I would have gone back and faced his mother, her taunts and jeers, his anger and doubt; I would have faced everything, but he called our child a bastard. How can I forgive him for that?"

I looked at her and said perhaps the most human words that ever came out of my mouth. "You can."

She was perhaps shocked at my response, hoping that I would agree with her decision. Taking my reply to mean that I didn't believe that she had gone through complete depression and disregard, she tried to withdraw her hand from mine, only to have me reach out and hold both her hands firmly in mine.

"Ariyana, listen to me. What you have gone through is unquestionably horrible. To fend all alone for oneself without any loved ones' support, and that too being pregnant, is horrible, especially while society does nothing but falsely label you and maim you for life. I understand your pain, Ariyana, and I am not asking you to immediately forgive your husband or to beg him to take you back. You are much too precious for that and your status as a mother is much too sacred to go on demanding acceptance. No. He will come for you when he realises that he has wronged you. I am telling you he will. And when he does, I think you should go back to him. Life is too short to let misunderstandings and hurt come in the way of people who truly love each other. You are lucky enough to find love, true love. Not everyone is. So when he comes back to you (which I am telling you again, he will), just forgive him and go back to him. You have been lucky. This is just a test of your love for each other."

"Thank you," she whispered. "Thank you."

She got off her stool, walked over to me, flung her arms around me and gave me a kiss on the cheek. I could feel my heart do a funny little flutter; I was happy for the fact that I had been capable of giving her happiness. She went and sat back on the stool. She was born to live in light, not in dark like me, and in respect for her light I would make sure she and her child never got a hint of the darkness in the world (at least not more than what they had got already). "Thank you so much for everything, really. I had nowhere to go and your family took me in. All I knew was that this village was once my father's ancestors'. I could have gone to England, but I didn't want anything to do with my mother's side of the family and what's more I didn't want to prove anyone wrong by just going abroad and them thinking I was following my mother's footsteps... my husband, my mother-in-law and father." She frowned, lost in thought. "Laila, can I now ask you a question?"

"Um-hmmm."

"Why don't you ever smile? I mean, when you do, it's as if it's forced – it's never truly from your heart."

I could feel myself turning red and wished nothing more than to just get up and leave, but then, realising my discomfort, she interjected and said, "I am sorry. Wrong question. Ummmmm, how old are you?"

"Twenty-seven."

"Really? I am twenty-five, going to be twenty-six soon! Are you married?"

"Yes. No. I mean, I was."

"Would it sound too nosey if I were to ask you what happened?"

"Oh no! Not at all. You just shared your problem with me. The least I can tell you is about the misery that had befallen me. Unlike you, I wasn't so fortunate in the man I ended up marrying. I don't know if he loved me; perhaps he did in his own way, but that way was not the one that I had always dreamed of or one that any woman would cope with. He used to beat me and rape me every time he wished to have me or every time he would get drunk, which was pretty much every day. He would use me in every way he pleased and when I told my mother and father that I wished to not be married to the monster anymore, they sent me back to him. When I left again the second time, they cut me off and refused to have any connection with me. I went to the court myself and got a divorce. My ex-husband was initially extremely reluctant to agree to the divorce, thinking that society would believe me and look down upon his freak self, but he was unnecessarily alarmed; no one blamed him for anything. He was from a distinguished family, wealthy, educated, so handsome. I was the weird one, the artist, the wrong woman that he had married. Like you, both society and the court tarnished my respect, my izzat; they squeezed out every drop of respect I had even had for myself and ended up labelling me as the only thing people can do to ruin a woman and called me a whore – something that meant doing a thing I would never have had the courage to do. By the time the divorce was final, even I had started to believe that I had been the wrong one in the marriage while at the same time wishing that I could show everyone this."

My voice was as calm and cold as Ariyana's had been passionate and engaging, and as I lifted my shirt to make visible the cigarette burns, bites, bruises, and nail scratches, I could hear Ariyana gasp and silently weep.

I pulled my shirt back down.

"You know, I had become used to these marks, used to the pain that he gave me. I never loved him, but, yes, I liked him very much (enough to marry him) and like every girl, I had hoped that I had met my prince charming, but most men somehow find a way to break that dream, you know. I was hurt by the fact that my husband wasn't what I thought he was and that, irrespective of the fact that I knew that he wanted to destroy me and got a sadistic thrill out of it, I knew that he would only be able to if I let him. So I discounted every physical assault on my body as the external outpourings of a very sick mind, but when my family turned against me, then I was really, really hurt, Ariyana. I was hurt when they called me a whore, hurt when society decided to hold me culpable for something that was not my fault, and why? Just because I am a woman and don't have an entire fortune to my name any more as my husband does, just because it is easier to blame people who have no support, money, or power to fight back? Yes, I was hurt at the injustice of it all."

I hadn't shed a single tear at this point.

"And so the only thing I could do, I did. I cut my hair. Well, I cut it the first time I left him, but it was only to my shoulders and then my mother sent me back. I loved my hair – well, at times I did – but so did my husband and I did not want to keep anything on my body that would be a reminder of his insanity and my subsequent destruction." I laughed then as I ran my fingers through the spikes that were growing out of my head, slightly nostalgic for the long tresses that used to brush the back of my knees. "The second time around, I cut it all."

Ariyana continued weeping and I felt more pity for her grief at my unfortunate marriage than my own misery because of it.

"Don't cry, Ariyana! It's okay. That was a really, really bad dream and now I am awake and I am going to live. I am not going to look back and I am not going to let my past define my future. I will make my life what I want it to be. I will be the sole programmer of my software, the sole baker of my cake, the sole teacher and student in the school of my life. I am done letting a society arbitrarily either throw me out like trash or accept me. I don't need their acceptance anymore. I don't need people to tell me that without a man I cannot survive, that I am incapable of fulfilling my hopes and dreams and must rely on some man's charity to give me what he wants, when he wants, and how much he pleases. No, no, no. I am through with that. I don't need someone else to complete me, to make me feel like a whole. I am a whole individual. I survived the grossest kind of assault on my body and soul and I stand before you still dreaming, still wishing, still wanting to be alive. I don't need a man. I just need me."

Of course, by this time Ariyana had stopped crying and was staring all wide-eyed and open-mouthed at me. I never knew that I had all these thoughts or all these fierce emotions pent up like this. It usually takes one person to genuinely care, and like a match it ignites life in another person. I touched my face; I didn't even realise that while Ariyana had stopped crying, I had been continuously weeping. I didn't even know that my cool calculating voice had started getting both low and hoarse, with my shoulders and hands trembling until Ariyana walked over to me and placed her arms around me. I knew that

I felt extremely calm and peaceful in her embrace. I didn't want her to stop holding me. It felt so good to have someone's touch assure me and give me strength for a change.

"It is awful when society does that. It's so frustrating that they judge without knowing anything about me or even getting to know me. Just because I am half-white, it doesn't make me a whore," she said, angrily shaking her head. "Why don't they understand that their impulsive irrational judgments can ruin someone's life? They are critically passing these judgments about someone as if they were God, as if their decisions are what is the absolute truth and, to make matters worse, that is what everyone else will believe! Reputation is an extremely elusive trait – you do one thing right and people will tend to forget and one thing wrong (perhaps not even wrong, perhaps they just don't like you) and your entire personality is overgeneralised based on that one flaw. To make matters worse, irrespective of what you do, that initial mental representation they have of you – you can usually never change that image.

"No matter how many times I say I am not a whore and no matter even if my husband takes me in, people will always think I am one and that the only reason my husband took me back was either because he is one angel who is so magnanimous as to forgive me, or that my magic on him is too strong for him to break away from me. They will never understand the pain that I went through or how, no matter what happens, I will be fearful of being thrown out of my house for the rest of my life. I suppose I will be like other people in the judgment of my husband. If he does one day realise that I am innocent, and if by then his mother hasn't got him married again, I don't know if I will go back with him. I promised you I will think about it, but I don't know, because I will always be fearful of how he'd be capable of just throwing me out. I will always be dependent on him and as a result always afraid. I can never forget that look in his eyes and how in a minute I went from being the person he claimed he lived for to filth, filth he couldn't wait to get rid of." She shuddered. "And with having that fear in my mind, I think I can never ever be the same with him. We can never ever go back to what we were."

"Yes, you can. Holding on to the past will never let you go forward. You will only be stuck there. We make ourselves, Ariyana... we make or break ourselves. No one else has the right to do that. Only we have the power to do that. When the time comes, you must decide if you wish to let all these people

destroy you the way they wanted to or if you will recreate yourself into someone who has experienced destruction, but has had the power to move past that."

"What about you?"

"What about me?"

"How will you ever get back in?"

I laughed.

"I was never meant to. Ariyana, you are all life and full of light; I am night. I was never meant to be understood. I only always arouse fear and suspicion in others. I tried being a part of the world that every person in this country desires. And it wasn't just my husband, but the entire artifice, the social expectations, the backbiting, lying, taunting. I will not go back. I will find my own path. Don't worry about me."

We were silent for a few minutes, each reflecting on our own and the other's pain. It is hard to absorb so much information all at once and once all barriers have been prematurely broken, there is often an awkward silence associated with the disbelief that a stranger knows more about yourself than people you once loved and cared for.

Ariyana finally broke the silence. "Was your mother-in-law really a bitch?"

I laughed again. "She was a fucking psycho bitch. I mean, look at her son."

We laughed until Ariyana looked at the time and realised that it was nearly 2am. She got up to leave and I once again stared at her smile, her twinkling eyes, her mane of beauty, and felt a loss within me when she got up and left. I didn't want her to go. Later on, as I lay in my own bed, fidgeting and uneasily changing sides, I realised that I couldn't go to sleep. I did the only thing that in such moments gave me peace and calm; perhaps it is the urge to do it that keeps me uneasy. I picked up the brush and painted. I didn't know what I was making or how it just kept me so stable; all I did was let my hand take control and do whatever it wished. When I was done, I could feel light creeping into the room. Dawn was fast approaching and the night was slowly transforming into day. I suddenly felt very tired but looked at the picture before going to bed. I was shocked to see two bodies intertwined as one; you couldn't make out their faces, just the white and slightly brown skin of their bodies, but the most noticeable element was their hair – long tresses (black and blonde) that grew out of their heads and covered most of the canvas. They twirled and twisted into each other until they combined into this one mass of hair that flew out of their bodies and toward the end of one corner of the canvas and seemed to be fluttering out of the canvas, as if infinitely made into one.

I had never ever drawn another person before and as my eyes shut, all I could think about was Ariyana and her beautiful dark blonde hair.

ELYSIUM TO TARTARUS

LAILA WOKE UP to the sound of laughter. It was pleasant and comforting to hear human joy. She was still too groggy to understand the source of the peals, but as the melatonin started dissipating and it wasn't too much of a mission to even lift her eyes, she realised that they weren't exactly completely genial and light to the ears but a merry cacophony of many people's raucous relish. Her dream state was interpreting the joy as pleasant, but when she finally managed to wake up, like a dream, the purity of the bliss also dissolved with the reality of being awake. She was having a very pleasant dream.

She tried sitting up, but then fell back on the bed, frowning, contemplating the sources of the laughter, which were still continuing. She could easily make out Nile's boyish, not yet manly, roars, Maya's controlled little flutters, the servant's uncouth barbaric toothy jarring sounds, and this light, pleasant, heart-warming laugh. Laila frowned, yes, that's the one that she had heard, the one that had woken her up from the dream of the goddess and filled her heart with a moment of pure uninhibited joy for and with another person. "Argh," she said, running her hand through her hair. "Let it not be Ariyana's, let it not be…" But it was. And she knew it.

She tried to search her bed for her watch and when she saw that it was a little past noon, leapt out of bed, nearly knocking over her painting from the night before. She carefully removed it from the canvas and hid it in her cupboard, being too possessive and insecure about anyone else viewing her heart's various trajectories – even to her, her desires never formed a straight path. She didn't want anyone else analysing her deep-seated emotions and desires any more than she wanted to herself.

Pulling a *shalwar* over her shorts and a robe over her T-shirt, she pushed her feet into her slippers and, rolling and tripping while she walked out, finally emerged to the cordial group of seven – her two siblings, four servants including Mr Ars and Dai gee, and her. She straightened herself up and, avoiding looking at Ariyana, glanced at Nile and with a smile said, "Whatever is so funny?"

"Oh, Laila gee, you won't understand! You just had to be there to see the way that the cat was playing with the slipper." They were referring to the Persian kitten, which, like Nile, wasn't yet a grown cat, but not really a kitten.

She raised her eyebrows and still maintained a smile. "A slipper and cat and this much noise."

"Really, Laila, Nile's right, you had to be there to see it. I mean it made me laugh," said Maya, the lady.

"And you just had to see the way that it jumped up and all over Mr Ars, the caretaker and Cook's brother, and then how he threw the slipper over to Dai gee (who was now head maid under the children's direct employment, unbeknown to their parents) and how she was screaming and running all over the place and then merely laughing at her own screaming."

Laila smiled yet she shook her head. "Really guys, Dai gee doesn't deserve your ridicule, she deserves your respect! She works really hard to take care of us all. Don't forget that!" Laila was not much of a fan of humour, especially the kind that was derived from another's misery, at another's expense, and would have gone on about the evils of ridiculing others when Ariyana finally spoke.

"Oh, Laila! They are just children having fun with a cat. And Dai gee didn't mind at all. Really, you should have been there."

"Ah! Well, perhaps you are right," she replied, still avoiding looking at her. "Well, Simmy" (Simran, Dai gee's daughter), "could you please make me a cup of tea? I have an awful headache and am already late. Start making it in ten minutes; I am going to go have a quick shower." She left her brother and sister in slightly abashed spirits, which Ariyana was quick to rekindle. She wasn't kidding when she said she was going for a quick shower, emerging minutes later to find that the kitchen/dining area was empty save for Simmy making the tea.

"Where is everyone, Simmy?"

"Oh *bibi gee*! The servants have gone back to work. I think Nile sahib went to play cricket with the other village boys and Maya *bibi* is on the phone," she said, making the sign of a phone next to her ear. Of course, with Ali! Laila shook her head, glad that Maya had found a sanctuary where she was free to communicate with her lover, and that too under the motherly watch and support of Dai gee, but deeply upset about the fact that there was a remote looming possibility that they might never get to be together.

"And what about...?"

"The *maim*?"*

"Yes – I mean, no, she isn't a *maim*, Simmy."

"She sure looks like one, so white and beautiful."

"Yes, yes," said Laila, remotely pleased that she wasn't the only one afflicted by Ariyana's charms. "Where is she?"

"She was in her room... oh, no, there she comes."

Simmy put the black tea cup right in front of the counter and went away to clean the toilet where Laila had just showered. Laila and Ariyana were all alone, with tea in the kitchen again. And for the first time since that morning, Laila had to look at Ariyana – eye contact avoidance was no longer possible.

"Would you like a cup?" asked Laila.

"Oh no, no! I have had two since morning, can't overdo it on the caffeine."

"Did you wake up early?"

"Oh yes! I went around for my morning walk. You know exercise is good for both me and the baby."

"Ah yes! Good thinking." Silence.

"Did you have a good night's sleep?"

"Yes, yes, almost immediately fell asleep after our..."

"Listen..." They both spoke at the same time and then got embarrassed, turning away before looking at each other and smiling.

"You go first," said Ariyana.

"Uh-uh! You first, please."

"Okay, well." She looked down at the floor, the tops of her long thick lashes brushing the bottom of her brow. She then shuffled her feet and wrung her hands. Laila just wanted to reach over and embrace her to calm her and tell her that there was nothing to fear from her, but she refrained. "Well, Laila, I – I wanted to tell you that last night was really amazing. I have

---

* Foreign woman.

never opened up to anyone like that, the way I did with you, and you, you are like my first ever friend. I just…"

Laila reached over and squeezed Ariyana's hand, looking intently at her face. This wasn't what she had wanted to hear Ariyana say, nor was she exactly exhilarated by the tone of platonic companionship, though of course she wasn't aware at that time that the word 'friend' was what had actually irked her composure, and yet she swatted away her rising aggravation and tried to be pleased about the fact that Ariyana had successfully thawed the awkwardness between them.

"Yes. I – I agree," she said, smiling, wanting to stay forever amongst the aura of this woman who both calmed her and made her feel whole again, but she looked at the clock. It was 1pm and there were others who needed her more.

"Hey, Ariyana! I would honestly love to sit here and chat, but I am running late; I would love to come back and talk some more." She picked up what looked like a pretty heavy bag that was placed on the side of the counter.

"Oh sure! I am sorry, so, so sorry; that was very unintelligent of me… please, please go by all means. Don't worry about me at all. I'll be just fine here."

Laila was just walking out the door when Ariyana called her back. "Laila, where do you go every morning?"

Laila grinned. "Oh! An extremely special place in this already quaint little village, would you like to go?"

Ariyana's eyes sparkled and, as Laila looked into them, trying to become accustomed to their glitter, she momentarily forgot everything that she had been about to say. "Oh, yes! Please, that would be great."

"Hmmm. Sure, come on, but it's a long walk!"

"I don't mind walking."

"Do you want me to help you with that bag?"

"Oh no, dear! I carry it every day, never been a problem."

The two women adorned *dupattas* over their heads out of respect for the village norms and traditions and walked out of the house. Since all three of the siblings were back in the village it naturally made sense for them to move to their ancestral house (though Nile had to be talked into shifting from the cook's little abode). They crossed the wheat fields and the rice fields, they crossed broods of cattle, buffalos, and of course goats, they crossed the lesser refined village houses, they flowed past the women in their *chadors* working in the fields or ambling along after a child or five, they scurried past the men in a great hustle-bustle on tractors, around bull carts loaded with sugarcane and in the market past the shops where the barterers spat *paan* on the streets, and they giddily bounced past the little children whizzing and running about until after about thirty minutes, when Ariyana spoke again. "Laila, I don't mean to be so inquisitive, especially since you were nice enough to ask me to accompany you, but wasn't that the shoe smith's house? Aren't we nearing the edge of the village? I mean, I am pretty sure we will be on the main road soon."

Laila put a finger to her lips and quietly smiled. "Shhhh! We are almost there."

"Well, at least let me carry that bag for a bit. It looks super heavy."

"No, Ariyana! We are almost there. Please, no formalities."

It was only when they turned into perhaps the most deserted and dilapidated part of the entire village that Laila stopped. It was ailing and fraught with being debilitated and doddering on the point of collapse. Ariyana could almost feel the poverty and the sickness wrapping itself around her, choking her. She wanted to be far from here, but she glanced over at Laila, at the calm serenity that accompanied her visage, and she calmly followed her into one of the weary flaccid houses.

"Laila, what..." she whispered.

"Shhhhh," said Laila, putting her finger over her lips again.

Ariyana was quiet and soon she walked into the house and realised that it was composed entirely of mud and cow dung; other than a back window it had no other openings for ventilation of air, which was much needed, since at least twenty women sat on the floor. They had cast their *chadors* aside to reveal extremely fatigued, feeble, decrepit bodies, but as soon as Laila walked in, it seemed like she carried with her the secret of life and immortality. Their eyes shone as if the universe had offered them the secrets of its celestial importance, as if their misery and affliction, their poverty, was but an illusion that Laila had dispelled. Ariyana knew instantly that each one of the women in the room worshipped and loved Laila and as she walked and sat down, she was curious to know why.

"*Asalam aleikum*, Laila *bibi gee*," they shouted in a unanimous chorus.

"*Waleikum Asalam*, ladies... and how are you today?"

"Not bad, Miss Laila," said one of the younger women. "All of us have been waiting for three hours, so eager for you to come."

"Oh, I am so sorry for being late, please forgive me."

"Laila *beti*," said an old wrinkly woman of about sixty-five, "P didn't mean that. All of us would honestly wait for days for you. She meant we were all assembled anxiously as always."

"Well, R. *ama* (older mother/woman), I know she didn't mean that. I still had to apologise for making you late. Well, ladies, this is my lovely friend, Ariyana." The women said their salaams to Ariyana and for the first time since she had been in a gathering of women, they didn't envy either her body or her white skin, or pay much attention to her, save for the fact that she was a woman just like them. "Ladies, I know you have a number of household chores to get taken care of so I believe we should get started."

There was a great deal of exuberant agreement and Laila opened her bag to take out a sketchbook and many different types of fabric. It didn't take Ariyana long to figure out that Laila used the sketchbook to create the designs and would then hand out the fabric to the women to do hand embroidery on.

Astonished, Ariyana nudged Laila and whispered, "Laila, how, where?"

She smiled a saintly smile. "Some of them already knew how to sew and the ones that didn't, I taught. I mean, I didn't really teach them something that wasn't theirs to know already. They are some of the most hardworking, honourable women that I have ever met. I feel honoured to be working alongside them, to have my designs transferred by them onto fabric. I send them to my friend back in the city; it's been a month now and the first batch was a modest sale, but for these women it was not just the opportunity to actually have money for a change, but also gave them the ability to have some control over their lives."

"Laila, this is remarkable. I had no idea what an incredible task you were accomplishing every morning."

"No, no, no. They just needed someone to guide them, to show them their potential. They always had it in them. And you know what? You haven't seen the best part yet. V, V," she called out to one girl. "Where are they?"

"Oh, Laila *gee*, Hashim saw you walk in, he has already gone to round up the others. They should be here any minute." She had barely finished her sentence when Ariyana heard the pitter-patter of feet, squeals, and giggles and in ran a brood of children, twice – nay it seemed almost thrice – the amount of the women in the room. Both little girls and little boys aged three to fourteen were shyly looking at Ariyana, smiling and giggling except for one little golden-haired Pathan boy who leapt into Laila's lap and gave her one big hug, screaming, "Laila *didi*," and kissed her hands.

"Hashim," said Laila, laughing. "Were you a good boy today?"

"*Nahi gee nahi*" (literally translated to no way José). "Hashim and good boy," said a golden-haired Pathan woman, presumably his mother. "The little food that I scrounged around for is completely eaten by the time I get back and then I have nothing to feed the other little two and the baby. I mean…"

"G. How many times have I told you? Don't restrict Hashim from eating. There is so much extra food at the house. Please let me offer to give you some."

But G was a proud Pathan woman and one who would never live on others' charity. "No, Laila *gee*, we may be poor, but we don't beg," she said and, embarrassed, she turned back to her needle and thread.

"Ah, well," sighed Laila, "who is up for some treats?"

Hashim was still lodged on Laila's lap, making it hard for her to move, so she signalled to Ariyana and asked her to open the bag and distribute what was in the bag to the children. Ariyana opened Laila's bag of wonders to reveal Mars and KitKats and crisps such as Lays and Pringles, and as she handed out the junk to these children, she could tell that they had never, before the advent of Laila, in their lives, ever presumed that these goodies were ever within their reach. As she handed over things and saw the smiles of gratitude and the eyes of eager childish want fulfilled, Ariyana knew what Laila meant when she said that they were in the most special place in the village. For the first time, her mother leaving her seemed so miniscule and immaterial and yet she thought about how she had let that event time and time again haunt her and manipulate her daily activities.

Laila ran out for a breath of fresh air with the children and Ariyana turned to this woman, probably in her late forties. "Did Laila *gee* teach you embroidery?"

"Yes," said the woman. "May Allah bring nothing but happiness for that girl. She, she has had faith in those whom it seemed even Allah had spurned for a while, but," she said laughing, "Allah never spurns his creation. We each have to suffer to come to know the meaning of happiness, and in Laila *gee*, Allah sent us a *farishta*.* We are women with no families to call our own and a whole brood of children to feed."

---

* An angel.

"Why?" said Ariyana, amazed. "Why don't you have family?"

"Because some of us are widowed, some of us are in an immoral line of business, some of us had acid thrown on us by a man in a jealous fit of anger and passion, and yet for some of us, like myself, our husbands have kicked us out."

Yes, thought Ariyana, *I know what that's like*. "Why did he?"

"Because he married a younger woman who would bear him sons and overnight my three daughters became illegitimate and I became a whore and society treated us like we were *achoot*,* until Laila gee came and she saw in each and every woman in this room something that none of us knew existed. She gave us a chance when no one would." Ariyana shed a tear along with the woman, feeling a tugging at her heart for Laila, a love that had just grown out of nowhere and that respected her soul and essence. After all that Laila had been through, she still had the capacity to love, to give so, so much love, and she, Ariyana, had never nor would ever respect anyone more. In Laila, she saw the hope and potential for man to regenerate, to grow out of the depths of hell and find a luminous existence that guides all out of the darkness.

When Laila came back in, she felt Ariyana looking at her in a peculiar way – almost in the same deferential manner that the other women in the room did. She didn't know whether she liked that any more than 'friend' and was determined that they be on equitable levels in their emotions and respect for one another.

As both women walked back, they were just as silent as on their walk to the house, though this time the silence had more to do with the absorption of the day and less to do with the anticipation of the showing and being shown of one's heart.

"Lai—"

"Ari—"

"You go first."

"No, now this time you should go first."

"Well, Ariyana, I just wanted to tell you that I hope you keep today a secret. I don't want anyone else to know."

"But why?"

"Because…"

_____

* Untouchable.

"Laila, both Maya and Nile need to know what it is that you do. I know you think that they are too young, but they really aren't. Nile is going through an existential crisis and this village has given him some sort of purpose, and Maya, I don't even think I need to tell you how society is ripping apart her very core and humanity. They can handle the truth, Laila. I know you wish to protect them, but there is no purpose in protecting people from the truth. They will find out eventually. It is better that you elucidate them with the facts yourself. And I don't know if you know this, but before coming here Maya was teaching Fehranaz for so many years and will continue to do so, she said, once she goes back home. Perhaps she could teach the children. I am sure Hashim would be an avid learner."

"Hmmm," said Laila, proud of her siblings for once. "You know, I suppose you are right."

They were walking past the *lohar** when Ariyana suddenly realised something. She smiled and told Laila that she would catch up with her. When Laila asked her where she was going, Ariyana merely laughed and ran, telling her that she wanted to go thank Lala Ibrahim's wife for sending her *kheer*** the other day.

Laila muttered something about how she wouldn't have minded coming along but Ariyana was not within earshot. Had she been, she still wouldn't have had the chance to reply. There was a flash of bright light and all went black.

---

* Iron smith.
** Rice pudding.

CATASTROPHIA

THE FLASH OF light was so unbearable, perhaps even more painful than the sound that accompanied it. It was as if God had extended his hand from the heavens and blinded out all memory, all reality, and all existence. There was just this persistent wiping out, clearing away, reducing to nothing. Complete obliteration. Complete silence, and then seconds after that momentary vacuum of the senses, a tirade of their reigniting. So much frenzy and dust, dust everywhere and covering everything, mixed with panic and noise. The fleeting lapse of death and destruction abates only to have life muster every ounce of energy to fight back.

When Laila came round, her entire body was aching. She was lying face-down and spat out a great deal of dirt. Where was she? What was she doing on the ground? She tried to get off, to get up, but she couldn't move. Why was everyone around her shouting? She tried getting up again but her right arm was in a great deal of pain; she couldn't move it, even her leg felt numb. Why was everyone in such a great panic? She tried feeling her left arm and leg. Good, she could feel them! Wait, did she just hear Nile? Why was he shouting at her, calling her, telling her to not move? Why did everyone's voices just sound like a loud, jarring sort of amalgamation?

"Don't move, Laila, DON'T MOVE! I think you have broken your arm, and your leg is injured!"

His face was inches away from her and betrayed an expression of extreme confusion and panic. "Nile, Nile, what happened?"

"We don't know, Laila, Lala Ibrahim's house is gone... anyway, all this is immaterial right now, you don't move. Please don't move, Laila. The men are creating a sort of semi-stretcher and the women are coming to take you inside one of their houses. Just don't move."

"Wait… wait! Where are you going off to?"

"To get Ariyana out!"

A wave of panic took a hold of her now. "Wait, Nile, what happened to her… ?NILE!" She was using every ounce of her energy to shout at him now. "WHERE IS SHE?"

"Under the rubble," he shouted back. "She and Lala Ibrahim's wife were just a little further away from the house. She is fortunate to have survived. I am going to go get her out."

"NILE!" she shouted back. "STOPPPPP!" Laila screamed, but knew that nothing could perturb Nile's newfound courage. She gave up, lying back on the ground, frustrated and anxious. She was worried about Ariyana's safety, but perhaps just as nervous about her little brother going to get her out. Let's not jump to hasty conclusions; Laila did indeed feel a surge of pride that her kid brother was trying to be the hero in this moment of utter desolation, that he had the ability to be resourceful and dauntingly resolute, but she simultaneously knew that it wasn't safe.

Nile, on the other hand, ran as fast as he could to the site of the explosion. He was most concerned about everyone's safety, as those who have been touched by the blessed duality of both bold strength and empathy often are. He had met his life's calling in this village and was determined to save and protect it while at the same time keep his 'self' alive. Whether it was a rise in his adrenaline or testosterone, Nile was wilfully choosing to follow his heart. He couldn't and wouldn't at any point give up on the place that had taught him the meaning of life and no one he loved would suffer under his watch. Ariyana was a kind, generous woman and did not deserve to suffer. No. He would make sure she didn't.

He ran and, panting, stopped over at the area where pretty much an entire house was plastered atop of her. Nile had the common sense to stand and assess the situation as it was. There were a couple of men trying to move the rubble away, but at that rate she would lose all potential oxygen and be buried alive. It wasn't safe for her; they had to get her out fast.

He ran up to what used to be Lala Ibrahim's house and shouted out, "Ariyana, can you hear me? Ariyana?"

"Nile, get me out of here… Nile… please," she was both hysterically crying and shouting. "Nile, there are dead bodies next to me. Nile, PLEASE

GET ME OUT. My baby, Nile, please save my baby," Ariyana wailed.

"I will get you out, I promise. Just hang in there!"

"Nile, please, I can't feel my legs, Nile," she kept deliriously crying. It only made him more impassioned to help her but at the same time prevented him from concentrating, so he asked her what any man with common sense would.

"Okay now, Ariyana, I want you to please stop crying and feel the roof of where you are. Does the rubble seem sturdy, because I don't want it caving in if we try to move."

"Yes," she said, moving her hands to feel the earth around her and simultaneouslly, realising that her frenzied agitation would not be conducive to the rescue mission. She stopped wailing. "Yes, there is an opening that you can get to."

Nile was confident enough that there would be no way that the ground would crush Ariyana were they to move the upper layer of the brick and wood that had enclosed her. Now the predicament was that there was no way any man, let alone a twenty-one-year-old boy, could possibly remove the debris and heavy brick trapping Ariyana. After thinking for about five minutes, his O level physics finally came to some use. Nile asked one of the villagers to run to his house, which was less than a mile away and had withstood the explosion, and grab some sturdy rope. He meanwhile asked another one to get a bull cart and a third to grab a large hook-like object that they used for ploughing. When the man brought back the rope he tied the contraption into the debris and asked the men to make the cattle pull the heavy remnants. He repeated the procedure a number of times and finally created an open space from which he could see Ariyana clinging to a rock, huddled in a corner with what looked like parts of Lala Ibrahim's wife splattered next to her.

"Ariyana, hold on. I will jump in and pull you out. Please don't move in case something is broken; we don't want any harm to come to your baby." He tied one end of a rope around himself, removing the huge claw-like hook that had been crucial in removing the bricked waste, and left the other end still attached to the cattle. He lowered himself into the giant hole that had formed and landed right next to Ariyana. Her face was bruised and bleeding; part of her *kameez* was torn and there was blood all around her. Afraid for her child, as he was pretty sure that the pressure on her ribs would have resulted in a pretty slim survival rate, he chose to remain quiet and instead extended himself and removed the rope, attaching it around her to make sure that there would be no damage to the baby – if there was even any possibility that it was still alive.

Five men peered into the opening and as Nile signalled to them they shouted out to the man in charge of the cattle and, like a decently self-designed crane, the cattle pulled her up to the ground. The men threw the rope down and Nile attached it to his waist, but before they could pull him back up, he slipped on a piece of rock and fell on the pile of rubble near him, upsetting the balance of the earth around the opening. The earth fell around him, enclosing him in a much more fatal living grave than the one Ariyana had been trapped in only moments before. One clumsy step and your entire life literally can come crashing down. The last thing he thought was *Oh shit* as five moustached heads shouted and screamed to an Earth that listened to no one but its own force of nature.

A WORLD BECOMING FLAT

HIS EYELIDS FLICKERED once and then once again before shutting again. He tried opening them again, but the light was too piercing. Where was he? The roof looked white, too white. Arghhhhhh – what was that light? Too, too bright, much too fluorescent… it wasn't his room, definitely wasn't his room. Well, then, where was he? This jumbled incoherent split-second assessment was momentarily halted. He tried to breathe but felt something choke him, gagging even the very next thought that was formulating. He looked to his right for any sign of an authentic indication to his objective reality and saw the curtains around the bed, tried to move, and found that he was connected to all the dials and gadgets on the wall. God, where was he? Perhaps there was a scar near his stomach that might betray the absence of a kidney. No. Thank God. It didn't seem like he was missing one. He tried to get up, to remove this thing that felt like it was trying to choke his throat, but felt like every fibre in his body was extremely opposed to his mind's current extremely ambitious aspiration. He lay back down and looked to the left for the first time in the past thirty seconds.

Indeed, he did look to his left and that is when he saw her, seated on the chair. Her grey eyes beautiful and expressive, straight nose, full lips, and what was perhaps the most unconventional of all, he saw her dressed in the most humble *shalwar kameez*. Yet to him, she had never looked more beautiful than she did at that moment. In between all this confusion and jumbled delirium, he could feel his heart still do the familiar little jump it always did when her vision physically or sublimely infiltrated his mind. If Arzoo was here, and he thought that he could tangibly perceive her, then that could only mean one thing: that after so many days he was finally in the most glorious dream he had had for a long time and no longer had the desire to expunge this horrible deranged state.

He tried to speak, but his throat felt much too dry. It burnt and all he had was an inexorable need to consume every gallon of water that existed on this planet. He could see her getting up and within seconds she was standing next to him; his flesh sparked at the place where her soft hand lightly yet firmly touched his arm and he could feel his face getting hotter. She reached over and expertly pulled out whatever was blocking the air from him and within seconds enabled him to breathe again.

"Wa-wa-ter," he managed to croak. She nodded her head and walked across the room, pouring water into a cup from a glass. Putting the cup around his mouth, Arzoo slowly tipped it so that it was easier for him to take one gulp at a time. The first few sips felt like fire trickling down his throat, scorching his oesophagus, but ignoring the pain, he let her give him the water and slowly the pain subsided only to calm his throat. Strange dream. Queer little conundrum of pain and pleasure, of confusion and familiarity, where water feels like fire only to vacillate back to its original state.

"How do you feel, Nile?"

He stammered, more at the fact that her grey eyes were trying to peer at him with their almond enclave than the fact that his voice was still slightly hoarse and it scratched his throat to try and speak. "I am... fine."

She looked worried. "I think you should try and rest, Nile; I don't want you to... maybe I should call a doctor. Yes, I think I should, he needs to tell you."

Arzoo was rising from the side of his bed when he stopped her.

"Wait, we are in a hospital?"

"Yes!" Suddenly the white walls, roof, the various tubes and pipes around his arm, and what's more, the damnable construct in his mouth, made sense. As is often the case with a puzzle where one gets the first piece, or a darkened way that has suddenly been illuminated, the problem suddenly seemed to increase in proportion. Numerous other questions started haunting him.

"Wait. What am I doing in a hospital?"

She got up this time. "Let me go get the doctor, Nile."

"No. Please. Stay. What are you even doing here?"

"I came back two weeks ago."

"Two weeks and it took you this long to get in touch with us?"

She kept staring at the floor, perhaps too ashamed to meet his eye. *What is she hiding?* he wondered.

"Where are my parents?"

"Oh! They were here until yesterday; my mom and I decided to stay behind. They've gone to your Lahore house; your father had some important business that he needed to take care of."

"So where am I exactly?"

"Peshawar!" she mumbled.

"WHAT? What am I doing here?"

She kept looking at the ground, but finally looked up, looking at him straight in the eye, hoping that perhaps he could see the sincerity in her intentions for trying to keep the truth from him.

"Your parents left with Maya yesterday, but Laila is…"

Arzoo didn't have to finish her sentence. Just the mention of Laila brought back a recollection of a horrible sound, a jarring, deafening sound, the kind that makes you forget what a sound even is. He remembered the blood, the glass, the dead bodies; he remembered his sister and…

"Laila, Laila, Laila, Arzoo, where is she?"

"She is fine and…"

"What about Ariyana?"

"She is fine too. She still hasn't left yet even though… well, she lost her baby." Nile nodded, remembering how he knew then that it was impossible for the child to have survived. "But she hasn't left, even though everyone has been telling her that she needs to rest and has been through such a rough ordeal, but she really was waiting for you to get up. She said that no matter how long it took she wouldn't leave the hospital till you were well up, but I mean, it's like 3am and everyone went back to get a good night's rest. I just couldn't go back. I thought someone should stay here with you, so I did."

Nile, feeling a surge of warmth for her little display of compassion, ignored that which was pertinent to his heart to inquire about that which was necessary to his mind. "Up? How long have I been here?"

"About three weeks, I guess."

That's when Nile recalled what he should have at the onset, the five moustached faces and the earth caving in…

"I need to get up, Arzoo. I am completely fine now. I… Why can't I get up? Wait. Why can't I feel…"

"Nile, wait. Let me get the doctor first. He will explain."

"Why do you keep mentioning the doctor? WHY CAN'T I GET UP?" he panicked.

Nile finally had enough strength to move his arms, threw away the covers, and saw to his utter horror his right leg lying next to a stump.

"ARZOOOOO, ARZOOOOOOO, WHERE IS MY LEG? Where is my leg? Where is my leg?"

"That is what I kept trying to tell you," she whispered. "The doctor wanted to be here when you woke up."

"WAKE UP!" he screamed. "WAKE UP to this? NO, NO, NO, NO. This is a dream," he said. "This is a dream! You are not real. You aren't real. This isn't real."

Nile kept denying that which was glaringly obvious to him now, but irrespective of the number of times that he kept negating the obvious to himself or the number of times that he kept trying to push Arzoo and her hands away, he couldn't get away from the fact that he no longer possessed a right leg. It would be a Bedlam hell to wake up and find one's limbs gone, to realise that you are no longer one complete person as you saw yourself, but must now learn to adjust. As a young boy with many dreams and wants from running to driving, as someone whose testosterone would have guided an impulsive existence for at least a few more years and to whom losing a leg meant partially losing the identity of being a man, Nile's denial would seem an appropriate means of coping with this new turn of events. He had just begun to find himself; he had just realised his life's greatest mission. Must he now lose all purpose when he had only begun to understand the hazy shadow of his print in this world? Nile was inevitably in purgatory, but as is the case of the cruellest of trials, he would only be guided into an even deeper understanding of who he was and could be. But for now, he first had to come to terms with his loss.

His anguish loitered around his body in the way he clenched his fists and warded off Arzoo's advances, but as soon as it again travelled up from the stem to his stomach, through his chest and neck to his brain, he knew that his one pure act of heroism had inevitably been the cause of his own imminent undoing. He let his hand unclench and stopped screaming and let the sorrow find a way into the core of his being and out through his eyes. Arzoo finally got around to the other side of Nile and as she saw the tears silently trickle down his face, she thought that he was perhaps the most honest and noble of all men she had seen to be able to articulate his grief so gracefully in front of her. It touched her heart more than even the lack of his leg had. So she did the only thing she could have. Perhaps, it might not have been the wisest thing to do in a hospital in Peshawar with thousands of judging little beady eyes posted at every nook and cranny, but they were in a private room and she couldn't care less what the doctor or his little opinionated posse of nurses thought of her.

Arzoo softly crept on the bed beside Nile and put her arms around him. All she wanted to do at that moment was to assure him that he would never be alone in his unfortunate forfeiture of young carefreeness that had actually just dissipated with his leg. He grabbed onto her with a need that neither of them had felt – it was pure and instinctual. It was the extremely austere and unsullied need for human companionship and support. And as he wept in her arms, she, not an alien to grief and loss, cried too, letting out all the fear and pain that she had held inside her for a very long time. They stayed like that in each other's arms for a long time, long after they had stopped crying and even after they had gone to sleep – neither was willing to let go.

The nurse who found them in the morning was quite excited about the prospect of seeing such a blatant display of 'unmarried affection' and rushed in to tell the other morning orderlies. She was a foolish woman to have assumed that the purest of human bonds must always be denigrated to a physiology of the body and hormones.

THE THREE FATES

MAYA SAT ON her bed, once again contemplating her oxymoronic existence. The infiltration of her thoughts was making her weary now as the same emotions and beliefs kept circulating around and around in her head. Her mind kept oscillating between her, her parents, the lover, and the cousin, until all that she could play in her head were the numerous ways her marriage could work out. How does she appease her sense of duty and gratitude or her newly developed self? Why must it even be a choice between her parents and the boy she loved? Why couldn't her inner turbulence once and for all end? There is no greater agony than that of being stuck in between, not knowing and just being in the interim where, like a spectre, you are neither alive nor dead. Just your mere existence itself is a huge question haunting those around you and more than anyone else, plaguing you to no end.

As she turned and tossed, weeping, she felt her passion rising and a familiar emptiness entrap her. She was all alone; no one could help her. Not her friends, not her lover, no, not Laila, not Nile, no one. She had barely thought of Nile when in he walked with three of her aunts. He was hobbling on one leg; it broke her heart to even imagine the pain he was going through, being without a leg. It made her want to scream at the world, scream at the injustice, hold it by the neck and throttle it to nonexistence. *Yet, stop, it isn't injustice's fault.* Like the leaves of a tree, it just flows to wherever it is directed; unfortunately though it affects all in its path.

"Maya, do you have a minute? These women wish to talk to you."

Aunt number one: "Look, Maya, you need to stop thinking that we are your enemy; we are not. We want what is best for you."

391

"Haaaa," smirked Maya. "And I don't know? And you, a foreigner to my wants and needs and the inner trajectories of my thoughts, are better versed in what is best for me? Please do enlighten me." She sat up, snarling, her eyes gleaming with the possibility of no longer being constricted but finally speaking her mind and pouncing on the well-deserving prey.

Nile shook his head in an attempt, I suppose, to tell her to not appear like she wasn't in control of her emotions and to rationally address these infuriating menaces.

Aunt number two: "Well, Maya dear, we didn't come here to either fight with you or incite any trouble. All we want is to tell you the facts."

Aunt number three: "Yes, dear, we aren't opposed to you, we are your family. We will only want what is best for you."

Maya: "Oh, cut the histrionics and get to the point."

Aunt number one: "Look, you must do this for your parents."

Maya: "I thought this was about me."

Aunt number one cut in, "Dear, your parents are and should be the most important people in your life."

Maya: "We are talking about my marriage, which has suddenly become the harbinger of destruction to everyone. We aren't talking about my parents or my marriage to my parents, nor are we discussing how neither of my parents will have to marry the man that they have destined for me. I WILL! AND I CAN'T!"

Aunt number two: "What an ungrateful girl, tsk, tsk. You MUST do this for your parents. For all that they have done for you, clothed you, fed you, sent you to the best schools, sent you to Harvard."

Maya: "So now I have to be grateful to them for sending me to Harvard for two and a half years. I must be indebted to them for having the paternal love to give me permission to go to HARVARD?" Maya's voice was rising in emotionality and losing an observer's notion of rationality. "DO YOU KNOW WHAT YOU ARE TALKING ABOUT, YOU DAFT WOMAN?"

"My, my," said one of the aunts. "This girl still hasn't changed! So much hubris. It is indeed permissible to not send girls to college."

"My going to Harvard was a product of my hard work and my intellect, though as you say, since I am a girl perhaps I should be indebted to them for enabling me to have this opportunity," retaliated Maya further.

Aunt number three: "Indeed you should! You know that no girl before you has gone to college in the States, it was by your parents' grace that you even went."

Maya, mumbling, inaudible to the others except Nile: "And by their good graces that I am not at Harvard anymore."

Aunt number three said with harsh finality, "Enough is enough, Maya! You must marry and soon. Your cousin is ready. You made a commitment and you must stick by it."

Maya: "I never made that commitment. You all did. I merely momentarily and falsely complied. I was nineteen and unsure about my own self, let alone what I wanted from life. And while you were all playing gods planning my life, I realised I didn't want it and was showing my reluctance and dislike since the beginning. I GAVE HIM A FOUR... A FOUR. None of you cared about what I wanted, you had already made up your mind and my choice mattered little... AND if in my religion a divorce is permissible, then why not the ending of an engagement?"

Aunt number two: "Yes! Of course we did what we thought is best for you! We are not here to scream at you or be mad at you. We are just explaining the potential possibilities. If you want us to leave, we will, Maya, but it is a lost cause if you don't marry him. Everything will be gone. I am just saying. You should think this through."

Maya: "I have and I will not raise my funeral pyre the same day as they raise my *doli*.* I will not marry him. There is nothing common between us. Forget the fact that he fails to touch my mind, my heart, my soul; I am not even remotely attracted to him! His touch repulses me. He is my cousin, for God's sake! I wish to marry for love; I always have and that is the only condition under which anyone should even marry in the first place. By my logic, it is not fair on him either. He deserves to marry for love too."

Aunt number three: "He loves you."

Maya: "HE DOES NOT LOVE ME AND DON'T EVER SAY THAT AGAIN. He doesn't know me, so all he is doing is lusting after this superficial flesh, not the essence of what exists inside. And if he did love me he would learn to let go."

Aunt number one: "Wow, this is the first time that we have heard this logic. He is such a distinguished lovely young man, willing to marry you even after he knows about you, what you really are, and what's more, this is something all you educated young women must learn – a wife is inferior to a husband."

---

* Traditional carriage for a bride, that is carried from her house to her husband's house; usually the brothers of the bride carry her in this structure.

Maya chuckled. "So according to you he loves me because he wishes to possess my flesh and satisfy his depleted male ego? HA HA HA. So he loves me because in spite of my complete ambivalence to him and hatred for this prospect, in spite of my incessant pleas and desire to do anything but marry him, he still will marry me and I AM INFERIOR TO HIM?"

Aunt number two: "Laugh all you want, Maya. It is not a lost cause if you marry him. You will develop feelings for him, eventually. He will give you everything you want. He has a family, which will ensure that. Now the thing is, you've blocked your mind to the possibility of liking him. You've been doing this for quite a bit now. But you should just think that in the future he would be the better one. So, no, it is not a lost cause this way."

Maya, weeping now: "Why don't you all understand? If I don't like him, shouldn't that be indication enough of the fact that I SHOULD NOT be forced to marry him? You can't be forced to marry someone, you just can't. It isn't like, 'Oh, Maya, don't wear this dress to the party' or, 'Oh, Maya, those shoes and bag don't match,' or 'That hairstyle doesn't flatter your jawline...' this is a husband we are talking about, the man I am to spend the rest of my life with, the man who will be with me through most other aspects from now on, the man who I will have kids with and grow old with. If I feel displeased and disgusted with him holding my hand, how can I have his children? If every moment is a miserable forced expectation I will die *ghut ghut kay*[*] before I ever even get to be old."

Aunt number three: "Maya, dear, look at me! You have no choice." She stroked Maya's hair. "This world is unfair, but you must learn to – to give in."

Maya: "I will never be the victim."

Aunt number two: "Look at them. Your mother almost died. She can and will never accept the fact that you won't marry your cousin. I am not trying to blackmail you, just relaying a fact. The number of times you refuse or he complains to her, it kills her internally. She will die if this falls through, so do keep that little consideration in your calculations."

Aunt number one: "Yes, and your father, dear, just look at what's become of this family. Your brother has lost a leg, your father is facing political repercussions for the drone strike, with the media blaming your poor brother for being involved in the Jammat-i-Dua."

---

[*] Suffocation.

Aunt number three: "And you know how sick your father is. What kind of a daughter will you be if you leave your parents in such dire straits?"

Aunt number one, nodding her head: "Really, what kind of a daughter?"

Aunt number two: "Only you can save this family and make it whole again. Fix it, Maya! Fix everything around you."

Maya, whimpering and crying, holding, clutching, and pulling the forefront of her hair, whispered more to herself than anyone else, "But what about me? But what about me?" She shook as she kept repeating, "But what about me?" like a fish that had been caught and struggled and frantically palpitated its desperate body for a last glimmer of life.

Maya too drowned in this perception of what others viewed as best for her but was in fact suffocating and crucifying her. Her father, mother, and cousin – these people loomed over her mind and, extending their shadowy insistence, occupied any recesses of light that remained. She cried and whimpered until aunt number two touched her. But by then the events of living in a claustrophobic beautifully erected prison cell had permanently trapped her sanity and lodged it in the past, safely away from reach. An influx of negative emotions, both paranoia and anger, took an irrational hold of Maya and she screamed, pushing her aunt aside, her words foaming at her mouth.

"HOW DARE YOU TOUCH ME? HOW DARE YOU? GET OUT, GET OUT!" Screaming and kicking, she tossed and turned on the bed again, throwing cushions and pillows at the aunts. For once, the aunts, harrowed with fear, backed away, terrified as much by the vagaries of Maya's behaviour as the prospect of having her rampant irrepressible rage unleash on them. They slowly edged out of the door just as Nile hurriedly hobbled over to Maya and held her wrists, restraining her anarchic passion.

"Maya, stop... Maya, stop!" She kept tossing and grinding her teeth. "MAYA," he said, shaking her furiously now.

"GET OUT!" she screamed at him. "JUST GET OUT AND LEAVE ME ALONE, ALL OF YOU. JUST GET OUT!"

Nile looked at his sister, at the sad pathetic animal that she had been reduced to and, feeling a stab of pain greater for her handicap than even his, hobbled out of the room and went to the only person who could perhaps reach Maya at some level. Within minutes, Laila came running into Maya's room to find her still kicking and weeping.

She ran up to Maya and gave up shaking her, so she calmly went and lay next to her, putting her arms around her. Laila didn't let go till Maya stopped crying, after which, snivelling and turning to Laila, she hugged her back.

"Laila, please, Laila, please take me away from here. I am so tired, I really don't want to live anymore; I want out of my body; this flesh is trapping my soul. Laila, please save me."

"Shush, Maya, shush." She kept hugging her, kissing the top of her head. "It will all be fine. You are the strongest person I know. I take my inspiration from you and the way that you have been resilient in the wake of all these bullshit trials and tribulations."

"No, no! You don't understand Laila, I just… I am so tired. Don't you see that? I just don't know what to do anymore."

Laila was deep in thought for a few minutes then she looked at Maya and whispered, "How would you like to go and see Ali? You know our parents have gone out for dinner. I think you should see him." Laila knew that where she could be emotional support for Maya to some degree, she needed to meet the man that she loved to give her hope again. She knew being the upstanding loving boy that he was, he would help Maya from the perilous whirlpool of dejection and despair that she had flung herself into.

"But I haven't seen him in over a year now… I think it's almost been two years. Will he even want to see me after all that has happened?" Maya suddenly seemed perplexed and confused, but Laila knew that her feeling this normal worry was better than the blank emptiness she had been experiencing moments ago. Laila smiled.

"Maya, now you are being silly, of course he will! We both know that he loves you immensely and if it makes you feel any better, I will call him and let him know. Okay? I think I would prefer calling him in the other room if that is permissible to you?" Laila wished to call him separately so that she could inform him of the delicacy of the situation without Maya being affronted or wanting to conceal the reality of things from him.

Maya nodded and as Laila went into the other room to get her phone and call him, she mumbled, "Thank you!"

Laila stopped, came back, and gave her a big hug. "Anytime, baby sis… anything for you."

While Laila drove, she knew she was forbidden from driving by her parents, but she honestly couldn't care less. They had a son without a leg, a daughter who was losing her mind, and yet in order to try and save any remnant of her father's political career, her parents would still attend the Governor of Punjab's dinner party. In fact, they had all moved to Lahore not just for Nile's treatment (Lahori doctors were, after all, better) but also because the governor was offering her father a district, and in light of the explosion he had renounced his pledge to her father, one that her father was again willing to seek. As the eldest in the family, she could at least hold onto the small semblance of sanity that remained and try and propagate what she knew was the right thing to do.

"Laila, do I look okay?"

"Maya, you have asked me that a hundred times; of course you do, my dear. You are beautiful and Ali loves you – he doesn't care what you look like."

"Yeah, you are right. I am just really nervous. I haven't seen him in such a long time. What am I going to do?"

Laila reached over and squeezed her hand. "Just be yourself; it will be all fine."

They reached Ali's friend's house. The friend's parents were gone for the weekend and Ali craved the same complete privacy that Maya too desperately desired. He was standing outside, pacing up and down in anticipation, and Laila smiled at the tempestuous ardent nature of young love. He was just as excitable as she was. He rushed to the car and opened the door for Laila; she got out of the car and approved of not just his appreciable manners but once again of his handsome face and honest eyes, and knew that her sister had chosen well. He greeted Laila, but she knew that he was anxious to open the door for Maya as well.

She smiled and indicated toward Maya, encouraging him to open the door. How respectful, humble, and caring he was, how unlike her own husband and yet her foolish parents couldn't see how happy he would make Maya. Didn't they want at least one of their daughters to have the life she deserved? Hadn't they learned from her experiences? I suppose some people are fated always to be in the dark and not only to never know the truth, but also expound the unreality of the dark onto other poor hapless souls.

He smiled at Laila and went over to the other side of the door. Maya was looking down, trembling and quavering; she didn't have the power to look up. He put his hand under her neck and made her look up. When they finally looked at each other, Laila could see their simultaneous joy and pain, their desire to be together and their fear of losing each other. He pulled her out of the car; they still hadn't said a word to each other. All three walked in the house and Ali asked Laila if she would like anything to drink or eat; she politely declined. After a few more minutes, where he talked to Laila, but was looking only at Maya, Laila told the two that she was going to go shopping in the market nearby. Of course, she didn't have to buy anything and was only trying to give the lovers time to be together and reconcile their separation with their tender *ishq* for one another. They needed to give each other strength and couldn't possibly do that with her just sitting there, making things even more uncomfortable. She could tell that they were both grateful that she left, but as he sat down and put his arms around Maya, they didn't even notice her looking at them with such sadness in her eyes. They didn't even know when she left, for you see, they had eyes for no one else but each other.

NO MORE CHOICES

I LOOKED AT him and could do nothing other than reminisce about how each and every part of him had been and would always be a part of me. I looked at his hands and remembered the way those fingers caressed me; I looked at his arms and remembered the way he would always hold me, the way they would wrap around me and cushion me both physically and emotionally. I looked at his mouth and remembered the way that it would feel – his lips' plush softness tempting, seductive, and yet eerily reassuring. I looked at his cheek, his nose, but when I looked at his eyes, at the deep pools of green, I felt myself burn with the desire to connect on an even deeper level.

His eyes were his and his alone – they alone failed to bring forward a memory that was blinding and distracting me from the present. They entrapped me and held me rooted, unable to move and just leaving me capable of feeling, of feeling his soul knocking at the doors of his pupils and rushing, hitting the tunnel of his vision, out and into me. I didn't hear myself breathe or feel myself gulp or know that my heart was suddenly pumping blood at a rate that matched the increasing anguish at even the little distance that remained between us.

He seemed to hear my inner coveted yearning, for within minutes he was sitting next to me and had wrapped his arms around me. I felt myself melt, melt into his being until I could feel, think, smell nothing but him. My essence latched into his and forgot its own origins as it found its destination. I didn't even know that I was holding onto him until he disengaged himself and got up, pulling me up with him. He held my hand and together we walked into the room. I sat on the bed and he turned the light off, taking his shirt and trousers off.

Passion interlinked with the desire to be immortal in the act of love-making yet, realising that each moment was perhaps the last that they would share together, the very venture became all the more sacred, all the more definitive and special. Each kiss etched itself on her lips' memory; each caress was implanted permanently on her skin. When they lay minutes later in each other's arms blissfully smiling, they had successfully created a sanguine sanctuary that knew no human law or code and just obeyed the queries and pleasure of the soul.

He touched her hair, pushing it back, giving her a kiss on the forehead. She smiled. They started speaking for the first time in that hour.

"Maya," he whispered into her hair. "What are you going to do?"

"What do you mean?" she said, pushing him a little further back so that she could fully read his face, but the harder she tried, the harder it was for her to understand his current intentions. Her confusion broke their bond of comfort and led her to be tense and on her guard again. He kissed her head and held on tighter than before, relaxing her body.

"Shhhhh, Maya, I just asked you a question. What are you going to do?"

She shrugged. "Keep fighting until they see that you and I are meant to be."

"No," he said. "No. You won't do that. Look at me, Maya. Please. I know you are going to argue with me. I know it. But please just listen to me." She was quiet, tears streaming down her cheeks. "Maya, my love." He held her face in his hands. "Listen to me. Laila told me everything that has been happening and I really can't stand what is happening to you. Maya, your parents are never going to acquiesce. You are going to slowly and steadily decline into nonexistence. I can't let you do this."

"You think I won't die without you?" she said, screaming and crying at the same time. "How can you ask me to do such a thing? I don't know how to exist without you. I don't know how to spend one second without you. I can't."

"Yes you can, Maya, and you will, for me. I have to save you, Maya, and I will do anything to keep you safe and happy, even if that means giving you up."

"So you don't love me anymore." She stopped crying, both shocked and horrified.

"Maya, how can you say such a thing? I love you, which is why I have to do this. You think this won't be hard for me? It will be even more distressing to me to be without you. Maya, I have never been with nor will ever have any other girl in my life, save you. I mean it, Maya, you were my one and only. Please, I am already internally dead without you, but I cannot superficially function if I know that they treat you like an animal and have taken all semblance of life and liberty from your being. No, Maya," he said, a solitary tear running down his cheek and touching the top of her hair. "I don't know how to live without you. But our love isn't just meant for this world, my little girl. Love and the coupling of the soul is a vow deeper than that of life. It exists internally. My soul is yours. They will be together always. And I know, in fact I am sure, that one day we will find a way. We will. You just wait and see."

And for the first time, Maya actually understood and didn't argue back.

The two wept and cried in each other's arms and it wasn't until Laila called Maya that she had any inkling of the fact that she had to get up and leave. She got up to go, but he held her wrist. "Five more minutes, please."

She stopped and once again intertwined herself into his arms, transiting recollections of his visual, nasal, and tangible self permanently into her heart. She savoured his being for one last time, lingering till there wasn't any more she could ingest, but still she retained so much more of an appetite to stay.

Maya put on her clothes, turned the light on, and turned around to him to say, "Goodbye."

He lay on the bed and nodded his head. "No, no, never any goodbyes between us, ever, so until we meet again."

She nodded, smiling, tears still running down her face. "Yes, stay in touch," she whispered, knowing in her heart that this was perhaps the last time he would talk to her like this, face to face.

"Yes, I will. Take care of yourself. You will always be in my heart and prayers."

Maya stumbled to the car, quite an anomaly compared to her usually self-poised grace. She didn't even look at Laila when she sat in the car and just stared out the window, snivelling and wiping away silent tears. Of course, Laila decided to let her be but couldn't help but keep glancing over at Maya, worried that she had fallen again into her empty helpless woe.

"Maya, what's wrong?"

"Nothing," she said, not taking her eyes off the road.

"Darling, I thought seeing Ali would help you."

"It did."

"Well, what conclusion did you guys come to?"

"Hmmmm. One that will please everyone else."

"What do you mean?"

"I will marry the cousin."

"WHAT?" Laila braked so hard, Maya hit her head against the car window.

"Watch it," she angrily turned around to snap at her big sister.

Happy that Maya still retained some spark in her, but extremely perturbed by this sudden announcement, Laila said sheepishly, "I am sorry," and then with more urgency, "but what do you mean?"

"What, I just… I am marrying the cousin!"

"But, Maya. How can you do that? How can you give up just like that?"

"I AM NOT GIVING UP!" she screamed and then said more calmly, "Ali suggested it, and you know what? He is right. I have been dying in that house, dying in that infinite stream of abuse and disparagement aimed at my soul. Enough is enough, Laila. I will protect my integrity and myself from any further abasement. It is the least I can do for him."

"So Ali's giving up? Don't you think that just giving in now is worse than anything else that you could do at this point?"

"No. I know what you are thinking, that I have come this far and shouldn't give up on those values that I have held so dearly to me, but Ali is right. Our love isn't transient and temporal… merely existing in this one realm. It will exist forever. Don't you see, Laila? I must do this to prove to them that even if they can physically pry us apart, they will never keep our souls asunder. And I know in heart that we will still find a way because we are meant to be. Nobody can change that."

"I don't get it. If I were you guys, I wouldn't give in."

"But you aren't us and you won't get it," she smiled. "He and I will always be one. I underestimated the amount that he did indeed love me." She smiled again, tears sparkling around the edges of her eyes. "He loves me enough to let me go, knowing that he and I will always be one."

FORGIVENESS

Y WAS STANDING outside the huge doors of his house, pacing impatiently up and down his driveway. There was no sign of his two new confidantes whose comradely nature had abruptly been sent his way. *Allah's designs*, he thought. *Who can say anything? We plot and plan our lives and don't even know what is to come next.* He stopped, gravely lost in his meditations. *Right now, if I ask myself, I have planned my entire life since I knew what the term meant and since I became old enough to deal with my life without most of my mother's intervention, and yet hardly any of my life events followed the route that I had intended to set out for myself. Just take now, for instance. I have been the perpetrator of my wife's injustice and the moment that I saw her I swore to protect her and never imagined bringing any harm to her, let alone being the cause of it. What have I done?* He paced up and down the driveway at an even greater rate, as if his speed would absolve him of the crime that he had unknowingly committed. It wouldn't, of course, but did ease his hyped-up tensions for the time being.

He had been waiting for over three-quarters of an hour and wouldn't have minded waiting any longer except it was June and the summer heat was increasingly unbearable to deal with, so wiping the sweat off his brow, he slunk away into the air-conditioned inside. Letting out a sigh of relief, Y plopped onto the sofa and turned the television on to the news station. He had barely started listening to the newscaster's report for the highlights of the day when the front door opened and in walked the odd pair. Mrs S, slender, had quite a petite frame and walked with long impatient strides, while Mrs J, stout and round, huffed and puffed, trying to keep up with the other's dynamic vitality. With Mrs S, of course, came all life, loud and

403

glaringly boisterous. You could hear her all the way from the front door to the lounge and Y put the television on mute and almost chuckled, shaking his head at the energy that this woman possessed. Mrs S had that capacity to make you squirm under her gaze and yet always create a soft spot in your heart.

She stormed into the lounge and within a single breath sat down and ordered the servant to stop gawking and get both her and Mrs J glasses of orange juice. Fanning herself with her hand, she too tried to get rid of the droplets of sweat that had accumulated on her foundation-caked face.

"I am so sorry we are late, Y; my godforsaken generator short-circuited last night and there was virtually no electricity all night. I swear to Allah I don't know how the poor do it. I was boiling to death."

"Yes, we all read your WhatsApp update about the generator," said Mrs J. "I am sure Y wants to know about his wife."

"Ah yes! Well," said Mrs S, ignoring Mrs J's direct comment about not making the present conversation about herself, "I would have been on time, but the mechanic was such a buffoon. It took him three hours to fix something that should have taken him twenty minutes and I had to stand on his head to make sure that he did his job.

"Anyway, I inquired about your wife. Well, there weren't any friends who she could have stayed with really, and her father, quite a rude man, refused to tell me about her whereabouts ,so I questioned the gatekeeper at Ariyana's father's house, nice old man, has been in the family for years and had quite a soft spot for the girl. Well, he told me that there was only one place that Ariyana could go to – I mean, naturally, if not your father or friends you try for extended family—"

"She is at her father's village," interrupted Mrs J, wishing for once Mrs S would get to the point and fast, especially when that poor man was trying patiently to listen, all the time just wanting to bounce off his seat. He smiled a kind thank you to Mrs J and she nodded back.

"Ah yes! She is at the village. Well, I do believe that we should make our way there immediately. I fear what the poor girl will be doing there all alone; I mean, she has white blood in her and…"

But as Y turned his face toward the television screen, in a split second he saw the latest headline running at the bottom of the screen, taking his heart out with it. He removed the mute and heard the newscaster inform the viewers about a drone strike that had hit the village that Ariyana was in and that there were was a great deal of chaos, with the roads being blocked and emergency measures being taken to aid the injured. He did also report that there were a few deaths. Y felt his heart come out of his body – for minutes he sat there frozen, not feeling the beating of his heart or the rushing of his pulse, save the fact that perhaps he had lost his wife forever.

Mrs J, quite an empathic little observer, saw his ashen face and the horror of impending dread resting itself actively on his brow and in the tight clench of his jaw and realised that it was Ariyana's village that was on the news. He needed just one thing right then so she, Mrs J, left Mrs S, who was still oblivious of the fact that the newscaster had just mentioned Ariyana's village and was still ranting on and on about the summer heat and how Ariyana's porcelain skin would lose its whiteness in the village sun and how Americans don't value anyone else's life who isn't an American, and went to the kitchen to get a glass of water. She emerged huffing and puffing and came and sat right next to Y, putting a hand on his shoulder and offering him the water.

It took him a while to register that Mrs J had a glass of water up in front of his face, and even longer for Mrs S to realise that the two weren't paying attention to her sermon of using skin protection against the fretful sun, which can tan your skin.

"Why, whatever is the matter, Y?" asked Mrs S.

But his jaw was locked and his tongue couldn't find the words to express the anxiety his heart was experiencing. His lips were sewn shut with temporary pain; he couldn't afford to open them for fear that doing so would tear upon the seams of his fears that he was trying to contain.

So instead Mrs J replied, calmly yet with much remorse, "That is the village where Ariyana is, the one that they were talking about in the news."

Once the truth was voiced, Y had no other choice but to accept it and for the second time in his life, his shoulders heaved and he cried in front of the two women.

"It is all my fault, all my fault, and now Allah will punish me for letting the one perfect thing in my life get away, for slighting the most amazing woman on this planet. It is my entire fault. I did this to her, I DID THIS TO HER," wailed Mr Y.

His words not only caused Mrs J to hold his hand firmly but also caused Mrs S to bounce up from the chair in an extremely flurried motion and implode a sonorous rhetoric of extremely frantic proportions. "WHY, WE

HAVE NO TIME TO WASTE THEN... stop crying, Y. This is about the hundredth time that I am going to repeat myself: crying is never of any consequence. There is no point; just pull yourself together and if you feel that you are to blame for what you have done to your wife, then you already did the act, it has already happened and gone and if you must rectify the future then fix the present, for in the present lies a man's appeasement from retribution."

Even though Mrs J wouldn't exactly have been quite so insensitive as Mrs S, she did admit to herself that the woman had a point. There was no point in just sitting and weeping over the past when it would be clearly more worthwhile for him to try and find a viable solution out of this predicament.

"But – but what am I going to do?"

"Oh, but please, boy! Have you lost your senses along with your manhood? Why, you have so much money, get one of your helicopters to take you there."

Y stopped crying. Mrs S had made him realise that since the situation hadn't approached an inevitable conclusion, there would always be a way out.

So that is how the trio found themselves seated inside Y's private helicopter, descending onto the drone site. The entire journey from Peshawar, Y had been anxiously moving his legs and had bit each and every nail on his hand at least six times. The helicopter had barely touched the now demolished 'desecrated' site when Y leapt out and ran, inquiring if anyone had seen his wife.

In the mayhem of the aftershock, disgruntled and anxious people could not remember seeing a white-skinned woman. Finally Y came across a woman who seemed that she was in a greater degree of control than the others. She luckily turned out to be the woman that Ariyana had conversed with whilst accompanying Laila and, as the latter had been kind to her, the woman too would now unknowingly aid her. The woman told the *sa'ab* that the last she had heard of the white woman was that she had been near the house that was struck. Fear would have shackled him to the ground, but hope and the desire to aid his wife if she were in trouble made Y take directions and run in the direction that the woman pointed. When Y finally came to the site he saw five moustached men and a screaming white girl, bloody and fearful, pointing to the ground, surrounded by a group of women. He ran up to his wife sitting on the ground. She was unable to stand but kept pushing anyone that tried to approach to help her. But when he came, she let him come near; even in the mayhem of the aftershock her body welcomed him. She put her arms around him and, screaming, pointed to the ground. "SAVE HIM! OH GOD! SAVE HIM SOMEONE, PLEASE!"

If you asked Ariyana, she too had plans; she never dreamed that she would be in the village of her forefathers or that her husband would have kicked her out. In fact, if you had asked her a day ago what she was feeling for her husband, she would have told you that she wouldn't have forgiven him. In light of things, even his extremely unforgivable act was forgiven. The warmth of his arms expunged half her frantic worry, for she knew only he could make everything right again. She wept into his arms, screaming, "Please save him!" And eventually, that is how an unconscious Nile was in a helicopter along with Ariyana to Peshawar. At least he would now wake up about three weeks later, still alive, albeit without a leg. We humans don't even know if we will be alive the very next minute, so how can we plan and then feel miserable when life doesn't turn the way we meant it to? All we can hope is to have the courage to be above what life gives us, for the moral of our existence is that it too, like everything else, shall pass.

The clock kept ticking, but every time I stared at the incessantly slow rotation of the second hand, time did not seem to be moving at the rate he intended. He stood there, heart beating, pulse throbbing, and when every single worst possible outcome had been envisioned and relived and he couldn't stand it anymore, Y began to pace up and down the room. Of course, Mrs S rebuked him twice, but realising that the doctor was still not out of the OR, she too started getting jittery and fidgeted with her leg. Mrs J, also quite anxious, was made to feel more rattled by the superfluously shaking knee and so she stuck her hand out and placed it on Mrs S's leg to both make her stop and give her physical comfort.

Y had literally pleaded with every nurse and every surgeon that walked up and down the hall for any information and was about to walk into the OR, when after a few words were exchanged, Y rushed into the ER where his wife was relocated.

"They didn't save the baby," said Mrs J.

"Yeah, I am not surprised," replied Mrs S.

"Poor girl... I don't even have any children and yet I can only imagine what pain it must be to lose one that you have."

"Mrs J..."

"I am going to wait until husband and wife have their moment and go offer my condolences and give comfort," Mrs J thought aloud.

"Mrs J..."

"But a wretched Fool in fortune's draw, no evil intention or action, just an inherent goodness that was unbelievably more threatening to all those..."

"Mrs J..." Now Mrs S shook the other woman, determined to get Mrs J's attention; honestly, Mrs S was never used to being slighted or ignored but the other one was in a trance of both self and selfless empathy, lost in attempts to gauge why the hapless must always be the easiest of victims. "Well, I was wondering if you could do me a favour."

"Sure," said the jovial plump woman, forgetting her momentary deliberations into nature's injustice, eager to offer aid.

"You see, I don't... I... I just thought of something, something I don't know why I never thought of before. I think you are the most noble woman I know, but, well, you know Fehranaz has decided to not keep the baby. She's so young and, what with any future prospects of both marriage and yes, even education, it seems like the smart choice. Well, I was wondering if I should keep it, but that I don't think I could bring myself to... well, like I said, you are the most honourable woman I've met and... well, would you be willing to take Fehranaz's baby as your own?"

Mrs J nodded, tears in her eyes.

While Fehranaz's baby found itself a welcoming home, Ariyana's was left untainted by life's experiences. She was still partially unconscious when Y rushed into the room and held her hands, kissing her forehead.

"My baby," she groaned. "My baby... is my baby okay? Is my baby okay?"

"Ariyana, please darling, you need to relax. The doctor said you mustn't take any stress. Please, darling, I need you to get better. You have broken ribs and your arm..."

"But my baby," cried Ariyana. "WHAT ABOUT MY BABY?"

"Didn't survive the procedure," said Mr Y solemnly.

Ariyana howled and Y broke, seeing her in so much pain.

"Please, my love...please, please..."

"BUT MY BABY," she screamed, her chest heaving and probably adding further injury to her damaged diaphragm.

He put his arm around her lightly and cried into her hair, the tears matting the blonde, and whispered, "Please, my love, don't! I am just so sorry... so sorry. If only I could make my tongue akin to the language of my heart, I could tell you how truly sorry I am. Please forgive me, because I will never forgive myself."

"No," she said, shaking her head. "No, it is not your fault. You were falsely duped. If only I hadn't gone to see that CEO, but…"

"Ariyana, please," he said, wiping her tears, "don't try to lessen the burden of my guilt. I have abused you in ways that no husband should be allowed to live after and as I stand before you alive and unfortunately in good health, I still have a price to pay. The child is my penance, not yours… not yours, my love."

Embracing each other, they cried over the loss of the unborn life of their dead child. For the rest of her life, every June, Ariyana would remember her night at the hospital and feel that pain in her heart, more acute, deeper, and more frightening than the earth that had enveloped her.

SHADI GHAR

SHADIS (WEDDINGS) HAVE magical effects on things. The Ks' house was finally a place of laughter and gaiety. The morbid shackles were removed from their hinges, happiness flitted and danced into every hallway, into every corner, inside every room, save, of course, one. After about five years, Mrs K finally had the second biggest project, the marriage of her second daughter, and since it was in the family, it would be an even bigger affair. The servants finally let go of their petulant unwelcoming stance, Mr K's political career (thanks to his new son-in-law-to-be) was rocketing; even Laila became engrossed in the designing and ordering of the breathtaking *langay* (beautiful and very heavy skirts), and Nile, well, his new impaired body was slowly beginning to heal with matters of the heart. In their exuberance over all that was coming – the food, the clothes, the guests, the relatives, the dance practices under a skilful choreographer, the caterers, the jeweller, the wedding planner(s) (everyone wanted a hand in a K wedding), they all forgot about the most important ingredient in a wedding – the bride.

Arzoo had been frequenting the K household more and more. She would come every morning and stay all day long until the night threatened to give way to the eager sun. Yes. She of course came for Maya, to, along with Nile and Laila, dissuade her from the preposterousness of the situation, and yet when she realised that Maya was obstinate in not only her decision but in remaining locked up in her room, Arzoo was determined to give her as much love and support as she could in virtually every way. It can be hard to bolster that which you so vehemently disagree with and yet Maya was her sister and for almost a year, in light of her own foolish mistakes, she condemned herself the most for failing to be there for Maya. She wouldn't make the same mistake twice and so, day in and day out, she would come and stay for as long as it took, sometimes sitting opposite Maya in silence, sometimes crying with her, sometimes shouting with her, sometimes aiding the elders in the house in their preparations, but always a persistent safeguard against a relapse into an endless misery.

Arzoo was right now standing in the hallway preparing *gajras* (flower bracelets) for the Mayoon the next day. The Mayoon is one of the earlier celebrations in Pakistani weddings; and subcontinental weddings, as everyone knows, can last from five days to a fortnight or even longer. Maya wished to be alone; Fehranaz was over today as well and in the midst of her final sacrifice, Maya secretly took solace in the education she was imparting to another person. She was adamant that her lessons with Fehranaz not be halted at any cost and that at least her mind was something that she could keep alive when she had willingly burned her heart to embers. Moreover, it made her feel good to see this young girl every day, full of life and yet so much sorrow, full of naive innocence and yet a wisdom that surpassed any she knew, full of eagerness and yet a reluctance to embrace what she could. Seeing her go through a horror at such a tender age, an apprehension that only envisioning makes most women quiver, and seeing her still not only not give up on expecting from life, but also greet each new day with a remarkable zeal, gave Maya strength and the patience to go ahead with her own ordeal. Arzoo quickly came to realise how significant these few hours every day with Fehranaz had come to be to Maya and so, even though she was a little miffed that Fehranaz could do for Maya what she couldn't, she would skilfully creep away and let the exchange of ideas and words flow through a two-way connection.

Except perhaps today; today, when Maya had earlier told Arzoo that Mrs S was on her way to drop off Fehranaz, Arzoo remained rooted at her spot on the settee, gazing out from the French balcony into the garden.

"Arzoo?"

"Hmmmm."

"It is usually me who is lost in a whirlpool of contemplation. What's troubling you?"

Her grey eyes smiled. "Oh! Nothing."

"I've known you since forever, Arzoo. You can't lie to me. Just tell me, what is it?"

She smiled. "I told you, nothing, Maya. You think too much, cooped up in this big room all by yourself."

"Loneliness gives you perspective sometimes, and right now, you're over there. Stop trying to change the topic by preventing me from accurately assessing and turning my attention to myself." She gave Arzoo a playful gaze, one that the latter hadn't seen in such a long time that she regretted having to tell her what was bothering her; it ruined the innocent playfulness Maya had been craving to indulge in.

"Is it the baby?"

She turned around and smiled at Maya, holding her stomach. "It is always the baby. This thing has been with me through everything. Funny thing how I have begun to love it almost like, like, well, the way I love myself. I know it sounds selfish and you probably won't get it, but this baby is me. It's been a part of my thoughts, my decisions, but, like myself, I will never take it for granted."

"Then what is it?"

Arzoo was looking out of the window.

Maya followed her gaze and saw Nile standing there, trying to feed all the stray cats in the neighbourhood. They all flocked in the courtyard at sundown, rubbing past each other and slyly charming Nile for a bite and he, privy to their cunning, would be standing there waiting to give.

"Oh!" said Maya. "I see."

"What?" said Arzoo, finally giving Maya her full attention. "What do you see, huh?"

"You have been afflicted after all with the disease... the disease that comes from within, that grows irrespective of how close or far you are from the cure, that makes you all hot and cold, nervous and sure, that gives you hope and yet makes each moment fearful. It is the most elusive, most threatening of all diseases and yet you wouldn't part with it any more than you would part with your life."

Arzoo turned red. "It – it is not like that."

"Oh!" replied Maya. "But it is. I am your best friend." She came over and sat next to her on the window seat, putting her arms around Arzoo. "What are you afraid of?"

"I don't know," she replied.

"If you don't try, you will never know. Just give it a shot. The universe has a way of surprising us when we least expect it!"

When Fehranaz knocked and entered Maya's room, she saw her seated on the settee, looking out at the garden the same way Arzoo had. It was dark and she, of course, could not see anyone but was only visualising a particular face in her mind's eye. She turned to Fehranaz with a queer twinkle and strangely hopeful smile.

Arzoo, on the other hand, now sat crouched on the flowers, playing with the white jasmines. Of course, a skilled man had promised to undertake the making of the *gajras* specifically for the K marriage, but Arzoo wished to aid him and add her own touch to the garlands. She wound them around her hands, smelling their sweet earthly fragrance, before picking one up and putting it in her hair, because she was happy that Maya had been so receptive to her inner turmoil and because she thought that no one was watching, as everyone was passing by, goaded by one errand or the other. She didn't realise that Nile was standing at the end of the other corridor through the central courtyard, peering at her. He was watching the way the flower added to her ethereal beauty and felt like laughing as he saw the corners of her lips turn upwards for no other reason than the smell of the jasmines. As he stood there and watched her he was struck once again by how happy she made him. To him, she had always carried a joy that had the capability of turning his sorrow into serenity. He secretly wished that she would sometimes come stay at their house to see him but knew that his childhood crush would only remain that – a one-sided infatuation. He stood for a while, contemplating whether to interrupt her little session of self-amusement. Finally, he walked over to where she sat and tapped the floor with his leg (his father had of course managed to get him a prosthetic leg).

"Ahem!"

She turned, letting her cascade of beautiful curls flow around her. "Oh! Hello, Nile," she said and smiled, making his heart leap and his face turn red. "Didn't know you were standing there... or more like creeping around."

"Ummmm," he tried, flustered with his attempts at speech.

"Ha ha ha," she said. "I was only kidding *baba*," and she patted the ground next to her, indicating for him to come sit next to her.

"What have you been up to? I see you have been fortunate enough to get a brand new leg." (She was of course teasing him about an extremely awful tragedy and yet he knew that she did it to make him feel normal. She was the only one who did.)

"Yes, well?"

"Sadly the rest of us are completely stuck with the bodies that we have and can't get any new spare parts." He saw her unintentionally reach for her stomach. In her loose *kurta* it wasn't even visible. He chose to ignore her subconscious action and instead changed the topic.

"How are things at home?"

"Well, they are getting better. I, of course, couldn't immediately expect Mother and Father to forgive me, but we all had dinner yesterday and, well," she smiled a sweet sad smile, "it felt like old times."

He didn't like the sadness that took a hold of her. No. He just wished to see her happy, to fulfil her every need and desire in each and every way he could.

"I am sorry."

"Oh! Don't be. It was all my own doing and, well, there are still certain things that they don't know about, like… well, forget it. I don't know what you will think of me either."

"Try me," he said, looking her right in the eye. She was amazed at this sudden tenacious resolve in his gaze and actually looked down, biting her lip.

"Well…"

He put his finger under her chin, causing her to look up. They were both startled with this unexpected meeting of their flesh. The effect was counterintuitive on Arzoo, making her unburden her secret. "Well, you see, Nile, I am preg—"

"I know."

"What do you mean? Did Maya tell…"

"No, she didn't tell me. We slept together that night that I regained consciousness, remember?" Pause. "I know you've never had a bump over your stomach before and I know that loose clothing isn't very characteristic of you."

Now it was her turn to get flustered and look down at the floor, red in the face. This was especially so because neither had talked about that night since it happened, both turning right and left in their conversations, always avoiding the huge block in the middle of their linguistic road.

"I have made so many mistakes, Nile, so, so many. I just wish, ahhhh, that I knew then what I know now. It would have saved everyone so much pain." She turned away; her eyes were brimming with tears.

He didn't know how he got the strength to say it – perhaps it was the refreshed aura of the house. "Make one more mistake. Marry me."

"What?" she said turning to face him. "But…"

He held out a hand, stopping her from saying anything more before he lost his newly sparked nerve. "I know what you are going to say. You are going to say no, but please hear me first. I know I am younger than you, I know I am far from perfect. Let's face it, I am a one-legged cripple and I know all that you've been feeling for me is pity due to my lack of a leg and I mustn't confuse it for any serious emotion, but, Arzoo, I will make you the happiest woman on this planet. I've loved you ever since I saw you, since before I even knew what the word love meant, perhaps even before I had a memory of anything but you, but you never ever noticed me. Every time you would come over in your pigtails, running around, getting Maya to run and put down her book, I would watch you… up trees… in alleys. I followed wherever you led. I always loved you from a distance, always too afraid to approach for fear that you would reject me."

He looked down now.

"You always liked all those older guys with their rugged good looks and suave charm. I know I am not a charmer, Arzoo, nor am I some white athlete. I know I am not your type nor ever will be. I know one thing: I will always take care of you. I may not be the man that you wanted to spend your life with, but maybe you can marry me, even if it is just to hide the fact that you're pregnant. We could get married instantly and then no one would ever have to know or even if they do, they won't say anything because you'll be my wife. Even if you say no, I will always love you and will always be there for you. You actually make my life so much better. Every second that I think of you or every second that I see you, I just thank Allah for giving me the opportunity to live, even if it were just to gaze at you." He stopped and when he looked at her, tears streaked her cheeks.

She didn't hesitate for a second and reached up and kissed him. Now it was his turn to be shocked. "Oh, Nile!" she said. "You little fool. I wasn't going to say no. Haven't you seen how happy you make me or how I secretly try to spend as much time as I can (when I am not with Maya, of course) around your room, hoping that you would come talk to me. You are the most perfect, kindest man I know. You are the man I have always wanted but never known. You have been right here under my very own eyes the whole time and I have traipsed all around the world trying to search for you. I am such a fool. Such a fool."

She started weeping and he put his arms around her. After a few minutes she stopped, a huge smile plastered on her face, only to be clouded with a frown again. "But how will you accept this child, Nile? It's not even yours. I don't even know…"

"Shhhh!" he said, wanting her back in his arms. "If it is a part of you, it is a part of us. I will love it more than even our own children."

"Oh, Nile!" she said, collapsing into his arms. "I don't deserve you and yet I feel like after all the ceaseless miles that I have walked to find my destination, it was always where I started. I finally feel like I am at home."

He kissed her hand. "Yes. Should we – should we just get married as soon as possible? I don't want to really spend another moment where you and I aren't together."

"Yes," she said, beaming and kissing him (much to the horror of the servant girl, who spread it around the house, adding quite a lot of fuel to everyone's gossip-famished ears and marriage joy). "I don't even want any of this elaborate princessy wedding nonsense. You have always accepted me for who I am – something no one ever did, at times not even Maya. All I wanted was the man of my dreams and I finally have him."

"I really think our parents will be extremely happy with the news." Indeed, they both were. Arzoo's were ecstatic that she had found a decent Pakistani boy and was ACTUALLY getting married, and when Nile told his they were exhilarated by the fact that not only had he found a wife but had actually even wished to wed after his traumatic experience. Though I will say for Mrs K, she was deeply upset that she couldn't have the most elaborate of all weddings for her only son, but ah, well, at least he was getting married… though wait, she did have an afterthought that it was too soon and too unexpected. The whole house had been noticing the chemistry between the two, but she hadn't assumed it would amount to this.

"You wicked little boy. Who knew that you were fabricating your own little romance behind the scenes?"

Mr K: "Ah well! He is my son, after all. Charm and good looks run in the genes."

Mrs K: "The only thing that runs in the genes is the capability of keeping a secret. Hmph!"

Mr K: "Oho, darling! Why do you internalise everything? I was just fooling around with the kid."

Mrs K: "Hmph! Well, I always loved Arzoo, much better than that fast niece of yours who would always have her eye out for my poor baby at dinner parties. I wholeheartedly approve of your choice, son. Those grey eyes… my grandchild will have such white skin and colourful eyes." (Well, unbeknown to Mrs K, her first grandchild undoubtedly would.)

Nile was only too pleased that his parents approved; it saved the house another drama.

Nile: "I say we should get married now."

Mrs K: "I daresay, such impatience… he really is your son."

Nile: "No, Mother! You misunderstand me. Life is too volatile to be left against the test of time, I know that; not a minute without the people you love."

Mrs K was still unconvinced. "But – but the plans I had for your wedding. I was going to invite Sharukh Khan and a couple of other Bollywood actors. NILE!"

Nile: "Well, you have a week until the actual really important events begin. Just let your dreams guide you and imagine the hype."

Mrs K: "Well, fine, we are having a double wedding then. You are right – it'll be double the fun," (and double the pomp and admiration). She would of course immediately call Mrs N, congratulate her and plan out the affair, the cards, the jewellery, the bridal outfit… Oh, the amount of work, but oh, how her relationship with her best friend was now translating to an actual familial bond.

Mrs K was again struck by the sudden urge for this emergent wedding. She shrugged the annoying little thought away, as, like I said, the list of caterers and guests for tomorrow had to be organised. The wedding took precedence in her priorities.

THE WEDDING DAY

THE MARRASSI DRUM roll had ceased its beating, the jumping and swirling movement of frolicking feet had dissipated, the last *gulab jaban* had been consumed and the *mehndi* tents had flapped their last. (The *mehndi* is perhaps the most festive and colourful event in a wedding full of dances, both choreographed and spontaneous, actual *mehndi* or henna and the joyful noise that is synonymous with most Indian or Pakistani weddings.) Alas, it came to pass that the festivities were coming to an end, where the trappings of a gilded happiness or a liberated sorrow must come to their natural conclusions. Fehranaz stood staring at Arzoo. She, along with all the other women (Mrs S, Mrs J, Mrs N, Mrs K, and Ariyana, to name but a few) were standing outside the makeup artist's room, spellbound by the beauty that he was further embellishing with his art. Flamboyantly gay, he was just adding the finishing touches to her lips when he saw the horde of ladies peering at him and was immensely perturbed by both their audacity to disturb his work of creation and their impetuous 'commoner' mentality for not having the patience to appreciate a majestic work of divine faculties in progress by trying to sneak a peek at it with their mortal eyes. He waved his arm about and in a nasal voice asked his terror-stricken assistant to 'tell the people that if they ruin his mood they might not have a bride to see.' The embarrassed women scurried away, only to be ushered back in fifteen to see a fully ready or, as the artist claimed, 'finished', Arzoo. Decked from head to toe in a Bunto Kazmi (a very famous female designer in Karachi) *lehga choli* (traditional wedding dress consisting of a short blouse and big heavy skirt), she looked like a picture to behold. Fehranaz had indeed seen so many brides on each of her visits with Mrs S but none that radiated with the vivacity and the glamour that Arzoo did.

He had very intricately blended in the pink, green and gold in and around her grey eyes to mirror the shades in her *lehanga*; her pink mouth was smiling and even the baby bump was hidden in the heavy work done on the *lehanga*. Of course, Arzoo had opted for wearing the unconventional pink, green, and gold instead of maroon and to be quite honest, reader, I assure you she couldn't have chosen better. The diamond and emerald choker that her parents gave her dangled around her neck while matching accessories adorned her ears. She smiled and each and every one who saw her was lured into her sparkling eyes, instantly struck with the rapture and contentment that radiated from within her soul out into the world.

"Oh my!" said Mrs K. "My new daughter looks like a *heera*, a *heera*." (A diamond, meant to emphasise the extreme rarity and immense appeal of the girl, of course, by comparing her to a commodity of intrinsic value.)

Mrs N beamed, appreciating the fact and counting her blessings that her best friend would be her daughter's mother-in-law. She knew that, in spite of the very many faults that Mrs K could be implicated for, not accepting Mrs N's daughter as her son's wife with wholehearted zeal was not one of them. He was, of course, her only son, and to most Pakistani mothers that in itself is the greatest glory they could have achieved (though most, unlike Mrs. K, are reluctant to share such an honour with anyone else, including his bride). "My son is so lucky to have you," she announced, kissing her head so as to not leave an imprint on her newly made face and yet still making her mark.

"Well, believe me, I am more than fortunate to have him."

"Well, it is an auspicious day," intervened Mrs J. "Both best friends getting married together."

"Well, actually…" Of course, Mrs S wanted to point out that it in fact wasn't considered very fortunate to have two weddings at the same time (superstitiously speaking, of course one wedding never makes it) but for the first time, Mrs J shot her a look of such an entitled force that Mrs S immediately shut her mouth (again, quite a novel occurrence).

Fehranaz smiled shyly as Arzoo walked by and mumbled, "You look beautiful." Fehranaz no longer carried the baby, so in spite of the fact that her stomach was flat, her eyes carried with them a much more harrowed, mature deepness than her young years should.

Arzoo nodded and smiled in return, anxious to glide away to her almost-husband for their private photo shoot before the wedding. They had hardly slept the night before. Even though the *mehndi* had ended at 3am, they wanted to spend every moment on the phone telling each other all the secrets that they had always wanted to share with a respected other but had never managed to find the right person to unburden their soul to. Of course, by sunrise Mrs N had got up for *fajr* (morning prayers) and had thus the opportunity of finding her daughter giggling and so blissfully happy that she almost didn't want to interrupt, but knowing it was a special day and one for which Arzoo would later wish she had conserved her strength, she had swiftly approached her daughter's side and humorously told Nile that he would have her all to himself the very next night. Embarrassed, he hung up and Arzoo and her mother burst into laughter. It was only after the laughter abated that, with tears in her eyes, Mrs N looked at her daughter and told her that she had barely got her daughter back and now here she was, going again. Arzoo, too, wept and as mother and daughter embraced, Arzoo tried not to let her little belly seem obvious while her mother hugged her, and was relieved that she hadn't noticed. "You did what you had to, I suppose, but now you are finally a woman and I am just so proud of you. I just don't have words to tell you." She knew that she had to let her daughter sleep, a point she had acutely made her son-in-law aware of, but what could she do? She was a mother, after all, and was going to get up when she saw Mr N standing at the doorway, tears in his eyes.

"Oh, Daddy! Didn't realise you were standing at the doorway." She tried to get off the bed.

"No. No, remain lying, *beta*. I just came to give you this big hug and kiss," which he did, "and to tell you that no matter where you are or how old you are, even if you are a grandmum, you are always going to be Daddy's little girl."

Keeping her family's happy thoughts abundant in her head, Arzoo, with the help of the other women, carried her mermaid-tailed *lehanga* (the kind that trails behind you) into the car and to the photographer's place. She was delirious with impatience and the desire to be one with the man of her dreams, but for now she was excited about poking fun at him during the shoot – it would be his first night, you see.

Fehranaz saw Arzoo's car take off and knew that Maya, who had her makeup done before Arzoo, and hair after, would be ready by now and so she scurried over, desperate to see how beautiful Maya looked. If you have ever seen a Pakistani bride, you will understand Fehranaz's uncontrollable anxiety – they do something to you, these brides with their excess of jewels and flamboyant colours surrounding them while they remain this frail little thing in the centre of this 'so much', bearing the weight and making it look like beauty's ultimate lure. Even though Fehranaz had concluded that Arzoo was the most beautiful bride that she had ever laid eyes on, Maya literally took her breath away.

It wasn't that either Maya or Arzoo was any more gorgeous than the other; every passer-by would rate them as being roughly of the same blessed gene pool. Yet where Arzoo inspired warmth and light-hearted femininity, Maya was the centre of this morbid awe. This fascinating stew of tradition and power that combined with her beauty had the magnetic pull of summoning Fehranaz to its core, of entrapping her gaze and making her vulnerable to its aura. Maya spoke volumes in her silence, standing there in the traditional gold and maroon *lehnga* with heavy *polki* (gold) jewellery. She looked as Fehranaz approached, having informed everyone that she would like to get ready in peace, and smiled an empty smile at her. Perhaps she was practising for when she would have to be on stage. (Yes, the bride and groom sit up on a stage for all the world to remark and gossip about – can be quite uncomfortable if you don't really like being stared at or are not comfortable with putting on a show!) Her honey eyes were laden with gold and black, her lips a foreboding red. Oh! The world would have quite a lot to say about the lure of her face tonight.

"Is the car here?" she asked quietly.

Fehranaz was about to answer when Mrs S and Mrs N flew past her and, in a flurry of movement and words, they both began to exclaim in hurried tones before stopping short. "Maya jaan, whatever are you doing? The car is..."

Mrs S was the first to break the spell. "Maya, you look..."

"...incredible," finished Mrs N. "I knew you were going to make a stunning bride, but you have by far exceeded my expectations."

"Oh! Mine too," said a frank Mrs S, who was blunt and indeed did speak her mind about everything, and even if uncharacteristic of the rest of society, it was a genuine compliment she was paying.

"Is Laila here?"

"Why, yes. Let me go ask the driver to bring the car to the door so you won't have to walk that much."

Mrs N was still staring at Maya mesmerised by the way she looked and more so by the hurtful resolve in her eyes. "What is the matter, dear?"

"Nothing," she said, and she bit her lip to stop the tears from running down.

"Oh, there now! You can tell me. It is that boy, isn't it?"

Maya remained silent.

"Well, I don't know how you had the fortitude and will to come to this conclusion, and for that matter I don't even know how you even had it in you to go through all that, but you need to know a little secret. I have been rooting for you all along. Shhhhh! Wipe those tears. I am proud of Arzoo, but dear, I am even more proud of you. What you are about to do for your family is nothing less honourable than a soldier who goes to war, foolish and manipulated by the times and yet able to make a sacrifice for something that he believes in. You believe in your love, *jaani*; it will come back to you one day. No sacrifice of this magnitude should go unrewarded, nor will it, I'm sure of it."

Maya hugged her, feeling the love and warmth of a mother she so desperately craved at this point. "Thank you. Thank you."

"*Beti*," said Mrs N, weeping now, "I just pray for your and Arzoo's happiness all the time and I know that Nile will always take care of my little one. It is you who I fear for. I sometimes can't sleep at night when I think about what your family is putting you through."

But they never got a chance to finish, for gleeful Mrs K, completely dressed and ready to play head host at the wedding, popped in. "Oh, Maya… well! What's going on here?"

"Oh nothing, nothing!" said Mrs N, wiping her tears. "Maya just looks like such a little porcelain doll, can't imagine them all grown up. I held her when she was born. I mean, I am the one who named her, after all."

"Oh, yes," said Mrs K, and after a moment appropriate to the emotion, she lifted her head again and said, "Well, Maya, you must hurry. Come now, we can't keep your cousin waiting all day; he has already arrived there and just called to let me know." (Mrs N did all but roll her eyes.) "And, Maya, please be pleasant and don't forget to smile while the pictures are being taken, and if he tries to put his arm around you and be close, let him – he is your husband now."

Maya neither refuted nor agreed, just silently followed. Fehranaz offered to hold Maya's *lehanga* for her, and in between her mother's instructions managed to whisper, "Maya *baji*, you look ravshing."

"It's 'ravishing', dear, with an 'i' in the middle, and thank you." She practised her smile once more.

The journey from the parlour to the photographer and then the excruciatingly difficult task of maintaining a feigned calm whilst having her pictures taken with 'him', and then the way from there to the wedding hall, seemed like a terribly long one for Maya. Arzoo had already gone in before and while people laughed and became boisterous in her presence, a hush went through the crowd as Maya walked up to the stage to take her place next to 'her' contract upholder. Each and every person felt that they hadn't witnessed such sorrowful grace and elegance till this night (of course they didn't know that it was Maya's grief that made her all the more mortal and beautiful in their eyes). They just felt as we all often do without knowing what it is. Maya could hear Arzoo and Nile laugh and giggle and she made small conversation with her cousin, intermittently smiling whenever her mother looked her way. But her eyes, oh, they searched and searched in anguish for that one face that alone could give temporary peace to her unsettled soul, and it wasn't until the *joota chopai* that she saw him entering the hall.

If you are not familiar with the custom of the *joota chopai,* let me acquaint you with it. *Joota chopai* literally means the hiding of shoes. Now everyone knows how eager a groom is on his wedding night to behold his prize, and the bride's female relatives take advantage of that fact, hiding his shoes until and unless he pays them a ransom before taking his bride. In between the to and fro of the witty exchanges and the bargaining for the shoes (or symbolically, dare I say it, the bride), the bride is just expected to sit there and smile, and so no one noticed the simultaneous panic and reassurance in Maya's eyes as she stared at the face of the man she loved with all her heart and soul. I could not even tell you the thoughts that went through his head – he was seeing the wife of his soul marrying the flesh of another man. As it was, Arzoo was the only one who saw him enter the door and catch this unspoken exchange of agony. She glanced at Maya, perhaps as full of sudden terror as she, but she looked at Maya with an 'It's okay, I am here for you' look and smiled. It helped Maya to know that Arzoo was right there – it made her feel all the more close to her sister, as if in essence they too were getting married to each other.

The *rasm* (tradition) of the *joota chopai* over, both fathers came to walk their daughters out the door. Arzoo's *rukhsati* (farewell, as they call it) was a teary one where both parents and daughter wept. Maya knew she would never let this be the end. As it was, she had no tears left to give and so she held her head up high and walked up to the door, only to turn around and look at someone for a brief second. It would have taken an expert observer to notice the silent tears that dripped out of her eyes and the sad smile that touched the corner of her lips… and then, just like that, she was out the door.

EPILOGUE

"HELLO, LADIES AND gentlemen, this is the Captain speaking! We will be descending into Lahore shortly. I hope you had a pleasant flight. Thank you for flying with us through Emirates."

As the seat belt sign switched on, the man next to her got up to head over to the restroom – a typical involuntary action of most Pakistanis. It was almost as if the seat belt sign indicated a permanent cessation of action where all is indelibly forbidden and disallowed, though I suppose when you need to go, five minutes can make all the difference.

She looked down outside her window, down at the sparkling lights. It was interesting looking down from above. It was perhaps as interesting as looking the other way around; everything glittered and seemed so far away. Yet when she looked down at the shimmering expanse that stretched as far as the eye could see, it awakened in her this familiarity, this nostalgia that she hadn't experienced in a long time. She could smell the curry being cooked at the *dhaba*,* she could hear the sound of *rikshaws* and the perpetual honking of all the road rage, disclaiming the politeness that Lahoris are used to; she could even feel the riverbed as the children leapt in the water, and yet it was night time. All that she saw, heard, and felt was in her mind.

"Ma'am, may I take your glass away?" The air hostess smiled at her; she seemed a little intimidated and in spite of fearing the potential to offend, she still managed to smile so as to appear pleasant enough whilst attending the passengers. She smiled back at the woman, trying to make her relax.

"Yes, of course," she said, and continued looking out the window.

---

* Roadside shack.

The bittersweet conundrum kept enveloping her until she felt giddy with excitement. She was coming back home after a long time.

Would everyone have changed? Perhaps they had stayed the same and maybe she had. Perhaps they were now all in completely different situations and thus adapted to the way around them, making her an outsider to their world. Yet she never had been an insider in this city, which had displayed to her both the extremes of passion and the turmoil of fear. It had both embraced and rebuked her, simultaneously welcoming and rejecting her. Perhaps it wouldn't be that different after all. The man returned; he too was a doctor, a heart surgeon.

"I am telling you, hospitals in Pakistan need better doctors; all the crème de la crème go abroad for practice. I am so glad you decided to come back, a doctor as young as you and a neurosurgeon no less – you will quickly build quite the reputation, you know." He looked at her again, struck by how beautiful she was, and full of admiration, applauded both the tenacity on her brow and the polite reserve of her etiquette.

"*Gee*," she said, "I always wanted to come back."

The plane hit the tarmac now; no matter how many times she flew, that moment when the plane touches and runs on the runway always felt like the most devastating crash. It is hard to think of anything but the sound and the roar of the impact – yes, even that which won't escape you in the nightmares you experience every night.

She thought of home again and why she was returning. She had thought about the village that had been torn to shreds by a drone strike. She thought again about the people who had mattered most to her and once again debated about their proposed evolution. Had they changed? She felt the same concoction of nervous vertigo again.

The seat belt sign came off and she got up to pull her bag down. As she turned to leave, hair pulled back in a ponytail and wearing white pants with a black turtleneck that ironically covered her body yet still managed to portray her form, he called out to her again.

He sheepishly looked at her and said, "I am so sorry, doctor. I remember everything, but have a horrible memory when it comes to names. What was it again?"

"No worries. I know what that's like. Memory has a tendency to make us forget things we most want to remember and deals with us on quite opposing terms when we wish to forget. Anyway, I ought to stop rambling."

Realising that being in Business Class, they were the first to leave, and that there was quite a queue developing behind them, she shook his hand. It was a firm handshake with a conviction and self-assertive confidence that had been acquired over time.

"It's Fehranaz. Dr Fehranaz."

 Matador